THE MERCY OAK

Also by Kathryn R. Wall

In for a Penny

And Not a Penny More

Perdition House

Judas Island

Resurrection Road

Bishop's Reach

Sanctuary Hill

THE MERCY OAK

KATHRYN R. WALL

ST. MARTIN'S MINOTAUR ❧ NEW YORK

This is a work of fiction. All of the characters, organizations, and events portrayed in this novel are either products of the author's imagination or are used fictitiously.

www.minotaurbooks.com

Library of Congress Cataloging-in-Publication Data

Wall, Kathryn R.
    The Mercy Oak / Kathryn R. Wall.—1st ed.
        p. cm.
    ISBN-13: 978-0-312-37534-8
    ISBN-10: 0-312-37534-4
    1. Tanner, Bay (Fictitious character)—Fiction.   2. Women private investigators—South Carolina—Hilton Head Island—Fiction.   3. Hilton Head Island (S.C.)—Fiction.   I. Title.

PS3623.A4424 M47 2008
813'.6—dc22

                                                            2008003304

First Edition: May 2008

10 9 8 7 6 5 4 3 2 1

As always, this book is for Norman.

ACKNOWLEDGMENTS

Those readers who live in the Hilton Head area may recognize a name or two in *The Mercy Oak*. This is due to the generosity of two couples who placed winning bids for naming rights at the silent auction held in conjunction with the 2007 Cooks & Books fund-raiser sponsored by Literacy Volunteers of the Lowcountry. I hope they enjoy their namesakes' roles, although "Harry" may have a difficult time expressing his opinion.

The legend of the tree I've dubbed the Mercy Oak is entirely fictional, although the context is as historically accurate as I could make it.

My thanks, as always, go to my writing pals, Jo Williams and Vicky Hunnings, who slog through multiple versions of the manuscript and never fail to offer invaluable insight and critique. I'm indebted to my agent, Amy Rennert, and to my editor, Jenness Crawford, for their guidance and concern.

My husband, Norman, deserves extra stars in his crown for putting up with the craziness that is the daily lot of someone married to a writer. He accepts the hectic travel and conference boredom with equanimity and good humor. Even after he's sat through another speaking engagement and heard my spiel for the hundredth time, he still manages to come out smiling. I am truly a lucky woman.

THE MERCY
OAK

CHAPTER ONE

F I'D TAKEN TIME TO READ THE PAPER THAT MORN-
ing, I might have been better prepared for my involvement in the Montalvo girl's death. Or maybe not.

But with Christmas less than two weeks away, I'd simply
skimmed the front page, then grabbed the Belk's ad from among the
dozens that nearly doubled the usual girth of the Sunday *Island
Packet,* and raced off to join the pre-holiday madness.

I generally despise shopping, especially as a recreational activity.
Living on a subtropical island off the southernmost tip of South Carolina allowed me to spend most of the year in shorts and T-shirts. I
ran the office on a pretty casual basis as well, so I had no professional
wardrobe to worry about, either.

My business—Simpson & Tanner, Inquiry Agents—was still
hanging on by its fingernails. My late mother's trust fund and my
own investment portfolio had been keeping us afloat, with the occasional request for a background check providing a meager supple-
mental income. The local attorney I'd worked for briefly on the
Dumars murder case had also thrown a couple of things our way, but
we'd yet to attract another major paying client.

After the events of the past summer, I'd kept my promise to my
brother-in-law, Red Tanner, and backed off from any potential case

that even hinted at the possibility of personal jeopardy. That suited my associate, Erik Whiteside, just fine. His own close brush with death had unnerved him, and for a while I'd been afraid he might decide to abandon our struggling enterprise altogether. His uncanny ability to coax information out of the most stubborn computers and databases made him highly employable, and I knew he could make a lot more money somewhere else. His personal loyalty to me kept him showing up three mornings a week at our tiny office near Indigo Run, and I was more than professionally grateful. The bond we'd forged in the heat of danger had made Erik as much family as my one remaining partner, retired judge Talbot Simpson, who also happened to be my cantankerous father.

The Mall at Shelter Cove lies about midway down Hilton Head Island, screened from busy Highway 278 by a narrow belt of trees. The cars in the parking lot near the big department store overflowed onto the landscaping. I wandered the lanes for a few minutes and finally lucked into a spot when a gray Mercedes backed out and pulled away. I slid my new Jaguar into the narrow space and hoped my neighbors would be gentle with their doors. I'd managed to total three vehicles over the past few years. Though none of the incidents had been technically my fault, my insurance agent had stopped taking my calls.

I tucked the newspaper ad under my arm and drew in a deep breath, preparing for battle. I had my fingers wrapped around the door handle when my cell phone chirped. Although it carried our coastal area code, I didn't recognize the caller's number. I hesitated for a moment before pushing the button.

"Bay Tanner."

A short pause. "Mrs. Tanner?" The words came out in a terse, choked whisper.

"Yes?"

"This is Bobby Santiago."

Caught completely off guard, I slumped back in the seat. Why would one of my housekeeper's children be calling me on a Sunday morning? My first thought was, *Why isn't he at Mass?* And then I re-membered that Roberto, Americanized to Bobby, had been the sec-ond of Dolores's very Catholic children to head off to college. He wouldn't be the first freshman to backslide once out from under his parents' thumbs.

"Is something wrong, Bobby?" I asked.

"Yeah. I mean, I think so. I mean—"

"Slow down. Is it your mother?"

Dolores Santiago had been attacked a couple of years before by intruders in my beach house. Through perseverance and fortitude, she'd managed to overcome her injuries, but the effects still lingered. I felt the familiar flush of guilt creep up my throat.

"No, Mom's fine as far as I know. It's . . . Did you see anything in the paper this morning about a hit-and-run? On the island?"

Dear God, I thought, *not Angelina or Alejandro.* Dolores would die if anything happened to one of her kids.

"Just tell me, Bobby. Quickly. Is it your brother or sister?"

"No! I— *Infierno!* I'm making a mess of this!"

I heard him draw a deep shuddering breath.

"I think a . . . a friend of mine died last night. I thought maybe you might have seen something about it."

"I didn't read the paper this morning. I'm sorry about your friend." I waited, but Bobby didn't rush to fill the silence. "Is there anything I can do?"

His voice, when it came, was soft, almost apologetic. "I think maybe it wasn't an accident."

I had hoped to spend a productive hour of Christmas shopping, grab some lunch, and be home in time for the one o'clock kickoff of the Carolina Panthers football game. Red had promised to try and make it over by halftime. Instead, I found myself pulling out the chair from the desk in my cramped office at the agency. I'd stopped at the drugstore and bought another copy of the *Packet* along with a couple of packs of cheese-and-peanut-butter crackers to tide me over. I pulled a Diet Coke from the mini-fridge and spread the front section of the paper out on the glass-topped desk.

I would probably have skipped right over the brief mention on page three if I hadn't been looking for it. The accident—which was what the paper was calling it, despite Bobby Santiago's shocking suggestion of murder—had occurred shortly after one that morning, which explained the lack of details. A female had been struck and killed while crossing 278 on the north end of the island. No witnesses, at least none that had come forward by press time, and no description of the vehicle involved. A passing motorist had nearly run over the body in the road and called it in. Again, no name given.

I pulled up the *Packet's* Web site, then moved on to those maintained by the local TV stations, but none of them had anything new to report. I had just retrieved my personal address book from my bag when the rattle of the doorknob made my head snap up. My hand groped automatically for the tiny Seecamp pistol before I remembered it lay nestled in the floor safe in the walk-in closet in my bedroom. Another promise I'd made to Red.

"Hey! What are you doing here?" Erik Whiteside stepped around the door, his tall, lean body clad almost identically to mine in jeans and a gray Panthers sweatshirt. "Did I lose a day somewhere?"

"I could ask you the same thing."

A smile creased his boyish face and crinkled his soft brown eyes. "I'm working on something at home, and I forgot one of the disks I need."

He crossed the narrow strip of carpet and perched on the corner of his desk, which would have doubled as the receptionist's if the amount of business we generated had justified another employee.

"I got a call this morning," I said, leaning back in my swivel chair. "You remember meeting any of Dolores's kids?"

"No, I don't think so. Why?"

I told him about Bobby's strange call.

"How did he know about it? I mean, if he's at College of Charleston, and the name didn't even make our local paper."

"A friend of his—whose name he won't divulge—called him about it."

"And the friend knew how?"

In the few years Erik and I had been working together, I'd come to admire the way his mind worked. Maybe it came from his fascination with computers and with unraveling their mysteries and secrets. Whatever the reason, he had the ability to zero in on the heart of a matter.

"Another good question to which I don't have an answer. All Bobby would tell me was that this girl—" I checked the notes I'd scribbled on the back of a deposit slip from my checkbook, the only paper I could put my hands on when I took the teenager's call. "Serena Montalvo. She was killed by a hit-and-run driver early this morning. Bobby thinks it was deliberate."

"Why?"

I shrugged. "I don't know. I mean, I think the kid's got an idea, but he didn't want to talk about it."

"So what are you supposed to do?"

"Check around and see how the sheriff is handling it. Bobby's aware of my . . . connection to Red. So far all he wants to know is if they're treating it like an accident or not."

Erik stood and paced the short stretch of gray Berber carpet between his desk and the door. "I take it this won't be a paying gig," he said.

"Probably not. The kid doesn't have any money, and I wouldn't take a cent from Dolores if she tried to hold me down and force it on me."

Erik nodded. He knew as well as I did that Dolores Santiago had saved my life. After I'd witnessed the explosion of my husband's plane and been severely injured by the rain of hot metal, the tiny Guatemalan woman had cared for both my body and my spirit, urging me back into life when all I wanted was to curl up and hide from the world. Rob's murder had nearly killed *me* as well—emotionally more than physically—and I had Dolores's calm faith and stubborn determination to thank for my deliverance.

"Have you talked to Red yet?" Erik asked, and I shook my head.

"I wanted to get a little more information before I broach the subject with him. If I even hint that we're investigating something that might involve violence . . ."

I let the thought trail away. Sergeant Redmond Tanner of the Beaufort County Sheriff's Office and I had come to an understanding of sorts. Part of our decision to explore the possibilities of a relationship had included my swearing off putting myself in any more danger, and I had succeeded so far in keeping my end of the bargain.

"So what's the plan?" Erik's voice broke into my thoughts. "Anything I can do?"

"I was just going to call Gabby Henson at the *Packet,* see if she had anything to share."

"Or you could just ask Red to check it out. That would be a lot simpler."

"Maybe. But with Red there are always strings attached." I glanced at my watch. "Speaking of which, I need to finish up here and get home. He's expecting to be fed during halftime of the game."

"We're a demanding bunch, aren't we?"

"Definitely high maintenance." I sobered. "Can you take a few minutes and check the girl out? See if there's anything on the Net about her?"

"Sure."

I printed the name on a slip of scratch paper and handed it over. "Don't go to a lot of trouble."

"No problem. I'm settling in for the game, too." He paused. "Stephanie might drop over later on."

I nodded, unwilling to rise to the bait he'd just dropped into the conversational waters. Ben Wyler, my late partner, and his daughter were subjects I didn't want to discuss, and he knew it. Erik and Stephanie had developed a friendship that appeared to be blossoming into something more, but it was none of my business, and I intended to keep it that way. Irrational probably, but we all deal with grief in our own ways.

"Tell her I said hello." I avoided his eyes and flipped through the pages of my address book.

"Sure." I heard him pull open a drawer, and a moment later he added, "I'll let you know if I find out anything."

"Thanks. Enjoy the game."

"You, too."

The door closed softly behind him. I exhaled deeply and punched in Gabby's cell phone number. She answered on the second ring.

"Bay Tanner! Long time, no hear. What's up?"

"Hey, Gabby. I need to pick your brain."

"Sorry, I leave it at the office on Sundays. Unless, of course, you've got something juicy to trade?"

I had to smile. Gabby fancied herself the Lowcountry's version of Bob Woodward. If there was a scandal brewing, especially in the rarefied strata of the high society into which I'd been born, Gabby considered it her moral duty to ferret it out.

"Not yet. I just want to ask about a blurb in this morning's paper. About a hit-and-run on the north end. A girl was killed."

"Nothing much more to tell you. She hasn't been identified yet, at least not according to our night reporter who got the initial call. It isn't technically my story, but I'll probably end up with it. Why? You have something I can use?"

"No. And they're sure it was an accident?"

"What else would it be? Bay? If you're holding out on me, I'll—"

"A client heard about it and called me. That's all I can say."

I'd learned from past experience not to give Gabby even a millimeter of an opening or she'd drive a Mack truck through it, mowing down anyone who got in the way.

"And this *client* implied it wasn't an accident? You can't just leave that hanging."

"Sorry, Gabby, that's the best I can do right now. Can you give me a call when you confirm an ID on the victim?"

For a moment I thought she was going to refuse, but finally she said, "Yeah, I can do that. Just remember our deal. Quid pro quo. Right?"

"Thanks. I'll be home all afternoon."

"Tell the handsome deputy I said hey," she quipped, and I hung up on her wicked laugh.

I should have known there would be no keeping secrets from Gabby Henson, even about something as personal as who I was sleeping with these days.

CHAPTER TWO

PULLED INTO MY DRIVEWAY IN PORT ROYAL PLANTATION a little after one. Across the dune that separated my house from the Atlantic, a lowering sky crowded the horizon, melding with the gray-green of the rolling waves. A steady onshore wind rippled through the stands of palmettos, the rasp of their needle-sharp leaves sounding like the dry cackles of old women.

Inside, I touched a match to the kindling in the great room fireplace. We have so few chilly days, even in the dead of winter, that a roaring fire is a luxury. On the way by, I flipped on the television before climbing the three steps into the kitchen. The Panthers trailed the Cowboys 7–0 in the first quarter. I set the oven and pulled out the casserole dish of beef stew Dolores had left for me in the freezer. I didn't mind feeding Red, but I refused to miss a football game while stuck in the kitchen peeling and chopping.

The phone rang just as I slid the dish onto the counter. My heart dropped when I recognized the caller ID.

"Dolores, how are you?"

"Bien, Señora. Y usted?"

"I'm fine." The momentary pause told me a lot. "What's the matter?"

"Is Roberto. He no answering *teléfono.*"

Bobby hadn't told me to keep his call confidential—and in spite of what I'd told Gabby, he wasn't technically a client—but I felt as if I owed him at least some discretion. Still, I hadn't anticipated having to dance around the truth with his mother. "Probably out with friends," I said. "You know how college boys can be."

"No, *Señora.* Every Sunday we call. *A la una.* He never miss before."

Being required to report in at precisely one o'clock every weekend seemed like a lot to ask of a teenager with his first taste of freedom. Still, Dolores and Hector had brought up three pretty great kids. I knew Angelina came home often from Athens, where she was an accounting major at the University of Georgia.

"Maybe he's studying and lost track of time." I tried to analyze why I felt this urge to make excuses for Bobby's absence. Maybe it actually was something to be concerned about, especially considering his suggestion that the death of Serena Montalvo might not have been an accident.

"We worry, *Señora.* Hector, he says we must go to Charleston."

"You might want to hold off on that," I said, perhaps a bit too quickly. "Give him some time. There could be lots of reasons why he's not picking up. Maybe his cell battery's dead."

"*Sí, es posible.*" A gentle sigh. "*Gracias, Señora.* I ask Hector to wait."

"I think that's best. Give me Roberto's number, and I'll try, too." I scribbled it on the back of the Imperial Dragon's takeout menu stacked with half a dozen others on the built-in desk. "If I reach him, I'll tell him to call you right away."

I hung up and sat staring at the wall. I didn't like it that Bobby had dropped off the radar screen so soon after his conversation with me. Could be there was no cause-and-effect relationship whatsoever, but I've never been a big fan of coincidence. I punched in the numbers and waited through seven rings, but the call never switched over to voice mail.

The stove *ding*ed, and I rose and slid the casserole into the oven. A moment later, I heard the garage door roll open. I smiled at the sound of Red's steps on the stairway leading up to the house. I met him at the door.

"Hello, sweetheart," he said, and his hug engulfed me.

At nearly five-ten, I stood just a couple of inches shorter than the rangy sheriff's sergeant, and I had to tilt my head up only slightly to receive his kiss. Even after several months, I still found my knees buckling a little at his touch. I'd avoided Red's less-than-subtle advances for the better part of three years after Rob's murder. I told myself it was because I thought of him as a brother, that our romantic involvement would constitute something bordering on incest, but that had just been an excuse to avoid risking the pain of loss again. I'd been an emotional coward. I was working on that.

"Dinner's in the oven, and the game just started," I said, clutching his hand and pulling him with me into the great room. On the wide white sofa, I snuggled into the curve of his arm.

"Getting nasty out there." Red worked off his running shoes and propped his feet on the coffee table. "Temperature's only around fifty, and the wind makes it feel a lot colder."

As if to punctuate his words, a flurry of rain spattered against the glass of the French doors out to the wraparound deck.

"Let it snow," I said, and he laughed.

"Not quite that bad. But the fire feels good."

I told myself to relax, to savor the warmth and the serenity I felt nestled against a man who swore he loved me without reservation. I ordered the nagging voice in my head to shut up, but fate had other plans.

Red stroked my hair and sighed. "Glad we finished up with that hit-and-run before the weather turned bad."

In for a penny, I told myself. "You were on that? The one up on the north end of the island?"

His eyes turned wary. "What do you know about it?"

"A couple of lines in the paper this morning," I said. Not exactly a lie, but not the entire truth, either. "Any idea who she was?"

"Hispanic teenager. I hate it when we have to deal with kids."

I knew his thoughts, like mine, had drifted back to the grisly contents of the Styrofoam cooler I'd pulled from St. Helena Sound a few months before.

"Any leads on who might have hit her?"

Red slid his arm away and leaned back to study my face. "This is more than just your usual nosiness, isn't it? What's your interest?"

"Nothing," I said, jumping up and heading for the kitchen. "Just making conversation. I need to check on the stew."

"Bullshit." Red strode after me. He took my arm and spun me around before I could reach the oven. "I know that look. If you have information, I need to hear it."

I resisted the urge to jerk my arm out of his grasp, and a wave of déjà vu swept over me. We'd had this same conversation way too many times. In the past, it had led to harsh words and bruised feelings. I didn't have the heart for it on that rainy Sunday afternoon.

"Nothing," I repeated and stepped in to wrap my arms around his neck. "Forget about it."

A cheer went up from the Panther faithful as I ended any more talk of death with a long lingering kiss.

Despite the closeness of the game, Red fell asleep on the sofa shortly after we'd finished the stew, eaten off plates balanced on our laps. I took the opportunity to try Bobby Santiago's number again. This time his voice mail picked up, and I left a terse message for him to call his mother. And then me. I told him I was working on his problem but so far had nothing to report. The moment I clicked off, the phone rang in my hand.

"Bay, it's Erik."

"What's up?"

"I found something about the Montalvo girl I thought you'd want to hear."

The sudden knot in my gut told me I probably *didn't* want to hear it, but I said, "Tell me."

"Well, she was involved in some sort of organization at the high school. The group's been in trouble a few times. Nothing too serious, a couple of protests and sit-ins, and some of the kids got suspended. Incidents made the papers."

"Protests about what?" I asked. Red mumbled and resettled himself on the sofa. "Hang on a second."

I moved down the hall and into the bedroom my late husband and I had used as our office. I dropped into the desk chair and pulled a legal pad from the right-hand drawer.

"Okay, go ahead."

"The protests mostly had to do with the persecution and exploitation of Hispanic students. From what I can gather, it started with a kid from somewhere in Central America, hotshot soccer star, who had his offer of a college scholarship yanked because he didn't have a valid Social Security number. Serena and her friends organized a walkout."

"When was this?"

"Last spring. Right before the end of the school year. Why don't I just e-mail the story to you? Might be easier."

"Okay," I said, tossing the pen onto the desk. "Anything else?"

"Nothing I could find on a cursory sweep. I'll keep looking if you like."

"No, don't go to any more trouble. Just shoot that story over to me. I'll see you in the morning."

"Sure." A pause. "Stephanie sends her regards."

"Tell her I said hey."

I disconnected and sat staring at the computer screen. I was going to have to speak to Erik about his heavy-handed efforts to put Stephanie and me together. I'd been trying for weeks to analyze my feelings about my late partner's daughter. I'd finally come to the conclusion that it was guilt, the emotion with which I felt most familiar, that kept me from returning her overtures of friendship. *The whole damn thing is backwards,* I thought. Stephanie should be avoiding *me.* If I hadn't . . .

I was saved from wandering down that same nonproductive path by the flag on my cyber-mailbox. I opened the article and scanned through it. Seemed like kid stuff to me—demands by a student activist group for the administration to intervene with the small college in the Upstate that had pulled the boy's scholarship offer. As if that would make any difference. The law was the law. The story contained an interview with the leader, Serena Montalvo, about what she viewed as rampant discrimination against Hispanics in her school, and then went on to describe the ceremonial parade of about a hundred students out of the building.

There were pictures of the group milling around in the parking lot, waving signs and no doubt chanting slogans. I could barely remember the antiwar demonstrations of the seventies, and these kids hadn't even been born yet, but they seemed to have the technique down. The sheriff's office had sent deputies to disperse them, and they'd returned to their classrooms with only a couple of minor scuffles. Alerting the paper had gotten them what they really wanted. The article concluded with the information that Serena had been the driving force in organizing both the group itself and the demonstration. She had been an honors student, although no mention was made of any college plans.

"Bay?" I turned at Red's voice in the doorway. "What are you doing?"

"Just checking on something for work." Without conscious thought, I clicked on the desktop, effectively blocking out the story I'd just been studying. "Erik called, and I didn't want to wake you."

"You're missing the end of the game. We've got the ball first and goal with less than two minutes left. Still down by four." He held out his hand. "Come on. Leave that for tomorrow."

I nodded and followed him back into the great room.

After the Panthers pulled it out, we couldn't get interested in the second game, and Red left a little before six. He'd been working crazy hours for the past few weeks. Generally fall and winter were the quiet times in our corner of the Lowcountry, the tourists and the golfers having already spent their precious vacation days or headed south to Florida's warmer climate. But a spate of armed robberies all over the county had everyone at the sheriff's office pulling extra shifts as they dealt with the unusual crime spree along with their everyday duties of protecting an exploding population spread over a wide geographic area. Living in paradise has its downside, too.

Back in the office, I tried Bobby Santiago and again got his voice mail. I'd begun to worry more as the afternoon wore on, and I still hadn't heard from him. I toyed with the idea of calling Dolores, but I didn't want to alarm her. Maybe he'd already reported in at home, I told myself. If so, my housekeeper would eventually let me know.

Concern still niggled at the back of my mind as I straightened up the kitchen and threw a few more logs on the fire before curling up on the sofa with my latest project. Having devoured all the John D. MacDonald and Dashiell Hammett novels, I had recently embarked on the complete works of Agatha Christie. Dame Agatha had been so prolific, I decided to divide her books by protagonist. I'd finished the Miss Marples and had begun on the Hercule Poirots. I was saving Tommy and Tuppence Beresford, my personal favorites, for last.

I found my place in *Peril at End House*. Three pages in, the slamming of the front door sent the book flying. I leaped up to find Dolores Santiago dripping water onto the hardwood floor she spent so many hours fussing over. Behind her, the hulking form of her husband, Hector, loomed like a giant over my diminutive housekeeper.

"What is it?" I asked in a breathless whisper a moment before Dolores flung herself into my arms.

"My Roberto, *mi bebé*!"

My heart dropped into my feet as I held the tiny trembling woman. I looked across her head to the stoic face of her husband.

"*Desaparecido,*" he said softly.

Gone.

CHAPTER THREE

I BREWED TEA WHILE THE TWO OF THEM SHED THEIR wet coats and huddled around the small table in the breakfast alcove. Heads together, they murmured to each other, primarily in Spanish, so I missed most of the conversation.

"Okay," I said, handing mugs around, "tell me what's going on."

They exchanged a look, then Hector spoke, a note of quiet defiance in his voice. "You say wait, *Señora,* but we go to Charleston. To Roberto's place. His friend, his . . . *compañero de habitación?*" He glanced helplessly at his wife.

"Roommate?" I asked, and he nodded.

"*Sí.* He is a good boy, we think. James Fenwick. He is Anglo. From the North. He says Roberto go home, but . . . no." Hector shook his head, and Dolores's lip trembled. "How he get here, eh, *Señora?* Roberto no have car."

I didn't want to suggest that Bobby had hitchhiked down from Charleston, but that's probably what he'd do. Kids that age, especially boys, thought themselves invincible. And immortal.

The tea sat untouched before the two distraught parents, but I sipped at mine while I tried to formulate some response that wouldn't scare them more than they already were. I toyed with divulging the substance of Bobby's call, but that could only make things worse for them.

"Why don't you go home and wait for him? I'll bet he shows up tired and wet and hungry before the evening's out." I forced a smile. "You can chew him out for making you worry."

Dolores nodded. "*Sí.* We . . . scold him very hard."

"Okay. In the meantime, I'll see if I can track him down. And if he doesn't come home tonight, you can call the sheriff in the morning. I'll help in any way I can. I don't have any experience with teenaged boys, but I think maybe this isn't that unusual. Try not to imagine the worst."

I hoped my babbling was offering Dolores and her dour husband some comfort. I wished I believed even half of what I'd just said.

After Hector's landscaping truck disappeared into the rainy Sunday darkness, I tried the number they'd given me for Bobby's dorm room at College of Charleston. I didn't hold out much hope, but surprisingly, someone answered on the third ring.

"Yeah?"

"Is this James Fenwick?"

"Yeah?"

"My name is Bay Tanner. I'm a friend of the Santiagos, Bobby's parents?"

"I told them he's not here. He said he was going home."

"Well, he hasn't arrived. Exactly what did he say and when did he leave?"

"Is this gonna take long? I've got an English lit exam tomorrow morning, and I need to study."

I chewed on my lower lip a moment to keep my anger and anxiety from spilling out onto this ill-mannered kid. "If you answer my questions, it won't take long at all."

His sigh held eighteen years' worth of frustration at the inexplicable ways of adults. "He said he needed to take care of something at home. That he'd be gone a couple of days and would I cover for him. You know, say he was sick if anybody asked."

"Anybody like who?"

"You know, his profs. Or Chad, our house mother."

I stifled an inappropriate laugh. "Does Chad have a last name? How I can get in touch with him?"

"Chad Pickering. Call the switchboard and ask for him, okay? Look, I really need to study for this exam. Lit isn't my best subject." He paused. "I'm gonna be a lawyer."

Just what the world needs, I thought.

"What time was this, James? When Bobby left?"

"I dunno. After lunch. We sent out for a pizza, then he got this call, and—"

"From whom?"

"I don't know! Look, lady, we share the room, okay? I'm not his mother."

And this was the child Hector Santiago had described as a good boy. I took a deep calming breath.

"What time, James?"

"Maybe around twelve thirty? I'm not sure." He heaved his own exasperated sigh. "I was *studying.*"

I got the sarcasm. "Okay. Thanks for your time. If you hear from Bobby, or he comes back, have him call his parents. Or me. He's got my number."

"Sure, no problem." His next words did a lot to rehabilitate him, at least in my estimation. "He's probably fine. His parents shouldn't worry too much. Bobby's about as straight-arrow as they come."

I thanked him again and hung up.

I spent the next hour pacing the length of the great room and back, jumping at every gust of wind that continued to fling bursts of rain against the French doors. I'd tried connecting with Chad Pickering, the dorm monitor, but he wasn't answering. Twice I'd picked up the phone to track Red down, then changed my mind. Finally, I strode into the office and pulled up the article Erik had e-mailed me and read it through again. Another name besides Serena Montalvo's had figured prominently in the newspaper account: the boy whose scholarship had been revoked, Enrique Salazar.

There were four listings in the local phone book, but I had no way of determining which one had a college-age son whose life had been turned upside down by his parents' illegal immigration status. It wasn't a question I wanted to ask strangers, especially if I expected their cooperation. As I pondered my very limited options, the phone rang.

I grabbed it up without checking the caller ID. "Bay Tanner."

"Hey, I'm not interrupting anything, am I? I mean, if you and the sergeant are in the middle of—"

"Give it a rest, Gabby. I'm alone."

"Sorry to hear that, Tanner. Since my own love life is basically in the toilet, I was hoping . . ."

"Do you have something for me?"

She laughed. "You're no fun at all. Yeah, I've got a name on the dead kid. Theresa Montalvo. Sixteen, junior at Hilton Head High. Beautiful girl. We got a picture from the parents. We'll be running it in tomorrow's paper. Shame."

"*Theresa* Montalvo? Are you sure?"

"Father identified the body. The face was pretty much intact. Why?"

I swallowed hard at her callousness. I supposed it was standard emotional armor for a reporter who had to deal with so many tragedies, but it grated on me nonetheless. "It must have been awful for him, the poor man."

"Of course. But you were surprised at the name. Why?"

"That . . . client I told you about thought it might be someone else. Did Theresa have a sister?"

I could almost hear Gabby's antennae quivering across the crackling phone line. "Let me check my notes. Yeah, Serena. Older. And two younger brothers. What's going on, Bay? You're holding out on me. I can feel it."

"I have to think about this. Let me call you back."

"Oh no you don't. This isn't how the game works, and you damn well know it. I want the name of your client and why he—or she—assumed the dead girl was this Serena. Cough it up, Tanner."

"I'll call you. Thanks, Gabby," I added and hung up.

I imagined I could hear her shrieks of frustration all the way from Bluffton. I shrugged. She'd get over it.

I pulled the legal pad toward me and began a list. Suddenly there were a lot of players in this gruesome scenario: Theresa and Serena Montalvo. Enrique Salazar. Maybe James Fenwick. And Bobby Santiago. Where the hell was the kid? I'd be willing to bet the phone call he'd received a couple of hours after he'd talked to me had been about the Montalvo girl's death. That might explain his taking off in such a hurry, although I hadn't yet worked out exactly why. I hated to disturb Dolores and Hector, but I needed information.

The hope in my housekeeper's voice made me cringe.

"Dolores, it's me. Bay. You haven't heard from him yet?"

"No, *Señora.* You have news?"

"Sorry, no. But I wanted to ask you a question. Does Roberto have a girlfriend? Someone he dated before he went to college?"

I could picture her round olive face creased in concentration. "There were girls, but not one. Not that he tell me."

I shuddered at the obvious pain in her long sigh. Dolores was wondering if there were a lot of things her beloved middle child hadn't told me.

"Okay. It was just a thought. Have you been in touch with any of his friends here? Someone he might have called to come pick him up?"

"*Sí.* Hector, he try all we remember. No one has heard from Roberto."

"How about Angelina?"

Bobby and Angie had seemed fairly close the few times I

remembered seeing them together. He might have confided in his big sister.

"We have asked, *Señora. Mi hija,* she say she no hear from Roberto."

At least not that she's telling her parents, I thought. I'd never experienced the joy—or aggravation—of brothers and sisters, but my best friend Bitsy and I had kept all manner of secrets, especially from our autocratic mothers. The us-against-them mentality would surely be even stronger among siblings.

"Well, try not to worry too much. He's a pretty level-headed young man."

"*Sí, Señora. Gracias,*" she whispered before disconnecting.

I wandered back into the great room and did some more pacing. I flipped the TV back on, more for background noise than for any interest in what might be playing. A news break, just before the hour, brought my head snapping around. I grabbed the remote and cranked up the volume.

The hit-and-run was the lead local story. I missed the first few seconds, but I caught a pert blond reporter shoving a microphone into the face of a twitchy young man with a scraggly beard and eyes that looked everywhere except at the camera. The words superimposed on the screen read, JASON EARLY, REPORTED BODY.

"It must have been quite a shock, coming upon the remains like that in the middle of the road," the girl was saying. "How did you feel?"

The witness fumbled for words. "I, uh . . . I mean, it was awful. At first I thought it was a dog maybe, you know? I had to swerve to miss it. But then I saw that it, you know, had clothes on and stuff, so I stopped."

"Did you realize right away that Ms. Montalvo was dead?"

Jason Early looked at the reporter as if she'd lost her mind. "Well, yeah. I mean, she was sort of, uh, mangled, you know? Like if you hit a raccoon and . . . And Ter— I mean, the girl was so pretty. Kinda made me sick." The boy wiped away an invisible tear. "So I

called the sheriff on my cell phone." He delivered the next line looking straight into the camera. "Right away."

"A terrible ordeal, I'm certain," the reporter purred into the microphone. "Another young life senselessly snuffed out here in the
Lowcountry. Our hearts go out to the Montalvo family. Anyone with
information on this shocking hit-and-run should call the Beaufort
County Sheriff's Office at the number on your screen. Reporting
from Ridgeland, this is Becca Thompson. Back to you, Carl."

There were only three listings for Early in the Hilton Head
phone book but more than a dozen in the section for the northern
part of the county that included Ridgeland. No Jasons. I checked the
clock over the sink in the kitchen. At a little after ten, most people
would still be up but probably not terribly receptive to being interrupted by a stranger, especially one who had only a one-in-twelve
chance of having the right number. I decided it could wait until
morning.

I turned off the TV, picked up my book, and settled again onto
the sofa, but I couldn't get my mind back on the adventures of Poirot
and Captain Hastings.

Jason Early had known the victim of the hit-and-run before he
chanced on her body in the middle of 278. He'd almost called her by
name during the interview, catching himself just in time. And he'd
been a little too earnest about insisting he'd called in the accident
immediately.

The boy knew more than he was willing to tell the perky reporter,
and I wondered why.

CHAPTER
FOUR

THE STORM RAGED THROUGHOUT THE NIGHT, SENDING pine cones and dead tree branches bouncing off the roof of my beach house and jerking me awake every few minutes. I finally gave up a little after six and stumbled into the shower.

By seven, as I sat at the small table in the kitchen alcove sipping Earl Grey and studying the morning paper, the worst of it had moved out to sea. A thin line of blue appeared along the horizon, although heavy waves continued to slam against the dunes that separated my deck from the ocean. My yard looked as if a giant hand had shaken every tree until the ground was thick with stripped leaves and shattered limbs.

Hector Santiago and his landscaping crews would be busy today, I thought, and pointed the remote at the little TV mounted under the counter. The seven o'clock update had nothing new on the hit-and-run, just a rehash of the previous night's report. I downed the last of an English muffin with extra-crunchy peanut butter and refocused on the *Island Packet*.

Gabby Henson had indeed been given the lead story, and her flamboyant style brought the gruesome details to life on the flimsy page. A blurry photo of the confused, desolate parents of Theresa Montalvo nearly broke my heart. Often over the past couple of years

I'd had occasion to grieve the fact that Rob and I had never had children. At times like these, I could almost feel grateful.

I jumped at the shrill bleat of the telephone in the morning stillness.

"Mrs. Tanner, it's me. Bobby Santiago."

My relief that he wasn't lying sprawled in the road somewhere
quickly morphed into anger. "Where the hell are you? Do you know
your parents have been looking all over the damn state for you?"

His voice didn't quite match the contrition of his words. "I
know. I'm sorry."

In the background I could just make out what sounded like the
clatter of dishes and the low hum of conversation punctuated by an
occasional raucous laugh.

"Where are you?" I asked again.

"We're . . . I'm okay. Really."

I wasn't about to let that little slip go unchallenged. "Who's *we*?"

I expected him to ignore the question, and he didn't disappoint.
"Will you let my folks know I'm all right?"

"Why can't you call them yourself?"

"I don't want to get into a big hassle. I've got some things I have
to do. Just tell them not to worry, okay?"

I was losing him. "Bobby, wait! Let me help you." I took heart
when he didn't immediately hang up. "Tell me what's going on. You
said yesterday you thought Serena Montalvo might have been killed
intentionally. Are you aware it wasn't her, that it was her sister,
Theresa?"

He took a long time to answer. "Yeah. But it was a mistake."

"What was a mistake? You mean the identification? Her father—"

"No! Terry shouldn't have . . . I mean . . ."

A woman sobbed, close enough to Bobby's phone that I could
make out a few choked words in Spanish, although I had no idea of
their meaning. It sounded like *a skull cap mean,* which made absolutely no sense at all, but I scribbled the phrase on a scrap of paper
on the desk anyway.

"Who's with you, Bobby? Is it Serena?"

"I have to go now. Did they find out who . . . who was driving the car?"

"No, not yet. How are you involved in all this, Bobby? What are you afraid of? Please, let me help you. You can trust me."

"I'll call you later. I promise. I just have to check out a couple of things first. I . . . we'll be careful."

"Wait!" My mind groped for some way of keeping the kid on the phone, of holding him until I could figure out a way of reaching him. "Do you know someone named Jason Early?"

"What's Jason got to do with anything?"

"So you do know him. He's the one who discovered the . . . Theresa. He called the sheriff to report the accident."

"Jason? Are you sure?"

Again I heard the mumbled Spanish in the background, unaccompanied this time by sobs. Instead, the voice sounded clipped, angry.

"He was on the news last night," I said. "He sounded as if he might have known Theresa. Before. What does he have to do with this?"

"I have to go, Mrs. Tanner. I really will call. I think we might need your help after all. Tell my mom not to worry."

Before I could open my mouth, he was gone.

I stared at the phone a moment before replacing it in its cradle. The caller ID had revealed only Bobby's cell number, so he could have been anywhere in the country. Or even out of it, for that matter. No clues there. It had definitely been restaurant noise in the background, but again that told me nothing, other than that it had sounded more like a diner than a fast-food place.

And then there was the girl. I'd bet my next dividend check it had been Serena Montalvo. Young, Hispanic, scared. And devastated by the death of Theresa, as you'd expect her to be over the loss of a younger sister. Idly, I picked up the scrap of paper on which I'd scribbled the strange words and carried it with me back to the table.

A skull cap mean. I repeated it to myself several times, but it still came out as gibberish.

How was I going to let Dolores and Hector know their son was all right without divulging the reason for his contacting me? Bobby wasn't my client, so no confidentiality to hide behind. He was eighteen, in some respects legally still a child. His parents had a right to know—what? That was the problem. What could I tell them for certain? All my conclusions were based on guesses and suppositions. All I knew for sure was that the kid was alive and well. For now. I hoped that would be enough.

I didn't have the number where Dolores was working, so I tried Hector's cell phone. He answered immediately, and I could hear the hope in his voice.

"*Señora. Buenos días.* You have news?"

"Yes. Bobby . . . Roberto called me just a few minutes ago. He asked me to tell you and Dolores that he's fine," I said in a rush. "He'll be in touch soon." A small but forgivable lie.

I'd expected Hector to blow a fuse, rail at me for a while in Spanish so I couldn't translate the curse words. He hadn't been shy about letting me have it in the emergency room a few years ago when his wife lay unconscious, bruised and battered by a pair of intruders who had made her pay for defending my home. I'd deserved it then, and I would certainly understand if he wanted to vent at me again.

But he surprised me. "*Gracias, Señora,*" he said softly. "He is not hurt? Not in trouble?"

"He's fine," I said with more conviction than I felt. "He wouldn't tell me anything about where he is or why he doesn't call you directly, but he did sound . . . fine."

"I will tell *mi esposa. Gracias.*" I could almost see his chin rise, the fierce pride I'd always admired in all the Santiagos constraining him from asking for my help. Not a problem. He'd get it anyway.

"You're welcome, Hector. Try to keep Dolores from worrying too much. Your son is a good young man. I think you should trust him."

I'd stepped over the line. I could tell by his terse, "*Sí, Señora. Adiós.*"

I glanced at the scrap of paper I'd been crumpling nervously in my hand. "Wait! Can I ask you something, Hector?"

"*Sí.*"

"It's about Spanish. I heard . . . someone say something that I didn't understand." I smoothed out the paper. "It sounded like *a skull cap mean.* Does that make any sense to you?"

"Say again, please."

"A skull cap mean."

"This has something to do with my Roberto, *Señora?*"

"I'm not sure. Why, what does it mean?"

"I believe you have said, '*Es culpa mía.*'" Hector paused. "In English, it would be, 'It is my fault.'"

The phone rang again almost as soon as I'd hung up. Gabby Henson, no doubt looking for her quid pro quo. I let the machine record her rant about what an ungrateful jerk I was while I cleaned up the kitchen. I promised myself I'd make it up to her as soon as I could.

I pulled into the parking lot of the one-story complex that housed our office just ahead of Erik. I shivered a little in my light jacket as I waited for him to climb down from his Ford Expedition. The Weather Channel had predicted a return to the high sixties by midafternoon, but the wind still swirled off the water, bringing with it a sharp, salty tang and a definite wintry bite.

Inside our neat, compact reception area, I flipped the thermostat over to heat and raised the temperature to seventy-two.

"We'll be sweltering by noon," Erik said, sliding his laptop onto the bare desk. He wore a heavy cotton sweater, its deep green color contrasting nicely with his light hair and fading tan.

"I'll live with it. You got anything going on this morning?" I stepped into my office and draped the jacket across the back of my swivel chair.

"Let me check messages," he said, reaching for the phone.

I felt too chilled for my usual Diet Coke, so I retrieved a pad from the center desk drawer. From my bag, I pulled the page of notes I'd made earlier at home.

"Hot damn!" Erik's grin lit his handsome face.

"What?"

He crossed the carpet and deposited himself in the client chair in front of my desk. "You remember the deal I've been working on with the recreation association?"

"The contract to do all their background checks on employees and volunteers? Don't tell me we got it?"

My associate raised his hand for a celebratory high five. "We certainly did. They want to meet with us later this week to finalize details."

"Nice work. That should keep the wolf from the door for a couple of months."

"It's even better than that. They think the county will want to use us as well, so it won't just be the island. If it pans out, we could get a lot of local government work, maybe even the schools. That would really put us on the map."

I smiled at the obvious pride on Erik's face. Contacting the recreation folks had been his idea, and he'd done the lion's share of the work on it. A chance conversation with a member of the board while the two of them were working out at a local gym had been the catalyst, and Erik had pursued it doggedly. All that effort was about to pay off, and he deserved every bit of the credit.

"I think this calls for a raise," I said, surprised when he shook his head.

"Not until we get everything signed on the dotted line. And then I'd like to see how profitable it really turns out to be."

I laughed. "You're turning into a worse Scrooge than I am. Are you sure you didn't used to be an accountant, too?"

His face still held the thoughtful, sober look. "I'm aware we might still be on shaky ground with . . . with Ben gone. I know the fact that he used to be a cop got us the license, and without him . . . Well, you said yourself you aren't sure if they're gonna let us renew next year. So I just don't want to get too excited about this in case it all ends up falling down around our ears."

"Okay, spoilsport," I said, unwilling to let his worries put a damper on his accomplishment in landing the account. "We'll see how it goes." I waited until he looked up. "I'm proud of you."

The blush reached his ears. "Thanks."

He rose but turned when I called his name.

"I want to run this thing with Bobby Santiago by you. Got time?"

"Sure. Just let me call Jack and set up an appointment. Is Friday good for you?"

I flipped open my nearly pristine desk calendar. "That's fine. Work around your own schedule."

Erik's part-time job at the office supply store took up almost all the hours he didn't spend at Simpson & Tanner. I hoped the new client would give me an opportunity to pay him enough to make his second job unnecessary. We'd been pretty much treading water for the past year, and I sincerely hoped this new opportunity would finally kick-start the business.

While he talked, I took a few moments to arrange my notes and my thoughts so I could present him with a coherent report of my conclusions regarding Bobby Santiago and Serena Montalvo, including her admission in Spanish that her sister's death had been her fault. That part scared me more than any other.

The front door banging inward made me jump, and I looked up to find Red Tanner storming across the room, his olive green jacket damp across the shoulders as if he'd been standing under a dripping tree. In a few angry strides he stood in the doorway of my office.

"Hey," I said, confused and more than a little taken aback by the scowl on his face. "What's up?"

"You're involved in this hit-and-run, aren't you?" Before I had a chance to open my mouth, he railed on. "I specifically asked you about it yesterday, and you didn't say one damn word. I have to hear it from that scandal-mongering reporter pal of yours. How do you think that makes me look?"

Behind him, I saw Erik hang up, and I hoped Red's outburst hadn't made it through to Jack Ogilvy's phone at the recreation board.

Silently, I cursed Gabby Henson and all her ancestors. "Calm down before you have a stroke," I said with what I hoped was just enough lightness to defuse Red's anger. "Have a seat. Want a Coke?"

"No, I don't want a damn Coke! I want an explanation." Some of the fury eased out of his voice as he pulled out the client chair and sat. "I thought we had a deal."

I glanced up to find Erik hovering, unsure whether this was a situation he needed—or wanted—to get involved in. "Close the door, will you, please?" I asked, and he complied.

"Listen, Bay, I—"

"No, you listen," I said, leaning over the desk so he had to look me squarely in the eye. "Don't ever do that again, do you hear me? Do not come barging into my office and chew me out in front of Erik, especially when you don't have the first damn idea of what the hell you're talking about. Wait!" I said through clenched teeth when he opened his mouth to interrupt. "We do have a deal, and the problem is that you keep forgetting your side of the bargain. I run my business the way I see fit. I don't answer to you for any of it. All I promised was that I'd be careful. And I am. That's all you need to know."

We glared across the desk at each other, neither of us willing to be the first to look away.

Finally, Red sighed and leaned back in his chair. "You and that Henson broad made me look like a fool in front of the sheriff."

"Then you should be over at the newspaper chewing *her* ass out," I said with more calm than I felt. "I thought we'd gotten past all this protective crap," I added. "I don't need a keeper, Red. You're very much mistaken if that's the job you think you've signed on for."

We'd been down this road before, and I completely understood his fears. I had a few of my own every time he went out on a call, especially with armed robbers routinely holding up convenience stores and bars all over the county. I didn't want to be burying another Tanner, either.

"I know all that. But Henson said you knew the name of the victim before it was reported anywhere in the press and that you had a lead on the driver. You know damn well you can't withhold stuff like that from us, Bay."

"Gabby's wrong, at least about my knowing the driver. The rest of it isn't pertinent to your investigation. If I had anything solid, you'd already have it. If you can't trust me at least that far, then I don't know what the hell we're doing here."

"We're having a lover's quarrel, in case you hadn't noticed," he said, that grin that reminded me so much of his dead brother's suddenly replacing the scowl.

I closed my eyes and willed Rob's face out of my head. "Go away, Red. If I run across anything that will help identify the perp, you'll be the first to know."

His laugh drained all the tension from the tiny room. "Perp? No one talks like that except on *Law and Order* reruns."

I smiled back. "Get out of here, please. Go hassle a speeding tourist or something. I have work to do."

"I'm sorry, sweetheart," he said, reaching across the desk for my hand. "I worry about you, that's all."

"I know," I said, returning the pressure of his fingers. "Try for a little balance, though, okay?"

"Okay. Call you tonight?"

"Fine." I watched him open the door and nod to Erik as he stepped outside.

"What was all that about?" he asked, replacing Red in the client chair.

I sighed and ran a hand through my tangled mop of hair. "He thinks I'm holding out on him about the hit-and-run."

"Are you?" Erik asked.

"Sort of," I said, and he frowned.

CHAPTER FIVE

"HERE'S HOW I SEE IT," ERIK SAID, HANDING ME A Diet Coke and opening a Sprite for himself. He hesitated, waiting for my reaction.

"Go ahead."

"Dolores's son, the Montalvo sisters, and this Early guy all know each other, maybe from school. If Bobby is Serena's boyfriend, he's probably mixed up in her immigration causes, too. Maybe she stuck her nose in the wrong place or rattled the wrong chain. But for some reason, the whole group is willing to accept that someone tried to kill her and got Theresa by mistake. Serena and Bobby are on the run from these same people. I don't know where Jason fits into it. Could he be the one who called Bobby about the hit-and-run?"

I shook my head. "I don't think so. I'm pretty sure Jason knew it was Theresa. He slipped and almost called her by her nickname on the TV interview. Why would he have told Bobby it was Serena who'd been killed when he knew it wasn't?"

"So there's another player to be named later."

"Maybe this Enrique Salazar, the one who got his scholarship yanked. I'm assuming he'd be in the forefront of Serena's movement, since he seems to have been the catalyst for the walkout last spring."

Erik swallowed soda before replying. "Lots of assuming in all this, when you think about it." He smiled across the desk. "You taught me that could be dangerous."

"So is holding out on the sheriff. Much as it pains me to admit it, Red is right about that."

"I know. But if these kids know something about the girl's death, they're all in danger."

"But from whom? If I can't get Bobby to open up to me, I really don't know where to go next. Add to that the fact I don't have a clue where the hell he is, and we don't even have a place to start."

"Sure we do." Erik waggled his fingers at me. "The magic box. Let me see what I can coax out of the Net."

"It would be good to know if Serena Montalvo has a car," I said, "or access to one. Jason Early obviously does, but he was home last night being interviewed live on TV, so I don't see how he could be the one transporting Bobby around."

Erik rose. "Let me play with it a little, see what I come up with."

"Fine. Then give me the proposal you've been working on for Jack Ogilvy. I'll do some polishing and get all the supporting documents together."

We worked steadily at our separate tasks for the next hour, the only sound the click of our keyboards and the occasional *whoosh* of warm air when the heat pump kicked on. The phone, when it rang, sounded particularly shrill in the silence of our small office.

"I've got it," Erik called from the desk in reception. A moment later he stood in my doorway. "Gabby Henson."

I rolled my eyes. "Did you tell her I was here?"

"I didn't say."

"What does she want, do you know?"

"She said she had some information you might find interesting, but that you were gonna have to 'cough up' first."

"Tell her I'm on the other line, and I'll call her back." I looked past Erik when the outer door swung open. A few dead leaves swirled into the room followed closely by the *Packet*'s ace crime reporter, her phone still stuck to her ear.

"Bay, Bay, Bay," she said, flipping her cell closed and dropping it in the pocket of her brown leather bomber jacket. "Trying to avoid me again?"

When I'd initially encountered the reporter a couple of summers ago, it had been roughly twenty years since our paths had first crossed on the campus of Northwestern University. I'd been shocked to see the impish girl I remembered carrying an extra fifty pounds, the result, she claimed, of three sons and a cheating ex-husband. I knew she'd been determined to shed the weight, and it looked now as if she'd been working hard at it. It was a trimmer, more sprightly Gabby who marched across the carpet and stuck out her hand.

"You must be Erik. I can't believe we've never officially met. Gabby Henson, Intrepid Girl Reporter."

Erik took the offered hand and smiled down at the smaller woman. "Pleased to meet you."

"Is it a rule that Bay only lets hunky-looking men hang around her?" Gabby winked up at Erik, who predictably blushed.

"You might as well come in," I said, leaning back in my chair. "I have a feeling it would take an act of Congress to get you out of here now."

"Don't scowl, Tanner. It makes wrinkles." She set her battered leather satchel on the floor and dropped into the client chair. "Got any coffee?"

"No. There's soda and water in the fridge." I indicated the compact unit next to her right arm. "Help yourself."

"Handy." She pulled out a Diet Coke and popped the top.

"You look good," I said, meaning it.

"About fifteen more pounds to go, and I'll be back to where I was before Rory was born. I don't think I'll ever shake what I put on with the first two, but I can live with that."

"How are the boys?"

"Two teenagers and a wannabe. What do you think? You could cut the testosterone level in my house with a knife."

"I like your hair." The sparse light filtering in from the single window in the reception area glinted off blond streaks in what I remembered from our previous encounters as a mousy brown mess.

"Cost more than my damned car payment," she said, "but worth it. Believe it or not, I've actually had a couple of dates. Drives old what's-his-name crazy. So enough of the pleasantries. Let's talk turkey."

"Sure. You go first."

Her bark of laughter reverberated off the walls. "Nice try. Fool me once, and all that." She reached down and pulled a creased and smudged notebook from her briefcase. The pen appeared in her hand as if she'd had it tucked up her sleeve. "Theresa Montalvo, sixteen, daughter of immigrant parents from El Salvador, was struck and killed Saturday night on Route 278 near the intersection of Spanish Wells Road."

"That sounds like the opening line from the newspaper article. Tell me something I don't already know," I said.

"Unh-uh. You called me assuming the dead girl was the sister, Serena. Why?"

"I told you. A friend of hers heard about the accident and thought it was her. Obviously—" I swallowed down the *he* I'd been about to blurt out. "Obviously this person was mistaken."

Gabby stared across the desk at me, and I held her gaze without flinching. "You also implied it might have been deliberate. Did this *person* tell you why?"

"No," I answered with complete honesty.

Gabby was obviously resisting the urge to run a hand through her carefully arranged and expensively colored hair. Instead she vented her frustration by tossing her pen onto the desktop. "Look, Bay, we could help each other. I've heard a couple of hints around the sheriff's office that the scene didn't exactly support the idea of an accident, either. Your handsome brother-in-law nearly tossed me out on my can when I brought up the subject. If we pool our resources, we might be able to get to the bottom of this. If someone deliberately ran down that poor girl, don't you want to nail the scumbag?"

Gabby knew me too well.

"Of course I do. But you've never been able to wrap your re-porter's head around the fact that I have confidentiality issues the same as you do. You regularly protect sources, and I'm damned sure you'd go to jail to honor those commitments. I can't tell you any more than I already have."

She snatched up the pen and tossed it and her notebook into the briefcase. She pushed back the chair as she rose. "Okay, I can respect that, I guess. Like I told you before, we could make a formidable team. But I'm willing to play it your way—for now."

After Gabby breezed out the door, Erik stepped back into my office.

"Is she always like that?" he asked, settling into the vacant chair.

"You mean like a pudgy, bad-tempered tornado?"

He laughed. "Yeah."

"Pretty much. It's part of what makes her good at her job, though."

"Sounds like we're gonna have to stay a couple of steps ahead of her."

"You mean if we want to keep Bobby Santiago out of her clutches."

"Right." He paused, and his eyes slid away from mine.

"What are you thinking?" I asked.

"Well . . . I really hate to bring it up, but it could have . . . ramifications down the road."

"You're thinking something about this could come back to bite us?"

Erik squirmed in the chair and hitched his leg across his knee. "Not *us* so much as you."

"Spit it out," I said, my stomach fluttering a little at the solemn look on his face.

"Okay, it's . . . What do you know about Dolores and Hector? I mean, about their . . . status?"

"You're asking me if they're legal, is that it?"

"Yes."

I bit back the angry words that sprang immediately into my head and drew a long breath before I spoke. "That's a legitimate question, I guess. I know Dolores came from Guatemala when she was pretty young. Not a kid, but maybe a teenager. I'm almost positive she met Hector here." The fluttering had turned into a full-scale rumbling in my gut as I realized how little hard information I really had. "He has to be legal because he's got a license for the landscaping business. I mean, he must have, right? The town has been cracking down pretty hard on that, so—"

"Assumptions," Erik said softly.

I sat back in my chair and mulled over the implications. I was certain all the kids had been born here, which granted them automatic citizenship. But Dolores could—

"Wait!" I nearly shouted the word, and Erik jumped. "I report what I pay Dolores to the IRS. If there was anything fishy about her Social Security number or immigration status, it would have set off alarm bells in the system long before this."

"That's good. Look, Bay, I'm not trying to cause trouble for them. I'm just thinking that having Bobby involved in this investigation about the hit-and-run could maybe send someone like your friend Gabby—or the sheriff's office—digging into stuff you'd rather they didn't." He paused, then added, "I can do some checking if you want."

The thought of rooting around in Dolores's past seemed like the worst kind of violation of our friendship, but Erik was right. Better if we discovered a problem than if a reporter or someone official ferreted it out. At least we could do damage control.

"Okay," I said. "See what you can find out." I held out my hand as he rose. "But discreetly, understood? I don't know how I'd explain it if she got wind we were sniffing around her family's personal business."

"Got it."

"And Erik?" I said, and he turned back. "Just for the record? I don't like this."

"I know," he said softly.

I sat for a few moments staring off into space, the clacking sound of my partner's fingers on the keyboard chattering in the stillness. *He won't find anything,* I told myself. With a sigh, I pulled the proposal for Jack Ogilvy and the recreation board toward me and tried to concentrate on proofreading Erik's figures. But Dolores's sweet face as she bustled around my house kept sliding into my vision. After ten minutes of rereading the same section about a hundred times, I tossed the papers aside and reached for my jacket. I slung my bag over my shoulder and paused in front of Erik's desk.

"Listen," I said, "I need to get out of here."

"Okay." His eyes studied me expectantly.

"I'm gonna run up to Ridgeland and see if I can get a line on this Jason Early. The fact that he knows . . . knew the dead girl—and Bobby and the sister as well—is giving me bad vibes."

"Okay," he said again. "Anything I can do to help?"

"Just find me proof that Dolores and Hector don't have anything to worry about. From Immigration, anyway. I'll sleep a lot better knowing they're in the clear."

"Understood. You coming back?"

I shook my head. "Probably not. I may have to do a lot of legwork to track down the right Earlys. There were a ton of them in the phone book. And I think I'll stop in at Presqu'isle while I'm up that way. I haven't seen the Judge in a week or so."

"Give him and Lavinia my best," Erik said. "I'll call you if anything comes up here."

"Thanks."

I hesitated, wanting to tell him it wasn't his fault that the whole county—hell, the whole *country*—had gone crazy over the subject of illegal immigration. That I was certain he wouldn't find anything that could hurt the sweet woman who had nursed me back to sanity. Instead, I simply nodded and bolted through the door.

CHAPTER SIX

*T*HE TRIP UP TO BEAUFORT IS PRETTY STRAIGHTFOR-
ward when the roads aren't clogged with our two million annual visitors, although we get a slight increase in the trickle of
winter tourists as we get closer to the holidays. I settled into the soft
leather seats of the Jaguar and breezed through every single traffic
light before taking the off-ramp to 170.

At the vocational school, I hung a left and headed north through
thick stands of pines and hardwoods. Interstate 95 would have been
faster, but I'd felt the need for the tranquility of the nearly deserted
two-lane road, flanked occasionally by low swales of swampy ground.
Off to my right, the pale winter sun glinted off dry brown marsh
grass, and my eye was caught by a trio of great blue herons startled
into graceful flight by a swooping red-tailed hawk. Sometimes, in
the madness of traffic and visitors and hubbub that was Hilton Head
Island a good bit of the year, I forgot how breathtakingly beautiful
and pristine the Lowcountry must have been before humans stamped
their indelible mark on it.

A few miles farther on I passed the tiny hidden cemetery where
the remains of Thomas Heyward Junior, a signer of the Declaration
of Independence and one of South Carolina's most famous sons, lay in
relative obscurity. His marker rose in the midst of a small enclosure

constructed of tabby, our local building material made of oyster shells and lime. Most people have no idea it's even there. My best childhood friend, Bitsy Elliott, and her sister members of the DAR made an annual pilgrimage to clean and preserve the site.

I turned left again and eventually wound my way into Ridgeland. The old town had recently undergone a renovation, and once sagging, neglected buildings and houses gleamed with fresh paint and pride. I parked near the center of town and pulled my list of Earlys out of my bag. I'd printed it and a street map off the Internet, and I took a moment to orient myself. A few phone calls had eliminated the ones listed for Hilton Head, and that had been a long shot anyway. If I hit on the right Jason Early, I wanted to be able to confront him without the nearly hour's drive giving him an opportunity to skip out on me.

I uncapped the bottle of water I'd snagged from the mini-fridge on my way out of the office, took a long swig, and punched in the first number.

The woman sounded elderly.

"May I speak to Jason, please?" I asked.

"I'm sorry, dear, there's no one here by that name. My husband is Charlie. Well, Charles, really, but everyone calls him Charlie. Except his mother, God rest her soul. Our boys are Ralph and Ambrose. Family name, Ambrose. Really, I didn't want to burden him with that, all the kids calling him Rosie like they done, but it's an old family name, and Charlie—"

"Thank you for your time," I managed to get in when she paused for breath. "I'm sorry to have bothered you."

I clicked off and smiled to myself. It always astounds me how much people are willing to tell you if you just shut up and listen. Of course, sometimes it's information you could have lived very well without. I shook my head and moved on to the next number.

I hit pay dirt on the fifth try.

"Are you a reporter?" The thin voice sounded weary. "We ain't talkin' to no more reporters."

So much for that. On to Plan B.

"No, ma'am. I'm investigating the hit-and-run accident, and I need to ask Jason a few follow-up questions."

I'd had to caution Erik any number of times about impersonating a police officer, the kind of rule-bending that could get our license yanked on the spot. His argument had always been that he never said he worked for law enforcement. If people chose to misinterpret the words *investigator* or *detective,* that wasn't his problem. A fine and shaky line, and I was stepping right up to it.

However, Mrs. Early—if that was in fact who I was speaking with—had apparently been around the barn a few times herself. "Are you with the sheriff?" she asked, her tone making it sound like an accusation.

"No, ma'am. I'm a private investigator."

The long silence made me wonder if she'd quietly set the receiver back in its cradle and walked away.

"Ma'am? Mrs. Early?"

"Who you workin' for?"

"I'm not at liberty to divulge that information, ma'am. Let's just say it's an interested party."

"Let's just say you leave my boy alone."

This time there was no doubt she'd hung up. I clicked off my cell and consulted the map. The phone had been listed under *M. Early,* so I assumed there was no husband around. A woman's attempt to avoid advertising that she lived alone by using only her first initial seemed pointless, but I knew many still harbored the illusion. My own listing sprawled across the narrow line with my entire mouthful of names: Lydia Baynard Simpson Tanner. *If someone wants to find me,* I thought, *let them come.*

The Early address lay south of town off Route 17. Houses were sparse, intermingled with peeling billboards and abandoned produce stands. As I scanned the roadside, I passed an open field, barren now in the week before Christmas, with a massive live oak standing like a lonely sentinel at its center. It was an old tree, its girth approaching twenty feet, I guessed, its twisted lower limbs crawling across the brown stubble like writhing snakes. I wondered how many decades it had stood watch over the death of the gracious old ways and the noisy intrusion of what we liked to call progress.

It took me only another minute to locate the right mailbox. A dirt driveway wound back from the road, alongside a defunct gas station, its bare concrete islands testifying to the one-time existence of two pumps. Graffitied squares of weathered plywood covered the windows. A block addition looked as if it might once have housed a repair or body shop. The rutted lane ended in a weed-choked yard in front of a sagging bungalow that hadn't seen a paintbrush for at least a decade. There were no cars pulled up beside the house. I parked and shut off the Jaguar's engine. From my bag I retrieved the small leather wallet that held my PI license ID and my business cards, tucked it into the pocket of my jacket, and stepped out into the warm afternoon sun.

The slamming of the door set off a frenzied barking that sounded as if it came from the rear of the house. I hesitated, my fingers still clutching the handle in case I had to make a diving retreat back into the car. When no slavering mongrel came charging at me, I moved cautiously toward the narrow porch. An ancient glider squatted there, and its matted stuffing spilled from a dozen tears in the dirty vinyl upholstery. The rents looked as if they could have been made by powerful claws. I swallowed hard and rapped on the flimsy screen door. From inside, I could hear the canned laughter of a TV show.

I waited a full minute before knocking a little harder. The door rattled on its rusty hinges, and a moment later I heard the click of shoes on linoleum. I flipped open my license.

The woman who approached wore what looked to be a permanent scowl, which was a shame because her even features hinted at a prettiness worn down by time and discontent. Her thick dark hair was caught up in a clip at the back of her head, and a few escaped tendrils curled around her slender neck. Nearly black eyes regarded me with suspicion.

"Mrs. Early?" I said through the screen mesh when she made no move to open the door. "My name is Bay Tanner." I held up my license. "We spoke a few minutes ago."

She didn't give my credentials even a glance. "And I told you to leave us alone. Jason said everything he had to say to that other woman from the Beaufort sheriff's."

Woman? I wondered if a female officer had been sent to interview the boy. Or perhaps—

"Do you remember her name?" I asked.

"What's it to you? Somethin' foreign. Polack, maybe."

I cringed at the crude epithet, but it told me what I wanted to know. Lisa Pedrovsky, the detective who might have been more than a friend of my late partner, Ben Wyler. Someone other than Bobby Santiago had to think this was more than a tragic accident. Lisa generally got the big cases, especially homicides. Although a hit-and-run could technically be called manslaughter. Still—

"You wanna get off my porch now?"

Her voice snapped me out of my pointless speculation. "I wonder if I could speak to Jason. Just for a moment." I watched the refusal spring to her lips. "I know a couple of his friends. From school."

She hesitated. "What friends?"

"Bobby Santiago and Serena Montalvo, the dead girl's sister. In fact, I'm trying to locate them. I thought maybe Jason could help me."

"Jason don't have no spic friends."

She turned and walked away, and again I listened to the tap of her heels on the floor. A moment later, I heard a door slam toward the back of the house, and the frantic barking rose to a screeching howl.

I bolted off the porch and threw myself inside the Jaguar just as Jason Early's mother rounded the corner. The massive animal strained against her hand wrapped around the metal choke chain. From the safety of my car, I stared back at her, a sad, bitter woman in too-tight jeans and a tattered sweatshirt. Her smile made the hairs on the back of my neck stand up. I shook off the shiver of fear and wheeled across her scruffy lawn, past the derelict gas station, back toward the highway.

When I glanced in the rearview mirror, she was still standing there staring after me, the snarling dog lunging against her restraining hand on its collar.

Presqu'isle couldn't have been more of a contrast to the rundown shanty Jason Early and his strange mother called home.

As I eased into the circular drive in front of the towering antebellum mansion on St. Helena Island, I tried to shake the feeling of unease the encounter had left me with. Ignorance and bigotry generally go hand-in-hand, but that half smile on Mrs. Early's face had hinted at something more elementally . . . what? Devious? Cunning?

I stepped onto the gravel of the drive and mounted the sixteen steps up the split staircase to the wide verandah that encircled the house. I pushed through the thick oak door and into the hallway that bisected the lower floor.

I headed straight for the kitchen, where I could almost always find Lavinia Smalls, Presqu'isle's housekeeper for as long as I could remember. She'd all but raised me, buffering me from my mother's erratic mood swings, most of which could be directly traced to the level of bourbon in her system. It had been Lavinia's bony chest that had cradled me after some hurt or childhood scrape, her soft brown hands that had stroked my wild chestnut hair off my face and dried my tears.

After Emmaline Baynard Simpson's death, Lavinia had stayed on to tend to my father. I'd become aware some time ago that their relationship had evolved over the years into something far deeper than either of them felt comfortable discussing with me. The thought that they'd found that kind of happiness at this stage in their lives made me smile.

"Lavinia?" I called, stepping into the spacious kitchen washed in soft light from the mullioned windows that faced St. Helena Sound.

As usual, everything gleamed, spotless and immaculate, with not a dirty glass or spoon to mar the sink or counters. Lavinia ran a tight ship. I moved back down the hallway and paused to stare into the main drawing room. Here chaos reigned amid the gilt silk upholstery of the antique furniture my mother had treasured far more than the people in her life. Boxes of Christmas ornaments littered the deep blue-and-gold-patterned carpet, and a fresh pine garland looped across the mantel of the Italian marble fireplace. I stepped inside to find the jade and ivory crèche already set out in its place of honor on the round mahogany table in the center of the room. A red leather-bound journal lay open on the settee, and I knew Lavinia had been consulting the account of a long-dead Baynard/Tattnall mistress of Presqu'isle as to the placement of my mother's family heirlooms. These traditions, kept intact from the earliest plantation days, should have angered Lavinia; but, in a way I'd never understood, she held them in as much regard as Emmaline had.

I ducked back out and turned toward my father's room, once his study before a series of small strokes had confined him to a wheelchair. The downstairs space had been converted into a bed/sitting room remodeled to accommodate his special needs. I stuck my head around the door and found him just where I'd expected to: stretched out in his recliner, an afghan across his nearly useless legs, the ashes of an earlier fire dying now in the grate of the blackened fireplace.

"Vinnie?" His voice, raspy with sleep, made me jump in the familiar stillness of the old house.

"No, Daddy, it's me." I moved around to where he could see me.

"Bay? What are you doin' here?"

Most of the time retired judge Talbot Simpson drove me crazy with his irascible temper and his constant harping at me about everything from my clothes to my love life. But in moments like these, with his still abundant white hair sticking out at odd angles and the slackness of sleep still softening his stern features, I almost felt as if I could drop onto the floor and lay my head in his lap as I had done countless times as a child.

The illusion didn't last long.

"Where the hell is Vinnie?" His eyes strayed to the clock on the carved mantel above the fireplace. "She said she just had to pick up a few things for all that confounded decorating she's been doing. Waste of time, if you ask me, which of course no one's bothered to do."

"Nice to see you, too, Daddy."

He ignored my sarcasm, as he usually did. All his years on the bench, exchanging verbal blows with defense and prosecution attorneys alike, had made him impervious to my pitiful slings and arrows.

My stomach rumbled, reminding me that I'd skipped lunch. "I'm going to see if I can scare up a sandwich. You want anything?"

The judge used his powerful right arm to bring the back of his recliner more upright. "Tea," he said, "hot. You could hang meat in here. Vinnie let the fire go out."

"It's almost seventy degrees outside," I said, but crossed to the fireplace and poked the embers back into feeble flame.

"And am I outside or in?"

I gestured toward his motorized wheelchair tucked up in its assigned corner. "You want some help getting up or shall I bring your tea in here?"

"I can manage," he said gruffly.

I moved the chair close to his recliner and left the room. Almost as much as his infirmity, my father hated displaying his helplessness to anyone except Lavinia. Especially me.

I set the kettle on the stove and found some leftover ham in the refrigerator. I cut two slices from a loaf of homemade bread, slathered on some mayonnaise, and had just pulled out a chair from the scarred oak table when I heard the whir of the Judge's wheelchair and the hiss of its tires on the heart pine floor. I poured his tea as he slid into his place across from me.

"Thank you, sweetheart," he said when I set the cup in front of him.

His moods were nothing if not mercurial.

"You're welcome." I bit into the thick sandwich. "So how long has Lavinia been gone?"

"Better part of three hours. She said she just had to run by the bank for some cash, then she had a couple of places to stop in Beaufort. Something to do with that mess in the drawing room." His smile softened his entire face. "I'm afraid I wasn't paying that much attention."

"I'm shocked," I answered, and he laughed, a short, sharp bark before his face sobered.

"It's not like her to leave me alone that long. She knows damn well there are things I can't—"

The ringing of my cell phone cut him off.

"Sorry. Let me see who it is." I recognized the number immediately. "Red," I told my father. "Hey, what's up?" I said into the phone.

"Where are you?" His voice sounded strange.

"I'm sitting in the kitchen of Presqu'isle with the Judge having a late lunch. What's the matter?"

"He can hear you?"

I glanced across at my father who was concentrating on stirring sugar into his tea and pretending not to eavesdrop. "Yes, of course. Why?"

"Can you move away? Out into the hall maybe?"

My stomach fluttered, and I pushed aside the plate with the half-eaten sandwich. "Business," I said to my father as I pushed back my chair. "I'll just be a minute."

I escaped from the kitchen before the Judge could demand details. Simpson & Tanner business was as much his as it was mine. I slipped into the drawing room.

"What the hell's going on?" I asked.

"Lavinia's been in a little trouble."

"Is she all right? What happened? Where is she?" I felt as if I couldn't draw enough breath into my lungs.

"She's not hurt. Well, just a little, but she'll be fine. She got caught up in the middle of an attempted robbery at the bank on Lady's Island."

"My God, Red! Tell me!"

"Calm down, Bay. I'm trying to. I don't have a lot of details my-self. She's here at the sheriff's office, the main building. The paramedics bandaged up the cut on her face, and she's working—"

"How did she get cut?"

"Bay, shut up a minute, okay? From what I can put together, she tried to help an old man who'd been knocked down by one of the robbers, and he tagged her, too. In the confusion, one of the tellers triggered the silent alarm, and we had a cruiser just a couple of miles away. Rookie. He hit the siren, and the guys ran. Lavinia's talking to the head of the task force right now, giving her statement. I'll bring her home in a couple of hours. I called so you could make sure the Judge is okay."

"And you're positive she's all right?" My mouth had gone so dry I could barely get the words out.

"Talked to her myself. She was more concerned about your father than anything else. I'll tell her you're there."

"You get her back here," I said. "Right now, do you hear me?"

"Daughter!"

I whirled at the sound of my father's booming voice.

"What's happened to Vinnie?"

I couldn't find the words. He reached up and grabbed the cell phone out of my hand a moment before my knees gave way, and I collapsed onto the gold settee amid the riot of boxes and tissue paper.

CHAPTER SEVEN

*I*F THE JUDGE'S LEGS HAD BEEN FUNCTIONING, I would have been forced to restrain him physically from tearing off on foot to rescue Lavinia. As it was, we had a towering, screaming argument that sent his blood pressure through the roof and made my head feel as if someone had taken a baseball bat to it. I left him cursing in the echoing drawing room and went in search of aspirin.

By the time I returned, my own temper under tighter rein, he'd managed to drag open the heavy oak door and wheel himself out onto the front verandah. The wind had picked up, gray clouds obscuring the weak winter sun, and I could see his shoulders shivering the moment I stepped outside. I turned back to his bedroom and retrieved the afghan folded over the arm of the recliner. He didn't comment when I draped it around him, but his one good hand clutched its warmth across his chest.

"Can we discuss this like civilized human beings?" I asked, moving around to lean against the railing in front of him. "We'll accomplish nothing by running off to the sheriff's office. Besides, I don't know if I can get you into my car. Red has things under control. He'll bring her back just as soon as she's finished giving her statement."

I waited for my father to respond, but he sat unmoving, like a stone Buddha, staring off at the empty driveway.

"Daddy?" I prompted, my earlier anger smothered by the fear that he might have worked himself into another stroke. "Are you okay?"

The Judge never so much as blinked in response, and my chest felt as if a cold hand were squeezing my heart. "Daddy?"

"Hmmm?" He seemed to pull himself back from some faraway place.

"Let's go inside. It's freezing out here." My own tremors had little to do with the temperature.

"I'm waiting for Vinnie." Again he spoke as if from a distance, more to himself than to me.

"We can do that in the house."

I didn't wait for a reply but gripped the handles of his wheel-chair and maneuvered him back into the hallway. He made no effort to override me with the electronic controls, and I positioned him so he could peer through the sidelight.

"I'll make some tea," I said, but he ignored me.

By force of will I quelled the trembling in my icy hands as I re-heated the water and filled two large mugs. I'd intended to lace my father's with a generous splash of bourbon, but I suddenly wondered if that would be a good idea. I had no clue how alcohol would affect him if he was in fact on the verge of another . . . incident.

Lavinia would know, I said to myself.

I settled for stirring in two heaping teaspoons of sugar and car-ried the tray out into the hallway.

"Here, drink this." I thrust the mug into my father's good hand, thankful when he took it without protest and lifted the steaming tea to his lips. His color had returned almost to normal, and that vacant look had retreated.

"Thank you, sweetheart," he said, and a thin smile lifted the cor-ners of his mouth.

"Are you okay? I'm sorry I yelled, but you went a little crazy there for a minute."

His sharp bark of laughter lifted my heart. "You weren't exactly a tower of reason yourself."

"I know." I set my tea on the console table and dropped onto my knees so that I could look him squarely in the eye. "I'm sorry. You scared me a little."

The old judge, the father who had always been my confidant and protector, peered out at me from clear gray eyes. "We're just too damn much alike, daughter. Curse of the Simpsons, that temper."

I laid my hand on his useless left arm, and again I resisted the temptation to rest my head in his lap. "Lavinia will be back soon. Let's go in by the fire."

The Judge had dozed off when I finally heard the front door open. I set down the book I'd picked up and clambered off the window seat. As I tiptoed past the wheelchair, my father's eyes snapped open.

"Vinnie?"

"I think so," I said. "I'll be right back."

I slid to a halt on the heart pine floor just as Red followed Lavinia into the hallway. A small square of white gauze was taped to her left temple, and I could just make out the swelling that extended beneath her bloodshot eye. But she stood ramrod straight, shrugging off Red's hand on her arm as we faced each other down the long expanse of gleaming wood.

"Don't start fussin' at me," she said with the authority born of forty years as Presqu'isle's mistress in all but name. "I'm fine. If I need help, I'll ask for it." She shrugged out of her sweater and set her sensible handbag on the console table. "I need to start dinner."

"I can do that," I began, but she brushed by me on her way to the kitchen.

"All of you just leave me be," she said over her shoulder, and I turned to stare after her.

A moment later, the Judge whizzed by, his wheelchair all but humming as he urged it down the hall. Red took a step in that direction, but I grabbed his arm.

"Let them have a moment," I said, and he nodded. "Come on in here."

I guided him into the drawing room and cleared the Christmas boxes and tissue paper from the settee. We sat, and Red pulled me into his arms.

"You okay?"

"I am now," I said, my head falling onto his shoulder. For a moment, I allowed myself to surrender to the luxury of his protective embrace before I straightened. "Tell me what happened."

"These guys are getting bolder with every job they pull. This is the second time they've hit a bank. The other one was a small branch, too. Apparently, two of them come in separately, loiter around at one of the tables where they keep the blank deposit and withdrawal slips, then get in different lines. No one at either place paid too much attention to them, so we're sort of piecing this together from several eyewitness accounts. They hit two tellers at once, notes with threats about handguns, although no one saw a weapon at the first job. And they were very polite. Most of the customers and the other bank employees didn't even know what was going down. They only took what the tellers had in their drawers. At the first bank, they put the money in one of those zipper bags and walked right out."

"So what happened this time?"

"Some old black man was talking to Lavinia in the next line and messed up their timing. One of the robbers tried moving him along, but he got incensed and proceeded to give him a piece of his mind. They panicked, and one of them shoved him out of the way." Red's expression said what he thought about someone who would manhandle an old man. "Lavinia came to his rescue and got hit on the head with something, we're not sure what at this point."

I cast a glance toward the kitchen. "So did Lavinia get a good look at them?"

"Not really. It's strange, but we haven't been able to get a decent description from anyone. They've done a couple of convenience stores attached to gas stations, a bar over in Bluffton, and another one just off the island. They change their outfits with every job. Sometimes they're dressed like painters or landscape workers. A couple of times they've been in regular street clothes. But they always wear caps of some kind, pulled low on their foreheads, so no one gets a really good look at their faces."

"Cameras?" I asked, and Red shook his head.

"Nothing definitive, from either bank. A couple of the stores had video, too, but the angle's been wrong. I hate to admit it, but these guys are either damn good or damn lucky."

I leaned down to straighten some of the mess I'd made by tossing everything onto the floor, one ear straining for the sound of my father's wheelchair or any other indication about what might be happening in the kitchen. Nothing. Old house, thick walls.

"Maybe it's not the same guys every time. Maybe that's why no one's been able to identify them."

"That doesn't make any sense," Red replied. "The MO's been pretty much the same."

"Until today," I said.

"A mistake. The task force is convinced we're dealing with the same pair."

"How do they get away? Is there a driver waiting outside?"

Red nodded. "But they use different vehicles. At least we can't seem to get a handle on one description."

I thought about that for a moment. "If they don't get a lot of money in each haul, I suppose that would explain why they keep at it. You'd think they'd move on to another territory, though. Every time they pull a job, they must leave more clues behind." I straightened up and smiled at Red. "They sound like amateurs to me."

It was a loaded word, one Red had been fond of throwing in my face whenever he thought one of Simpson & Tanner's cases might be treading on the toes of the sheriff's office. Sometimes we earned the title. But other times we'd been the ones to point the professionals in the right direction, and Red was man enough to admit it when we did.

"Amateurs have their place," he said, again pulling me close.

Our lips were bare millimeters apart when the discreet cough sent us springing away like two teenagers caught in the act.

"Excuse me. I need to speak with Bay," Lavinia said from the doorway. The white gauze on her forehead stood out in stark contrast to the polished oak color of her wrinkled face.

"I should be getting back." Red pulled me to my feet, then crossed to take Lavinia's worn hands in his own. "You sure you're all right, Mrs. Smalls?"

She disengaged herself gently but firmly. "I'm fine, Redmond. You're most welcome to stay to dinner."

"Thank you, ma'am, but I'm still on duty. Is there anything I can do for you?"

Her smile vanished. "Catch those awful men who injured Mr. Gadsden."

"We'll do our best," he said, then turned to me. "Walk me out?"

I glanced at Lavinia, who nodded. "I'll be in the kitchen," she said.

Out on the verandah, the wind whistled around the corners of the house, and I shivered. Red draped an arm around my shoulders. "You keep an eye on her," he said. "I don't think she's got a concussion, but the paramedic said to make sure she doesn't get woozy. If she passes out or anything like that, get her to the ER on the double."

I cast a look over my shoulder. "Was it that serious a blow?"

He shrugged. "Probably not. But it might not be a bad idea for you to stay here tonight. Just to be on the safe side."

"Okay." I thought of Bobby Santiago, gone from his dorm room now for more than twenty-four hours, on the run with Serena Montalvo from God knew what kind of trouble. Dolores would be frantic if she hadn't heard from him. I had some calls to make, but I knew where my duty lay.

"Okay," I said again. "When will I see you?"

"I don't know. Tracking down these robbers has become everybody's top priority. This was the first incident where anyone got hurt, but it's only a matter of time until they really panic and do something stupid. We need to get these dirtbags off the street."

"Call me," I said.

This time no one interrupted the kiss. I waved as the cruiser eased out of the drive, before turning back to the house.

I could see the anxiety on the Judge's face. His eyes never left Lavinia as she moved about the kitchen, setting a pan of water on to boil, pulling potatoes and onions from the bin in the pantry, and carrying them to the sink. Without a word, I took the peeler out of her hand.

"Bay—," she began, but for once I intended to have my way.

"Sit," I said in a voice she rarely heard from me. It startled her so much she actually obeyed.

"How many of these do you want?" I asked, attacking the potatoes.

"Put those down and come here a minute. I need to ask you something."

I studied her face for a moment, then dried my hands on a dish towel and slid into my customary seat at the weathered oak table where I'd taken almost every meal of my life until I'd gone off to college.

Lavinia gathered herself and stared directly into my eyes. "I won't be treated like an—" She literally bit her lip and glanced sideways at my father.

"Like an invalid?" the Judge said, a smile tugging at the corners of his mouth. "You can say the word, Vinnie. I am what I am."

She smiled back. "You're more than that, Tally Simpson. Much more, and you know it. Quit fishin' for compliments."

The look that passed between them made my eyes water. I cleared my throat.

"You've been feeding me for forty years. I can't return the favor?"

"That's not what I want to talk to you about," she said, her face sobering. "It's Romey Gadsden."

"Is that who tangled with the robbers? Was he badly hurt?"

"Twisted ankle. I called his daughter as soon as I got home here. Scared the poor old man nearly to death, but he'll be fine. No, it's what he said."

My father and I exchanged a look.

"When?" I asked.

"Right after that horrible man pushed him down and then struck me. We were huddled together, there on the floor, and everyone was yellin' and scurryin' this way and that."

She shivered a little, and I reached out to lay my hand over hers. Surprisingly, she didn't pull away.

"What did Mr. Gadsden say that has you so upset?" I asked softly.

Lavinia swallowed hard. "He said, 'Why on earth would he do something like that?'"

She paused, and I said, "I don't get it. It seems like a perfectly natural remark under the circumstances."

"Let me finish, child." She drew a long, deep breath. "Then he said, 'Naldo's always been such a good boy.'"

CHAPTER
EIGHT

"THE ROBBER WAS SOMEONE HE KNEW?" THE JUDGE BEAT me to the question.

"Apparently." Lavinia slid her fingers out from under mine. "I'm going to finish dinner. You sit," she added when I half rose from my chair. "I feel better with somethin' to occupy my hands."

I couldn't argue with that. "Naldo. That's an odd name. Short for Reynaldo, maybe?"

Potato skins flew from the peeler into the sink. Lavinia didn't turn around. "I don't know. I can't think of anyone with that name."

Within the close-knit community of the native islanders of St. Helena, there weren't many people Lavinia didn't know or hadn't heard of. "Could he have been mistaken? How old a man is Mr. Gadsden?"

"He has a daughter about my age, so I'd say somewhere around eighty."

"Don't be jumping to conclusions just because he's old," my father said. "I'm not far from that myself, and I'd sure as hell recognize somebody if I was staring right into his face."

"I'm not implying he didn't see clearly," I said. "But it was a pretty traumatizing experience. He could just be wrong."

"I don't think so," Lavinia said over her shoulder. She'd dumped the potatoes into the pot and started in on the onions. "I stayed right there with him until the medical people arrived. He repeated the name, and then he said, 'Maria will be so disappointed.' "

"The kid's mother?" I mused, not expecting a reply. "Or wife?"

"Maria. Reynaldo. Names don't sound like they'd be family to Romey Gadsden," the Judge said.

"You're right." I waited for Lavinia to comment, but she remained silent, her arthritic hands busy slicing and chopping. "What do you think?" I pressed.

"I don't know," she said.

I glanced at my father.

"Vinnie. Look at me," he said, his voice soft despite the gruff command. When she turned, he smiled. "Did you or Rom tell the sheriff about this?"

I knew the answer by the stiffening of her shoulders. "He asked me not to."

"That's crazy!" I began, but the Judge's good hand on my arm silenced me.

"Why would he do that?" he asked in the same calm tone.

"I think he doesn't want to bring trouble down on this boy's family," Lavinia said, crossing to the refrigerator to avoid looking at us.

"And does that make sense to you?" Again his soft voice carried none of the bluster and command we were used to.

I couldn't believe how my father was taking all this. A series of robberies had terrorized the Lowcountry for more than a month. A man who might be able to identify one of the criminals was refusing to do so. And had enlisted Lavinia's help in keeping the secret. That fell squarely into my definition of crazy, whatever the Judge might think. I opened my mouth, but once again his fingers on my arm silenced me.

"I don't know." Lavinia finally turned to face us, and I could see the pain and confusion etched into her dark eyes. "But I gave my word not to tell Redmond or anyone else official, and I didn't." She fixed her gaze on me. "Bay, I want you to find out who this man is. He carries a gun, and other folks could get hurt. He might even come after Rom if he comes to realize he was recognized."

"No, Lavinia, no," I said, shaking my head firmly. "I've learned my lesson about things like this. Painfully, I might add." Ben Wyler's face loomed up before me, and I pushed it away. "We're talking about armed felons—" I cut myself off. Red had told me no one had ever seen a weapon during the robberies. "You said he carries a gun? Did you see it?"

Lavinia folded her arms across her chest and dropped her head. A moment later her left hand rose to finger the square of gauze on her temple. "Of course I saw it," she said. "It's what he hit me with."

With no computer available at Presqu'isle, I slipped away to put in a call to Erik, giving him the sparse details and swearing him to secrecy.

"It's not much to go on," he said as I wandered the drawing room, idly picking up and discarding the precious ornaments and bibelots that had been an intricate part of every childhood Christmas I could remember.

"I know. Just do the best you can." I sighed, more troubled than I wanted to admit. "I think I'm probably going to have to talk to Mr. Gadsden in person."

"Lavinia won't want him to know she broke her promise," Erik said.

"Exactly. But unless you can come up with a name, I'm afraid she's going to have to get past it."

"What about Red?"

I waited a long time before answering. "I'll cross that bridge when I come to it."

"In other words, you're not going to tell him."

"Let's give it until tomorrow, okay? See what happens."

"You're the boss," he said.

"Anything to report on Bobby Santiago? Or Dolores?"

"I have a couple of leads I'm still checking on. One thing I can tell you for certain is that Serena Montalvo has a 1998 Ford Taurus registered in her name."

"So she's probably driving. That makes it more difficult. They could be anywhere."

"Don't give up on me just yet," Erik said. "I've got some other resources to tap."

"I'm staying the night here, so reach me on the cell if you come up with anything."

"Tell Mrs. Smalls I hope she's feeling better."

"I will. Keep me posted."

I knew my next move should be to check in with Dolores, but Lavinia's call from the kitchen gave me a welcome reprieve.

Dinner was punctuated by uncomfortable silences. No one felt like dessert, and it was a relief to escape after my help in straightening the kitchen had been firmly refused. For some reason, I found myself again drawn to the formal parlor. I took one of the wing chairs next to the empty fireplace and pulled out my cell phone.

"No, *Señora.*" Dolores sounded weary and afraid. "Hector tells me Roberto has said to you that he is fine, but we no hear from him."

I tried my best to reassure her, counseling against involving the sheriff at this point. But unless I managed to track down the runaway teenagers—and fast—I knew neither one of us would have a choice.

"Give me until tomorrow," I said.

I went on to relay my intention to stay overnight at Presqu'isle, providing just the bare bones of Lavinia's involvement in the robbery on Lady's Island. Dolores immediately offered to come to St. Helena if I thought she could be of help.

"We've got it pretty well under control," I said and thanked her. "I'll see you sometime tomorrow at home. Call on my cell if you hear from Bobby."

Just to be thorough, I tried the boy's number but had to leave another pointless message for him to contact his parents. I tried to take some comfort from the fact that his phone was still in operation. Jason Early and his mother weren't answering, either.

I rose and crossed the room to where the leather journal still lay spread open on the settee. The slanted handwriting was difficult to read, with its long looping letters and curlicues of an earlier style. Here and there, sketches amplified the written instructions. I ran my finger lightly over the page, conjuring up images of ancestral Baynard women hunched over this same book, squinting in the dim lamplight, determined to adhere to a ritual established long before even they were born.

I lay my head back, my eyes drifting closed, and a scene flashed into my mind. I must have been around eleven or twelve. I could see myself squirming on this very sofa, my bare arms and legs scratching against the stiff upholstery. It must have been a mild winter, because I remembered chafing at being forced to sit inside while the sun through the long windows beckoned me to far more adventurous pursuits. I could almost hear my mother's voice, low and exasperated. . . .

"*Lydia! Pay attention! I swear you are the most aggravatin' child. This is history —your history. My family has maintained these traditions for nearly two hundred years, and you can't spare five minutes? Lord, what have I done to deserve such an ungrateful—*"

"*But Mama,*" I heard myself say, "*all those people are dead. Who cares what they want? Why can't we have icicles and candy canes on the tree like everybody else? Jimmy Jefferson's mom —*"

"Bay? Are you talkin' to someone?"

Lavinia's voice from the doorway jerked me out of my half doze, and I snapped the book shut.

"Daydreaming," I said, shaking off the sadness the memory had left lodged in my chest. Maybe it hadn't all been Emmaline's fault. Maybe if I'd been a more dutiful daughter, tried harder to understand her veneration of the old ways and—

"Your mother could be a little obsessive about things," Lavinia said, reading my mind as she'd been doing for the better part of four decades. She made room for herself and settled in beside me on the settee. "You were always more your father's child. No fault of yours, honey."

I nodded. Our family, including Lavinia, had never been one for spontaneous physical displays of affection, and I restrained myself from an urge to take her wrinkled hand in mine. Instead, I passed her the journal.

"Surely you don't need this after all these years," I said, and she smiled.

"Not really." Her eyes scanned the perfectly proportioned room. "But I find as I get older that there's a certain comfort in tradition."

"But they're not your traditions," I said, realizing how ungracious the words sounded the second they were out of my mouth. "I mean—"

"I know what you meant, child, and there's some truth in what you say." She rose then and laid the book on the side table. "It'll seem more important to you when your father and I pass, and the responsibility for Presqu'isle is yours."

The simple statement opened up a hole in the pit of my stomach.

"But not just yet," Lavinia said with a twinkle. "Come on, help me get this room put to rights. I'll sleep a lot better knowin' this mess is all cleared away."

I swallowed back my tears and picked up a box of ornaments.

I lay awake long into the night, tossing in my old four-poster beneath the same goose-down coverlet that had warmed me since my childhood. I told myself I needed to stay alert in case Lavinia needed me, but the truth was that our conversation in the drawing room had awakened fears I usually kept shoved well back in my mind.

Sometime after four I must have drifted off, because it took me a long time to realize that my cell phone had been ringing. I stumbled out of bed, banging my shin on the edge of the nightstand and hopping to where I'd tossed my bag on the seat of the rocker. By the time I retrieved the phone, it had gone silent. I limped back toward the bed and flipped on the lamp, but the caller's number had been blocked. I checked voice mail, but no one had left a message. Outside, rain beat against the windows, and I shivered in my thin T-shirt and bare feet. Cold crept through the old wooden boards of the floor, and I sat down on the edge of the bed. *What kind of idiot calls someone in the middle of the damn night?* I was asking myself when the phone rang again in my hand.

"Listen, pal—"

A stranger's voice cut me off. "Stay out of our business, or someone else could get hurt. Bad."

I don't know how long I sat staring at the phone before I thumbed the Off button and slid back beneath the warmth of the duvet. I stacked the pillows up behind me and clutched the silent phone to my chest, my mind awhirl with the possibilities.

Dawn had just begun to seep through the thick layer of clouds hanging low over the Sound when I sighed heavily and keyed in Red's number.

CHAPTER NINE

ITH LAVINIA'S REPEATED ASSURANCES THAT SHE felt perfectly fine, I left her in the middle of scrambling eggs for my father and headed for Hilton Head.

Despite the cold rain, I kept my window rolled partially down to ensure I wouldn't fall asleep on the long drive. Battling our local version of rush-hour traffic forced me to concentrate on the road, a welcome diversion from the thoughts swirling around in my head. It took nearly an hour and a half before I pulled past Dolores's old blue Hyundai and into my garage. I dragged myself out and up the steps into the foyer.

I skirted the vacuum cleaner, abandoned in the middle of the floor, and found my friend hunched over a cup of coffee at the table in the alcove by the bay window. Her eyes lit with expectation for a moment, then clouded when I shook my head.

"You haven't heard anything, either?"

"No, Señora, nada." She pushed the cup away and rose. "I must do the floors."

Gently, I halted her with a hand on her arm. "Sit down, Dolores. We have some things to discuss."

I'd argued with myself during the drive from St. Helena about how much to reveal of Bobby's probable involvement, however peripherally, with the hit-and-run death of the Montalvo girl. I had no solid reason for assuming the disembodied threat in the middle of the night had anything to do with my attempts to locate Dolores's son, but I had a hard time imagining what else it could be about. The only thing resembling a case Simpson & Tanner had going was the vetting of employees and volunteers for the recreation center, and that wouldn't be official until Friday. We hadn't checked out a single person, so we couldn't be perceived as a threat to anyone's livelihood. Yet. And no one outside of Erik and the family knew of Lavinia's revelations about Romey Gadsden and the mysterious Naldo, who may or may not have been involved in the Lady's Island bank robbery. Logic forced me to admit the odds favored someone who didn't want me poking around in the teenager's death.

I drew a long breath. "Do you know a girl named Serena Montalvo?"

Dolores stared at me without speaking. Then, almost reluctantly, she nodded. "*Sí.* Her mother, she is in our church. The *chicas,* the daughters, I see not so often. *La pobre familia, pobre Theresa.* You know about—" She cut herself off in midsentence, and her olive complexion blanched. "*Señora!* Roberto, he did not—"

"No! He had nothing to do with the accident." I gripped her arm, the muscles taut with anxiety.

"*Gracias a Dios,*" she murmured.

I released my hold, and she crossed herself.

"But I think he might know something about it. Red's on his way over, and I'd like to tell the story to both of you at the same time. Is that okay?"

Her nod told me she'd heard me, but her face had gone white with fear. Without another word, she rose and clicked on the vacuum cleaner. Like the emotional coward I was, I retreated to the office, closed the door, and checked messages. A moment later, I dialed Presqu'isle.

*   *   *

"I don't like it," Lavinia said after I'd explained to her my need to speak with Romey Gadsden.

Erik hated to admit defeat, but he'd left a message before heading out to work at the office supply store that he'd been unable to locate anything about the bank robber Mr. Gadsden had recognized.

"I understand that," I said. "But if you want me to find out who this Naldo person is, I'm going to have to. Erik's the best at tracking things down online, but even he has his limitations. We need a last name. Or something else to go on." I paused. "You can ask him yourself, if you'd feel better about that."

She was a long time replying. "I'll speak to him," she said, "but I don't hold out a lot of hope. He had every opportunity to tell me yesterday there—" She floundered a moment before regaining her composure. "—there on the floor of the bank. And I'm afraid he has a tendency to wander a little, in his mind. But I'll try."

"Good." I started to tell her Red was on his way over, then thought better of it. Getting her to break her promise to Mr. Gadsden about not talking to the sheriff would take some convincing. "Good," I repeated. "Call me when have something. Are you sure you're okay?"

"I'm fine. Don't pester me, child."

"No, ma'am," I said a moment before she hung up.

The whine of the vacuum died as an idea struck. In the spare room, Dolores had just backed out into the hallway and begun winding up the long cord. Even though I spoke her name softly from the doorway, she still jumped.

"I'm sorry," I said, and she nodded. "Can I ask you something?"

"*Claro, Señora.*"

"Do the names Reynaldo and Maria mean anything to you? Maybe husband and wife? Or son and mother?"

"These people, they have to do with my Roberto?"

"No, no. Nothing like that. It's about something else. They may live on St. Helena or over by Beaufort somewhere."

She was shaking her head before I even finished speaking.

"No, *Señora*. I do not think so. There are many Latinos. We know only our friends, our neighbors, and those from the church, *sí*?"

"Of course." It had been a stupid question, one at which Dolores might have rightly taken offense. I didn't know every white person in Beaufort County. Why should I assume every Hispanic knew the others? Red was right. Sometimes my mouth did get way ahead of my brain.

"Never mind. Let's make some tea and wait for Red."

"But the cleaning—"

"Will keep. Come on."

With an arm around her shoulders, I guided her gently up the three steps into the kitchen. I'd just set the pot to steep when I heard the cruiser pull into the driveway.

"Promise not to panic," I said. "It will probably sound worse than it is, at least at first."

Solemnly, she nodded, and I went to open the door to Red.

"So that's it," I said, leaning back in the chair. "What do you think?"

Dolores had not spoken during my entire recitation. She rose silently and carried the kettle back to the table, lifted the lid of the teapot, and added hot water. I watched her jerky movements as she set the kettle back on the stove, and I had to resist the urge to fling my arms around her.

Red's first words were to Dolores. "Do you and your husband want to file a missing person's report, Mrs. Santiago?"

Dolores stood a little apart, her hands clutched tightly in front of her, her face unreadable in the bright overhead light of the kitchen. Although she'd gotten used to having Red around the house—more so now that we'd begun seeing each other—I knew the presence of a uniformed man brought back bad memories of her childhood. Even if Red and I should eventually marry, I didn't believe she'd ever feel entirely comfortable with him. Not that the subject of marriage had come up officially, but we'd certainly danced around it more than a few times.

"I must call Hector," she said, turning away.

"Of course. Use the phone in my office so you can have some privacy."

"*Gracias,*" she said and scurried down the steps.

A moment later I heard the door close.

"What do you think?" I asked, and Red shrugged.

"It's something, but I'm not sure what at this point. Obviously I need to talk to those two kids." His gaze softened, and he reached for my hand. "This has put you in a hell of a dilemma, hasn't it?"

"I'm glad you can see that." I squeezed his fingers. "As long as you keep doing what you do and I keep doing what I do, it's a problem that isn't going away."

"There's a remedy for that," he said, his smile fading.

I withdrew my hand and picked up my cooling tea. "Yeah, but I'd hate for you to give up your career just when you're about to make lieutenant."

I said it lightly, but his scowl told me he wasn't amused. Another one of those topics we skirted around without really resolving anything. Eventually, though, we'd have to face it.

Red checked his notes and changed the subject. "You said the Montalvo girl drives a Taurus?"

"That's what I hear," I said. It didn't seem necessary—or wise—to get into detail about how Erik came by his information.

"I'll get a call out on the wire. Check with her parents, although they haven't been very forthcoming so far." He paused and ran his hand across his freshly shaven face. "I hate to burden them with this on top of their other daughter's death."

"They have to be as frantic as Dolores if they haven't heard from Serena. Surely they expect her to be with the family at a time like this."

"So maybe they'll be grateful to know something about where she is."

"Keep in mind I'm just hypothesizing at this point. I have no proof the young woman I heard in the background was Serena."

Red's smile reappeared, lighting his entire face. "Your 'hypothesizing' usually turns out to be pretty damn good."

"*Señora.*"

I turned to find Dolores standing at the foot of the stairs, her heavy jacket pulled tightly around her and her handbag draped across her arm.

"What is it?"

"I must go, *Señora. Discúlpeme.* Hector, he says I must go home."

I rose and followed her toward the foyer. "Hold on! What's the matter?"

She ignored me. As she reached for the doorknob, I placed a hand on her shoulder. Even through the thick padding of her coat, I could feel her stiffen.

"Dolores, wait. What's happened?"

"*Por favor, Señora,* I must go."

"Have you heard from Bobby?"

She turned her head enough for me to see the mixture of fear and confusion in her black eyes before she yanked the door open. "*Por favor,*" she whispered, and I let her go.

I stood for a moment staring after her.

"Bay?" Red spoke from the edge of the great room. "Is something wrong?"

"I don't know. Whatever Hector had to say, she's scared. I wonder if Bobby called. Or maybe showed up at their place."

"I'll take a swing by on my way out, see if there's a strange car in the drive."

"If Bobby's hiding out at home, he'll have been smart enough to stash it someplace." Hand in hand, we climbed back to the kitchen. "But I don't think it's that. I'm more inclined to believe they don't want to deal with anyone official." I sank back into my chair. "Nothing personal, I'm sure. Bad associations."

I poured more tea for myself, but Red declined. "Understood.

I'm more concerned about that phone call last night. Nothing at all you can remember about the voice? Accent, anything like that?"

"Nope. Just a male voice. Not young, not old. He spoke softly, but the threat sounded real. I don't think it was a prank."

"You don't publish your cell number, do you? On your business cards or anything like that?"

I shook my head. "Ben advised me not to." Neither one of us spoke for a moment, the memory of my late partner hanging in the air between us. "I only give it out to clients who might need to reach me after hours."

"So how did this scumball get hold of it?"

"I have no idea. But one thing I've learned from Erik is that anyone can find out just about anything they want about you if they're determined enough."

"Then the question remains. Who would go to all that trouble to threaten you?"

If it had been a woman's voice in the middle of the night, I would have pointed the finger directly at Mrs. M. Early of Ridgeland. I would be a long time getting the image of her and her lunging dog out of my head. Of course, there was always Jason. . . .

"What's your next move?" I asked, shaking off the chill that suddenly slithered over my shoulders.

"I'll keep you posted." Red rose and reached for his jacket. "Let me know if you hear from Bobby Santiago."

I met his stern gaze with one of my own. "I said I would, didn't I?"

"Come here."

Before I could move, Red swept me into his arms and kissed me soundly.

"Be careful out there," I whispered against his cheek, and a moment later he was gone.

CHAPTER TEN

RED HADN'T LEFT ME WITH HIS USUAL ADMONITION to stay out of it, so I brought up switchboard.com and began a search for Enrique Salazar, the young man whose lost scholarship had sparked off the student protest at the high school the previous spring.

None of the local listings produced results. There were a few in Savannah, but there was no point in trying those. It had to be someone within the school district. I'd heard that a lot of single illegals rented condos together and tried to operate under the radar of immigration by not having phones or utilities registered in their names. Many never bothered to get a driver's license, either. A lot of the furor in our corner of the South stemmed from these practices, usually uncovered only after a traffic accident, or when a real estate investor came to inspect his one-bedroom rental property and found eight men living in it.

But the Salazars had a son, maybe more than one, who had been enrolled in the high school. I scanned the printout of the story Erik had forwarded to me from the *Packet* archives. Both parents had been employed in white-collar jobs, which meant they paid taxes and possibly owned their own home. How was that possible if they didn't have the proper documentation?

I realized I'd never asked Dolores if Enrique had been someone in Bobby's circle of friends. I paused, my hand poised over the telephone, then let it drop back into my lap. Something in her face as we'd stood staring at each other in the foyer caused a shiver to skitter down my back. She'd looked afraid, but of what? Surely not of me. If Dolores didn't know after all these years that I'd go to the mat for her and her family . . .

The ringing phone pierced the deep quiet of my empty house.

"Bay Tanner."

"It's Lavinia. I've just spoken to Mr. Gadsden, and he says now he must have been mistaken."

"About knowing one of the robbers? Did you believe him?"

The long pause said more than her next words. "Why wouldn't I?"

"Look, Lavinia, let's put our cards on the table. You're positive he recognized the man who struck him, right?" When she didn't immediately respond, I said, "Right?"

"I'm fairly certain, yes."

"So what do you think's going on here? Is he afraid of retaliation? Or is this person so close to him he can't bring himself to make an identification out of some sort of misguided loyalty?"

Her sigh made me wince. I needed to remember she'd suffered considerable trauma—both physical and mental—in the past twenty-four hours.

"I'd say he's either protecting someone, or he's just confused." Again she paused. "Romey Gadsden has been through a lot in his lifetime, seen some terrible things. I don't think he's afraid of much of anything."

Her assertion intrigued me, but I stored those questions away for another day. "Anyone else you can think of who might be able to shed some light on who this Naldo and Maria might be? Mr. Gadsden's daughter, maybe?"

"I could speak with Glory, but I'm not certain she'll know. Or tell me if she does."

"Then I think it's time we dumped this all in Red's lap." I waited for her to protest. When the silence had stretched out for long seconds, I added, "Don't you?"

"You're asking me to betray a confidence. Break my promise."

"I know, but what's the alternative? What if you keep quiet and someone gets shot at the next job these guys pull? Are you prepared to live with that?"

"No, I suppose not."

Again I waited, my fingers unconsciously reaching into the drawer where I used to keep a spare pack of cigarettes. My brain remembered I'd quit smoking a long time ago, but apparently the message hadn't gotten to my hands yet.

"Let me make one more call," Lavinia said.

"Okay. But if you strike out, I'm bringing Red over to Presqu'isle. And he'll want to interview Mr. Gadsden as well. You understand that?"

"I'm not an imbecile, Bay. I'll call you back."

The click sounded unnaturally loud. Gently I replaced the handset and wandered out into the great room. I paused in front of the French doors, staring out over the dunes to the gray rolling ocean. The storms had moved off, now only a dark line scuttling toward the horizon, and thin shafts of sunlight pierced the overcast. A few hardy souls had ventured onto the beach, the hoods of their sweatshirts and jackets pulled up to shelter them from the stiff wind that sent broken palm fronds and dead branches dancing across the wet sand.

With a sigh, I turned away and climbed the steps up to the kitchen. My stomach growled, and I stood for a few moments staring into the refrigerator before slamming the door closed. I wasn't accomplishing a damn thing, so I decided I might as well finish up my interrupted Christmas shopping. And grab a bite while I was out. I pulled on my leather jacket, slung my bag over my shoulder, and made certain the security system was armed.

I'm not an imbecile, either, I said to myself as I closed the door behind me.

Again the parking lot at the mall was jammed. I marched across the blacktop and pulled open the door to Belk's. The store was packed with people, mostly women, and the noise level would have done a small football stadium proud. Christmas music, broken occasionally by announcements about the endless sales going on, made me want to spin on my heel and scurry right back out into the cold. Instead, I drew a long breath and plunged into the bedlam.

I had a list. I always have a list. I don't seem to be able to function on any number of levels without one. For the better part of an hour, I slid sideways down aisles packed with merchandise and eager shoppers, jostled occasionally by scurrying women with bags hanging from both hands or piled high in strollers. Children cried and cajoled, and resigned husbands plodded along behind determined wives bent on searching out every last bargain.

I hate this, I repeated in my head as I worked my way toward the bottom of my assigned tasks. *Hate it, hate it, hate it. Internet next year,* I promised myself. *I swear.*

Finally, my rumbling stomach insisted I take a break. The wide, blessedly cool corridor was flanked by smaller, less hectic stores, and I flopped down on a bench to consolidate my bags. A moment to give my feet a rest, and I'd head on down to the center court and find something to eat.

I had just risen and turned in that direction when I collided with someone barreling out of Belk's. The impact nearly spun me around, and I grabbed the back of the bench to steady myself.

"Oops, sorry," I murmured, waiting for an answering apology, but the man ignored me, striding away without a backward glance. So much for the Christmas spirit. *Moron!*

"Hey, no problem!" I yelled at his retreating back. "I'm fine. Don't give it another thought."

He cast a brief glance back over his shoulder, but it was enough. Hard to forget that pitiful attempt at a beard and the shifty eyes I'd seen two nights before trying hard to avoid looking into the television camera.

I slipped my purse over my shoulder and set out in pursuit of Jason Early.

It's not a large mall by most standards, and it wouldn't have taken a genius to figure out I was trailing him. But Jason never looked back or even swiveled his head to peek into the heavily decorated windows of the shops he breezed past, not even Victoria's Secret. In only a couple of minutes, he'd passed into the center court where a sprawling display surrounded Santa's huge chair. The photographer's assistant tried to distract the squirming toddler on the red-suited lap as I paused to study my quarry's behavior.

The boy had stopped, his attention drawn to the line of parents waiting with their overdressed, fidgety children for the obligatory photo with the jolly old gentleman who was probably, under all the fake hair, just a regular guy with time on his hands. And more than his share of patience. I made a show of consulting my watch, then pulled out my cell phone and dialed the office. I responded to my own answering service with an occasional word or two to reinforce the charade while keeping my eye on Jason Early.

If asked, I couldn't have said what had made me trail after him. Something furtive in his manner. Or maybe it had been that lack of an apology for nearly running me down. I had just about decided to give up the foolishness and approach him directly when the boy suddenly veered off and headed down one of the arms of the mall that radiated from the center court. I slipped my cell back in my purse and followed.

When he stopped suddenly in front of the Bombay Company, I whirled and studied the wares in a high-end children's boutique whose name I couldn't remember, but whose prices for those tiny little dresses and shirts made me gasp. Again I hid behind the anonymity of my phone and cast occasional glances at Jason, who seemed mesmerized by Bombay's window. Having seen where he and his mother lived, I had a hard time believing he was shopping for furniture for the family homestead.

It was very neatly done, although when it was all over, I wasn't certain exactly what I'd witnessed. The tall Latino kid in a red-and-white athletic jacket moved away from fingering a pile of T-shirts at one of the kiosks, looked around, and ran straight into Early. They jostled for a moment, then stepped apart, nodding and bumping closed fists before the Hispanic boy moved off. I saw Jason slip his hand into his pocket and spin away. I had to scramble to keep him in sight as he strode directly through Saks Off 5th and out into the brightening afternoon. He paused for a moment, scanning the driveway in both directions. Suddenly a car whipped out from behind a row of shrubbery and squealed to a stop. Jason Early jerked open the back door and scrambled inside.

I had only a moment to register the driver, her face nearly obscured by a shimmering curtain of long black hair, before she gunned the engine and peeled away. An older car, four-door, faded red paint. South Carolina plates that began with 46-something.

And Bobby Santiago's startled eyes staring at me from the passenger seat.

CHAPTER
ELEVEN

RE YOU ALL RIGHT, MA'AM?"
I heard the words as if they came from inside a well.

"Ma'am?"

I blinked as the sun finally broke free of the hovering overcast and pulled my gaze away from the empty driveway. "I'm sorry?"

"I asked if you were okay." He stood a couple of feet away, a small black man with a wrinkled face, the creases around his eyes deepening as he squinted up at me.

"Yes. Yes, I'm fine, thank you."

"Looked like you seen a ghost," he said. His salt-and-pepper hair was cut tightly against his head, and his hands clutched several bags from stores inside the mall.

"No." I glanced off again in the direction the three young people had disappeared. "No," I repeated. "Just someone I didn't expect to see."

"Well, Merry Christmas to you," the old man said and shuffled off toward the parking lot.

"And to you, sir," I called after him. "Thank you."

I wandered back through the crowded high-end discount store and out into the mall. My feet found their way to a bench, and my hand had already extracted the cell phone from the depths of my bag by the time I sank onto the seat. I drew a long calming breath and waited for Red to pick up.

"I just saw Bobby Santiago," I said before he'd even finished saying hello.

"Where?"

I told him about my literal run-in with Jason Early, his strange encounter with the kid in the red-and-white jacket, and his escape in the Taurus that probably belonged to Serena Montalvo. "And Bobby saw me, too," I said. I closed my eyes and conjured up his startled face staring at me through the passenger window. "He looked scared."

"Of what? You?"

"How the hell should I know?" I took a moment. "I'm not sure. Maybe just surprised. I only saw him for a couple of seconds."

"I just got done running the girl's registration. That's her car. South Carolina plate 463GWX."

"So now what?"

"What do you mean?"

I bit down on my lip. "Are you going to look for them? It's an island, Red. There's only one way off. It shouldn't be that tough to contain them if you get on it now."

Red, too, seemed to be working hard at controlling his voice. "I can't request a dragnet for a couple of *possible* witnesses with *possible* information about what will likely turn out to be an unfortunate accident."

"It's still a crime to leave the scene. And you said you wanted to talk to them."

"I do, but I can't set up roadblocks, Bay. This isn't the movies."

"Okay, fine."

"Bay, honey, wait. Come on—"

He was still talking when I turned off the phone.

I needed food: hot, greasy, and bad for me. I hit a drive-through and devoured the double cheeseburger, pausing only long enough to stuff

French fries in my mouth. By the time I pulled into my driveway, I'd used up all the paper napkins and managed to drip ketchup down the front of my white sweater.

Back in the house, I washed up, changed into jeans and a sweatshirt, and called Dolores. The answering machine message was in both English and Spanish.

"It's Bay," I said, making certain to edit the anger and frustration from my voice. "Please call me. It's about Bobby." Just in case, I left my numbers, even though Dolores surely had them all memorized.

It was just coming up on four o'clock, and already the light had begun its slow fade into evening. We were fast approaching the shortest day of the year. I wandered out to the deck, hoping the sharp onshore breeze would sweep some of the cobwebs from my brain. All it did was make me cold. Shivering, I retreated back inside and pulled the drapes against the chill, then reset the alarm system. I threw some kindling in the fireplace along with the last two logs left in the basket and set them ablaze. I lowered myself onto the carpet in front of the raised hearth and stared into the rising flames.

In the silence, broken only by the crackling of the fire, I faced the ugly possibility that I had shoved into the back of my conscious mind from the moment Dolores had nearly bolted out my front door: What if she was gone for good? What if Hector had ordered her to leave and not come back?

I raised my freezing hands to the fire, but it didn't seem to warm them.

She wouldn't do that. She wouldn't desert me with no warning, no explanation. *Get serious,* I ordered myself. *Of course she has a reason. You brought the law into her life, even if it is in the person of someone she's known for years.*

But I'm trying to help Bobby, I argued. *To keep him from getting hurt. Surely she sees that.*

Of course Dolores would understand. She knew me better than almost anyone except Lavinia. In the long months after Rob's murder, she'd tended to my every need, both physical and spiritual. We shared an intimacy that was hard to explain, one on which I'd relied in the years since to anchor and sustain me. With her unwavering faith in God and her unshakable belief in the basic goodness of her fellow human beings, she'd become my touchstone, my rock when the world around me turned ugly.

But Hector . . . That was an entirely different story. In Dolores's male-dominated culture, would she be able to hold out against her husband's insistence that she abandon me?

I pulled my knees up and wrapped my arms around them and ordered myself not to cry.

"No sense borrowing trouble." I could hear Lavinia's words, spoken so many times during my volatile childhood. I swallowed down the tears, hauled myself to my feet, and stretched out on the sofa. The light from the fireplace glowed in the darkening room. I pulled the throw down over me and snuggled into its warmth. In a matter of seconds, I was asleep.

I awoke to utter darkness and the ringing of the phone.

The fire had long ago burned itself down to a few embers, and the great room felt cold when I swung my feet onto the carpet. My head felt as if it had been stuffed with old newspaper, but I managed to get to the telephone before the answering machine kicked in.

"Are you okay?" Red's voice, anxious and tinged with anger, exploded into my ear.

"I'm fine. What's the matter?"

"Open the door."

"What are you talking about?"

"I'm standing on your front porch. Open the damn door."

Still in a semi-fog, I stumbled down the steps and into the foyer. I had to concentrate on the alarm code but managed to punch it in and turn the knob. In a second, Red had me wrapped in an embrace that nearly drove the breath from me.

"Jesus, you scared the hell out of me. I've been knocking for five minutes."

I pushed away and drew a gulp of air. "I fell asleep on the couch. I hardly slept at all last night at Presqu'isle."

"I should have a key."

I slipped my hand into his and pulled him along with me into the kitchen, snapping on lights as I went.

We'd had the "key" conversation a couple of times, and I thought he understood. We had a relationship. Some, including Red's ex-wife, Sarah, might even call it an affair, although we were both free and single. But some part of me balked at giving up my independence completely. Alain Darnay, my Interpol agent lover, had moved in, insinuating himself into my life in a way no one had since Rob. And that had ended badly. This was my home, my haven. I needed to know it was secure against . . . what? I couldn't explain it, not even to myself. I just knew it wasn't time yet for Red to have total access to my life. Someday, maybe, but not yet.

"What time is it?" I asked, filling the tea kettle and setting it on the stove. "I'm starving."

"It's ten after nine. And we will talk about this, Bay."

"But not tonight. I'm going to fry some eggs. You want any?"

I busied myself with a frying pan and butter, then pulled out bread and the toaster. I kept my back to Red, but I heard him shrug out of his jacket and set his gun belt on the built-in desk.

"I'll have a couple," he said. "Over—"

"Easy. I know." I turned then and smiled at him, and a moment later his arms snaked around my waist.

"Got any sausage? Or bacon?"

His warm breath in my hair made me shiver.

"Home fries would be good, too," he murmured against my ear.

"Hey, this isn't Cracker Barrel. Don't press your luck."

I tried to disengage his hands, but he turned me deftly until our faces were an inch apart. "I can wait. For breakfast."

I felt the familiar weakening in my legs. I pushed hard against his chest, and he let me go. "Food first, Sergeant." I kissed him lightly on the lips. "You'll need your strength."

I used my last bite of toast to scrape the remains of egg yolk from the plate and sat back. "Okay, I feel human again."

Across from me, Red set down his mug of tea and smiled. "That was great. My mother always cooked the blasted things to death." He watched my face for a reaction when he added, "Rob and I always said we could use them for hockey pucks. If we played hockey."

Red had refrained for a long time from any mention of his late brother, my murdered husband. We'd worked our way through that, at least I hoped so. If comparisons were being made, they were happening in his head, not mine. Mostly.

"Dolores is a good teacher," I said a moment before the fear tumbled back into my consciousness. "I'm afraid Hector won't let her come back," I blurted and felt the treacherous tears pooling in my eyes.

"No, sweetheart, I'm sure that's not it." Red's hand covered mine. "They're upset about their son. It's understandable. Give her a little time."

I swiped my free hand across my eyes. "Come on, let's clean up."

He helped me carry the plates and silverware to the dishwasher. I scrubbed out the frying pan and left it in the drainer.

"She'll be back, honey. Don't worry about it."

Something in his tone put my back up. Maybe it was the endearment, tossed out so casually. Or maybe I was just being pissy. It had been known to happen from time to time.

"Don't patronize me, Red. You don't know Hector. He's not my biggest fan to begin with, and I've heard some rumblings that he doesn't like Dolores to work. Makes him look bad to his macho buddies, like he can't support his family on his own."

"I'm just trying to make you feel better." He smiled and held out his hand. "And obviously not doing a very good job of it. Come here."

I let him pull me down into the great room and onto the sofa. I tucked my legs up under me, and he draped the afghan around me.

"Let me get some more logs. I think I can coax this baby back to life."

I let him pamper me, mostly because it seemed to make him happy. I snuggled down into the cushions and watched him dump the wood in the basket. In a few minutes he had the fire roaring. He slipped off his heavy shoes, settled on the couch, and gathered me into his arms.

"There. That's what I've been looking forward to all day."

I let my head droop against his shoulder. "Nice," I murmured, wishing I could let myself go, shut off my brain and just enjoy the moment. I tried. For a long time we sat huddled together, both of us mesmerized by the flickering light from the fireplace, before the words just sneaked out of my mouth.

"Are you sure Theresa Montalvo's death was an accident?"

I felt him stiffen, then force himself to relax. "I had a long talk with Lisa Pedrovsky today. There are a couple of things she's not happy about."

"Like what?" I leaned back so I could see his face.

"No skid marks. I mean, that's a busy intersection, so of course there've been other accidents. But nothing recent."

"So whoever hit the girl didn't try to stop."

"That's what it looks like. There is a set that begins about a hundred yards past the actual point of impact, but the techs can't say for sure they came from that particular incident. Could even have been made by the Early kid when he realized he'd just driven past a body in the road."

"What about him?"

"Who, Jason Early?"

"Yes."

"What do you mean?"

I wriggled myself upright. "Don't you think it's strange that he's the one who reported the accident, and two days later he's riding around with the dead girl's sister?"

Red's face crinkled into a frown. "I thought you said they all went to school together. It's a small island. I don't find it that unusual."

I almost felt the click in my brain. "But Jason Early lives in Ridgeland. He wouldn't have gone to Hilton Head High."

"True. But maybe he stayed with relatives down here. I understand Jasper County schools have got some problems."

I shook my head. "I can't see his mother worrying that much about his education."

"When did you meet his mother?"

I'd forgotten I'd left my foray into Ridgeland out of my account that morning. Obviously my brain still wasn't firing on all cylinders. "I wanted to talk to him. No big deal."

I could feel the tension bunching again in Red's shoulders. "How did you know about him? With Wyler dead, I thought your pipeline into the sheriff's office had been cut off." It was unnecessarily cruel, and he knew it. "I'm sorry. That was uncalled for."

"Damn right." I sat up and put some distance between us. "I saw him on the news Sunday night."

"Right. I forgot about that. I'm sorry, sweetheart," he said again.

"So maybe someone did deliberately run that girl down. And her sister and Bobby Santiago and this Jason character know something about it. So why didn't you want to track them down when I called you this afternoon?"

"We have to tread carefully here. The Hispanic community is feeling under attack from all sides with these tougher immigration ordinances. The county solicitor doesn't want us to appear to be profiling."

"Jason Early isn't Latino."

"I know, but all the same . . . Look, we're on it, okay? Just leave all this to us for now." He pulled me back into his arms, and I let him. "We're really pretty damn good at it, you know?"

"So you say," I murmured a moment before his lips found mine.

We didn't discuss it again until morning. In fact, we didn't talk much at all.

CHAPTER
TWELVE

W E ENJOYED A QUIET BREAKFAST, BOTH OF US PRE-
occupied with our own thoughts and the *Island Packet.*
Bright sunshine poured through the windows of the French doors,
and the paper said we might hit seventy by afternoon. Winter in the
Lowcountry could be a roller coaster. Over a second cup of the coffee
he'd brewed himself, Red set the sports section aside and smiled
across the table at me.

"You going into the office today?" he asked.

"Of course. We've got to firm up the proposal for the recreation
board. We're meeting with Jack Ogilvy on Friday. Why?"

"I'm going to stop in and see Dolores this morning. I thought
you might like to come along."

"And run interference for you?"

A brief look of annoyance flitted across his face.

"She won't be there," I said, "at least not if she's keeping to her
schedule. She works for a family in Palmetto Dunes on Wednesdays."

"I'll call first. I just thought it might make things easier for her
if you were there. Considering how she feels about men in uniform."

I felt the guilty flush on my cheeks. "Oh. Sure, if you think it
will help."

Red slurped down the last of the coffee and stood. "I had a chat with Detective Pedrovsky while you were in the shower. They're officially calling Theresa Montalvo's death 'suspicious circumstances.' "

"So now you 'officially' need to talk to Bobby Santiago."

Red fastened his laden gun belt around his slim waist and situated the holster more comfortably against his hip. "The difference between your job and mine is that I have rules to follow." He softened the words with a smile. "Not that there aren't times I wish I could just chuck it all and listen to my gut, but that's not how it works. Those kids have now become persons of interest in vehicular manslaughter, maybe homicide. All bets are off."

I didn't like the tone of that last statement. *Persons of interest* sounded innocuous enough, but I knew they could slide into *suspect* status without much of a shove. "There's no reason to think they had anything to do with the death itself. If they have an idea about who or why, they could be in danger themselves."

"All the more reason for us to locate them fast. Lisa had a couple of deputies drive by there last night, but there wasn't any sign of them at the Santiago house." Red slipped on his jacket and cupped my face with his hands. "If you hear from Bobby, tell him to come in. We can offer them protection. If someone orchestrated the girl's death and they know who it was, they're sitting ducks out there."

"I know." I leaned up and kissed him lightly. "Call me at the office before you head for Dolores's. I want to go with you."

"I will, sweetheart. Talk to you later."

I sat for a while, my fingers caressing the warmth on my cheeks where his hands had rested, the same hands that . . .

I smiled at the images the sharp ringing of the phone interrupted.

"Don't push your luck, lady. Sleeping with a cop won't help you if you don't stay out of our business."

"Who the hell is this?" My head swiveled to the big bay window in the kitchen. "Where are you?"

"Close enough. Drop it, if you know what's good for you."

"Drop what?" I demanded, but I was talking to dead air.

Again I checked caller ID and found the incoming number had been blocked.

I dropped back down into my chair and stared at the phone. I closed my eyes and conjured up the voice. Male. Not young, not old. No accent. Gruff, as if he had a cold. Or maybe a longtime smoker. Definitely the same jerk who had found my cell number and called Presqu'isle in the middle of the night. I scribbled down his exact words on a notepad on the desk, then rose and worked my way around the house, checking the view from every window. Nothing. No strange car out on the road, no sign of anyone. Even the beach was empty except for one solitary woman jogging along beside her golden retriever. I marched into my bedroom closet. Pulling up the carpet at the back, I worked the dial on the floor safe and removed my pistol. In a minute, I had it loaded and tucked into the pocket of my slacks.

Red would have to get over the idea of my packing a gun. Like my American Express card, I wasn't leaving home without it. At least for a while.

I kicked out of my low-heeled pumps and pulled on my running shoes, shrugged into a jacket, and slipped out onto the front porch. One hand wrapped around the gun in my pocket, I trotted down the steps, my eyes scanning the walkway and surrounding shrubbery for any signs of disturbance. The ground was damp from Tuesday's rain, but much of it lay covered in fallen leaves and pine straw. I crossed the drive and skirted the deck, trying to step carefully. A mockingbird squawked over my head, and I jumped. My eyes swept from side to side, pausing at every tree trunk and bush. I was beginning to feel like a complete fool when I found the cigarette butts.

Three of them, just to the side of the wooden walkout that spanned the dune. Unfiltered, tossed onto the mud and wet leaves. They looked fairly dry, which meant they'd been dropped after it stopped raining. I turned back to the house. In the kitchen, I cut a plastic storage bag into a couple of squares and rummaged around in the drawers until I located a handful of wooden skewers. From the closet in the foyer, I pulled my yellow rain slicker from its hanger.

Back outside, I laid the plastic carefully over the cigarette butts and secured it on all four corners with the skewers. It felt a little melodramatic even as I was doing it, but I'd learned a few things sleeping with a cop. And from being addicted to old murder myster- ies. Just to be doubly sure, I laid my raincoat over the entire area. I did another quick sweep but found nothing else out of place.

I left my sodden shoes on the porch and transferred the Seecamp to a clean pair of slacks. I left a message for Red and double-checked the alarm. A few moments later, I gunned the Jaguar out of the garage.

I walked into the office only ten minutes late despite my foraging around for evidence of the watcher.

Erik looked up and grinned. "It's not often I beat you in here. Oversleep?"

I tried not to read anything into the question. Although Erik knew Red often spent the night at my place, he seemed as pleased about it as most of my friends. The general reaction when it became known I'd taken up with my brother-in-law had been, *It's about time.*

"No. Something weird's going on."

Over my first Diet Coke of the day, I told him about the two phone calls and my discovery of where the guy had probably stood, watching my house and smoking.

"But what's it about?" he asked when I finished, his eyes scrunched up in a frown of worry and confusion. "We're not involved in anything that would generate that kind of threat." He paused. "Are we?"

"You know everything I do. We're trying to get Bobby Santiago and his friends to come in. By the way, the Montalvo girl's death is officially suspicious as of this morning."

"That's not good. What do you suppose those kids know about it anyway?"

"Motive is my guess. And I'd bet it's something to do with Serena

Montalvo's involvement with immigration issues. I can't think of what else it could be."

"So you're thinking if they know *why* they might know *who?*"

"Exactly. That makes them dangerous to someone. And remember, Bobby originally thought it was Serena who'd been killed. If she was the target, then they—whoever the hell *they* are—screwed up. They may be looking to correct their mistake."

"What else?" he asked.

"The bank robber Mr. Gadsden thought he recognized."

"But no one knows about that, right? I mean, you didn't tell Red."

The last wasn't a question, but I nodded. "Right. Not yet. Just the Judge, Lavinia, you, and me." I thought for a moment. "I mentioned it to Dolores, but just the broadest information. Nothing specific about this Naldo. Of course, we don't know who else Mr. Gadsden might have talked to."

"But still. Even if he told his whole neighborhood, why would anyone connect that back to you? I mean enough to give them reason to threaten you."

"I have no idea. But what other than those two things could it be? We don't have a client, and we haven't even signed a contract with the recreation board."

Erik tossed a folder onto my desk. "Speaking of which, I've got the firm quotes for the services we'll need to subscribe to in order to do the background checks legally."

I looked up to meet his smile.

"The temptation is great, isn't it?" I asked. "I know you could hack into most of these databases and save us a ton of money, but we need to do this on the up-and-up. My figures show it will still be profitable, especially if we can get some of the other county agencies to jump on board."

"Agreed. Do you have the proposal proofed? I want to get everything together and take it down to the store. They can copy and bind it into something professional looking. I'm thinking we should have enough for every member of the board."

"Good plan. Just give me a few minutes to put in the changes, and I'll have it ready to go."

I pulled the file out of my drawer and looked up to find him still standing in front of my desk. "Something else?"

He reddened in that charming way he had. "Just about this guy calling you. Have you told Red?"

"Not about the one this morning. I'm waiting for him to get back to me."

Again he seemed half-embarrassed to ask the question. "Carrying?"

I nodded and patted my right-hand pocket.

"Good," he said and turned back to his desk.

Half an hour later we'd finalized all the presentation material for Friday's meeting, and Erik was on his way to the office supply store to make copies. I busied myself with bringing our financial records up to date and collecting the things I'd need to prepare our tax return. In years past, when I'd still been involved with public accounting, December had been a mad rush to get my personal life in order in anticipation of the madness of tax season. I smiled, remembering the ritual Rob and I had gone through every New Year's Eve. We'd shunned the dozens of invitations to parties around Charleston, where we'd lived and worked during the week. Instead, we'd ordered in a lavish dinner from one of the city's finest restaurants and spent the last night of the year alone. We'd toasted each other at midnight, made sweet, quiet love, and agreed to meet back there again on April 16.

Rob had never scolded or fussed at me for the exhausting hours I put in that time of year. Missed meals, unfinished laundry, absolutely no social life—he'd borne it all with good humor and patience. Even now, after all this time, I could feel the emptiness in my heart at his loss.

"A penny for them."

I jumped back in my chair to find Red smiling down on me.

"How did you get in here?"

"The door, like everyone else. Good thing I'm a friendly burglar." He leaned down to kiss me lightly on the lips. "I could have walked out with the furniture, and I don't think you'd have flinched."

"Sorry." I hoped he hadn't noticed the betraying flush of color in my cheeks. "I was contemplating."

"Where's Erik?"

"Out getting some copy work done." I cleared my throat. "You got my message."

"I got something. I think the dispatcher must have garbled it. She said you found cigarette butts in your yard." His grin chased Rob's lingering image back out of my head. "I've risen a little past handing out tickets for littering, you know."

"I got another call." I pulled the note from my bag and tossed it across the desk to him. "Just after you left."

He scanned the few words of the threat. "Same guy?"

I nodded. "Sounded like it. I did a little reconnoitering and found where he'd been watching."

"The son of a bitch! What the hell's this all about anyway? You have any idea?"

"Nope. All I can think of is that someone knows about Bobby and Serena being in touch with me and isn't happy about my sticking my nose in, although I'm damned if I can figure out how. Besides, I haven't done anything except talk to them." I looked up to find him studying my face intently. "I swear, Red. I'm not involved in anything else."

It wasn't technically a lie. There was no way anyone could have found out about my interest in Romey Gadsden. Besides, all I had there were a couple of first names. How could that be a threat to somebody?

I told him about my precautions to protect the evidence.

"I don't know what it will accomplish, or even if you think it's worth collecting those cigarette butts, but I thought it might be a good idea."

"It was. This has moved from harassment to stalking. That's a felony." He used his cell phone instead of the mike on his shoulder. "Dispatch, this is Tanner. I need to talk to Detective Pedrovsky." He smiled across at me. "Don't worry, honey. We'll take it from here. Detective?" he said into the phone. "I need someone to come out to my sister-in-law's house. That's right. She's being stalked, and there's some evidence I need collected. Right. Okay, thanks."

He tucked the phone back in his pocket.

"What's happening?" I asked.

"She'll send a tech over to photograph the site and collect the evidence. You should meet them there in about half an hour."

"Okay, thanks. Did you get hold of Dolores?"

He shook his head. "You were right. I talked to her husband. She's working today."

I waited, but he didn't continue. "Just tell me, Red. I've already prepared myself for bad news from that quarter."

"I don't have anything to tell. I'm meeting them at the house around five. You can still come along if you like, but Lisa Pedrovsky will be in charge. We'll just be there as a courtesy."

"Hector didn't say anything to you about Dolores not coming back?"

"No, honey, he didn't. We'll know more tonight. I'm sure it's going to be okay."

"Are you coming with me to the house now?"

"Can't. I have to be in court in a few minutes. Traffic accident with injuries case. I could be a while."

Erik stepped through the door at the same moment the phone rang. "I'll get it." He dumped a large box on the floor and crossed to his desk.

"Go testify," I said with a smile. "I have work to do."

"I'll call you about this afternoon. I can pick you up if you want."

"We'll see."

Erik filled the doorway. "It's Lavinia. Want me to take a message?"

"No, I'll get it," I said, and Red stood.

"Talk to you later," he said and nodded to Erik. "Good to see you."

"You, too," my partner answered as I picked up the phone. "Hey, Lavinia."

"Are you busy right now?" Her voice sounded subdued, but with a current of excitement running just below the surface.

"Why?"

"We have a chance to talk to Romey Gadsden if you can get over here quickly. He's got a doctor's appointment at one, to have his ankle checked out, and his daughter has to go in to work. I said I'd carry him over to Beaufort."

I glanced at my watch. If the sheriff's tech showed up on time, I might just make it.

"I'll do my best. Shall I pick you up at the house?"

"No, I think it'll be better if you just meet us at the hospital. I'll wait for you in the lobby."

Out in the reception area, I could see Erik unpacking a pile of black folders from the box and stacking them on his desk. He looked up and gave me the thumbs-up sign, and I nodded.

"Bay?"

I jerked my attention back to the phone. "Okay. I have a couple of other things to take care of, but I should be able to be there close to one."

"You best be. Don't leave me to handle this all by myself."

"What has you so agitated?" I asked.

She drew in a long breath and lowered her voice to a whisper. "I think I've figured out who Naldo and Maria are."

CHAPTER
THIRTEEN

I PULLED INTO A PARKING SPACE AT EXACTLY ONE thirty and hurried across the blacktop toward the main entrance to Beaufort Memorial Hospital. Traffic on Ribaut Road whizzed by as I approached the front door to find Lavinia seated on a bench under a covered portico.

"Sorry I'm late," I said, dropping down beside her.

The tech from the sheriff's office had been prompt, but we'd wasted a little time chatting about Malik Graves, the deputy who'd been run down a few months before while accompanying Red and me to an interview out at Sanctuary Hill. His shattered leg had responded well to rehab, and he hoped to be back on light duty in a few weeks. When the tech had finished extracting the cigarette butts with tweezers and dropping them into a plastic evidence bag, I'd asked him to give my best regards to Malik. Although I had no earthly reason to do so, I still felt guilty about his injury.

"No matter," Lavinia said in response to my apology. "They're runnin' behind as usual. Mr. Gadsden just went in a couple of minutes ago."

"So tell me about this revelation of yours. How do you know Naldo and Maria?"

Some of the suppressed excitement I'd heard earlier in her voice crept into her next words. "I don't know them, not personally. But I was fixing dinner last night, thinking about all this, and I remembered that Romey has a visiting nurse that comes to him once in a while when his hip acts up and he can't get around. Spanish woman. I've heard Romey talk about how kind she is, but I didn't remember ever hearing her name. And she has a son, boy who did some odd jobs around his place and once in a while for his daughter, Glory, after Romey moved in with her." She beamed at me. "It has to be them, right?"

I smiled back. "Seems like good deductive reasoning to me, but not exactly evidence. Did you ask Mr. Gadsden about them?"

She shook her head. "I didn't find a good opportunity while we were drivin' over here. I told him you were meeting us for lunch afterwards, and maybe you could help. That's all I said."

We looked up as the glass doors *whoosh*ed open, and the wizened old man, leaning heavily on an ornate wooden cane, shuffled out. Both of us scrambled to our feet, but Lavinia reached him first, slipping a hand under a bony elbow.

"Now, Romey, I told you to have them come get me when you were ready."

"Don't fuss at me, Lavinia Smalls. We'd be sittin' here 'til doomsday if we had to wait on these young folks. Bustlin' here and there, so busy, with their papers and their telephones. In my day, old people got more respect."

"Hello, Mr. Gadsden," I said, smiling at his indignation. "I'm pleased to see you're feeling better. I hope your injury wasn't serious."

"Well, Lydia Simpson! Ain't seen you in dog years, girl." He looked up from his slightly bent stance and studied my face. "My goodness, I'd forgot how *tall* you are. Near puts a crick in my neck just to look at you. How old you be now? On for fortyish?"

I laughed. "Yes, sir."

"Bad business about your man. Don't know if I ever said how sorry I was to hear of it."

"Thank you, Mr. Gadsden."

"Now, you call me Mr. Rom like all the other young folks." His throaty cackle multiplied the deep wrinkles on his weathered brown face. "Could prob'ly be your granddaddy, way I figure it."

"Come along now," Lavinia said, urging the hobbling man toward the parking lot.

"Why don't you get the van?" I suggested. "And I'll wait here with Mr. Rom."

"Fine. But you make him sit down, now, hear? That ankle doesn't need any more stress on it."

I nodded as Lavinia strode off. Romey eased himself down and rested the cane beside him.

"She's a fine woman, that one," he said, nodding to himself. "Always lookin' after folks like she does. She takes right fine care o' your daddy."

"Yes, sir. I don't know what we'd do without her."

People trickled in and out of the hospital's doors, some nodding in recognition and speaking briefly to the old man as they passed. A little breeze drifted in off the river, but the sun sparkled on the shiny leaves of the dormant shrubs along the walkway.

"That was a terrible thing that happened to you the other day," I began, deciding I might as well test the waters. "I hope it didn't upset you too much."

He snorted, a guttural *harrumph*. "Didn't upset me so much as make me fightin' mad. Peoples work all their lives tryin' to put a bit by, make things better for their families, and others think they can just waltz in and take it for theirselves. If I'd a had my walkin' stick with me, they woulda thought a little harder about it."

I smiled and glanced at the intricately carved shaft of wood, the finish worn down from years of use, the handle looking as if it might once have represented the head of a cat—a lioness or maybe a tiger. "It's beautiful," I said, deciding to work my way cautiously around to the subject of Naldo. "It would have been a shame to break it across the skull of some lowlife bank robber."

Romey caressed the stick, ignoring the opening I'd given him. "Belonged to my great-granddaddy, Luther Tait. Born on a plantation over to Hilton Head he was. Carved it himself, or so they say. First one of my daddy's family to get free. Wasn't but nineteen when the Yankee boats come blastin' their guns into Port Royal Sound, and all the white folks went runnin'." Again his cackling laugh reminded me of dead leaves underfoot on a crisp winter's day. "Skedaddled, the lot of 'em. And good riddance, too, far as I can tell." His rheumy eyes touched briefly on mine, then glanced away. "No offense, honey."

"None taken, sir."

I'd been about to steer the conversation back to the twenty-first century when Lavinia eased the van to a stop in the drive. I practically lifted the old man into the high seat and helped him strap on the shoulder harness.

"I'll follow you," I said to Lavinia. "Where are we going?"

"Deke Coley's place," Romey Gadsden said with determination. "Ain't nobody does better barbecue. Boy uses mustard, just like my mama done. None o' that red, runny tomatoey stuff." He paused a moment, waiting for one of us to contradict him.

"Deke's it is," I said and closed the door. "See you there."

The ramshackle diner on the banks of the Beaufort River reminded me of the Shack, one of Red's and my favorite places on Hilton Head, where seafood was cooked over an open fire and shoes were optional. Traffic was heavy across the bridge to Lady's Island, and by the time I pulled into the crushed oyster shell parking lot, Lavinia and Mr. Rom were already being seated at a prime spot overlooking the water. Most of the lunch crowd had headed back to work, and only three other tables were occupied.

Unlike the old black man, I prefer the runny, tomatoey kind of barbecue, so I ordered a fried shrimp sandwich and iced tea. Outside the spotted window, a few pleasure boats and a trawler glided silently by on the placid river, bright sunshine sending flickers of reflected light dancing across the surface.

"What'd the doctor have to say about your ankle?" Lavinia's voice broke the somnolent quiet.

"Stay off of it and soak it in some Epsom salts," Mr. Gadsden said. "Don't know how much he'll be chargin' the Medicare for that piece o' wisdom, but it's a right sin. Already figured that out for myself."

I smiled. "It's good nothing's broken. It might have been a lot worse."

I registered the slight tremor of his shoulders, but I didn't know how else to extract the information without making him relive the terror he must have experienced. At least here, in a place where he felt comfortable, with people who cared about him nearby, maybe it wouldn't be too bad. I glanced at Lavinia, lowered my voice, and forged ahead.

"Mr. Rom, I heard you might have recognized one of the men in the bank that day. Can you talk to me about that?"

His arthritic brown hands fastened themselves around the sweating glass of sweet tea and raised it to his lips. He set it carefully back on the plastic tablecloth before replying.

"I thought so at the time, but I believe I must've got that part mixed up."

He tried to hold my eyes, but the lie forced him to glance away.

Again I consulted Lavinia with a look, and she nodded.

"But you said a name, didn't you? Naldo? And then you said something about Maria being disappointed. Is she Naldo's mother?"

For a long time I thought he wasn't going to answer. I could almost hear the internal battle raging inside his head. That he might have misgivings about sharing his secrets with a white woman, especially one he hadn't seen in a number of years, didn't bother me. I even understood it. As much as I could.

"Yes," he finally whispered and bowed his head as if in prayer.

I felt like Torquemada, the Grand Inquisitor, trying to squeeze a confession of heresy out of some poor fifteenth-century peasant. I almost backed off then, but Lavinia's face urged me on.

"Is Maria your nurse? The one who takes care of you once in a while?"

I could have strangled the pretty black waitress who chose that exact moment to slide her heavy tray onto the next table.

"Here we are," she said brightly. "Mr. Gadsden, Deke told me he made sure you've got a fresh bun for your barbecue and some extra coleslaw on top, just how you like it."

The old man smiled sweetly at the young woman. "You tell that Deke he's an old rascal, and he don't need to be tryin' to butter me up. I can still whup him at gin rummy any time I've a mind to."

"Yes, sir, I'll tell him." Plates delivered, she topped off everyone's tea and left us with the admonition that we should call if we needed any little thing at all.

Romey tucked into his sandwich as if someone were going to come and snatch it away. He was a beanpole, without an ounce of fat, but he ate with gusto. I let it go and slathered my crispy shrimp with cocktail sauce. Lavinia had ordered catfish, and we ate in silence for a few minutes before the old man suddenly spoke up.

"Lazarus Tait—that would be my granddaddy—he was the first one born into freedom. He and my grandmama Pea worked them acres the Yankees give us over to Hilton Head. Mitchellville, the town was called back then. She bore nine children, and most of 'em was carried off when they was little. Fevers and such. Only Uncle Juke and my mama died of old age."

I had no idea where this was going, but I kept silent and let him talk.

"Times was hard back then, Lydia, for white folks as well as black."

"I'm sure they were, Mr. Rom. It's always been difficult, trying to make a living from the land."

His faded eyes studied me across the table. "You right about that, girl. Took a special kind o' people. Tough. Ornery." He smiled.

"Don't know what they'd be thinkin' of me, quivering with fear like a old willow branch." He stuffed the last of his barbecue into his mouth and followed it with a long swallow of tea.

"It was Naldo all right. I looked up square into his face. And he knowed it, too. Looked as if he'd seen a ghost. Reynaldo Velez." He shook his head. "Poor Maria."

I laid my hand on his scrawny arm. "Thank you, Mr. Rom. I'll try to keep your name out of it if I can, but you understand I have to let the sheriff's office know. I don't think you need to be afraid, but it would be good if you didn't tell anyone else about what you saw."

His sharp chin lifted, and he stared straight into my eyes. "My mama saw them hang a man from the Mercy Oak when she wasn't but five years old. Stood up and pointed out the men what done it, too. I reckon I won't be worryin' about no boy who don't know no better than to steal other folks' money and beat up on old colored men. No sir, I reckon I won't."

On the way back to Hilton Head, I broke one of my own cardinal rules and called the office from my moving car.

"I've got something for you to check out," I said when Erik picked up. "Those two names I gave you Monday night?"

"Naldo and Maria. I remember."

"Their last name is Velez. And his is actually Reynaldo. The mother is a nurse who sometimes looks after Mr. Gadsden."

I could hear Erik's fingers already pounding on the keys. "Private, or does she work for the county?"

"I didn't ask."

Romey had closed up after giving me the last name, and I figured that was a good thing, so I didn't push for more. As I'd told him, the fewer people who knew about his recognizing his attacker, the better. I hoped I'd made that plain enough as I'd helped him again into the high seat of the Judge's van.

"I may be old, but I'm not a fool, Lydia Simpson," he'd snapped.

"Just see you don't bring any more grief than you have to down on poor Maria's head, hear?"

"Nothing's popping right up," Erik said, jerking me back as I rolled past the turnoff to Parris Island.

I glanced at the clock on the dashboard. "I have to meet Red at Dolores and Hector's at five, so I'm going straight there. Call me if you find anything. I'm going to make sure he gets this information to the task force."

"Will do. Listen, Bay, are we all set for Friday then? For the meeting with Jack Ogilvy?"

"Far as I know, unless you've got something else in mind."

"No, I think we're good." He hesitated before adding, "Do I need to wear a suit?"

I couldn't control the bark of laughter.

"What's so funny?" He sounded annoyed.

"Nothing, sorry. Just whatever you'd wear to work is fine. Jack may be dressed up since we're meeting at his insurance office, but business casual is great."

"I want to make a good impression," he said, his tone still carrying a hint of irritation.

"Don't worry about it. Let's meet at the office at nine, get everything organized, and drive over together. That sound good?"

"Sure. I guess I'm just a little nervous."

"You'll be fine." I couldn't resist one last barb. "Do you even own a suit?"

"Goodbye, Bay," he said and hung up on my ripple of laughter.

My good mood didn't last long.

When I pulled up in front of the Santiago house on the winding dirt road, the yard was already filled with a cruiser and a dark gray Crown Victoria whose unadorned exterior and county plates screamed unmarked cop car. Hector's landscaping truck sat in the driveway, but I didn't see Dolores's old blue Hyundai. I turned around in the middle of the deserted road and eased the Jaguar onto the muddy verge.

Red stepped out of the cruiser as I walked up the gravel drive lined with winter cabbages, their purple leaves catching the last rays of the dying sun. Behind the house, the golden marsh grass waved softly in a chill breeze. I shivered and closed the top button on my jacket.

"Dolores isn't home yet," my brother-in-law said. "And Hector didn't invite us in."

"That's strange. She always leaves my place by four so she can be here to get dinner started," I said, a little flutter of unease whispering through my chest. "What about Alex?"

Alejandro, the youngest of the Santiago children, was a junior in high school, a good athlete who played on all the sports teams but excelled at track.

"I don't know. He hasn't shown up yet either." He turned as Lisa Pedrovsky joined us.

"Bay," she said tersely and nodded in my direction.

"Detective. I'm just here to run interference with Dolores." I figured I might as well forestall any objections she had about a civilian horning in on her case. "She's a little jumpy around uniforms."

"So I've heard. Just leave the interrogation to me, got it?"

"Fine," I said.

We stood there quietly as night crept over the marsh and the birds fell silent. I shivered a little, but Red made no move toward me. I smiled to let him know I understood.

"Sergeant tells me you've talked to those two kids." Lisa Pedrovsky's voice seemed to come out of the darkness.

"Yes. I'll be glad to give you a statement. I'm worried as hell that they've gotten themselves involved in something dangerous."

"And you saw them yesterday."

I nodded, then realized she probably couldn't see me. "That's right. At the mall. Just a glance as they drove away, but I'm certain it was Bobby in the car."

The sudden *click* sounded loud in the stillness of the Lowcountry night, and the flare of the lighter hurt my eyes. A moment later, I inhaled the smoke wafting from the detective's cigarette and barely controlled an urge to snatch it out of her hands.

"I suppose you've got some theory about what's going on," she said.

I wondered if I was imagining that hint of hostility in her words. "A couple," I said, "but nothing more than speculation."

"So speculate," Lisa Pedrovsky said, exhaling a cloud of smoky breath into the cold. "We don't have anything else to do. Without a warrant, we're going to have to wait for an invitation."

As I talked, lights bloomed inside the neat little bungalow and sparkled in the windows of the larger, more expensive houses across the marsh. When I finished, Lisa returned to her unmarked to make some calls.

By six o'clock, Dolores still hadn't come home.

At six thirty, I gave myself permission to panic.

CHAPTER FOURTEEN

I DIDN'T EVEN TRY TO SLEEP.

I sat on the sofa in the great room with all the lights on and fed wood into the fireplace, but still I couldn't seem to get warm. I clutched my cell phone in one hand and the land line in the other, willing one of them to ring. Even bad news would have been better than the incessant waiting. . . .

Earlier, back at Dolores's, Red had tried to stop me from pounding on the door of the small cottage, but I'd jerked out of his grip.

"God damn it, Hector! Talk to me!" The metal of the storm door had rattled under my assault but remained firmly closed. "Alejandro! We just want to help," I hollered. "You know that, damn it!"

Red's efforts to pull me off had me rounding on him as well. "You scared her away! Who knows where the hell she's gone now, or what kind of trouble she's in!"

Lisa Pedrovsky obviously shared my frustration, but she handled it much better. "I'll put out an alert on her car," she said, pulling a cell phone from the pocket of her thin jacket. "Chill out, Bay," she called over her shoulder before moving away. "Your ranting isn't helping the situation any."

"You can go to—," I began, but Red spun me around and shook me.

"Knock it off!" With a quick glance toward the unmarked car, he'd pulled me into a quick embrace. "Come on, honey," he whispered. "Quit reacting and think. Where would she go? Who are her friends?" He stepped back and dropped his arms. "Do you think Hector knows what's going on?"

I drew a shaky breath. "Of course he does. He wouldn't stand for not knowing exactly where Dolores is. But he's not going to tell *us*." By force of will, I quieted my trembling fear. "Maybe it would be better if I left. Hector doesn't like me. He might open up if I'm not here."

Red had encouraged me to go home, to eat and try to get some rest. I let him think he'd talked me into it and climbed into the Jaguar with a brief kiss and his assurance that he'd keep me posted. It had taken me only ten minutes to reach the office, another three to locate the address.

Serena Montalvo's family lived in the same condominium complex where I'd tried tracking down a murder suspect the past summer, so it felt eerily familiar as I coasted down the winding drive. Light spilled from their apartment tucked back in the farthest reaches of the property, and all the parking slots in front of their building were full. None of the cars was a dented blue Hyundai. Or a faded red Taurus.

I had pulled across the drive and doused my lights, my eyes fastened on the door tucked back up under a narrow roof over the steps. My instinct was to pound on that door as I had on Hector's and demand entrance. Common sense and decency held me fast in the soft leather seat of the Jag. These people had lost a daughter, suddenly and violently. For all I knew, they had no idea where her sister was, either. Even my fear for Dolores couldn't justify adding to their burdens.

After fifteen minutes, I'd turned for home. . . .

A log, partially burned through, collapsed in a shower of sparks. I reached for my mug, but the tea had gone cold. I plodded up into the kitchen and turned the burner on under the kettle. I tensed at a flicker of lights on the street in front of my house, but they moved on by.

As I stood leaning on the counter, waiting for the water to boil, it occurred to me that I'd never told Red about Mr. Gadsden's identification of one of the bank robbers. *A perfect excuse to call and see what's going on,* I thought as the tea kettle whistled. I filled my cup, and then added a large spoon of sugar. I punched in Red's cell number and waited through a dozen rings before hanging up, then tried my partner.

Erik answered almost immediately.

"How'd it go with Dolores?" he asked after assuring me I wasn't interrupting anything more important than a basketball game on ESPN.

"She never came home."

"What do you mean she never came home?"

I swallowed my irritation. It wasn't Erik's fault my nerves were rubbed raw. "She supposedly went to work this morning, in Palmetto Dunes, and never came back."

"Do you think something's happened to her?"

"I don't know what to think at this point. I'm more inclined to believe she's hooked up with Bobby and is doing what she can to protect her son." The sigh came out shakier than I'd intended. "At least that's what I hope she's doing."

"How about the other kid? Alex, is it?"

"Yes. Alejandro. He finally showed up around six forty-five. Basketball practice after school. Like his father, he clammed up the minute he saw the cop car. Neither Red nor Lisa Pedrovsky could get a thing out of him."

"Did you have a run at him?"

"I tried. Apparently I'm firmly entrenched in the enemy camp, at least as far as the male Santiagos are concerned." *And maybe in Dolores's mind, too,* I thought and shivered.

"I know it's pointless to tell you not to worry," my partner said.

"I'll bet you're sitting around in the dark cooking up all kinds of nasty scenarios in your head."

"Not totally in the dark, but close. You know me too well."

"Would a little company help?"

I smiled at the offer. Erik had become like the little brother I never had, and his innate kindness never ceased to astound me. For one still so young, he had an amazing capacity for doing and saying exactly the right thing.

"Thanks, but it's late. I'll go turn on some lights and quit brooding. Promise."

"Listen, I found a couple of things online this afternoon about the Velez woman. I was going to call you tomorrow before I left for work."

I carried the fresh cup of tea and the phone back into the great room and curled back onto the sofa. "Go ahead."

"Well, she doesn't work for any of the county agencies, far as I could tell. She ran a couple of classified ads in the *Beaufort Gazette* a while back. She's more like a temporary companion for old people when their primary caregivers are away or they need some kind of special attention. I don't think she's technically a nurse. At least she didn't claim to be in her ads."

"Interesting," I said. "So probably no business license or anything like that. I wonder what her immigration status is."

"Why?"

I shrugged. "All the media attention, I guess. That and this mess Bobby Santiago seems to be embroiled in. We have Hispanics working all over the county, and it never occurred to me to wonder about them before. Now it's almost the first thing that pops into my head." I sighed. "I'm beginning to feel like a bigot or something."

"Don't be ridiculous! You're the farthest thing from a bigot I've ever known."

"I'd like to think so. But I have to admit it makes me uneasy that so many people seem to come and go across our border as if they were crossing the street for a carton of milk. Especially in the times we live in."

"I know what you mean," Erik said.

"Anyway, we're not going to solve—"

A horrible shrieking sent lukewarm tea sloshing onto my hand.

"What the hell is that?" Erik's voice was almost drowned out by the noise.

"The alarm. I'll call you back."

"No! Bay, wait—," he yelled, but I hung up.

Almost immediately the phone rang in my hand.

"Mrs. Tanner? This is Coastal Security. Your perimeter alarm has been activated. May I have your password?"

"Mr. Bones," I said. The name of the stray cat that had briefly graced me with his presence a couple of years before had seemed a safe choice. No one but Dolores would remember him.

"Are you in need of assistance or did you set it off accidentally?"

Without thought, I crossed to where my bag rested on the console table, pulled out the Seecamp, and dropped it into my pocket. "No. I mean, no I didn't set it off."

"We're sending plantation security and the sheriff. I'll stay on the line until they arrive."

"Fine."

Back in the great room, I picked up my cell phone and called Erik, keeping the handset against my other ear.

"What the hell's going on?"

"Someone tried to break in," I said, amazed at how calm I sounded. "The security company's on the land line. They're sending people."

"Where are you? Get away from the windows."

"Why? You don't think—"

"Just do it!" he yelled and I stepped into the hallway leading to the bedrooms.

A moment later I heard a pounding on the front door, and I moved cautiously into the foyer.

"Mrs. Tanner? It's Deputy Sanchez. Beaufort County Sheriff's."

I could barely hear him over the shrieking alarm.

"Look through the window. I'm holding up my badge."

I did as he instructed, then punched in the cancel code and yanked open the door.

"They're here," I said to the security company dispatcher. "Thank you."

"Glad to be of assistance. Take care."

It took me a moment to realize Erik was shouting at me from my cell phone.

"Bay! What's happening?"

"Sorry. There's a deputy here. I have to go."

"I'm on my way," he said.

"You don't have to—," I began, but he was already gone.

"Just sit down, ma'am," Deputy Sanchez said, steering me toward the sofa with a gentle hand under my elbow. "My partner is outside checking the perimeter. I'll do a walk-through of the house, but I think the alarm probably scared him off."

I dropped obediently onto the couch and let my hand slip into the pocket of my sweatpants to caress the pistol resting against my thigh.

Damned good thing for him, I thought, fear hardening into anger as I curled my finger toward the trigger. *Damned good thing.*

CHAPTER FIFTEEN

RED AND ERIK ARRIVED ALMOST ON EACH OTHER'S heels.

By that time, the deputies had assured me the house and grounds were secure. I'd told Sanchez about the phone threats and the cigarette butts I'd discovered earlier in the day.

"Any idea who it might be?" he'd asked in a soft voice.

"No. None at all."

"Well, line of work you're in, ma'am, you must make some folks a little angry now and again. Maybe some husbands who aren't real happy."

I'd bristled. "We don't do divorce work, Deputy. Trust me, this has nothing to do with some philanderer who can't keep his pants zipped."

If he was shocked, he didn't show it. "As you say, ma'am. We'll keep a car in the neighborhood for the rest of tonight, but I don't think he'll be back. Probably kids looking to make some mischief or grab something they can pawn for drug money. Once they know a place has an alarm, they usually don't come back."

Usually. I tried to take some comfort from that.

Red burst through the door then, shouldered Sanchez out of the way, and nearly smothered me in his arms. I had to wriggle free, embarrassed by his display in front of his fellow officer. The deputy didn't even pretend to look away.

"Are you okay?" Red's face in the bright lights of the living room looked chalky.

"I'm fine. The deputies have assured me no one's lurking in the closets or under the bed."

Red didn't see any humor in the situation. "I'll do another pass," he said, nodding at Sanchez. "No disrespect intended, Rudy, but I'd like to check things out myself."

"No problem, Sarge. We'll leave you to it. Ma'am," he said, touching his forehead with two fingers, "you take care."

"Thank you, Deputy. Goodnight."

The poor man took another body block as Erik bounded up the front steps.

"It's okay," I called as Sanchez's hand went automatically to his holster. "He's my business partner."

The deputy shrugged and disappeared into the night.

"Bay! What's going on?"

I stepped back in case Erik had plans to crush the breath out of me, too. "Someone tried to break in and set off the alarm." I shrugged. "They seem to think it was kids looking to score something they could turn into crack or whatever. Red's checking the inside again."

"Do they know about the threats you got? And the guy watching the house?"

"I gave them the whole package. I don't think they were impressed." I turned and walked up into the kitchen. "Are you hungry? I didn't have anything for dinner except some peanut butter crackers, and I'm starving."

I heard him follow me up as I peered into the refrigerator. "I've got some marinara sauce frozen. Wouldn't take long to whip up a couple of plates of linguine."

"No, thanks. I'm fine. What are you going to do about this?" he asked.

I handed him a can of Coke, and he popped the top.

"What am I supposed to do about it? That's why I spent a fortune on the alarm system, and it turned out to be worth it. I'm about as safe as I can be anywhere."

"I've got a spare room. Nothing but an air mattress, but it's pretty comfy."

I smiled at him and set the frozen sauce in the microwave. "I appreciate that, but I'm fine right here." From down the hall I could hear doors opening and closing. "Besides, I think it'll take dynamite to get Red out of here tonight."

"Good. I don't like this, Bay. I wish to hell I knew what's triggered it."

"Me, too." I set a pot of water on the stove and took a package of pasta from the pantry. "It has to be about Bobby Santiago."

"But why? I mean, who knows you're even involved with him and his girlfriend?"

"Jason Early." Red's voice was stern as he climbed the three steps. "And his mother. And whoever the Santiago kid or Serena Montalvo might have told. Plus Dolores, Hector, their other son, and anyone they might have confided in."

Red sat down at the table across from Erik, and I brought him a Coke as well. "You have no idea how far this might have spread. It's a tight-knit community. If you've been perceived as a threat, someone might have decided to take it in his own hands to scare you off."

I put the defrosted sauce in a pan and turned on the burner. "That's a pretty sweeping statement. I'd venture to guess that most of those people are too busy trying to make a living and raise their kids to be worried about me or Bobby Santiago."

"Don't be too sure. Whether we want to believe it or not, there are a lot of illegals in the Lowcountry. Some of them are in debt to their coyotes, and those people play rough. Remember that case in Florida last year? The baby that got kidnapped to coerce his parents into paying what they owed the guy who smuggled them into the country?"

"But not around here," I said, stirring the sauce with a wooden spoon. "I mean, okay, I guess I can see Florida. Haitians and Cubans. And Arizona, California. Maybe Texas. But we don't exactly share a border with Mexico."

"We've got a coastline and practically nothing but a few scattered patrols to guard it. You know that as well as I do."

I threw a handful of salt into the boiling water and turned to Red. "You want a bowl of pasta?"

I could always count on Red to make cooking worthwhile. "If it's not any trouble."

"Erik, you sure?"

"Well, if you're positive there's enough."

I smiled and dumped the entire box of linguine into the pot.

"Anyway," I said, "you may be right, but I'm having a hard time wrapping my head around it. Maybe it was just an isolated incident. Or maybe they have me mixed up with someone else."

"Playing ostrich isn't the answer," Red said. "You need to be on your toes, aware of your surroundings at all times. I'm going to make certain a car swings by here on a regular basis, especially on the nights I can't stay over."

"Good," Erik said.

I turned my back on both of them and busied myself with ladling out our midnight dinner. I had my own agenda, and it didn't involve being a captive inside my own house. *"Quivering in fear like a old willow branch,"* Mr. Gadsden had said earlier.

The watcher would be back, and I'd be ready.

Erik left shortly after scraping the last remnants of sauce from his bowl. At the door, he patted my shoulder awkwardly. "You'll be fine."

"I know that. See you Friday at the office."

He nodded, and I could tell he waited on the porch until I reengaged the alarm.

Back in the kitchen, Red was rinsing dishes and setting them haphazardly in the dishwasher.

"Let me do that," I said, using a hip to ease him out of the way.

"I've got it." He pushed back, and I laughed.

"I have a system."

"I know. But hey, what the hell? Live on the wild side. I'll bet they'll get just as clean if all the edges of the plates aren't lined up perfectly and the forks and knives aren't in separate compartments."

I retired from the field and poured myself a cup of tea. "I need to talk to you about something."

Red glanced over his shoulder. "That sounds ominous."

"It's about Lavinia and Mr. Gadsden at the bank Monday."

He closed the door of the dishwasher and dried his hands on a towel before crossing to take the chair across from me. "What about it?"

"Mr. Gadsden thinks he might have recognized one of the robbers."

I could tell by the tightening of his jaw that the news didn't sit well. As I had known it wouldn't.

"It's like with the Santiagos," I said, reaching across the table to take his hand. "Some people don't have the same faith in the justice system as we do. It's nothing personal. But there's no denying some folks just don't like talking to the police."

"Tell me something I don't already know." He shook his head. "There are a lot of crimes in the native island and immigrant communities that don't get reported because they're more afraid of us than they are of the criminals."

"I know, but it's not just about that. I don't know the whole story, but Dolores has hinted at atrocities where she comes from that were committed by the army and police. And people like Lavinia and Mr. Gadsden haven't always gotten the best treatment." I could see the anger rising in his eyes. "I know you're all super-sensitive now, Red, but there's a history. You have to admit that."

"What did Romey Gadsden tell you?" he asked, and I didn't like the way he squared his shoulders. "That he—and Mrs. Smalls—felt they couldn't tell me?"

I sighed. "You have to promise you're not going to hassle him—or Lavinia—about it, okay?" I raised my voice a fraction. "Okay?"

"You know I can't promise no one will want to interview him. And he'll definitely have to make a statement." He frowned. "*Another* statement. He may be the best lead we've had on grabbing these dirtbags. Come on, Bay, give it up."

"He's scared. And rightly so. You take it easy on him, you hear me? He's old and frail."

"I'm not going to beat it out of him, for God's sake. I just might take you across my knee, though, if you don't spit it out."

"Promises, promises," I said, then sobered. "He saw the face of one of them after he got knocked down. His name is Reynaldo Velez. His mother, Maria, has looked after Mr. Gadsden on occasion. He didn't want to make trouble for the woman, that's why he didn't come forward."

I saw him glance toward the clock over the sink.

"Let it go until tomorrow," I said, rising. I still held his hand in mine. "Come on, let's get some sleep."

"Okay. There's no one on the task force working at this hour anyway. But we're going to have to interview Mr. Gadsden. You know that."

I nodded and pulled him to his feet. "Just make sure they're gentle with him. And you have to keep his name out of it."

Red didn't reply, but he let me lead him into the bedroom I'd once shared with his brother.

"I need a shower," he said and headed for the guest bath across the hall.

I took the one connected to the bedroom. We hadn't quite progressed to the level of intimacy that allowed us to share a bathroom.

Outside, the roar of the ocean provided a muted backdrop as I washed my face and brushed my teeth. I pulled on my old chenille robe over my nightgown and brushed out my hair. I worked cream into my skin and tried not to dwell on the tiny lines beginning to radiate from the corners of the eyes staring back at me from the mirror.

Where was Dolores? Was she safe? Had someone taken her as a way to bring Bobby Santiago and Serena Montalvo out into the open? Or would I awake on Thursday morning to find her bustling about the kitchen, muttering in Spanish about the sloppy way I'd cleaned up after our midnight meal? I thought about praying, but I did it so seldom, it seemed presumptuous of me to believe anyone would be paying the least attention.

I gazed at my reflection. "If she's not here tomorrow, I'll find her," I promised myself. I flipped off the light and stepped into the bedroom.

In the dim glow from the bedside lamp, I could see Red already settled under the duvet, hair still damp from the shower, his eyes closed and his chest rising and falling rhythmically. I shed the robe and slipped in beside him. He grunted and reached for me. I wriggled closer and laid my head gently on his chest. He smelled like soap and shampoo. And safety.

I curled my body against his and slept.

CHAPTER
SIXTEEN

NEXT MORNING, I FLUNG MY ARM ACROSS THE cold, empty space Red had occupied and squinted at the clock. 7:37. I threw back the covers and snatched up my robe. Barefoot, I stepped out of the bedroom onto the chilly hardwood floor of the hallway. A rattle of pans sent me dashing toward the kitchen, skidding to a stop at the foot of the steps.

"Dolores?" I called, hope a palpable presence in the center of my chest a moment before I registered Red standing at the stove.

"Sorry, sweetheart, it's only me."

I tightened the belt on my robe and pushed the mass of hair out of my face before plodding up to join him.

"Good morning," I said, doing my best to mask the deep disappointment. I turned my head and took his kiss on my cheek. "I haven't brushed my teeth yet."

"Tea water's hot." He gestured toward the kettle as he expertly flipped an egg. "Pour me a coffee, will you?"

We moved about the kitchen in silent harmony until breakfast had been laid out on the small table next to the bay window and we'd both seated ourselves.

"I tried Hector first thing this morning, but no one answered. Screening, probably."

"I'd like to strangle him," I said around a mouthful of crisp bacon.

"He has to know where she is. From what I've seen of him, he'd be tearing the island apart if he didn't."

"She's with Bobby," I said. "I'd bet everything I've got on it. You're right. If Hector thought she was in trouble, he'd tell us. Even as much as he disapproves of me, he knows I'd be there if Dolores needed me." I sipped the sweet, hot tea. "At least I hope he does."

"I talked to Lisa this morning, too. She's our liaison with the robbery task force. I gave her the info on Mr. Gadsden and this Velez guy. They're running him through the databases, but it's a long shot."

"Why?"

"If he's never been arrested before, he's not going to show up. Or if he's illegal or using a false name. There's a pretty brisk trade in forged documents. He could even be using someone else's papers. We've run across a lot of that lately."

"So what do you do?" I asked. "I mean, that's out of your jurisdiction, isn't it? Do you turn them over to INS?"

"It's ICE now. Immigration and Customs Enforcement. I don't interact much with them. Way over my pay grade."

I sat back and regarded him across the rim of my cup. "I need to find Dolores and Bobby. You have any suggestions?"

Red carried his empty plate to the sink. "You know there's nothing we can do about Dolores. There's no hint of foul play. She seems to have left under her own power and by her own choice." He turned and leaned against the counter. "Don't you know any of her friends?"

I shook my head. "She's a very private person."

"Well, her son is on our radar screen. We'll eventually track them down."

I watched him remove his gun belt from the small built-in desk and strap it on.

"What are you going to do with yourself today?" he asked.

Good question, I thought and decided he wouldn't like the answer that had just popped into my head.

"I've got some errands to run. Maybe I'll stop in at Presqu'isle. What's on your agenda?"

"Chasing bad guys and making the world safe for democracy. The usual."

His grin made me feel even guiltier, and I rose and hugged him hard. "Be careful."

"You, too." I could feel the tension where my hands rested against the muscles of his shoulders. "I'm not completely convinced that business last night had anything to do with kids hunting drug money."

"Neither am I," I said, staring straight into his eyes. "I don't know why someone's watching the house or making those threatening phone calls, but I'm taking it seriously."

"You might want to think about getting the Seecamp out of the safe," he said, and I had to suppress a smile.

"If you think it's a good idea."

"Just keep it handy. I took a look around outside this morning when I went to get the paper. There's nothing to indicate they did more than try a door or window before they set off the alarm." Suddenly, he pulled me into a hard embrace. "I don't like leaving you alone."

I slid myself out of his arms and stepped back. "Don't start hovering, Red."

"Just be alert," he said, all trace of his smile gone. "And call me if anything spooks you."

"You're going to be late." I kissed him briefly on the lips.

"Call me," he said again and trotted down the steps. "Set the alarm," he yelled over his shoulder a moment before I heard the door close.

I waited until I heard the hum of the cruiser's powerful engine fade into the bright morning air before I padded back down the hallway to my office. In less than a minute I had accessed the archives of the *Island Packet* and found the follow-up article on the hit-and-run death of Theresa Montalvo. I'd remembered correctly that, even though the body hadn't yet been released by the coroner, a Mass was being said for the girl at ten o'clock that morning at Holy Family on Pope Avenue. I peeled off my robe on my way to the bathroom. If I hurried, I just might make it.

There were a few other Anglo faces in the small gathering, but I knew I was conspicuous in my dark blue suit and navy pumps, towering over most of the Hispanics who huddled together in the center of the sanctuary.

I'd waited until the last possible moment to slip inside, but still heads had turned as I seated myself in the last row of pews. The priest stepped to the pulpit, and I bowed my head, rising and sitting when everyone else did, although I wasn't really following the words of the ritual. My eyes scanned the backs of the heads of the fifty or so people who had taken time off to pay their respects, but I didn't recognize Dolores's tight bun or Roberto's unruly mass of tangled black curls. One or two of the women had long, silky dark hair, but I couldn't have picked Serena Montalvo out even if I'd seen her full-face. That one brief glimpse I'd had as her old Taurus sped away out of the mall parking lot hadn't given me much to go on.

My mind wandered to the watcher and why he had targeted me for his attentions. What if it did have something to do with this poor child's death? Red had mentioned coyotes. I'd heard the term on television programs about the growing illegal immigration problem. I knew these men—both Anglo and Hispanic—extorted large sums of money from their clients, largely poor people desperate to escape the grinding poverty of their home countries for a chance at a better life in America. As I'd told Erik, I sympathized with their plight, but I couldn't bring myself to condone their methods. Still, like most homegrown American citizens, I didn't have a clue about what obtaining legal status entailed. I made a mental note to do some research.

Movement jerked me back to reality, and I rose quickly as the mourners began filing into the aisles. I spotted the bereaved parents surrounded by their friends, accepting hugs and sharing tears. Two young boys, squirming self-consciously in dark suits and ties, seemed eager to be away from the clutching hands and sweaty embraces of weeping women in black. There was no sign of the missing daughter or her boyfriend.

Back outside, the air had warmed, and I felt a trickle of perspiration run down the back of my neck as I slipped on my sunglasses. I'd parked the Jaguar at the far end of the treed parking area, and I sat for a while watching the sad procession of family and friends. Finally, only the Montalvos and their sons stood at the wide door. I saw Serena's mother embrace the elderly priest, and her husband shook hands solemnly before shepherding his diminished family toward one of two vehicles besides mine remaining in the graveled lot. The four of them squeezed into the seat of a Ford pickup truck which pulled out onto the wide avenue and disappeared.

As I reached for the key, a sudden movement in the thick stand of shrubbery bordering the church on the side farthest from the road made me jerk my hand back. Without thinking, I slid down in the seat, banging my knees on the steering column and forcing me to bite back a shriek of pain. Through the narrow strip of windshield, I watched Jason Early and a slim girl who had to be Serena Montalvo glance around before scurrying across the parking lot and slipping into the white Dodge Neon.

I waited for a full ten seconds after they turned left onto Pope Avenue before I eased out after them.

I followed the Neon into the left lane and had to let a few cars get between us before I could merge into the Sea Pines Circle. As I anticipated, Jason Early took the exit to Palmetto Bay Road. Over the Cross Island bridge and approaching the tollbooths, he moved into the cash lane while I slowed before gliding through with my Palmetto Pass. I glanced at the gas gauge, which showed me a little short of half a tank. I'd be okay unless he was headed to Charleston or Atlanta.

Where was Bobby? I wondered, dropping back again to allow traffic to flow in between me and the tiny white car. With Dolores, maybe? I thought of calling their house, then decided I didn't need the distraction while I was trying to keep Jason and Serena in sight. Time enough when I found out where they were going.

The Neon bypassed the exit for Gumtree Road, so he wasn't taking the girl home. Swooping down onto 278, we caught the red light at Spanish Wells Road, just a few yards from where Theresa Montalvo had been struck and killed. And where Jason Early had supposedly "happened" upon the scene shortly thereafter. I'd seen him twice now with the dead girl's sister, and that coincidence was becoming harder and harder to swallow.

We made the next green and moved with the flow onto the bridges to the mainland. Just past the entrance to the newer of the two outlet malls, brake lights began to flash on ahead of us. In the middle lane, I slowed as Jason maneuvered the Neon to the far right. Around the bend, I could see blue and red emergency lights strobing in the bright sunshine a moment before traffic came to a complete standstill. Behind me, I heard the wail of a siren.

A few moments later the fire engine roared by, riding the berm because there was nowhere for the solidly packed lanes of cars to go. I pushed the gearshift into Park and reached for my cell phone.

"Sergeant Red Tanner, please," I told the dispatcher.

"One moment."

Up ahead, drivers were flipping on their right-turn signals, so the accident must have blocked at least the far left lane. I glanced in the rearview mirror to an unbroken line of vehicles backed up as far as I could see.

"Ma'am? I'm sorry, but Sergeant Tanner isn't available. Would you care to leave a number?"

Because I was pretty sure everyone in the department knew about our relationship, I felt awkward, like a lovesick teenager bothering her boyfriend at work.

"This is Bay Tanner. Please have him call me on my cell. It's important," I added, although I could almost see the knowing smile on the woman's face.

"I'll give him the message," she said.

I tried his personal cell, but it was out of service, either because he'd turned it off or he was in one of those dead areas for which rural Beaufort County is famous. Horns blared as drivers tried to nose into the far right lane, and I pulled the gearshift down and edged forward six inches. My one consolation was that Jason and Serena wouldn't be going anywhere, either.

For the next fifteen minutes we crept forward, some kind souls allowing their fellow drivers to move over, but most staring straight ahead, intentionally oblivious to those trying to worm their way in. Our traffic jams, especially on 278, are legendary. Even after the only road leading to and from the island had been widened to six lanes, a serious accident could tie things up for hours.

As we crawled forward, I was finally able to see around the bend approaching the entrance to Colleton River Plantation and got my first look at the pileup. Two cars and a furniture delivery truck lay scattered across the entire westbound stretch of road. An ambulance crew was loading someone onto a gurney, and several other people milled around the smashed and broken vehicles. Two sheriff's cars were on scene along with the fire truck, and a deputy was directing cars onto the right-hand shoulder.

I flipped on my turn signal, but I didn't have a lot of hope. With growing dismay, I watched the white Neon edge closer to the deputy until finally he waved them through, and they sped off down the highway.

I glanced frantically to my right, nosing the Jaguar toward a minuscule opening behind a van with Pennsylvania plates, but the following driver obviously hadn't heard of Southern hospitality. I banged my hand on the steering wheel and cursed while Jason Early and Serena Montalvo disappeared into the distance.

CHAPTER SEVENTEEN

ALF AN HOUR LATER, I FINALLY REACHED THE turnoff to Beaufort without having sighted my quarry. There were any number of side roads they could have taken, not to mention dozens of shopping areas whose vast parking lots could have hidden a hundred little white Neons. At the exit ramp, my hand hovered over the turn signal lever, then dropped back onto the steering wheel. I drove on, bypassing the entrance to I-95 before heading up Route 17 toward Ridgeland.

I almost never traveled that road, and I was amazed at how much had changed. A lot more development than I remembered, but nothing compared to the expected explosion of this area in the next few years. I shuddered to think how many more problems that would bring, how much more pressure on our resources and the fragile natural beauty that drew so many visitors and eventual transplants. I'd never before thought about leaving the Lowcountry, not seriously, but maybe it was time to reassess.

Don't be ridiculous, I told myself. What about the Judge and Lavinia, Dolores and Erik, Bitsy, Neddie? And Red. Except for a few years away at college up north, this had been my home forever. And my family's. Generations of Baynards, Tattnalls, Chases, Simpsons. Tied to the land and the history . . .

One day, though, my father would be gone. No escaping that painful truth. Though he had deeded Presqu'isle over to me on my fortieth birthday, it would always be his home for as long as he lived. But after? Would Lavinia want to stay on alone in that rambling old house? Maybe she'd want to live with her son, spend her remaining years being waited on herself. Lord knew she'd earned it.

Besides, where would I go? Nowhere on the southeast coast seemed safe from the kind of population explosion we'd been experiencing for the past twenty years. And the approaching retirement of the entire baby boomer generation wouldn't make things any better. For the first time, I thought seriously about it. California? Earthquakes and fires. Florida? Their problems were worse than ours. Nowhere cold, that was for certain. Mountains didn't appeal to me except as nice vistas to be viewed from a distance. Despite the trouble I'd run into there, the islands of the Caribbean might be a possibility. Surely there were some that hadn't been overrun by tourists. Anegada had seemed charming, although my impressions had been somewhat tempered by the hurricane. Still—

The part of my brain that had been keeping the car on the road while I mentally wandered the world suddenly registered a familiar landscape. With a quick glance in the rearview mirror, I slowed and let the Jaguar drift into the rutted driveway past the abandoned gas station and coast toward the old bungalow. I stopped well short of the house, but I had a good view of the yard. No white rental car.

So Jason Early hadn't brought Serena Montalvo home to mama. Recalling the woman's wild eyes and unrepentant racial epithets, I decided it was probably a good decision on the boy's part. So where in hell were they? I sat for a moment, the Jag's engine idling quietly, while I pondered possibilities and came up empty. My hand had just settled onto the gearshift lever when a distant barking penetrated the hushed silence of the car's interior.

The back wheels churned up a cloud of dust as I whipped back onto the highway.

* * *

I wasted nearly an hour cruising up and down the streets of Ridgeland, exploring small lanes and big parking lots. I grabbed a sandwich at Burger King, then widened my search grid. I finally
admitted defeat and turned south toward Beaufort. Wherever Jason
Early had decided to hide, he'd done a damn fine job of it.

Presqu'isle dozed in the early afternoon sun. As I climbed the
steps, Lavinia turned from the wide front door, a hammer clutched in
her hand. She stepped back and smiled at me when I joined her on
the verandah.

"How's that look?" she asked.

The live wreath had a few small pine cones embedded in its
branches, and a cluster of red silk ribbons formed a perfect cascading
bow.

"Lovely. Understated and elegant."

"Good! That's exactly what I thought." She bent to place the
hammer in a small tray of tools. "You hungry?"

"No, ma'am. Just ate. Has the Judge gone down for his nap yet?"

Her snort of laughter made me jump. "Yes, but don't let him hear
you say that. He insists he just rests his eyes in there all afternoon."

I followed Lavinia into the house and back to the kitchen. She
stored the tools in the cupboard under the sink and set the kettle on.
"Gonna be about time for iced tea again before too long, but I always
think hot is much more appropriate this time of year, don't you?"

I took my assigned seat at the oak table and watched her familiar movements as she set out the paraphernalia for the Southern version of the tea ritual. "Have you heard anything from Mr. Gadsden?"
I asked.

She paused in the middle of taking the second-best china cups
out of the cupboard. "No. Did you have a chance to talk to Redmond?"

Lavinia was the only person who insisted on calling Red by his
full first name.

"Yes, I did. I told him to take it easy on him, that he was frail and not in the best of health. I know Red will do his best to be gentle with him."

"You're a good girl," Lavinia said, and the sudden lump that rose in my throat surprised me.

"Thank you."

The comfortable silence settled over us, interrupted occasionally by the tap of an oak limb against the side of the house and the muted ticking of the grandfather clock in the hallway. I have no idea what made the question pop into my head.

"What's the Mercy Oak?"

She poured water from the whistling kettle into the teapot and turned. "Why ever do you want to know about that?"

I shrugged. "Mr. Gadsden mentioned it at lunch yesterday. He said his mother had witnessed a lynching at the Mercy Oak. I've never heard of it before."

I couldn't quite interpret the look that passed over Lavinia's eyes, but it disappeared as quickly as it had come. "I guess that could be true, although I'm not aware of that particular incident."

She set the steaming pot and the cups on the table, then added small silver spoons. Even though we were seated in the kitchen, she apparently intended to do it up right. She lifted a cloth from a plate on the counter and set it between us.

"Tassie cups?" I asked, eyeing the little hollows of pastry with amazement. "And lemon curd?"

She smiled. "I wasn't sure you'd remember."

"You used to make them for Christmas every year, but I haven't seen them in a decade. What's the occasion?"

Lavinia poured for both of us and passed the sugar. "I don't know. Maybe I'm just gettin' old. There's lots of recipes in that old journal you were looking at the other night. I read through it some after you left. Just put me in mind of how things used to be, back when you were a little girl and your mama was still alive."

I blew across the steaming tea before sipping. The cup rattled a little when I replaced it in the nearly translucent saucer. "Not necessarily good memories," I said tersely.

"I know, honey, but they weren't all bad, either. Christmas was Emmaline's favorite time of the year. Lord, the parties she used to throw! Sometimes we had more'n a hundred people jammed in here for one of her holiday soirées. Everyone dressed so fine, and the ladies with their best jewelry glittering in the lamplight."

"You make it sound magical. The trouble was, she usually ended up drunk and creating a scene."

"Sometimes," Lavinia said, her voice soft and seeming to come from far away. "But she was a beautiful woman, Bay. Wasn't a man in the place could keep his eyes off her when she made her grand entrance down the staircase."

"I used to watch from the landing," I said, "after she'd gone down."

Lavinia smiled. "I know that, child. Half the time you'd fall asleep there, and I'd have to come tuck you back into bed before she caught you." Finally the dreamy look faded from her eyes. "No denyin' your mama had a temper on her."

No denying, I said to myself. Then, with a long breath, I let it go.

"May I have one?" I asked, pointing at the plate of delicacies that conjured up good memories of Christmases past, most of them centered around this kitchen and this wonderful woman.

"I didn't spend the whole morning bakin' so you could just sit and look at 'em," she said.

Funny how much easier we felt with each other when we stuck to our assigned roles: willful but beloved child and cranky but beloved servant. I wondered if we'd ever truly move beyond it—our past. Did anyone?

My cell phone rang just as I sank my teeth into the tart lemon curd. I wiped my hands on the heavy cloth napkin and swallowed.

"Hey, it's me." Red sounded harried. "Where are you?"

"Hey yourself. I'm at the Judge's."

"I got your message. Sorry it took so long, but I was in a meeting."

"The task force?" I asked.

"Yeah. Some things happening there. We had another holdup."

I dabbed at my lips and sat up straighter. Across from me, Lavinia tilted her head to one side and studied me.

"Where?"

"A jewelry store on Hilton Head. New Orleans Road area."

"That's new. I thought they stuck to banks and bars. Sure it's the same gang?"

I could hear a lot of commotion in the background before Red replied, "That's the assumption. Same MO, at any rate. I'll be right there," he said to someone else, confusing me for a moment. "Look, honey, I gotta run. We're headed over there to take statements. What did you want to talk to me about? The dispatcher said it was important."

I gave it to him quickly, with no embellishment. "I was following Jason Early and Serena Montalvo out 278 off the island, but I lost them in a traffic jam after an accident near Colleton River. They were driving a white Dodge Neon, a Hertz rental, with a temporary tag that expires on January twelfth."

"So they can't have had the car long. Those tags are only good for forty-five days. Where did you pick them up?"

"They were at the memorial service for Serena's sister. Holy Family on Pope Avenue. They weren't in the sanctuary, so they must have been hanging around outside. Maybe Serena felt as if she needed to be there, even if she couldn't go in. I trailed them from the church."

Even though I knew Red was in a hurry, the silence stretched out. Finally, he said, "And what were *you* doing there?"

"Can you get the information out on the wire? I'd bet they can lead you to Bobby Santiago. And probably Dolores."

Again he didn't answer right away. "I'll take care of it. Are you heading home?"

"Soon," I said. "You should probably get going."

"We'll talk later," he said and hung up.

I sat for a moment before snapping the phone shut.

"Trouble?"

I looked across at Lavinia, whose worn brown face had puckered in concern.

"Another robbery," I said, "on Hilton Head."

Her hand went automatically to the small square of gauze on her forehead. "Lord have mercy," she mumbled.

"Amen," I whispered.

The brass knocker banged against the front door at almost the exact moment my phone rang again and the Judge's wheelchair rolled into the kitchen.

We stared at each other a moment before Lavinia rose from her seat at the table.

"I'll get the door," she said, pausing to lay her hand briefly on my father's shoulder before hurrying from the room.

I flipped open my cell. "Bay Tanner."

"*Señora?*"

"Dolores! Thank God! Where are you?" I turned as the Judge maneuvered himself up to the table, his bushy white eyebrows raised in silent question.

"Hector says the *policía,* they come to my house!"

"I know, Dolores. It was Red. And one of the detectives. I was with them. You didn't have to be afraid."

"I no afraid for me, *Señora. Mi* Roberto, he is *en líos, sí?*"

"I don't understand."

"Trouble? Roberto has the trouble with the *policía?*"

"What's the matter?" My father touched me on the arm, but I shrugged him off.

"Bobby is not in trouble with the police. They just want to talk with him. About the accident that killed Theresa Montalvo."

"He no have something to do with that! I swear by Santa Maria!"

An oath taken on the name of the Virgin Mary. In Dolores's world, you didn't get any surer than that.

"I know he didn't. But he has information about who may have been involved."

"No, *Señora*—"

"Dolores, listen to me. Bobby told me he thought it wasn't an accident when he called me on Sunday morning. Right from the beginning he believed that someone might have deliberately run that poor girl down. He knows something. And it's dangerous for him to be out there with that knowledge. Do you understand me? He could get hurt. You have to convince him and Serena to go to the sheriff." I looked up as Lavinia appeared in the doorway. "Are you listening to me, Dolores?"

"*Sí, Señora,* but my Hector, he says Roberto will go to the jail. He says we must send him away."

"No! That's the worst thing you can do." Lavinia appeared about to speak, but I ignored her, all my attention focused on making Dolores understand. "Where are you? Is Bobby with you?"

Her silence made my heart turn over. After all we'd been through together, she didn't trust me. I spared a moment to register how much that hurt.

"I will think of what you have said. *Gracias, Señora.*" And she was gone.

I stared at the tiny screen and checked the call report. It wasn't Bobby Santiago's cell. I keyed in the number, but it rang busy. With trembling fingers, I speed-dialed the office supply store.

Lavinia stepped a little farther into the room. "Bay, I need—"

"Not now," I said, then, "Erik Whiteside, please, in computers," when the singsong voice of the receptionist had finished her spiel.

"There's someone here to see you," Lavinia said, glancing quickly over her shoulder toward the long hallway. "I've put—"

I waved her to silence.

"Electronics, this is Erik."

"It's me. Can you get to a computer and check a phone number for me?"

"I guess. Why?"

"Dolores just called. She's with Bobby, but I couldn't talk her into bringing him and Serena in."

"Hang on a sec." I waited, unconsciously drumming my fingers on the worn wood of the table. "Okay, shoot."

I gave him the number with the 912 area code, which put the location somewhere near Savannah. "As soon as you have something, call me. On the cell or at the Judge's."

"Will do. Should just take a few minutes."

"Hurry."

As I hung up, Lavinia spoke. "There's a man here to see you. I've put him in the main parlor."

"A man?" I asked stupidly. "Why would someone come here to find me?" My mind still raced with the possibilities of what might happen if I didn't find Dolores and Bobby. And soon.

"I don't know, Bay. He wouldn't say anything except that he needed to speak with you."

"Did he give a name?"

Lavinia reached into the pocket of her apron and handed me a gold-embossed card.

"Harry Reynolds," I read aloud, "Special Agent." I looked up to find my father's eyes locked on my face. "Federal Bureau of Investigation."

CHAPTER
EIGHTEEN

*T*HE NAME HAD CONJURED UP A CLINT EASTWOOD LOOK-alike, craggy maybe and just going through the motions until retirement—a tough guy with a wrinkled suit and zero social skills. But Harry Reynolds could have made a good living as a male fashion model, and he knew it. I put his age at early thirties, although his smooth tanned skin and thick dark hair made it hard to judge. I could have been off by a few years either way. The perfectly tailored black suit hung nicely on his slender frame, and his brown eyes were almost level with my own when he rose and extended his hand. His grip was firm but not crushing. A good beginning.

"Mrs. Tanner. Thank you for seeing me."

"Agent Reynolds. Please, sit down."

Lavinia had put him on the dark blue settee with the gold fleur-de-lis pattern. I took the wing chair to his left, and he half turned to face me.

"Detective Pedrovsky at the sheriff's office said I might find you here." He studied my face, eager, I thought, to gauge my reaction. "Is Sergeant Tanner your husband?"

"Brother-in-law," I said calmly. "He and my late husband were brothers."

"I see. I'm sorry for your loss."

We stared at each other, and if I claimed those penetrating brown eyes didn't make my breath come a little faster, I'd be a liar. The man was seriously handsome, and I could tell the revelation of my status as a widow had pleased him.

I folded my hands demurely in my lap. "How can I help you, Agent Reynolds?"

He crossed one long leg over the other and adjusted the knife-edged creases in his trousers. "I understand you have some involvement in this string of robberies."

I smiled. "Are you accusing me of being a member of the gang?"

His laugh helped relax some of the stiffness in his shoulders. "I'm sorry. Bad choice of words. My mother the English teacher would be very upset with me."

I found it strange an FBI agent would be introducing personal family information into the discussion, but I kept the smile plastered on my face and waited for him to go on.

"I'm told you may have information regarding the identity of one of the suspects." In one smooth motion he pulled a notebook from his breast pocket and flipped a couple of pages. "A Reynaldo Velez?"

"I have no direct knowledge, Agent. I simply passed along information that came to me from someone who was present at the Lady's Island bank job. An old gentleman who thought he recognized one of the robbers. I can't verify that he's correct, only that he's telling the truth as he perceives it."

"Are you implying that his identification may not be reliable?" The warmth had fled from his eyes.

"No, I'm not implying anything of the kind. I'm simply giving you the facts as I know them."

"I see." Harry Reynolds uncrossed his legs and leaned forward, elbows on knees. "The sheriff doesn't want to trouble this *gentleman* if we don't have to. I understand he's quite elderly and not in the best of health. He vouched for you, as did Detective Pedrovsky. Can you tell me exactly what—" Again he checked his notebook. "—what this Mr. Gadsden told you?"

"Would you excuse me for a moment?" I rose abruptly and hurried from the room.

In the kitchen, I found the Judge and Lavinia sitting silently across from each other at the old table.

"What's going on?" my father asked.

"He wants to know what Mr. Gadsden said to me about Reynaldo Velez. Why is the FBI in on this?"

The Judge toggled the controls on his wheelchair and moved back a little from the table. "Bank robbery often falls under their jurisdiction, especially if one of the targets is a Federal Reserve branch. Or the sheriff could have asked for their help."

"So why aren't they interviewing Mr. Rom themselves? I'm not buying all this crap about not wanting to upset an old man. Are you?"

"Doesn't sound like standard operating procedure. Hearsay isn't worth a damn thing in a court of law."

"So what do you think he's up to?"

"I'm not sure. Want me to go back in with you?" Unconsciously he used his good hand to smooth down the tufts of white hair sticking out from the back of his head.

"Any tea left?" I looked toward Lavinia, who'd been unnaturally silent.

"Yes. Will he want to talk to me, too?" She looked as fearful as Dolores had sounded at the prospect of facing a member of law enforcement.

"I'll try to hold him off, but he might. Can you bring us in a tray? I'll keep him occupied, see if I can find out what he's really up to."

"Call if you need me," my father said as I slipped past him into the hallway. "And don't volunteer anything. I'll do some checking, see if anyone in town knows this Reynolds fellow."

When I stepped back into the parlor, the agent had risen and stood gazing down at the hand-carved manger scene displayed on the center table beneath the chandelier. He looked up at my approach.

"This is incredible," he said, reaching a finger out to brush one of the Three Wise Men. "Ivory?"

"And jade," I said and joined him. "It's quite old."

"And valuable, I would guess."

"I assume so." I moved back to my chair by the fireplace, forcing him to follow. Something about the look in his eyes as he'd handled the crèche made me uncomfortable.

"May we resume now?" The notebook reappeared in Reynolds's hand.

"I've asked Lav—my father's housekeeper to bring us a tray. We were just enjoying our afternoon tea when you arrived."

"I'm sorry if I've interrupted some longstanding tradition," he said and I detected a snide tone in his voice that matched the expression on his face as he'd studied the manger scene.

"Not at all. Despite Presqu'isle's trappings, we're very informal here."

I smiled, and he seemed to relax.

"I grew up on a farm outside Baltimore. I'm afraid afternoon tea wasn't one of our usual pastimes."

Again that personal information. Was he trying to get me to reciprocate? I wondered.

"Your family's still there?" I asked. Making small talk with a stranger. My mother would have been so proud.

"Yes. Both parents and two sisters. And a gaggle of nieces and nephews." His deep eyes held mine captive. "You have children, Mrs. Tanner?"

Lavinia saved me from telling him to mind his own damn business by gliding into the parlor, a gleaming silver tray displaying her best teapot and the Sèvres china. I rose and took it from her.

"Thank you," I said and she scurried away without once looking at Agent Reynolds.

Again I called upon my late mother's dreaded training in the ways a proper lady should conduct herself as I poured tea into paper-thin cups and offered sugar, cream, and lemon. The agent's obvious discomfort in trying to balance the delicate saucer on his knee gave me more pleasure than it should have.

"Lemon curd?" I asked. Lavinia had piled the serving plate high with the pastries.

"No, thank you." Reynolds sipped politely then set his cup back on the tray. "Now about this Mr. Gadsden."

"I told everything to Sergeant Tanner. I assume he passed the information along verbatim to his superiors and so to you. What exactly are you unclear about?"

"Look, Mrs. Tanner, let's quit fencing, shall we? If this gang is made up of illegals, it's a federal matter. We're running point, but ICE will eventually be involved and maybe Homeland Security. We need to know who and what we're up against—if it's coyotes or a foreign terrorist cell or something entirely homegrown."

"I understand, Agent Reynolds. And I applaud your diligence. I just don't know what else I can tell you. And neither will Mr. Gadsden. He recognized the robber who attacked him as Reynaldo Velez, the son of a woman who sometimes takes care of the old gentleman. He believes the boy recognized him as well, so naturally we're concerned for his safety. We'd all like this resolved as much as you would. You have a name. I feel certain, with the resources at your disposal, you can find an address. If by some chance Mr. Rom is mistaken, you'll be able to clear it up quite quickly. I fail to see what more you need from either one of us."

"I believe you have a Hispanic housekeeper, but I'm sure all her paperwork is in order." Without looking at me, he flipped more pages in the notebook. "Port Royal Plantation in Hilton Head. On the beach, isn't it? And you've recently acquired sole title to this place. Not bad for such a young woman."

There was no mistaking the undercurrent in his tone or the hostility in his eyes as he raised them to look directly into my face.

I'd often told people that, after years of dealing with IRS agents in my accounting practice, I was a hard person to intimidate. But Harry Reynolds didn't know that. Or maybe he did. Now that I thought about it, he seemed to know way too much about me for comfort.

"Since you already seem to have all the facts, I don't believe there's anything more I can add." I set my saucer on the tray and stood. "I'll see you out."

I didn't wait for him to reply. I walked briskly toward the hallway, my heels tapping on the pine floor in rhythm with my pounding heart. I flung open the door before turning to see if he'd followed me.

"Thanks for your time, Mrs. Tanner." The charming smile was back on his face. "Your government appreciates your cooperation."

He moved past me and out onto the verandah. At the top of the stairs, he paused. "We'll be in touch," he said and trotted down the steps.

I watched him climb into a gleaming black SUV that spewed gravel into the dormant rose garden as he roared out of the driveway.

Lavinia sat huddled over the table, staring at the Judge when I stomped back into the kitchen.

"Arrogant son of a bitch!" Lavinia didn't bother to call me on the profanity as I flopped down in my chair, suddenly realizing that my father held the handset of the portable phone in his good hand. He glanced up and scowled.

I sat back and crossed my arms over my chest. By the time he hung up, my breathing had returned to something resembling a normal rate.

"What did he say?" the Judge asked.

While Lavinia left to retrieve the tea tray from the parlor, I gave my father the unedited version of my exchange with Harry Reynolds.

"Hardly a typical interview," he said when I finished.

"Not even close. I always thought the feds were the ultimate in professional law enforcement. This guy sounded like something out of a bad Bruce Willis movie."

His snort of laughter helped relax the tension coiled in the pit of my stomach. "I've checked with the boys, and no one seems to know this Reynolds," he said.

The "boys" were my father's cronies, many of them former and current attorneys and government officials, who kept him up to date on all the goings-on around the county. In most cases, if one of them didn't have information about something, it wasn't worth knowing.

"The local office is in Bluffton," he added. "And there's another one in Charleston. The big field office is in Columbia, of course."

So that might explain why my father's network wasn't on top of Reynolds. Gabby Henson would know. I'd bet money on it. But I hesitated to kick that sleeping dog awake. We hadn't parted on the best of terms, and she would no doubt spend the entire time trying to pump me for information about Bobby Santiago's involvement in Theresa Montalvo's death.

"You should talk to Red." Again my father's voice jerked me out of my mental wandering.

"He's on the scene of the latest robbery," I said and gave him what scant information I had about it. "I'd bet he's going to be tied up for a while."

My mind flashed to Erik, and it suddenly occurred to me that he hadn't reported in about the number from Dolores's call. As my hand reached for my cell, the house phone rang. I nearly collided with Lavinia in the doorway of the kitchen as I raced for the console table in the hall.

"Bay Tanner."

"It's me. Got it." Erik sounded pleased with himself.

"Hang on." I found a pencil and notepad in the drawer of the ornately carved little table. "Okay, go ahead."

"It's a pay phone," he said, and my heart plummeted.

"Where?"

"You're not going to like it."

I opened my mouth to tell him to get on with it, when a series of connections snapped into place in my brain: White Dodge Neon. Jason Early and Serena Montalvo. Hertz. A 912 area code.

"The Savannah airport," I said.

After a short pause, my partner said, "Bingo."

CHAPTER NINETEEN

FTER ERIK HUNG UP, I STOOD FOR A LONG TIME staring at the portrait of some long-dead Baynard ancestor hanging above the console. I'd never paid that much attention to the pantheon of my forebears scattered across the walls of Presqu'isle. This whiskered gentleman had the family's piercing green eyes—evident despite the decades of accumulated exposure to light and dust—eyes that had made my mother so striking, the same ones that peered back at me every morning from the bathroom mirror.

Emmaline used to parade me through the house, attaching names to each of the imposing figures, but I had rarely paid attention, eager as always to shed the confining house for the freedom of the marshes, for the twisted limbs of the old oaks begging to be climbed. As I stood contemplating the dark curling hair and stern face of my ancestor, I heard Lavinia's soft voice next to my shoulder.

"Bay? Is anything wrong?"

"No. Well, yes, but—I'm sorry." I drew in a long breath. "It's okay. Just something I have to work out." I pointed to the portrait. "Who's that, do you know?"

"One of the Chases," she answered promptly. "Simon maybe? I'm not certain. There's a list somewhere. Your mother cataloged all the family likenesses and where they were hung not long before she died."

So my list-making, like my green eyes, had come from my mother as well, I thought. All in all, not a bad legacy.

The grandfather clock in the hallway began its deep-throated chiming, and I stopped to count the bells. Four o'clock. It would take close to an hour to make it to the airport, probably longer at this time of day. And there was no guarantee Dolores would still be there. But it was the only lead I had.

"I have to go," I said and headed back toward the kitchen.

"Where?" Lavinia trailed behind me as I grabbed my bag from the floor near my chair. "I'm just starting supper. Can't you stay and have a bite?"

I didn't want to take the time to explain. "Sorry. It's about Dolores and her son."

"Now, hold on, daughter," my father began, but I cut him off.

"I really have to go, Daddy," I said, brushing a quick kiss on the top of his head as I passed. "I'll call you later."

"But what about—?"

I missed the rest of his question as I pulled the heavy front door closed behind me.

I had been right about the traffic. Nearly an hour and a half passed before I gratefully whipped off I-95 onto the airport exit. Minutes later I strode into the lower level of the terminal.

Across from the luggage carousels, the various rental car counters made me pause, but I decided to save that for later. I scanned the area for a bank of pay phones, now pretty much obsolete with the advent of almost universal cell ownership. Nothing. I jumped on the escalator and rode the steps to the main lobby.

The holiday travel season had already begun, and I maneuvered through buzzing crowds around the atrium lined with shops and restaurants. I remembered once using a pay phone down by the gate area when one of Rob's flights had been delayed by weather, but there was no way I could check that out. Only ticketed passengers were allowed through the elaborate security apparatus. But unless Dolores was herself flying out somewhere, she wouldn't have been able to access them, either.

I found an empty rocking chair, one of many scattered around the atrium to make travelers feel more at home. I slumped into it and began to work a mental grid. My eyes roamed over the crowd, trying in vain to pick out my housekeeper's stern bun and tiny stature. I rose and made a slow tour of each business, then loitered a while in the ladies' room, and ultimately came up empty. With a sigh, I turned for the steps, trying to formulate some plausible reason for a harried clerk to tell me if she'd rented a Neon to Jason Early or any of his fellow travelers.

Just as I was about to turn toward the car counters, I spotted the lone telephone next to a pair of water fountains near the lower-level restrooms. In a moment, I had my cell out, dialing the number that had registered when Dolores called me at Presqu'isle.

I held my breath until I heard the sharp ring just a few feet away.

So she had been here. I glanced at my watch. The trouble was that had been nearly three hours before. With that kind of lead time, she could be anywhere, especially if she'd hung up and gotten on a plane.

But why would she? I asked myself. I could see her sending Bobby away, although I had no idea where. *Guatemala, maybe?* Surely she wouldn't have gone to that extreme, not unless she knew a lot more about how much trouble he was in than I did. Besides, that would require passports and visas and all kinds of complications. Much simpler—and cheaper—to hole up in some obscure motel. But then why had she called me from the airport?

I fumbled in my bag for aspirin and tossed down two with water from the fountain next to the phone. Asking myself unanswerable questions had given me a pounding headache. I slipped into the restroom and wiped my face with a wet paper towel, ran a brush through my mop of hair, and slapped on a fresh coat of lip gloss. I tried out a pathetic smile, then an angry frown as I stared into the mirror, running through possible scripts that might get me the information I wanted. I settled on the glare and stomped out toward the Hertz counter.

I'd lucked into a lull. The pleasant young woman in the crisp uniform beamed at me. "How may I help you?"

"I need to speak to your supervisor," I said.

The smile wavered. "Is there a problem, ma'am?"

I felt a momentary twinge of guilt, but my cause was just. "Of course there's a problem! I have a dent the size of a watermelon in the side of my Jaguar, and someone's going to pay for it. And I don't just mean monetarily."

"Were you involved in an accident with one of our vehicles?"

"Oh, no, it was no accident. The little punk deliberately rammed the door of that tin box into my beautiful new car out of spite! Just because I pulled in a little too close. He and his girlfriend could have gotten in on the other side, but no! He did it deliberately. I wasn't three feet away. And then he just drove off as if nothing had happened."

I clamped my mouth shut, afraid I'd already overplayed my hand. Sometimes I get so into my role I forget when to back off.

"And it was one of our vehicles? You're sure?"

"A white Dodge Neon with a temporary plate and your stickers plastered all over it. I didn't get the numbers, but the tag expires on January twelfth."

"All our vehicles are fully insured, ma'am." She reached under the counter and laid a form in front of me. "If you'd like to fill out—"

"I don't want to file a claim. I want that little hoodlum's name and address. I intend to prosecute him for malicious mischief and deliberate property damage."

I held my breath, but I could see the denial forming on her full lips even before she spoke. "I'm afraid I can't give you that information, ma'am. If you'll just complete this claim form, I'm sure we can come to a satisfactory resolution."

I gave it one more try. I whipped my cell phone from my bag and flipped it open. "I have my attorney on speed dial. Trust me, you do not want to tangle with him. All I want is a name and address."

The young woman had been well-trained. "I'm sorry. Mr. Hopkins, the manager, will be back in just a few moments. Perhaps you'd better speak with him."

I admitted defeat, whirled, and stalked back out into the cool winter night, leaving the poor clerk staring after me. As I slid behind the wheel of the Jag, I shook my head. I wasn't sure what I'd hoped to accomplish. I already knew that Jason Early—or Bobby or Serena—had rented a car. An alternate address would have been helpful. But even that might not get me any closer to finding Dolores and her son. Still, it had been worth a try.

On impulse I called the Santiago house on Jonesville Road. I was startled to hear Angelina's voice on the other end. If she'd been called home from college, it could only be bad news.

"Angie? It's Bay Tanner. What are you doing there? Is something wrong?"

"Oh, hi, Mrs. Tanner. No, Christmas break starts today. I just got in a couple of hours ago."

I let out the breath I'd been holding. "Of course." I stumbled around for a plausible excuse and decided just to go with the truth. "Is your mother there? I really need to speak to her."

Her pause lasted less than a beat. "No, she's not. Sorry."

No explanations, no chitchat. Very unlike the usual Angie.

"How about Bobby? Have you seen or talked to him lately?"

"Angelina!"

I heard Hector's voice in the background as clearly as if he were on the phone himself.

"I have to go," the girl whispered.

"Listen to me, Angie. I'm worried about your mother and Bobby. Get away from your father and call me." I rattled off my cell number. "Got it?"

"Yes."

"Good. Get back to me as soon as you can." I toyed with how much to tell her, but she was nearly a grown woman. And a smart one. "I think they're in real trouble. I want to help."

"Angelina!" Hector sounded as if he were right on top of her.

"I'm sorry," Angie said and hung up.

I had nearly reached the bridges onto Hilton Head when my cell phone rang. As my hand hovered over my bag, I ran down a mental list of possible callers and realized none of them was likely to be bearing good news. I slowed as I rolled down onto the island and pulled off onto the shoulder.

"Bay Tanner."

"Hey, honey. Where are you?" Red sounded nearly as exhausted as I felt.

"I'm almost home. How about you?"

"I'm still at the station. We're wrapping up on the robbery this afternoon. I should be able to bust out of here in another hour or so."

"Get anything new?"

"I can't talk right now. I'll fill you in when I see you. Have you eaten?"

I had to think about it for a moment. "No."

"I'll pick up something. Chinese okay?"

"Sure."

"See you soon."

I flipped the phone closed and tossed it onto the seat beside me. Almost immediately it rang again. I thought about all the years I'd resisted carrying one of the damned things, and here was exactly the reason. I'd always believed there had to be a few places where a person could be inaccessible to the rest of the world, islands of solitude amid the cacophony of everyday life: The bathroom. The car. I should have stuck to my guns, I thought.

"Mrs. Tanner? It's Angie." Her breathless voice sounded as if she'd been running.

I rubbed a hand across my temple. "Where are you?"

"I told Papa I needed some things at the store. He wanted to drive me, but I said it was 'woman' stuff, and he let me have the car."

I had to smile, and the very act eased some of the pain in my head. "Clever girl. Can you meet me? I'm just coming onto the island."

"I'm in your driveway. I'll just wait for you to get here."

"How did you get past the gate?"

"I've got Mom's car with the sticker on the windshield."

"But what's your mother driving?" I'd assumed Dolores had taken her Hyundai with her. It hadn't been in her driveway the night before when Red, Lisa Pedrovsky, and I had paced the front yard waiting for her to come home.

"I don't know. That's one of the things I need to ask you about."

"Give me ten minutes," I said and hung up.

I had hoped Angelina Santiago would have more answers than questions. It appeared I was destined for disappointment. Again.

I got caught by a red light at Spanish Wells Road and found myself glancing around. Strange how often during the past few days fate had brought me to the exact spot where Theresa Montalvo had died.

The light changed, and I gunned the Jaguar toward home.

CHAPTER TWENTY

HE SIGHT OF THE OLD BLUE CAR PULLED UP IN THE pine straw beneath the live oak gave my heart a little punch. What would I do if Dolores never came back? I swallowed hard and slid the Jag into the garage. By the time I had the door open, Angelina stood waiting for me in the harsh glare of the overhead light.

She'd always been a pretty girl, but college had changed her, matured her in some indefinable way. Maybe it was the jet-black hair, no longer hanging in a long fall down her back, but curved around her narrow chin in a style that accentuated her dark eyes and molded cheekbones. The simple turtleneck sweater and low-rise jeans clung to her slender frame.

Angelina Santiago had become a stunningly beautiful young woman.

Impulsively, I opened my arms to her, and she stepped in for a brief hug.

"You let your hair grow out," she said. "I like it."

"And you cut yours off. Very striking. I bet your father had a fit."

Her laugh hadn't changed. "He actually turned blue the first time he saw me. I was afraid he was having a stroke or something."

"But he got over it," I said, leading the way up the steps into the house. I dropped my bag on the floor. "Want a Coke?"

"Sure, that'd be great."

In the kitchen, Angie settled at the round table in the alcove of the bay window. I carried over glasses of ice and two cans. For a long moment we stared at each other.

"Where's your mother and—," I began, but Angie spoke at the same time.

"Do you know—?"

We smiled. "You first," I said.

"I'm sorry. I just don't have any idea what's going on."

"So you don't know where your mother and brother are."

She shook her head, and the light flashed across the sheen of her hair. "Papa said Roberto was having trouble at school, that he'd run away, and Mom went to see if she could find him."

"But you don't believe that."

"Why would she leave her car? I mean, how did she get to Charleston? And there's no way Papa would let her go off on her own like that."

I registered the undertone of disapproval in her voice. The next generation of Hispanic-American women would be less willing to buckle under to the rigid cultural paternalism her mother endured.

"You deserve to know what's happening," I said and spent the next few minutes giving Angelina all the information I had concerning her brother's involvement in the death of Theresa Montalvo, my sighting of him at the mall with the dead girl's sister, and ending with her mother's phone call from the Savannah airport. I watched the range of emotions that swept across her face and felt a twinge of guilt for dumping all this on the thin shoulders of a young woman not long out of childhood. Still, it couldn't be helped. Someone in her family needed to join forces with me, and it was a sure bet it wouldn't be her father.

"So where would she be going if she flew away with Bobby? Do you have relatives she might have sought help from?" I asked at the end of my story.

She shook her head. "No, there isn't anybody I can think of. Papa has a brother, but I've only seen *Tío* Jesús a couple of times in my life. I think I have cousins, too, but I've never met them."

The phone rang, a brash interruption, and we both jumped. "Let the machine get it," I said, turning back to Angie. "No one on your mother's side? Not even in Guatemala?"

I half listened for a message, but the caller hung up without speaking. I glanced toward the window, wondering if the watcher lurked somewhere beyond the thin light filtering from the kitchen out into the darkness. Red and I would do a sweep as soon as he arrived.

"She was an orphan when she came to the States."

I whipped my head back around. "I never knew that. How did she get here then?"

Angie shrugged. "I don't know all the details, but it was something to do with the church. They sponsored her as part of some program to get Guatemalan children out of the country."

I couldn't believe I had spent years in intimate contact with Dolores and never heard this story. She had witnessed me at the lowest point in my life: emotionally devastated over Rob's murder and physically tortured by the burns and scars that crisscrossed my back. She had bathed me, tended my ugly wounds, urged me back to a life I thought not worth saving. I'd wept in her arms, from grief and pain, and she'd cradled and soothed me as if I had been her own child. How could I not know something so important about her? How could she not have trusted me enough to tell me?

I swallowed back the tears threatening to spill over onto the glass-topped table. "How old was she?"

"I'm not sure. Maybe fourteen? She lived in a convent for a while, but I don't know exactly where."

"And she met and married your father here."

"Yes. He's from Mexico, I think, but he doesn't like to talk about the past."

Headlights flashed across the ceiling, and I recognized the low rumble of Red's cruiser. A moment later, a car door slammed, and I heard the tread of his heavy shoes on the garage steps.

"Who's that?" Angie half rose from her chair.

Before I could reply, Red stepped into the great room, his khaki uniform looking as if he'd slept in it. A couple of plastic bags swung from his hand.

Angie gasped.

"It's Red. My—" I couldn't force the word *boyfriend* past my lips. "Sergeant Tanner. My brother-in-law. I think you two might have met."

Red's engaging smile did nothing to cut the tension.

"No, I don't think I've had the pleasure." His eyes said he would have remembered a woman as striking as Angelina Santiago.

"This is Dolores's daughter," I said, and his grin faded. "Angelina. She's home from college for the Christmas break."

"Pleased to meet you," he said, setting the carryout boxes on the counter.

"You, too, sir." Angie's voice sounded small and frightened in the expansive kitchen.

"I've brought enough food for ten people," he said over his shoulder. "Do you like Chinese?"

"Yes. But— I mean, thanks, but I have to go." Angie jumped from her chair.

"Red's harmless," I said with one hand on her arm. "Sit down and have a bite with us. We're both concerned about your mother and Bobby. Red's been trying to find them, too." I could tell that didn't reassure her. "It's nothing to be afraid about. Really. The more people we have searching for them, the sooner we'll be able to find them."

"I know, it's just I told Papa I'd be back in a few minutes. He's going to be very angry."

I couldn't argue with that. "Will you call me if you hear from them?"

I followed her down the three steps into the great room.

"Nice to meet you, sir," she tossed in Red's direction and headed for the door.

"You, too, Angelina," he called, but she was already halfway through the garage.

"Call me!" I yelled after her a moment before she slipped into her mother's car.

I watched her wheel out onto the road without a backward glance. I turned and trudged back into the kitchen.

"That's pretty much spooked her," I said, crossing to the table where Red had laid out plates and silverware.

"Sorry. You should have called if you wanted me to stay away."

"I didn't have any idea she'd react like that. I thought her mother's thing about uniforms came from her childhood. About which I apparently knew nothing." I pulled up my chair while Red set the steaming containers on the table.

"I can't say I'm surprised about Angie. It's almost an epidemic. We're sure now this robbery gang is mostly Hispanic, but we're pretty much getting stonewalled in their community." He sighed and began ladling out food. "So how was your day?"

I let him spoon rice and shrimp onto my plate. The smell made me nauseous.

"Dolores called me from the airport in Savannah. I went there, but she was gone. And some creepy FBI guy named Reynolds grilled me at Presqu'isle about Mr. Gadsden and the robbery." I could hear my voice rising, but I felt powerless to control it. "And Angie said Dolores was an orphan, and nuns brought her here, and I never knew a damn thing about it and—"

"Honey, slow down. Eat something. You'll feel better after—"

"Stop it!" I pushed the chair back from the table and jumped to my feet. "Quit treating me like one of your kids." I registered the hurt on his face, but at that point I didn't care.

"I'm trying to help," he said, his eyes grave. "You sound ready to lose it."

"I'm fine." I drew in a long shaky breath, but it didn't help. "I'm fine," I mumbled again and burst into tears.

* * *

There's almost nothing I hate worse than crying. I avoid it at all costs.

I stared at my reflection in the bathroom mirror. Red-rimmed, puffy eyes squinted back. I wet a cloth in cold water and wiped my face, then wadded up some tissues and blew my nose. Despite the disastrous effect, I felt better. I squared my shoulders and marched back into the kitchen.

"I'm sorry," I said.

"I know." Red studied me, a forkful of fried rice poised halfway to his mouth. "Do you want me to heat this up for you?"

"I'll do it." I carried my plate to the microwave and stood for a moment watching the carousel spin. "It's like finding out that everything you thought you knew about your best friend was a lie."

"You mean Dolores?"

"Yes." I turned to find his eyes on me. "Erik suggested that maybe I should back off this whole thing, that digging around in a case that might involve illegal immigration could come back to bite me."

"You think Dolores is an illegal?"

I shook my head. "Angie's story rings true. The nuns would have done things by the book. The paperwork—naturalization papers and all that. Besides, I report her earnings to the IRS and Social Security. No, I'm thinking more about Hector. If he does come from Mexico, there's a chance he could be a border-jumper. And he has this mysterious brother that Angie's only seen a couple of times."

Red set his silverware on his plate and crossed the room. I could tell he wanted to comfort me, but my previous outburst made him wary. I solved his problem by taking one tentative step forward. In an instant his arms enfolded me.

"Do you have any legitimate reason to suspect either one of them?" His breath, soft against my hair, made me smile.

The bell on the microwave *ding*ed, and I leaned away. I carried my dinner back to the table, and Red followed.

"Nothing concrete. I'm just wondering why else Bobby would have gotten himself involved in Serena Montalvo's causes if there weren't some compelling personal reason."

Suddenly, I was ravenous. Red watched me shovel food into my mouth a moment before he answered. His smile looked so much like Rob's I had to turn away.

"You said the girl was attractive."

"I got a pretty good look at her at the church. She's quite beautiful. Reminded me a lot of Angie before she cut off her hair."

"And Bobby is what—eighteen? Trust me, a teenaged boy doesn't need anything more than a fine-looking woman to get him involved in any number of things he wouldn't even consider on his own."

"So you think Dolores's son is just tagging along because he's hot for the girl?"

Red shrugged. "Wouldn't be the first time."

I pushed the empty plate away. "You sound as if you're speaking from experience."

"No comment."

I returned his grin, my composure restored by his patience and a decent meal. "I have a lot of things to think about. I need to make a list."

I half rose, but the look on Red's face stilled me. "It'll keep until tomorrow," he said.

He was right. My emotions had had about all the hammering they could take for one day.

"I'll just clean up and—"

"It'll keep until tomorrow."

I let him take my hand and lead me down into the great room. I stepped away only long enough to turn out the lights and set the alarm. At the end of the hallway, we paused, and Red cupped my face. His eyes, shining with love, locked on to mine.

"I'll never let anyone hurt you again," he said and kissed me gently.

I sighed as we moved side by side into the bedroom.

I desperately wanted to believe him.

CHAPTER
TWENTY-ONE

I WOKE UP ALONE. RED WAS NOT JUST GONE FROM my bed, but from the house as well. I could sense the old familiar emptiness. I rolled over and pulled the duvet up around my shoulders. On chilly winter mornings I missed his warmth as much as his physical presence.

After our lovemaking, I'd set the alarm for seven, but I hadn't heard it go off. I cracked open one eye. A little past six thirty. I wondered what had called Red away so early. I hadn't heard the phone, but then I'd slept like the dead. Reluctantly I rolled out and crossed to the bathroom.

Half an hour later I carried my black wool blazer into the kitchen and draped it over the back of a chair. A quick glance out the French doors leading from the bedroom confirmed that the day had dawned dark and rainy. If the bad weather had blown in from the east, off the ocean, we could be in for another long siege.

I dumped the contents of the white cardboard cartons we'd left out the night before and ran the garbage disposal. I had to scrape the crust off the plates. I made oatmeal, something I'd loathed as a child, but which I'd come to appreciate in middle age, especially on cold, rainy mornings. By seven forty-five, I was at my desk in the converted guest room, a yellow legal pad in front of me.

What do we think, what do we know, what can we prove. Three columns. Rob's tried and true method for attacking a problem. I'd lost count of the number of times I'd sat like this trying to organize my jumbled thoughts into some semblance of order. Back when he'd been a special investigator for the state attorney general's office, we'd spent hours over charts like this one, tracking the illegal money generated by drug traffickers and other assorted felons.

I, however, was tracking people.

I started with Serena Montalvo, activist and advocate for immigrant rights. Possible target, adversary unknown. Girlfriend of Bobby Santiago? I added Theresa, Serena's sister, dead from a hit-and-run in what even Red's colleagues now believed might not have been an accident. Mistaken for her sister? That seemed likely. I made a note to check the *Island Packet* archives for the photo of Theresa that Gabby Henson told me they'd be running.

Jason Early. I had no idea where he fit into the picture, except he seemed to be attached to both Serena and Bobby like a barnacle on a ship's hull. Chances were he hadn't gone to school with them. So how did he know all the players? And why did they trust him? My mind flashed to the slick exchange of something between Jason and the mysterious boy in the red-and-white athletic jacket at the mall. What had that been all about? Drugs? It seemed an incredibly stupid place to carry out an illegal transaction, although most people probably wouldn't have caught on to it. If I hadn't already been zeroed in on Early, I might well have missed it myself.

And then there was Dolores. *Mother protecting child,* I wrote. That would stay firmly in the what-do-we-know column. No doubt at all. My friend would abhor being involved in anything remotely illegal or immoral, but she'd do whatever it took to keep her children safe. Period.

I stared at my scribbled notes for a long time. Around the edges I wrote the names Enrique Salazar, the student denied his scholarship, and M. Early, Jason's freaky mother. Bit players in this drama, I was convinced, but onstage nonetheless.

No pattern, or at least none I could detect. No motive leaped right out at me. I doodled some more, my mind swirling with the puzzle, until I jerked myself back and checked my watch. I tossed my pen on the desk. I'd promised to meet Erik at the office at nine to go over our presentation for Jack Ogilvy of the recreation board before our meeting. I slid my feet back into my black pumps and stood. I cast one more glance at the jumble of names and suddenly realized that unconsciously I'd added two more.

Along the left margin, I'd written *Hector* and *Jesús*. And a single word: *coyote*.

"I think that went really well."

I hung my raincoat on the rack in the corner and shook the dampness from my hair. The cold drizzle had continued to fall, not hard enough to warrant an umbrella, but just enough to turn my once wavy hair into a mass of fuzzy curls.

"Me, too," Erik said, punching in the number of the answering service. "With Jack signing off, it's just a formality now. We could be getting our first assignment by next week."

"Good work," I said, and he grinned.

I crossed into my office and pulled a Diet Coke from the small fridge. What I really wanted was tea, hot and soothing. *We need a hot plate,* I thought. *Or a microwave.* I glanced around, trying to figure out where we'd find room for one, when Erik spoke behind me.

"There's a message from Red. He says to call him as soon as you get in."

"I wonder why he didn't try me on the cell."

Erik shrugged.

I lifted the receiver and paused when I saw the look on his face. "What? Something else?"

"I think you better hear this one yourself," he said and turned back to his desk.

I followed, and he handed me the phone before pushing buttons.

The same gravelly smoker's voice: "You just don't listen, do you, lady? Last warning. Back off now, or someone's gonna get hurt."

The pause lasted so long I'd thought he'd finished. I'd just moved the receiver an inch away from my head, when the watcher added, "And you're really gonna hate who it turns out to be."

I didn't realize I'd been standing there, staring off into space, until Erik took the phone from my hand and set it back on its cradle.

"Bay?"

His voice seemed to come from far away. My brain had kicked into overdrive, scanning the list of names of everyone I held dear. I could feel my lips trembling, but I'd had my allotted bout of tears the night before.

"Can you save that?" I asked, clearing my throat.

"Already done."

"Can we get a copy?"

"Why?"

"I want to be able to study it. I took the other two calls directly." A thought struck me. "You know, as far as anyone else is concerned, I could have been making the whole thing up."

"That's ridiculous. Why would you do that? Anyone who knows you at all wouldn't even consider the possibility."

Unconsciously, I gripped my forehead with one hand. I hoped he was right.

I turned toward my office, the nasty voice replaying itself in my head. "How about tracing the call? Can they do that with the answering service?" I slumped down in my chair and kicked off my shoes.

"Maybe," he said, taking the client's seat across from me. "I'm not sure what their policy would be. It might take a subpoena or a visit from the cops. I just don't know."

"But can it be done? Technically, I mean?"

"I guess so. But don't you think this guy is probably using a disposable cell or something untraceable? That's what I'd do if I were making anonymous phone calls."

I slammed my fist onto the desk, and he jumped. "What the hell is this all about? It doesn't make any sense! I don't know a damn thing about *anything* that would make me worth all these threats."

"It has to be the hit-and-run and those kids."

I drew a deep shuddering breath. It felt as if there wasn't enough air in the room. "No. That's what I thought at first, but it's totally illogical."

"Aren't you the one who told me criminals are generally pretty stupid? That's why the jails are overflowing."

For no reason I could determine, the handsome face of Special Agent Harry Reynolds popped into my head. "The FBI came to see me yesterday."

Erik's face perfectly registered his confusion. "About the dead girl?"

"No. They wanted information about the robbery, what exactly Mr. Gadsden told me about recognizing one of the holdup men."

"And you think that's what the phone calls are about?"

"Hold on. Let me think."

I tried to do a mental time line, but my thoughts were too chaotic. I pulled a notepad toward me and rummaged in the center desk drawer for a pen.

"Okay. The robbery happened on Monday." I scribbled some more. "Lavinia told me that evening about what Mr. Gadsden said. About Reynaldo and Maria. I got the first call about four A.M. Tuesday morning."

"So, unless someone had Presqu'isle bugged, how could he know?"

I sighed and tossed the pen away. "You're right. It can't be that. Nobody who knew about it would be involved with the guy making the threats. It has to have something to do with Theresa Montalvo's death. But think about it! You know as well as I do I don't have a damn thing that could be a threat to anyone involved in it. Nothing!"

Erik folded his hands in his lap. "Maybe the bad guys are assuming you know more than you do. You're a PI. You're sleep—" He cut himself off.

"Sleeping with a cop?" I ignored the tinge of red creeping up his neck. "So you're saying this piece of garbage is hassling me and threatening to hurt my family on an assumption?"

"Maybe I'm wrong," he said. "It was just a thought."

I ordered myself to back off a few notches. "No, it's entirely possible. So how do I convince this idiot that I'm completely in the dark?"

We sat in silence for a long time, neither of us able to come up with a reasonable answer. Outside, rain splattered against the windows of the reception area. Over Erik's shoulder, I watched the rivulets running down the glass like tiny streams converging into larger rivers before emptying into the sea.

"What happened yesterday?"

His voice startled me. "What do you mean?"

"You haven't heard from this guy for a couple of days. What spooked him into calling again?"

It was a damn good question. I ran through it all, from my visit to Theresa's memorial service, tailing and then losing Jason and Serena, the arrogant FBI agent's appearance at Presqu'isle, and my fruitless trip to the Savannah airport. Any one of those actions could have precipitated the call. All of it, except for Harry Reynolds's inquisition, had been related to finding Bobby and Dolores. So why had the watcher waited until this morning to leave his message? Why not last night?

Angelina Santiago. The name popped suddenly into my head. Could Angie's visit have set him off? Or was it that he had no idea what I'd been up to the rest of the day? Was it only my beach house they had under surveillance? I tried out the idea. True, the first call had come at Presqu'isle, but it had been on my cell. Still, if they were watching the Hilton Head place, they'd know I wasn't home. So maybe not.

But they called after Red spent the night and again after Angie had been there. And there were the cigarette butts I'd found at the end of the walkway over the dunes. Maybe it wasn't some widespread criminal conspiracy that seemed to know my every move. If they had only one guy keeping tabs on me, that would explain why no one was upset about my visit to the church or my foray into Jason Early's driveway. Or the airport. Still . . .

I looked up to find Erik studying my face intently.

"You figured it out?" he asked.

"No, not really. But I think I'm beginning to get a glimmer."

"What can I do?" Erik asked, his eyes dark with concern.

I squared my shoulders. "Find out about tracing that last call. And get Red on the phone."

CHAPTER
TWENTY-TWO

*D*URING THE FORTY-FIVE MINUTES IT TOOK FOR RED TO return my call, I sat tilted back in my chair, eyes closed, my mind conjuring up and discarding scenarios in which all the scattered players might fit. Nothing worked.

Twice I'd straightened, my hand reaching for the phone, before I'd let it drop back into my lap. I felt as if I should warn Lavinia and the Judge. Maybe Angelina. Who else might this nutcase decide to go after? I glanced at my bag resting on the floor beside the desk and reached down to slide the Seecamp out of its compartment and into my pocket. Red could take care of himself. And so could I.

The jangling of the phone brought me up straight.

"It's Red," Erik called from the reception area, and I snatched up the receiver.

"Hey, sweetheart. Sorry it took me so long to get back to you. How did the meeting go?"

I didn't understand why he was wasting time with small talk. "Fine. Why did you call earlier?"

"Am I interrupting something?" His tone had dropped a couple of degrees.

"No. Sorry. It's just— I need to see you. Officially."

"What happened?"

"I had another one of those phone calls. At the office. I want to see if we can trace it somehow."

"Are you okay? Is Erik there?"

"Yes and yes. Do you have the capability to track down the caller from a voice mail left on my answering service?"

"I don't know, but I'll find out. Stay put. I'm on my way."

I hung up to find my partner hovering in the doorway.

"He's coming," I said. "He'll find out about tracking the voice mail."

"I already did," Erik said.

"What? How?"

"I have friends who have connections in interesting places. It's one of those things I think you'll feel better not knowing too much about."

I nodded. It wasn't the first time Erik had skirted the legal and professional constraints of our PI license, but I had to admit it had always been in a good cause.

"Friends with connections are good. So what did you find out?"

"A prepaid cell, just like I figured. No way to trace who it was sold to or who used it. Sorry."

"No, that's fine. At least we know that avenue's closed. I'll still have to let Red have a run at it, though. No point in compromising your sources."

"Understood."

I propped my elbows on the desk and let my chin rest on my hands. "So now what?"

"It seems something—or someone—at your house triggers the calls, right?"

"Yes."

"So let's set up our own surveillance. Maybe the sheriff will play, maybe not, but Red and I can do shifts when he's off duty. He might even have a couple of buddies who wouldn't mind picking up some extra Christmas money to join us. If you're willing to do that, I mean."

"I don't know." It wasn't a bad idea, but somehow the notion of surrounding myself with armed guards didn't sit well. It smacked too much of damsel-in-distress. "Let me give it some thought."

Erik turned at the sound of the door opening, and a damp gust of wind blew my brother-in-law into the office.

"Hey, Erik," he said, shaking the water from his clear plastic raincoat before hanging it on the rack.

"Red." My partner moved back to his desk and flipped up the cover of his laptop.

"Come on in," I said.

With a quick glance at Erik, Red planted a brief kiss on the side of my forehead as he stepped around me. "I'll need a copy of the call you had this morning. I'll get it to the tech people, and they'll see what they can do. I'll also need an authorization from you for the answering service."

"I'll get on that," Erik said. "You want to hear it now?"

"Damn right."

Erik punched some buttons on the phone, and the smoky voice filled the small office.

"Bastard." Red took the vacant chair across from me and reached for my hand.

"I'm fine, Red. Mad as hell, but fine. I'm getting used to people messing with me, but my family's off-limits. I want this guy's head on a plate."

"We'll do what we can." He stared straight into my eyes. "Are you carrying?"

"Absolutely."

"Good." He paused, and I could tell he'd thought long and hard about his next words. "Any chance you could back off this thing with the Santiago family?"

I stared back. "What do you think?"

"Okay. It was worth a try. How about taking a little vacation?"

"Is that an invitation?"

He smiled briefly, but it didn't quite reach his eyes. "Not that the idea doesn't appeal, but no. Too much going on right now. I was thinking more of you getting out of the way for a while. Out of the line of fire, so to speak."

"I know. And you can forget it. Or are you suggesting that I take Lavinia and the Judge with me? And Angie Santiago. And what about Erik? This jerk threatened my family and friends, remember? I'm not going anywhere."

"That's what I figured."

"Here's what you asked for," Erik said from the doorway. He handed a CD to Red and a sheet of our stationery to me. "You just need to sign."

I scanned the authorization to the answering service and scratched my name at the bottom before sliding it across the desk. Red took both and tucked them into the pocket of his jacket.

"How about lunch?" he asked.

"Aren't you on duty?"

"Sure, but they give us a few minutes to eat every day. I think it's in my contract."

I welcomed his attempt to lighten the mood. "Sure, why not? Erik, you want to join us?"

"No thanks. I think I'll get busy setting up our accounts with the agencies we'll need to run the background checks for the rec board." He spoke without looking up from his computer.

"Can I bring you something?"

"Thanks, that'd be great."

We settled on Applebee's, primarily because it was close. I slid into the booth, and Red took the other side. I ordered hot tea and French onion soup, hoping that one or the other of them would warm the cold, hollow place inside me. I'd been scared before, too many times in the past few years, but that had been mostly about myself. Only the Judge's kidnapping had opened up this yawning hole of fear in my gut. I didn't want to go there ever again. Ever.

"Your hands are shaking." Red reached across the wide expanse of table and wrapped his own around the warmth of the china mug of tea I clung to.

"It's the weather," I said, easing my fingers out from under his grip.

Red leaned in closer. "Bullshit," he said. "This guy has you spooked, and rightly so. You ought to consider going away. Just for a few days. If you're out of the picture, there's no reason for him to go after your family."

"Do you really believe that?"

The waitress forestalled his answer by sliding my soup onto the table.

"And what about Dolores and Bobby?"

He cut his cheeseburger in half and drowned his fries in ketchup. "We're on that, Bay. We're working on material witness warrants for both the boy and the Montalvo girl. If the county solicitor comes through, we can crank up the search for them. It's only a matter of time."

"Did you check out the airport?"

"Absolutely. I alerted Lisa Pedrovsky first thing this morning to the call you got from Dolores yesterday." His eyes dropped to his plate. "There's no record of any of them getting on a plane. Or even buying a ticket."

"Rental car," I said, slapping my hand on the table. Across the aisle, an elderly couple glanced nervously in my direction. "I should have thought of that! That's why she doesn't need the Hyundai. She and the Montalvo girl both dumped their cars. Makes it harder for someone to track them." I almost smiled. "For amateurs, they're not doing too badly."

"That's what I called you about this morning. We aren't as dumb as we look. Lisa got the info. Dolores is in a Ford Focus, gray. The Early kid paid for both that and the Neon he's driving. A week in advance. Cash."

I sipped the hot soup. "We know Dolores left her car at home. Where's Serena's Taurus?"

Red grinned. "The paperwork to have it towed back to Beaufort is in the works as we speak. We found it in the long-term lot at the airport."

I smiled back. "Right. Not as dumb as you look."

We ate in silence for a few minutes. When I'd finished, I waved the waitress over and ordered a steak sandwich and fries to go.

"Listen, there was another reason I called you this morning."

I looked up to find Red fidgeting with his paper napkin, ripping off tiny pieces and lining them up in front of his plate. I waited a moment, but he didn't continue.

"And?"

"It's about Christmas," he said, his voice low and uncertain. "It's a week from today."

"Yes, I know. What about it?"

"I, uh . . . I have a little problem."

"You're going to be with the kids. That goes without saying, Red. I know it's your turn to have them for Christmas. I never expected you to give that up."

Red's and Sarah's custody agreement called for Scotty and Elinor to spend alternating holidays with each parent. I smiled, remembering how a couple of years before Sarah had dumped them unexpectedly on Red over Thanksgiving. He'd brought them along to Presqu'isle, at Lavinia's insistence, and their presence had added a brightness to the staid old mansion that had been missing for decades.

"You're all welcome to join the Judge and me. It'll be just us, unless Aunt Eliza relents and agrees to come. We've invited her every year, but she doesn't like to travel. Lavinia's put up the tree in the front parlor." I was warming to the idea the more I talked about it. "You could all stay over on Christmas Eve, if you like. Then they could have their morning of tearing into packages just as if they were at home."

A fleeting picture of Red's dreary apartment flitted across my mind as the waitress set the Styrofoam box with Erik's lunch in front of me. I snatched the check from her before Red could make a move and handed her my American Express card. Much better for the kids to awaken to the magic of Presqu'isle in all its holiday splendor than the bleak, barren place their father called home. I'd have to do some more shopping, make certain they had a lot of packages to open—

"I had another idea."

I scribbled my name on the credit card receipt and looked up. "What?"

"Well, I was thinking maybe, I mean, if it wouldn't be too much trouble, that . . . Not that it would be, because I'd take care of everything. I mean, I know you don't go in for all that holiday stuff usually, but . . ."

"Red, for God's sake, spit it out."

He reached for my hand. "I want the kids to spend Christmas at your house. With us. Just us." He lifted his chin and held my gaze. "Like a family."

CHAPTER
TWENTY-THREE

J'LL THINK ABOUT IT."

That's what I'd told Red a moment before I dropped a brief kiss on his cheek and fled the restaurant ahead of him.

Like a family. His words stayed with me the rest of the afternoon as Erik and I set up our protocols and procedures for running background checks on the potential employees and volunteers at the recreation center. It was grunt work, and I was thrilled to have it to occupy my mind. Or at least part of it.

Like a family. What exactly did that mean? Was it an oblique proposal? After nearly five months of practically living together, we'd skirted around the subject a couple of times, but neither of us had ever used the *M* word out loud. We'd known each other for close to twenty years. As couples, Red and Sarah and Rob and I had led vastly different lives, but our paths had crossed often enough at dinners and holidays that I felt as if I knew almost as much about him as I had about my late husband. Still, I'd fought a long time against his hints and longing glances after Rob died. Only in the heat of the fire at the strange compound near Yemassee had I come to realize my feelings for him had changed, deepened into what I could only label *love.*

But was it enough? I was forty-one years old. Despite an occasional twinge, I thought I'd successfully repressed any maternal longings, telling myself I could be happy without children. Red seemed to be offering me a ready-made family. I'd never stopped to consider how I felt about that, taking Sarah's children in and treating them as if they were my own. I had absolutely no experience—zero, zip, zilch. Would I be packing school lunches and showing up at PTA meetings? Helping with homework? Wiping runny noses and patching up scrapes and bruises?

Don't be an idiot, I told myself. Red was a weekend dad. They'd spend the bulk of their time with their mother, just as they'd always done. We'd do the fun things, like trips to the zoo, baseball games, Disney World . . .

Out in the reception area, I could hear Erik humming to himself as he keyed in data. I wondered if he had longings for a family— wife, kids, picket fence. We'd never discussed it, although I knew his social life was anything but dull. Maybe it was different for his generation.

Or maybe this was a trial run. I sat up straighter as the thought settled and took root. I'd always been Aunt Bay to Scotty and Elinor, the one who gave extravagant presents, the kind their parents rolled their eyes at, someone who flitted in and out of their lives at birthdays and holidays. How would they accept me as a permanent fixture in their father's life? Or would they? The last thing I wanted was to cause any kind of breach between Red and—

"Earth to Bay, come in, please."

I jumped and looked up to find Erik standing in the doorway. "I'm sorry?"

"I was just asking if you have those information forms ready yet." He smiled. "I think you were out there in the universe somewhere."

"Right." I cleared my throat and dropped my fingers onto the keyboard. "I'll have them for you in a couple of minutes."

"Did you think any more about setting up some kind of surveillance at your house?"

It had completely fled my mind. "No, sorry."

"I think it's worth a shot." He paused, and I glanced up. "You sure you're okay?"

"Fine," I said and resumed typing.

Out of the corner of my eye, I saw him shrug and turn back to his desk.

I mentally shook myself and bent to my work. As Scarlett was fond of observing, I'd just worry about that tomorrow.

I had three messages on my answering machine when I walked in the house a little after five o'clock. I'd promised to meet Red at Jump & Phil's, our favorite local hangout, at six, but Lavinia's voice on the tape sounded strained. I shrugged out of my raincoat and dialed Presqu'isle.

"What's the matter?" I asked when she picked up the phone. "Is Daddy okay?"

"We're fine," Lavinia said, but the quaver in her words said otherwise.

"Tell me."

She sighed, a long exhalation that could have meant a lot of things, not many of them good. I felt the muscles in my chest constrict.

"That FBI man came back."

"Harry Reynolds? What the hell for?"

"Language, Bay," she said automatically.

"Come on, Lavinia. What did he want?"

"He asked me about the robbery. And about Romey Gadsden."

I wondered if he hadn't believed me. Or why he hadn't interviewed Lavinia when he was at the house the day before. Why come back? Maybe he'd wanted to interrogate her alone. But again, why?

"What did you tell him?"

I could almost feel her bristle. "The truth, of course. Your father was there, too. Agent Reynolds didn't like that, but Tally wasn't havin' any of his nonsense about it being private. He said he was my attorney."

I almost laughed. I felt certain the Judge's license to practice law had lapsed at least a decade before, but he would have bluffed his way through that with no problem. When my father got his temper cranked up, he could steamroll over just about anybody. The handsome special agent wouldn't have represented more than a small bump in the Judge's path.

"So if you told him the truth, what has you upset?" I asked.

"I don't like this, Bay. We live a quiet life here. Most of the time."

I thought her last words, uttered in that stern voice I remembered so well from childhood, had been intended to remind me that I generated most of the troubles that managed to disturb the tranquility of Presqu'isle. I snapped my mouth shut on a denial, because she was right.

"And things like this just get your father riled up," she went on. "He's been on the phone ever since that man left, fussin' at his old friends for information. I won't have him upset like that, Bay. I won't have it."

Again I wanted to leap to my own defense, the accusation clear in her tone. This was one set of circumstances that couldn't be laid at my door. But I swallowed down my retort. Calmly I said, "What can I do?"

"Your father thinks there's more to this than just the robbery. He's worried about you. He's convinced himself you're mixed up in something very nasty. I want you to come over here and calm him down."

The charge was bogus, and she knew it as well as I did. If the Judge was concerned about anyone, it was her. She and Romey Gadsden—and a gang of robbers—had set this particular chain of circumstances in motion. I chewed on my lip a moment before answering. "If you think I can help, you know I'll be there. I just have to get hold of Red and cancel our dinner." I glanced at the clock above the sink. "I can probably be there by seven."

In the silence, I heard the furnace kick on. Outside, the rain continued to drip from a leaden sky, dark and lowering as we approached the winter solstice.

"Lavinia?"

"Honey, I'm sorry. I don't know what's gotten into me." Again I heard that long heart-wrenching sigh. "I think it's this gloomy weather. Makes a body imagine all kinds of terrible things. You go ahead and have your dinner. I'll take care of things here."

The sudden reversal was out of character. "I don't mind. Really. Maybe Red and I can grab a quick bite, and we'll both come over. How would that be?"

"No. Thank you, Bay, but no. I'm being a silly old woman. I've got a lovely chicken pot pie ready to go on the table. We get some hot food into us, put a fire in the grate, and we'll both feel lots better. You go on about your business. I'll talk to you tomorrow."

"You sure?"

"Absolutely. Tell Redmond to treat you to a nice dinner. You two enjoy your evening."

I felt guilty and at the same time relieved that I wouldn't have to battle the nasty weather and the pre-weekend traffic for the hour or more it would take to drive over to St. Helena. "Okay, if that's what you want. How about if I call when we get home? Make certain everyone's doing all right."

"We'll be fine. Goodnight, honey. Have a good time."

After she disconnected, I stood for a moment with the phone still clutched in my hand. I finally set it back in the cradle and wandered down into the great room. I pulled aside the drapes over the French doors and stared out into the drizzle toward the ocean, obscured by the thin curtain of rain blowing across the dunes. I wondered if the watcher stood somewhere beyond the feeble reach of the single light on the deck, his back hunched against the wet and cold, his feet growing icy as water pooled on the already saturated ground. I pictured him in an old jacket, the turned-up collar offering scant protection from the weather. In my mind, I saw him cup his hands around the cigarette dangling from his lips as he flipped the lighter against the wind.

I shivered and let the drape fall back into place. My hand slid into the pocket of my blazer and fondled the tiny pistol. With any luck, the son of a bitch would freeze to death out there.

The bar at Jump & Phil's was crowded with locals, as it always was on a Friday night, with only a few tables occupied in the dining area. I flipped the hood back from my rain slicker and saw a hand pop up in the back. I wove my way toward Red and the flickering gas fire that bounced shadows off his face in the dim corner. He looked tired.

I draped my raincoat over the back of a chair as he stood to kiss my cheek. A few heads turned our way, but I didn't recognize anyone. I settled in, the warmth from the fireplace welcome against my back. A pot of tea and a mug sat in front of me.

"I wasn't sure you'd show up," he said, watching as I squeezed out the tea bag and added sweetener.

"Why wouldn't I?"

"You know. What I said. At lunch."

I'd thought long and hard about that conversation on the short drive from the house. Best to tackle it head-on, I'd decided. I stalled for a moment by raising the cup and breathing in the fragrant steam.

"If that's what you want, I'm willing to give it a try," I said and smiled as the tension in his face relaxed. "But have you run this by Sarah yet?"

His grin faded. "Not exactly. But the custody agreement says I have the kids from six o'clock on Christmas Eve until four in the afternoon Christmas. I don't think she gets to say what we do or where we spend our time."

The waitress, someone new, sidled up to the table, and we ordered.

"That's not the point. I know Sarah and I haven't been the best of friends, especially lately."

My mind flashed back to that horrible night, right about this time of year, when Red's ex-wife had demonstrated her courage and character. She'd saved a lot of lives, including my own. I'd hoped that might have been the start of mending our battered relationship, but I'd been wrong. She'd known about Red's feelings for me, maybe even before he'd been willing to own them himself. Even he admitted those feelings had contributed to the breakup of his marriage, despite the fact that it had been Sarah who initiated the divorce.

Now I was sleeping with him. And he wanted to bring his—*her*—children over and play house on Christmas morning. If I were Sarah, I'd throw a screaming, bloody fit about that.

"But I respect her," I continued when Red didn't reply. "And she's the children's mother. I need to know she's okay with this. She has a right to decide what's best for them."

Red's chin came up in a gesture I recognized all too well. His brother had reacted in exactly the same way whenever I made some sweeping pronouncement he disagreed with.

"I have rights, too. Remember what you told me that time at Thanksgiving when she was hanging out with the cowboy, that environmental wack job?"

I stifled a smile. "I was just thinking about that. And yes, I remember what I said. Something about Sarah's being entitled to live her life the way she saw fit. Without clearing it with you first."

"Exactly. She knows you'd never do anything to harm the kids. You love them." His eyes held mine. "Don't you?"

"Of course I do."

In a detached, avuncular sort of way, I thought. I saw them so seldom. And it always struck me how dramatically they changed from one visit to the next, the alterations in their appearance and manner so marked they almost seemed as if they'd morphed into completely different people. Of course I loved them. But not in the way Red meant. Not yet.

Our food arrived, and we ate in silence, the warmth of the fire and the underlying buzz of conversation from the bar providing a soothing backdrop to the thoughts careening around in my head. One of them lodged there. I looked up from my steak sandwich.

"What do you know about this Harry Reynolds guy? The FBI agent."

"Not much more than I told you last night. He works out of the Bluffton office. The sheriff brought him in on the task force. The bureau thinks there may be a Homeland Security issue because, although this gang seems to be mostly Hispanic, we can't rule out other connections. Too early to say for certain." He shrugged and twirled angel hair pasta around his fork. "I don't see it myself. That isn't the direction terrorist plots usually come from."

"He was back at Presqu'isle this afternoon. Lavinia called me."

Red stared back at me. "Why?"

"To question her. About Romey Gadsden and the guy he recognized. Why aren't they talking to him directly? I don't get all this skating around, asking questions of other people. Why not go right to the source? I mean, in a way I'm glad he's not grilling that poor old man, but Mr. Gadsden's the one with direct knowledge. The rest of us are just parroting what we heard from him."

"It is strange," he agreed. "But who ever understands how the feds work? They're in their own little world. Us mere mortals aren't usually let in on what they're thinking."

"Well, I don't like it. Reynolds has Lavinia and the Judge all upset." I laid my steak knife across my plate and poured more tea. "Any way you can get him to back off?"

"In a word, no. I'm sorry about his tactics, but like I said, they're a law unto themselves. Literally."

I let Red get the check, and we sat for a while in front of the fire, neither of us willing to brave the rain until we absolutely had to. We held hands across the table, both of us wrapped in our own thoughts. I almost wasn't surprised when his cell phone jangled. Peace had been awfully hard to hold on to in the past few days.

I watched his face draw into a grimace as he listened. After a couple of minutes, he glanced up at me, and his look froze me in place.

"Yes. Right here with me," I heard him say.

"What?" I leaned in. "What's the matter?"

He shook his head. "Yeah . . . Jesus! Okay, I'll take care of it . . . Okay . . . Right, got it . . . Thanks. We'll be there as soon as we can."

When he hung up, his eyes wouldn't meet mine.

"What's happened? God damn it, Red, tell me!"

Heads swiveled, but I barely registered them.

"Just take it easy. It's not terrible news. It's just—"

"What? Who's hurt?"

"Nobody. At least not that we know for certain." He winced as my nails dug into his skin. "It's Romey Gadsden. They can't find him."

"What do you mean they can't find him?"

"Apparently he's wandered off. His daughter Glory says he does that sometimes. Forgets or has a spell or something. Anyway, Lisa Pedrovsky took the call, and she thought you'd want to know."

I felt guilty for the wave of relief that washed over me. Not Lavinia. Not the Judge. Or Erik. "Why did you say we'd be right there? Where are we going?"

"Not long after Mr. Gadsden's daughter talked to Lisa, she called back to say she'd found a weird message on her answering machine."

"From whom? Weird how?"

Red clutched my hand a little more tightly. "Glory said the voice sounded gravelly."

I felt the bottom drop out of my stomach.

"He said she should ask you what's happened to her father."

CHAPTER
TWENTY-FOUR

THE RAIN HAD STOPPED BY THE TIME WE SQUEALED into the parking lot abutting the sheriff's main office off Ribaut Road in Beaufort. As I stepped down from Red's restored Bronco, I glanced up, relieved to see a thin sliver of moon peeking out from the thinning clouds.

Detective Lisa Pedrovsky met us at the door. "Good, you're here. I'm just on my way out to St. Helena."

"Any word on Mr. Gadsden?" I asked.

Pedrovsky shook her head. "Nothing. The whole neighborhood—hell, pretty much the whole damn island—is out there looking. We've got deputies working a grid out from the house." She dropped down into a worn chair in the waiting area. "Sit. Talk to me about this message the daughter got."

I took a seat, but Red moved toward the door to the offices. "I want to check on something. I'll be right back."

I watched him disappear before turning back to the detective. "Red told you about the threatening calls I've been getting?"

She nodded. "Yeah. And about somebody allegedly watching your house."

I felt my hands clenching. "Allegedly?"

"Sorry. Cop-speak. No offense."

I wondered but let it go. "Did you get anything from the ciga-rette butts your tech collected?"

She waved a hand in front of her face as if chasing off an annoy-ing insect. "Nothing yet. But it's early times. The lab is backed up, lots more pressing things to handle, but we're working on it."

More pressing things. I hated to think that it would take Mr. Gads-den's disappearance to move my troubles to the head of the line.

"So, the messages?" Pedrovsky's voice jerked me back.

"I have tapes of the last one. Deep voice, no accent, smoker's rasp, warning me to stay out of *their* business. Short, nasty, and to the point. The one from this morning said people I cared about could get hurt if I didn't back off."

"People like Romey Gadsden?"

Exactly what I'd been thinking all through the long, dreary drive from Hilton Head. But in the cold light of the sheriff's station—and Lisa Pedrovsky's staccato questioning—doubt had begun to seep in.

"It doesn't make any sense," I said. "My father would be the most likely target." I swallowed hard, remembering the time when he *had* been. I'd taken foolish risks, been perfectly willing to sacrifice anything—and anyone—to get him home safely. "Or Lavinia, his companion. My partner, Erik. Red. Dolores, my housekeeper." I tried unsuccessfully to suppress a shudder. "I've known Mr. Gadsden, off and on, for most of my life, but he's not a close friend. And certainly not family. I mean, I'm sick about his disappearance, but I don't un-derstand why anyone would think he could be used as a pawn to get me to do anything."

"That's what I've been thinking. Why go after an acquaintance when there are a lot more likely candidates closer to home."

I tried not to bristle at the casual way the detective tossed out the possibility of someone harming my family.

"But let's get back to the messages." Her hard eyes studied my face. "What 'business' is it you're supposed to stay out of?"

"I wish to hell I knew. I've been assuming it had something to do with the hit-and-run of Theresa Montalvo. I haven't exactly been keeping a low profile on that. I've stuck my nose in a lot of places over the past week. And Romey Gadsden has absolutely no connection to that."

"So this has to be about the robberies."

"But I'm not involved in that!" I looked up to see Red heading back in our direction. "If Lavinia hadn't happened to be there on Lady's Island when they struck the bank, I wouldn't know any more about it than what I read in the *Packet*."

The mention of the paper made Gabby Henson's eager face flash across my mind's eye, and I wondered why I hadn't heard from her in a few days. Something to think about. But later, after we found Mr. Rom.

"News?" The detective rose to meet Red. Her clipped delivery reminded me so much of my late partner, Ben Wyler, that I had to swallow hard against a sudden stab of loss. I glanced at Lisa and wondered how she was coping with his death. More than once I'd gotten the feeling she and Ben had had a thing going, at least from her side. But if she mourned him, she kept it to herself.

"No. I talked to Rudy Sanchez out on St. Helena. He says the rain pretty much obliterated any footprints. Some of the ladies from the church have set up a telephone tree, asking everyone to check their own property—garages, outbuildings, and sheds—anyplace Mr. Gadsden might have sought shelter from the weather. So far nothing."

"I want to help," I said, rising from the uncomfortable chair. "Are you going out there?"

"We've got plenty of people involved in the search." Detective Pedrovsky jumped in before Red could reply. "I want you to listen to that message."

I glanced at Red, who lifted his shoulders as if to say, *She's the boss.*

"Fine." I picked up my bag. "Then let's get going."

"Take the Bronco and follow us out." Red worked the ignition key off his ring and handed it to me. "I'll take a cruiser."

"I'm stopping at Presqu'isle first to make sure everything's okay there." I didn't phrase it as a question because it wasn't open for discussion.

"You know where the daughter lives?" the detective asked.

"Lavinia will. I'll get directions from her."

Pedrovsky jerked up the sleeve of her rain slicker and checked her watch. "We'll meet you there in half an hour."

Without waiting for a reply, she spun on her sensible black shoes and pushed through the door, calling "You're with me, Sergeant" over her shoulder.

Red cast a quick look around, then gripped my shoulders and pulled me into a brief embrace. "Be careful," he whispered against my hair before he, too, disappeared into the night.

I used my cell to check in at Presqu'isle before I sped toward the rain-slick causeway that connected St. Helena to Lady's Island, so I wasn't surprised to find Lavinia staring anxiously out into the dark when I climbed the steps up to the verandah.

"Any word?" she asked as I wiped my feet on the mat.

I slipped past her into the entryway just as the grandfather clock chimed nine. I shrugged out of my raincoat a moment before the soft whirring noise preceded the Judge across the heart pine floor.

"Hey, Daddy," I said, then turned back to Lavinia. "Nothing. What have you heard?"

For the first time I noticed that she wore a heavy sweater over her housedress and that tiny drops of moisture beaded her short white hair. "You've been outside?" I asked.

"Of course. I'll make tea," she added, leading the way toward the kitchen. "Did you have dinner?"

I trailed along behind the Judge's wheelchair. "Yes. And I can't stay. I just wanted to make sure everything was okay here." I stood just inside the doorway while Lavinia lifted the kettle from the stovetop. "I'm on my way to Glory's now. I need directions."

In a few words and gestures, she explained how to find Glory Merrick's house on Jenkins Creek.

"Thanks. I'd better get going."

"You have time for a cup of tea. Sit."

"Why were you outside this time of night?" I asked, not moving from the doorway. If she thought she could derail me, she'd forgotten that we shared the same stubborn streak.

"Checking to make sure Rom hadn't wandered this way." She poured water into the teapot, and, despite her brisk words, I could read the fear in her voice.

"If he's on foot, there's no way he got this far. Don't worry, we'll find him," I added with false confidence. "I have to go."

My father spoke for the first time since I'd walked in the door. "How involved are you in all this, daughter?"

I didn't know where to begin. Or how to explain, primarily because I didn't understand it myself. "I'm just trying to help. I'll let you know what happens," I said and turned for the door.

"Tell Glory we're praying for her and Romey," Lavinia said softly.

"I expect to hear from you," my father added in his courtroom voice that brooked no contradiction.

"Yes, sir," I said and slipped back into the rain.

Driving the narrow road that led to the house Romey Gadsden shared with his daughter and son-in-law was like traveling back in time. Occasionally, a single light glimmered through the misty fog that clung to the thick stands of longleaf pines and twisted oaks, but most of the way I felt like the last person left on earth. The wet blacktop sparkled in the headlights, and I drove more slowly than I wanted to in the unfamiliar Bronco. After what seemed like an eternity, I rounded one of the many sharp turns and saw ahead the strobing blue lights of several sheriff's cars reflecting back off the low-hanging clouds.

I pulled up on the verge and climbed down. Almost immediately, a uniformed deputy, his clear raincoat shimmering with condensation, stepped out of the darkness. Rudy Sanchez and I recognized each other at almost the same moment.

"They're expecting me," I said, gesturing toward the house blazing with light from every window.

"Yes, ma'am. Detective Pedrovsky said to escort you in as soon as you arrived."

I followed his broad back as he wove in and out of the dozen or so vehicles parked at odd angles in the front yard. A low buzz of conversation floated to me on the sodden night air. The breeze had dropped with the passage of the front, and the temperature had risen dramatically. I wiped away a trickle of sweat that slid down the back of my neck and stepped up onto the wide front porch.

I couldn't see much of the house in the mist and fog, but over the quiet voices coming from inside, I heard the distinct rush of water over stones. It must have rained a lot harder here than it had on Hilton Head, I thought. Jenkins Creek sounded swollen and running fast. I shuddered, hoping the normally placid little stream didn't play any part in Mr. Rom's disappearance.

I nodded at Deputy Sanchez and stepped into the light.

Several black faces turned at my entrance into the kitchen. Lisa Pedrovsky detached herself from where she stood speaking with a couple of her men and moved in my direction. A small woman, not much more than five feet tall, rose at the same time, her hand extended.

"Miz Tanner," she said, edging ahead of Pedrovsky, "thank you so much for coming. I'm sure you don't remember me, but I'm Glory Merrick, Romey's daughter."

She had the same bright, intelligent eyes as her father, and her fragile, tentative smile seemed more than I deserved.

I took her hand and clasped it in both of mine. "I'm sorry to see you again under such awful circumstances," I said.

"Do you know anything about what's happened to my father?"

I held her gaze steadily and said, "No, ma'am, absolutely not. I don't understand why someone would say I did, but I swear I'm as in the dark as everyone else."

"I didn't think so. Miz Smalls sets great store by you and your daddy."

"Thank you." Lavinia's stamp of approval apparently carried more weight than an anonymous phone call. I felt my shoulders relax.

"Is there any progress?" I swiveled my head to include the detective in my question.

"Nothing yet," Pedrovsky said. "But this is one of those no-news-is-good-news situations," she added, more for Glory's benefit than anything else, I thought. She touched my elbow. "A word, Bay?"

Glory Gadsden Merrick resumed her seat as we moved out into the hallway. Two of the people huddled in the kitchen resembled her enough to be her children, and the daughter took her mother's hand and squeezed it. *Like a family.* Red's words echoed in my head.

I followed Lisa into the living room with its overstuffed furniture and solid wooden tables, their polished surfaces gleaming in the lamplight. She stopped alongside a portable telephone with an answering machine attached.

"We've made a copy of the tape, but I wanted you to hear it for yourself," the detective said. She punched the Play button.

"Ask that nosey Tanner broad what happened to your old man. And tell her to back off."

That was it.

"Same guy?" Pedrovsky asked.

I nodded. "I think so." Something caught at the corner of my mind, then slithered away again.

"I listened to the copy of the one from your answering service on the way out here, and it sounds the same to me, too."

"Do you have the capability to do a voice comparison on the tapes?"

Her head was already shaking before I finished the sentence.

"The lab is so backed up we'd be lucky to get results on that before Easter."

"So what's the next step?"

"You're absolutely positive you have no idea whose toes you've stepped on hard enough to set this whole thing in motion?" I didn't imagine the accusatory tone in her next words. "You seem to have a knack for getting involved in things that turn out bad for somebody else."

I knew she meant Ben Wyler. I had no defense, so I let it go.

"Only what I've already told you." I met her hostile stare without flinching.

"I gotta get back to the office."

"Is there something I can do to help?"

"We've got more than enough bodies for the search. You'd just be in the way."

"Okay. Is Red around? I need to see what he wants to do about transportation."

"He's out checking on one of the search parties. He rode with me, so maybe you'd better wait." Her gaze drifted past me to where Glory sat at the old kitchen table. "You ought to go sit in the sergeant's car, though. I think maybe you being here isn't the easiest thing in the world for the family."

"Fine. Call me if there's anything I can do."

Without another word, she executed one of her trademark spins and left me standing alone in the deserted living room. I watched her speak to one of the deputies before striding out into the dark. I thought about saying something to Glory, but Pedrovsky's words about making things more difficult sent me heading for the door instead. I sloshed through the pools of water to Red's car and settled down to wait.

Three hours later I pulled into my driveway and shut off the ignition. My Jaguar, which we'd dropped off on our way to Beaufort, sat squarely in the center of the garage, and I decided I didn't have the energy to jockey cars around. Red's baby could sit outside for one night.

Red had been surprised to find me dozing in the front seat of the Bronco, the heater going full blast, when he finally slogged back into the Merricks' yard. When I told him Lisa had suggested I wait, he shook his head.

"She must have misunderstood. A lot on her mind, I guess. I need to hang here until we find— Until we get some resolution. You go on home. I'll grab a cruiser." His cold hand stroked my cheek. "I may not make it back at all."

I'd yawned and forced myself awake. "No word?"

"We haven't found any trace of him yet. But that's good," he added in response to the stricken look on my face. "We've followed the creek all the way down, so it's pretty certain he didn't fall in there. Don't worry. We'll find him."

I'd nodded, too tired and numb with worry to do much more. A brief kiss, and Red had melted away back into the gloomy night. . . .

I climbed down into my driveway and manually locked the Bronco. I'd forgotten to bring the garage door opener with me, so I trudged up the front steps, fumbling in my bag for the house keys. The security system had automatically turned on the outside lights at sunset, but I was concentrating so hard on locating my key ring that I stumbled over something lying on the doormat and smacked my shoulder into the siding.

I cursed softly and rubbed my arm. I stooped down to see what had sent me ricocheting off the side of my house and recoiled when my fingers encountered the intricately carved curves of the walking stick.

CHAPTER
TWENTY-FIVE

I LET MYSELF IN AND STOOD FOR A LONG TIME, THE end of the cane dripping water onto the hardwood floor, turning the old piece of oak over and over in my hands. It *looked* like the one Mr. Gadsden's great-granddaddy had carved, but I wasn't a hundred percent sure.

I shoved the Seecamp into my coat pocket, snatched up a flashlight, and barreled outside. I slogged through the wet pine straw and sodden leaves, scouring my property for any sign of the lost old man. I fondled the grip of the gun, my finger slipping inside the trigger guard every few steps. If I encountered the watcher, he'd tell me what I wanted to know. I even crossed the dune to search the beach a few hundred yards in each direction but came up empty.

I tried both Red and Lisa Pedrovsky on my cell, but neither picked up. In the end, I left a message at the Beaufort sheriff's office for one of them to call.

Back inside, I set the stick in the corner, slid out of my ruined shoes, and draped my coat over the closet door to dry. In the kitchen, I set the kettle on to boil, then retreated to my bedroom, where I stripped off my damp clothes and bundled myself into flannel pajamas and my old chenille robe. I retrieved the cane and carried it, along with a mug of steaming tea, into the great room. I built a fire, curled in the corner of the sofa, and pulled the afghan over my legs.

What the hell is this all about? I asked myself, my hands running over the smooth edges of the carved wood. Some kind of message? An attempt to lay the blame for the old man's disappearance at my door—literally? If so, it was a clumsy effort. Hadn't the anonymous phone call been enough? Besides, I had an airtight alibi. I'd been with either Erik or Red all day. I hadn't asked how long Mr. Gadsden had been missing, but it had to have been no more than a few hours before Red and I got the call from Pedrovsky at Jump & Phil's. So leaving the walking stick on my front porch had been overkill. And pointless.

I turned up the lamp on the side table next to the sofa and studied the cane more closely. It looked like the one Mr. Rom had proudly shown me on that bench in front of the hospital. I rose and retrieved my reading glasses from my bag. Although I'd seen it up close for only a few moments, Luther Tait's handiwork had been subtle and artistic, just like this. I turned it beneath the light, my fingers playing over the smooth head of the lion or tiger carved into the knob.

"Mr. Rom's," I said aloud, my words echoing a little in the silent house.

But why? That was the one question I kept coming back to. No way could I be blamed for the old man's disappearance. So what was the point? To rattle me? *It's not working,* I thought, at least not since the first shock of finding it had worn off.

Or to discredit me? I wondered. But in whose eyes? The sheriff wouldn't give it a second thought once I'd recounted my alibi. Even Glory Gadsden Merrick didn't believe I'd had anything to do with her father's disappearance. So what did this . . . *person* gain by such an obvious stunt?

I felt my eyes beginning to droop with exhaustion. I flipped off the light and slid down beneath the afghan.

Despite the turmoil of the strange day, in seconds I was asleep.

* * *

I wasn't certain if it was the shaft of sunlight stabbing my eyes or the distant ringing of the phone that woke me. Whatever the cause, I came instantly alert, my mind immediately filled with foreboding as if I'd been dreaming about Romey Gadsden's disappearance. I threw off the afghan and sprinted for the kitchen.

Red sounded past exhausted, but I knew the minute he said my name he had good news.

"You found him?"

"Yes. Well, I can't exactly say we found him. He just appeared on his daughter's doorstep."

"And he's okay?"

Red hesitated. "Pretty much."

"What does that mean?"

"Physically he seems not to have suffered any. He wasn't even very wet."

"How is that possible?"

"Hold on." He spoke to someone nearby, but I couldn't make out what he'd said. It was a moment before he came back to me. "I can't talk now. Mrs. Merrick went with her father to the hospital, just to have him checked out. But the poor old man wasn't making a whole lot of sense, so we're really not sure what happened."

"When are you coming home?"

Silence greeted the question, and it took a moment for both of us to realize what I'd said. *Home.*

Red decided not to comment. "I'm leaving now. I need to stop at the office, but I should be there in a couple of hours. What's on your agenda for today?"

I had to search my brain for a moment. *Saturday.* "I don't know. I haven't thought about it."

"Well, I need to get some sleep."

"I know. Be careful," I said automatically before I hung up.

Back in the great room, I folded the afghan and picked up the walking stick from where I'd dropped it on the floor next to the sofa. I'd forgotten to tell Red about it. Or maybe it didn't matter now that Mr. Gadsden had returned safely home. In the shower, I let the steaming spray roll over me, washing away the fear and anxiety of the night before.

Where had Romey been all those hours? How had he stayed dry? Someone had to have taken him away in a vehicle. There wasn't any other explanation. But why? And who? Toweling my hair, I padded into the bedroom. I needed to talk to him. Maybe Lavinia could help. I pulled on jeans and a light cotton sweater and slid my feet into my oldest loafers. In the kitchen, I set the kettle on and picked up the phone.

Lavinia sounded as relieved as I had. "Yes," she said, "I heard just a little while ago. Glory's daughter Ivy called. Praise God."

"What else?" I asked. "Any information about where he was all that time?"

"Nothing. It was around seven, just getting light. The sheriff's men had left or were out searching, and Ivy says her granddaddy just walked in the front door. Said he was hungry and had to go the bathroom." She laughed briefly, and I could almost see her head shaking in amazement. "Didn't seem to know he'd been gone all night, poor thing. I guess he doesn't remember anything about it at all."

"I'd like to talk to him. What do you think the chances are?"

"I don't know, Bay. Ivy said he was very confused, didn't understand why everyone was fussin' over him. Apparently he kept talking about the past, about things that happened a long time ago as if they were just yesterday. There's no telling when he'll be back to normal."

"Is that like him? I mean, when we had lunch, he seemed perfectly lucid. Does he do this often, fade back into the past and forget where he is?"

"Not often, but I've seen it happen to him before. He just sort of goes away for a spell, if you know what I mean."

It didn't sound promising. "Keep me posted on how he's doing, okay?"

"It's a strange thing, Bay. Makes me uneasy."

"I know what you mean." A thought struck. "Did he have his cane with him when he disappeared?"

"His walking stick? I have no idea. Is it important?"

"Maybe," I said. "Don't worry about it. Tell Glory I want to talk to her father, okay? When he's feeling up to it."

Lavinia didn't sound hopeful. "I'll see what I can do."

"Thanks. Tell Daddy I'll talk to him soon."

I hung up and made tea. Cup in hand, I studied the contents of the refrigerator. We were out of eggs and milk and lots of other things. Since Dolores did the shopping twice a week, I rarely saw the inside of a grocery store. I shook off the rising wave of fear. She'd come back. She'd be okay. I dropped the halves of the last English muffin into the toaster and scribbled out a list, another part of my brain refusing to ignore the nagging questions.

Where was Dolores? Where had Romey Gadsden been all night? Names and incidents swirled around in my head as I scraped the bottom of the peanut butter jar. I wolfed down the muffins, cleared the counter, and went in search of a jacket. I scribbled a note for Red, left the spare key where he'd know to look for it, and walked out into bright sunshine. The storm had washed the sky a brilliant blue, and a soft breeze carried the sharp, pungent smells of damp earth and wet leaves. I breathed deeply and forced myself to let it all go. So often, insight came to me from out of nowhere, appearing like a camera's flash, full-blown and complete. I slid into Red's Bronco and pointed it toward Publix and the madhouse that would be the huge grocery store on the Saturday morning before Christmas.

Three hours later I parked next to the cruiser and punched the garage door opener before I loaded my arms with bags. The house lay quiet as I deposited them on the counter and went back for the rest. I'd detoured to the plant nursery on my way home, and the rear compartment of Red's Bronco was piled with fresh pine wreaths and garland. I'd hesitated over a tree, then decided not to push it. There'd be time enough for that if things actually worked out. I left the greenery on a bench in the garage.

Inside again, I tiptoed down the hallway and peeked around the partially closed door of the bedroom. Red lay sprawled on his back across the middle of the king-sized bed, one bare leg flung outside the blanket. I watched the even rise and fall of his chest for a moment before sliding the door closed.

I stashed the groceries, leaving out the ingredients I'd need for Frogmore stew. I'd come late to cooking, and I didn't have an extensive repertoire, but I'd made this Lowcountry staple enough times that I could even do it without Lavinia's recipe. I found myself humming while I chopped onions and deveined shrimp, my mind wandering to the rapidly approaching holiday. Imaginary scenes of Christmas morning in the great room, a huge tree almost engulfed in shiny packages, shrieks of delight from Scotty and Elinor as they raced down the hallway . . .

"There won't be anything left of that if you don't quit scrubbing on it."

Red's voice made me jump, and I dropped the ear of sweet corn I'd been cleaning into the sink.

"What are you doing up?" I glanced at the clock. "You can't have been asleep for more than a couple of hours."

He yawned and stretched, the top of his sweats riding up to reveal a well-muscled stomach. "It was enough. I'm used to going on less when things start breaking on a case."

I cut the last ear of corn into two-inch chunks. "What's breaking?"

Red pulled the coffeemaker toward him and set about filling it. "I woke up with the feeling that things were going to start popping any minute. You ever have that?"

I moved aside so he could run water into the glass pot. "Yes, a couple of times. Sort of a tingling in the back of your brain, as if the answer is getting ready to jump into your conscious mind."

"Exactly. You should have been a cop."

"I'm close enough for comfort," I said, drying my hands on a dishtowel. "You hungry?"

"No, thanks. I stopped at McDonald's and wolfed down a few Egg McMuffins on my way home."

There it was again, I thought. That word. I let the silence last a few more beats while we both digested its implications. "I'm making Frogmore stew, but it won't be ready for a couple of hours."

"Sit down then." His tone had changed, and I looked over my shoulder to see his expression had sobered as well.

"What's the matter?"

He pulled out the chair at the small kitchen table. "I need to talk to you about something."

I sat, and he trotted down the steps, returning a moment later with Romey Gadsden's walking stick in his hand.

"Where'd this come from?" he asked.

I studied his face, but I didn't read any accusation on it. "I found it on my doorstep when I came home last night. It's Mr. Rom's."

"I know. His daughter described it pretty minutely. It wasn't at the house, so she assumed her father took it with him when he wandered off."

"Except he didn't. Wander off, that is." I paused, my eyes on his. "Did he?"

Red sighed and laid the cane across the table between us. "It doesn't look that way. We combed every inch of that ground for a solid square mile either side of Jenkins Creek. Checked every house, every garage, every old shed and barn. He wasn't within walking distance of the house. No way. Someone enticed him into a car and kept him away all night, then dropped him off in the morning. There's no other logical explanation."

I nodded. "That's what I figured. Did Glory or anyone hear a car early this morning? Were there still deputies at her place?"

Red's hand caressed the worn, weathered wood of the stick. "The family had all fallen asleep out of sheer exhaustion. We pulled in a new crew around six this morning and sent everyone out on the search. So no, no one heard or saw whoever brought him back."

"Damned convenient," I mumbled.

"Too damned convenient. They must have had someone watching the house."

"Any signs of a struggle? I mean when you first got there?"

He rose and poured himself a mug of coffee, then carried it back to the table. "No. Glory and her husband got home from work right on time Friday night, same as always. Romey was just gone. Along with his raincoat and his stick."

Red lifted the cane and studied its contours. "Mrs. Merrick said her father usually didn't take it when it was raining. It sinks into the ground and doesn't do him much good."

I watched his eyes, which kept darting away from me. "So someone came and took Mr. Gadsden without a struggle, bundled him into his raincoat against the weather, made sure he had his stick in case he needed it, and whisked him away without a trace. And then brought him back safe and sound twelve hours later."

"It's weird," Red admitted. Again he set the cane on the table. "And this is even weirder. You have no idea how it got here?"

"What do *you* think? If the interrogation's finished, Sergeant, I need to get back to cooking."

"Bay, honey, come on—"

I slapped his hand away as he reached for me. I banged a pan into the sink and ran water into it. I sensed him move up behind me, but he didn't touch me.

"I had to ask. You know that. I just don't understand why you didn't let me know about it last night."

"I tried. I left a message for you and Pedrovsky at the Beaufort office. If no one delivered it, that's not my fault."

"Things were a little crazy last night. It must have slipped through the cracks." He backed up as I swung the big pot onto the stove. "That's not important. But we have to figure out why you're involved with all this. You have to think about who's got it in for you and why."

I turned and leaned back against the sink. "Do you imagine I *haven't* been trying to figure this out? God, Red! Don't talk to me as if I were some suspect you're trying to trip up."

His arms still dangled at his sides, and his face still looked grave. "If I don't ask you, Pedrovsky will. I'll have to tell her about this."

"Of course you will. I would have told her myself if she'd bothered to call me back. Look," I said, forcing a calm I didn't feel into my voice, "it's a message of some kind. Someone's trying to tell me something. I just haven't figured out what it is yet."

"Or they're trying to get you involved in this whole bank robbery thing. But that's what's so strange. On the one hand, you've got some jerk warning you off, and on the other you've got whoever left Mr. Gadsden's walking stick almost inviting you to stick your nose in. It doesn't make sense."

A flicker of something sparked in the back of my mind for a split second, the same feeling I'd had the night before in Glory Merrick's living room. Before I could grab hold of the thought, I heard the sound of a car turning into the driveway. I stepped around Red and walked to the bay window behind the kitchen table in time to see the familiar blue Hyundai chug up the drive and pull onto the pine straw. I held my breath, daring to hope, and a moment later the door opened.

CHAPTER
TWENTY-SIX

"THEY'RE SAFE. I CAN'T TELL YOU ANYTHING ELSE. Please don't ask me."

Angie Santiago stood in the middle of the kitchen floor, her arms hugging her chest. She looked defiant, almost daring me to challenge her right to protect her family's secrets. Her eyes kept darting to Red, who had retreated with his coffee to the breakfast table.

"Not good enough," I said, and she flinched at the anger in my voice.

"Please, Mrs. Tanner—"

"Sit down," I said, hauling out the chair across from Red.

She hung back and shot a look over her shoulder, toward the front door, as if gauging her chances of escaping before I could catch up to her.

I stared her down, not speaking, and finally she edged past me and slid onto the padded seat.

Red picked up the paper and rose. "I need to take a shower. I'll leave you two to talk," he said.

I couldn't quite interpret the look he shot me on his way down the steps. I dried my hands on the dishtowel and took his empty chair.

"Where are they?"

Angie's shoulders stiffened. Her chin lifted, but she refused to meet my eyes. "I can't tell you. I just came so you could . . . so maybe you wouldn't worry about them."

"And *you're* not worried?"

She controlled the trembling of her lower lip. "Papa says you should leave it alone."

I eased back, lowering my voice. "Did he send you here?"

"No! Not exactly. I mean . . . He said you're putting them in more danger. He says you have to stop."

"Did you actually talk to your mother, Angie?"

I saw the temptation to lie flit across her eyes, then she sighed. "No, I didn't. But Papa says Mom called him and said she and Bobby are okay. She said you and your . . . Sergeant Tanner should back off."

I gave her a moment to consider her words. "Do you really think your mother said that? It certainly doesn't sound like Dolores to me."

"Papa wouldn't lie."

I bit back my immediate thought: *Wouldn't he? To protect Dolores? And Bobby?* Or maybe it was someone else. My subconscious had scribbled his name on my list, along with that of his mysterious brother, Jesús. Next to the word *coyote.* For the first time, I considered the possibility of his complicity in—what? It all came down to motive, and I didn't have a clue what Hector's might be.

"This is dangerous business, Angie," I said softly. "Dolores and Bobby can use all the friends they can find. And I think you know that."

"Papa says they're safe."

I pushed myself up and crossed to the refrigerator. I pulled out a Coke, retrieved a glass from the cupboard, and banged them both down on the table in front of Angie, a little more forcefully than I'd intended. Consciously, I unclenched my hands and relaxed my shoulders before sitting back down.

"Okay. Let's look at this objectively. Bobby and Serena Montalvo are involved in the death of Serena's sister." I shook my head as she opened her mouth to interrupt. "Not directly, I don't mean that. But they know who might be responsible. They're assuming—and so am I—that Theresa got killed by mistake. So they're in danger. Your mother's gone to help them hide." I waited a beat. "Do I have it right so far?"

The young woman averted her eyes and busied herself with popping open the Coke can. She jumped when I slapped my hand on the glass top of the table.

"Come on, Angelina. God damn it! Your father is a pigheaded man who hates my guts. But I love your mother like a sister. Do you honestly think I'd do anything to hurt her?"

The tears came from nowhere and slipped down her smooth cheeks. She dashed them away with the tips of her fingers and raised her head to stare directly at me. "You're asking me to trust you more than my own father."

"No," I said, "no. But he isn't equipped to handle something like this. I am."

Angie dropped her head again, and I glanced across her shoulder to see Red standing in the hallway. I shook my head slightly, and he retreated into the bedroom.

When I looked back, the young woman had taken control of herself. A half smile hovered on her full lips. "You can't let him know I've told you anything."

I sighed and felt my entire body relax. "Agreed."

An hour later, the Frogmore stew was simmering on the back burner, and Red and I had settled ourselves on the sofa. The fireplace lay cold, heaped with ashes, and the French door out to the deck stood open to a warm, soft breeze that carried the scents of damp, steaming earth and the squeaks and squawks of foraging birds.

"So you really don't know much more than you did before, do you?" Red stretched and repositioned his stockinged feet on the coffee table. "Just confirmation of what you already assumed, way I see it."

"Not exactly. But I think she told me everything she knows. I'll give Hector the benefit of the doubt and say he's trying to protect her by keeping the details to himself."

"Angie didn't give up their hideout?"

"I honestly don't think she knows. But they're close by. I'm convinced they're holed up in a motel somewhere around Savannah."

"Why not here?"

"Because they could have rented cars at the Hilton Head airport. Why drive all the way to Savannah unless they intended to stay around there? Besides, it's easier to get lost in a city than an island with only one way on and off."

"Logical." Red caressed my cheek with the back of his hand. "But not everyone thinks like you do, sweetheart. They had to have been panicked, scared."

"Jason Early's the key," I said. "Everyone's motives are pretty clear except his."

"You mean because everyone else is Hispanic?"

I set my cooling cup of tea on the side table and wriggled around to face him. "I know that sounds racist, but it's simply a fact. Dolores and Bobby, the Montalvos. Serena's involvement in the immigration thing. Sorry, but Early—and his mother—stand out like sore thumbs." I checked the clock over the mantel. "It's time to put the shrimp in." I rose, and Red followed me up to the kitchen.

"You said she sounded like the racist here. Early's mother. Why would she be involved?"

"Protecting her child," I said, lifting the lid of the bubbling pot and inhaling the fragrant steam. "That's at the heart of all this, when you come right down to it."

"I get that. But him . . . We need to make one of your lists," he said, his voice echoing as he stuck his head in the refrigerator. He emerged with a bottle of beer in his hand.

"I tried that without much success," I said. I dropped the shrimp into the pot and resettled the lid. "Just another few minutes." I pulled two large bowls from the cupboard. As I turned toward the table, movement caught my eye. "Who's that?"

Red followed my gaze to the window overlooking the drive. "Shit, it's Lisa," he said, and I watched the stocky detective slam the door to her unmarked Crown Vic.

"I'll set another place."

"That was great, Bay. I didn't realize how long it's been since I had a home-cooked meal."

Lisa Pedrovsky sat back, her hand reaching automatically into the pocket of her blazer before she jerked it suddenly back out.

I smiled. "You can smoke if you like. As long as you blow some of it in my direction."

I rummaged on the top shelf of a tall cabinet and finally located one of my abandoned ashtrays. By the time I set it on the table, she had already lit up.

"When did you quit?" she asked.

"Off and on over the past couple of years."

I cleared the table while Red and the detective sat in silence. Red had been flustered, embarrassed, I thought, for his superior to find us settled in like an old married couple in my house. I hadn't thought he was naïve enough to believe everyone in the department didn't know about us, but apparently having Lisa as an eyewitness had unnerved him a little.

"You want some coffee?" he asked, breaking into my thoughts.

I knew he didn't mean me.

"Coffee would be great," Lisa said, stubbing out her cigarette half-smoked.

Red retreated to the far counter, out of the line of fire.

"I got your message from last night," the detective said. "Let me see the thing."

Now that her belly was full and her bloodstream fortified with nicotine, she'd reverted to her usual rapid-fire delivery and slightly patronizing tone of voice. Still, a guest is a guest, even if uninvited, my mother's voice whispered somewhere from the back of my head. I took the three steps slowly and returned with Mr. Gadsden's walking stick. I laid it across the table and sat back down.

Lisa stroked the smooth contours of the carving, her fingers surprisingly gentle. "It's beautiful," she said. "How old?"

"Close to a hundred and fifty years, I'd guess. Romey Gadsden said his great-grandfather carved it sometime after the war."

Being Southern girls by birth, neither of us needed me to specify *which* war.

"Amazing it's lasted this long," Lisa said. She set it back carefully on the table. "Why you?"

Again, no explanation was needed. I knew exactly what she meant.

"I have no idea. I'm alibied by Red and my partner for all day yesterday." I paused a moment, then changed tack. "What do you think happened to Mr. Gadsden last night?"

Pedrovsky cast a quick glance over her shoulder in Red's direction, but he appeared mesmerized by the slow drip of coffee into the pot and didn't turn.

"Lots of theories floating around, but nothing that fits all the circumstances." She looked at me, and I stared straight back at her. "You seem to be the common thread here."

"You're right."

The admission caught her off guard, and I smiled to myself. There hadn't been too many times when I'd surprised her.

She recovered quickly. "Any idea why?"

"Not a clue. As I told you yesterday, I have no connection to the robberies, no information about the perpetrators, no interest other than as a concerned citizen who doesn't like the idea of a gang of thugs pulling heists in my neighborhood." I glanced over to see Red staring across the room at me. "If I had anything useful, I would have shared it with the sergeant already."

"I figured that." The detective pulled out another cigarette. She inclined her head in my direction, and I nodded. A wreath of smoke hovered over her as she exhaled, and I felt the longing in my own chest. "So what's your theory?"

202 ⌒ KATHRYN R. WALL

I shrugged. "I don't really have one. I haven't been able to make the pieces fit into any kind of workable pattern. You?"

She didn't like having the tables turned. "We've got some ideas, but like I said, it all keeps coming back to you."

"Any luck tracing Roberto Santiago and Serena Montalvo?" I asked.

Red set a mug of coffee in front of the detective along with the sugar bowl and a small carton of half-and-half. I wondered if he'd chosen that moment in order to give his fellow officer a chance to consider her answer, then shook it off. Red was on *my* side.

"The kids involved in the hit-and-run? We're on it. But I have to tell you, it's not a priority right now. There's nothing that points directly to one of them driving the car. And we haven't got anything that says they were on the scene, so . . ."

"So . . . what? You don't think they might be in danger?"

Red reached across the table to take my hand in his. I wasn't sure if the gesture was meant to reassure or to warn me against losing my temper. Either way, it didn't work.

"He's your housekeeper's kid, right?" There was a world of implication in the detective's voice. Red's fingers tightened.

"Yes, he is. What does that have to do with anything?"

"Like I said before, people around you have a way of getting themselves into trouble." This time she mashed the remains of her cigarette into the ashtray and picked up Romey Gadsden's stick. "We'll never lift any prints off of this. Too many bumps and ridges. I'll see the old gentleman gets it back."

Without thinking, I jerked it out of her hand. "If it's not evidence, I'll return it to him myself. Unless you have an objection?"

We glared across the table at each other, then Lisa Pedrovsky shrugged. "Suit yourself. Thanks for dinner, Bay." What passed for a smile touched the corners of her lips. "I really mean that."

Red walked her out to the car, and they stood in the driveway for a few minutes. Through the bay window, I watched the silent exchange, Red's arms gesturing, and Lisa shaking her head occasionally.

Finally, he stepped back, and she slid behind the wheel. Both of us watched her whip the big car around and roar out onto the street, sending dead leaves and loose stones flying into the quiet afternoon.

When he turned, Red caught me staring at him through the glass. His face was flushed with anger. A moment later he slammed the door from the garage and stomped up into the kitchen.

"What's the matter?" I asked.

"She knows something. I'm not sure what, but she's stonewalling."

"You think she's holding out on you?"

"Damn right," he said, pulling me into his arms. "And I intend to find out why."

CHAPTER
TWENTY-SEVEN

"YOU KNOW SHE BLAMES YOU FOR WYLER'S DEATH."
I bit back the denial that sprang immediately into my head and drew a long, slow breath. "Of course she does. I don't know what was going on between the two of them, but she took it hard. It's natural, I guess, to want to find somebody to focus your anger on."

Red leaned back away from me and studied my face. "She needs to get over it. And you don't believe any of that crap anyway, do you? If anybody needs to feel guilty, it's me. I should have taken the gun away from him."

I had to smile, despite the gruesome subject of the conversation. Red hadn't known my late partner nearly as well as I had. "I'm not sure you would have managed that without getting shot yourself."

After Lisa Pedrovsky left, I'd finished cleaning up the kitchen and now lay sprawled side by side with Red on the sofa, our feet propped up on the coffee table. The sun sparkled off the ocean just across the dune, inviting us to walk off our dinner. There were three college bowl games we could have watched. Or we could have napped, something both of us desperately needed. Instead we slouched, shoulders touching, and talked about death.

Red took a long time to respond. "Maybe." He turned his head to look at me. "But he probably saved Erik's life."

I shuddered. "That's over and done with. The question now is how much of Pedrovsky's personal animosity toward me is coloring her judgment about these two cases."

"Two?"

"The robberies and the hit-and-run."

"You think they're related?"

I didn't have to see his face. The skepticism fairly dripped from his voice.

"Come on, you heard what Lisa said. There's a common thread." I paused, waiting for him to fill in the blank. When he didn't, I said, "Me."

"That's bullshit!" Red's feet hit the floor, and he spun around to grip my shoulders in his powerful hands. "None of this is your responsibility—not Wyler, not the Hispanic girl, and not Mr. Gadsden. None of it."

I pried his fingers off my arms. "I know I'm not responsible, but there's no denying I'm connected."

"Coincidence," he said, his tone mellowing. "Hell, you know just about everybody in the damn county. It's like that six-degrees-of-separation thing."

That brought a smile. "Okay, let's look at it." I pulled myself up, hurried into the office, and returned with the legal pad I'd been doodling on a few days before.

"A list?" Red asked.

"Your idea. I tried it before, but I didn't get anywhere, probably because I was using your brother's method of laying out what I know. I can see now the problem is that I don't *know* much of anything. So maybe it would be more helpful to figure out what questions I need to ask."

We resumed our positions on the couch. Red crossed his hands over his stomach and stared at the ceiling. "Okay, I'll play."

I flipped over to a fresh page. "My number one priority is Dolores. And Bobby, of course. Where are they?" I said and wrote it at the top of the pad.

"You said Savannah, because of the car rental from the airport over there. Still convinced of that?"

I thought a moment. "Pretty much. So I need to check motels." I wrote that beneath the question. "Or make Hector tell me where they are. Can't you do that? I mean, if Bobby and Serena Montalvo are material witnesses in the hit-and-run, can't you force him to reveal their whereabouts? Lisa didn't seem all that concerned, but didn't you tell me the solicitor was working on warrants for them?"

Red yawned. "Sorry. She was handling that. I can ask her, but I'm not at the top of her hit parade right now."

I let that go and wrote his name next to Hector's. "Okay. Jason Early. What does he have to do with the girl's death? And who was the kid he met at the mall? What did they exchange? If I could just talk to Bobby! Maybe his roommate's heard from him. I've got his name somewhere . . ."

The soft snore startled me, and I looked over to see Red's chin slumped on his chest. I swallowed my annoyance. The man had been up all night tramping around in the rain looking for Romey Gadsden. He needed the rest. I edged myself slowly off the sofa and eased him down, tucking one of the pillows beneath his head. He stirred and stretched out. I laid the afghan over him and tiptoed down the hall to the office.

There had to be more than a hundred motels in the Savannah yellow pages, and I knew the local independent owners probably didn't have the money to advertise. Besides, even Erik couldn't hack into that many computers, and chances were some of the seedier ones operated on a cash-only basis.

So it came back to Hector. He'd never tell me a damn thing. I had to enlist Angie. Her halfhearted agreement that morning to find out where her mother was hadn't fooled me. She'd been twenty years under her father's iron rule. It would take more than a pretty speech from me to convince her to change sides. I scribbled myself a note to get her alone somewhere and put the pressure on.

The sound of Red's snoring drifted in from the great room and made me smile. *Must be lying on his back,* I thought. His brother had been the same way. The thought sent the smile skittering for cover. Was I completely nuts, sleeping with my dead husband's brother? There'd been a time when the very idea had given me the creeps, yet Red and I had somehow tumbled into this relationship that seemed to be headed—where? That was the question.

Or maybe tumbled wasn't the right word. Maybe he'd just worn me down. I cared about him; there was no doubt of that. We sniped and snarled at each other, but underneath I both liked and respected him. We'd been friends before we'd been lovers. Everyone said that made the best basis for a lasting relationship. I loved him. I did. But was that enough?

My mind flew to the pile of evergreens on the bench in the garage, to the Christmas tree I'd almost strapped to the roof of Red's Bronco. *Visions of sugarplums . . .* Scotty and Elinor gleefully ripping through bright wrapping paper and boxes, their father and I beaming across the room at each other . . . *Like a family.* Red's words, ones I had a difficult time relating to.

I could feel the lump rising in my throat. Was that what I was doing? Trying to recreate—no! *Create* a family? Did I think I could somehow wipe out the memory of my own sad childhood by appropriating someone else's? *The Brady Bunch.* Or those old black-and-white reruns on TV Land and Nick at Nite. *Leave It to Beaver. The Donna Reed Show.* Moms in high heels, neatly pressed aprons, and pearls. Dinner on the table every night at six. No shouting. No cursing.

"Shut up!" I said out loud.

I flung papers aside, finally locating the one with the number of Bobby's dorm room. I stabbed the buttons on the phone and glanced at my watch. Not quite five. No self-respecting college boy would be in his room on a Saturday afternoon. I waited through ten rings. No answer and no voice mail. I slammed the handset back in its cradle.

Christmas, you idiot! No doubt everyone had gone home. I tried to recall Hector's words as he and Dolores had stood dripping in the entryway a week ago. *James Fenwick. Anglo. From the North.* As if that narrowed it down. I pulled the keyboard toward me and searched Google with way too many results. Then another name popped into my head. Chad Pickering, the dorm monitor. Maybe he was local. I tried the online white pages using a fifty-mile radius of Charleston as my parameter and came up with six possibles.

I suddenly realized evening had slid into night, the monitor glowing brightly in the dim room. I flipped on the desk light and dialed the first number.

Chadwick Thomas Pickering lived in Mount Pleasant, a bedroom community off Route 17 just across the Cooper River from Charleston. After consulting a map, I'd saved this one for last. It seemed strange that someone who lived that close to the college would pay room and board instead of commuting, but there was no doubt this was the man I'd been searching for. His mother sounded like a typical Southern housewife, pleasant and accommodating, when I spun my tale of wanting to send a holiday gift to my son's friend. She even commiserated with me about my "boy's" inability to remember the correct address for James Fenwick.

"It just seems as if they'd forget their head if it wasn't fastened on, doesn't it? I swear sometimes I think Chad doesn't have the sense God gave an armadillo. But I'm not sure he'll be much help. All his records are probably still at the dorm. He's off with his friends tonight, but I'll surely have him call you the minute he gets home. If it's not too late, of course."

"Tomorrow will be fine." I gave her both my home and cell numbers and my name: Dolores Santiago. "Thank you so much, Mrs. Pickering."

"I'm happy to help, Mrs. Santiago. We mothers have to stick together, don't we?"

Though I'd become an accomplished liar in my short time as a private investigator, even I couldn't bring myself to respond to that.

How else could I go about finding Dolores? I tried to think like Erik, to tap the resources of the Internet and bend them to my purpose. What else did I know about her? I'd been shocked by Angie's tale of her mother's childhood, her being spirited away to the United States by the nuns. *Convent,* I said to myself. A place of sanctuary. It made sense. I plugged in the word plus South Carolina and hit Search.

What popped up were mostly schools or chapter houses connected to large Catholic churches. I thought I should be looking for a separate entity, like Mepkin Abbey, the Trappist monastery outside Charleston. Or maybe my idea of a convent was skewed. The very word conjured up for me drab, forbidding walls built far from old European cities, places where the disgraced or unmarriageable daughters of the wealthy were shut away to spend their lives in poverty and penance.

Ridiculous. Though I'd never visited, I'd seen pictures of Mepkin, a starkly beautiful building surrounded by gardens famous all across the Southeast. I narrowed my search to the corridor between Savannah and Charleston and checked each one. Only two seemed to have possibilities, and I copied their numbers onto the legal pad. Of course, Dolores's rescuers could have come from anywhere, but these seemed a likely place to start.

I chewed on the eraser end of a pencil, trying to come up with a believable story that might induce someone at a convent to part with information. In the end, I decided to go with some semblance of the truth. Even a backslidden Episcopalian can get edgy about lying to a nun.

I needn't have worried. Neither of the convents I called had ever conducted missions to Central America, and neither had a policy of harboring fugitives, although the concept was certainly part of their theology. But a very helpful sister, who sounded not much out of her teens, suggested I try Our Lady of Guadalupe, a small church on the outskirts of Savannah, which ministered to the growing Hispanic population in the area and whose priest had been active at one time in the mission field, she thought maybe in Central America. I took down their number with a rising feeling of excitement. I had my fingers poised over the keypad on the telephone when Red's voice over my shoulder made me jump.

"What are you doing?"

I turned my head to stare up at him as his hands settled on my shoulders. "Checking out convents."

His laugh brought an answering smile. "Surely I haven't been that hard to live with, have I?"

"Don't worry. I got the idea that maybe Dolores has sought sanctuary with the nuns who rescued her from Guatemala. I struck out there, but one of the sisters gave me some information on a church near Savannah that might be helpful."

"Then don't let me interrupt. I'm going to hunt down something to eat. Bring you anything?"

I shook my head. "Not right now. Thanks."

He padded out into the hallway, and I punched in the number of Our Lady of Guadalupe. The phone rang seven times before rolling over into voice mail. I left my name and number and followed Red into the kitchen.

"Any luck?" he asked.

"Nobody home. I'll try tomorrow. There certainly has to be someone around on Sundays." The idea simply popped into my head. "Or we could go to church. You game?"

Red slathered mayonnaise on two pieces of bread and began stacking thin slices of roast beef on top. "Sorry. I'm on duty at noon."

"I think I'll see if they have a Web site and get the time of the services. Might be easier to approach the priest if I can say something nice about his sermon."

"Homily." Red slapped on the top slice of bread and cut the sandwich neatly in half. "In the Catholic Church, I think it's usually called a homily."

"How do you know so much about it?" Red's and Rob's family had been staunchly Baptist for countless generations, although neither of the boys had carried much religion into adulthood.

He bit into the sandwich. "Old girlfriend," he mumbled around a mouthful of roast beef.

"I should have known," I said and carried a Diet Coke back into the office.

From the great room I could hear the whoops and shrieks of a college football game in progress. I located Our Lady's small site and jotted down the times of their services. I scribbled a few notes for myself, tidied up the office, and checked that my navy suit looked presentable enough for church. I found Red slumped on the sofa, about a third of the sandwich uneaten on the plate wavering precariously in his hand. The room lay in darkness, the only light provided by the flickering television screen.

I tiptoed in to slide the plate from his hand, tucked the afghan around him again, and turned off the TV. I thought about taking a turn around outside, to see if the watcher had come back, but somehow I couldn't bring myself to leave the warmth and safety of the house. Except for the call to Glory Merrick, he'd been quiet for almost forty-eight hours. I thought about Erik's suggestion of an armed patrol, glad I hadn't taken him up on it. I would have felt like a fool with off-duty deputies lurking behind trees and shrubbery and coming up empty. I satisfied myself with double-checking the doors and making certain the alarm was set.

By the time I'd showered and dried my hair, Red still hadn't appeared in the bedroom, so I slid beneath the covers alone and picked up my book from the bedside table. I half expected Chad Pickering to call, hopefully with the contact information for James Fenwick, but the phone sat stubbornly mute as I lost myself in the ratiocination of Poirot's little gray cells. I thought about climbing out of bed and dragging Red in from the great room, but the effort seemed too much. I fell asleep with the book spread open on my chest.

I dreamed about glass breaking. Or maybe not. I hung suspended between waking and sleeping, trying to focus on the clock beside my bed. The fuzzy red numbers finally came into focus.

It was precisely 3:16 A.M. when the alarm system went off.

CHAPTER
TWENTY-EIGHT

RED'S UNEXPECTED PRESENCE IN THE BED STARTLED me almost as much as the shrieking.

The phone rang. The man from the security company sounded like the same one as a few days earlier. I gave my password, and he assured me that help was on the way.

By the time I hung up, Red had tugged on his sweatpants and ripped his gun from its holster.

"Wait!" I shouted as he fumbled for his shoes. "They're sending a unit."

No response.

"Red!" I called when he disappeared into the hallway.

"Stay there!" he yelled over his shoulder. "I want this bastard myself."

I flung back the duvet, grabbed up my robe, and stumbled after him.

The cold hit me like a slap as I rounded the corner into the great room. The drapes billowed out from the French doors Red had jerked open. I hurried across the carpet, yelping when my bare foot crunched against the litter of broken glass. I felt the sliver bury itself deep in my sole. Cursing, I hopped back to the hallway and crawled up the steps into the kitchen, flinging on lights as I went. I scrabbled in my purse for the Seecamp, my breath harsh in my chest until my hand wrapped around the comforting grip of the little pistol.

I jerked my gaze in the direction of the bay window where blue lights suddenly lit up the driveway. I huddled on the steps, dripping blood onto the polished wooden floor, my head constantly scanning. Outside, I could hear voices, deep and male, bouncing off the walls of the house, ebbing and flowing, as identities were established and orders given. Through the thick twisted limbs of the oaks, I saw lights winking on in my neighbors' windows.

A few moments later, a shadow appeared on the deck, his silhouette dark against the glow spilling out into the night.

"Hold it!" I yelled and pushed myself erect. I leaned heavily against the wall and steadied the gun with my left hand.

"Officer!" the man shouted. "Lower your weapon, Mrs. Tanner."

Slowly, he moved toward the light, the sleeve of his brown jacket following the massive gun gripped in his hand. Then the other eased out, his badge glinting in the lamplight, and I felt myself relax. I lowered my arm and set the Seecamp on the counter of the built-in desk. I let myself slide back to the floor, the trail of blood from my foot smearing across the hardwood.

"You're hurt." He crossed the carpet in a few long strides, crunching glass under his heavy shoes.

"It's just a cut."

"I'll check out the interior, if you're sure you're okay."

I nodded and watched him move down the hall, gun poised, stepping cautiously into each room until he'd covered them all. He holstered his weapon and returned to kneel in front of me. As if in a daze, I let this stranger lift my foot and inspect the damage.

"I can see it in there," he said, his voice suddenly soft. "We'll get someone to look at it."

"Where's Red? Did you find anyone?"

The deputy shook his head. "No, ma'am, but the sergeant and my partner are still out there." He cast a glance over his shoulder.

"Looks like maybe someone just playing a prank. Doesn't appear they really tried to get in."

For the first time I noticed the can lying amid the broken glass. Even from my spot huddled on the kitchen steps I could tell it was Campbell's soup, its familiar white-and-red label clearly visible against the cream-colored carpet. I pushed myself up, the sudden movement taking the deputy by surprise. I hobbled closer, shaking off his hand under my arm.

"Ma'am?" I heard him say. "Mrs. Tanner? Maybe it's not—"

I skirted the glass and stared down at the can. I was only vaguely aware of Red's appearance in the doorway.

"Bay? Ah, Jesus, you're bleeding!" he said.

I felt his arms around me, his hand cupping the back of my head.

"It's vegetable," I murmured against his shoulder. "I hate goddamned vegetable soup."

Everyone wanted to call the paramedics, but I just wanted them out of my house. The deputies had found nothing outside—no footprints or tracks to indicate who might have stood on my deck and heaved a soup can through the French doors. I had no way of telling if either of them knew about the previous attempt to scare the hell out of me, or about the threatening phone calls, but at that point I didn't care.

Red talked to them for a long time out in the driveway before I heard him moving around, checking windows and resetting the alarm. He found me perched on the closed lid of the toilet with a pair of tweezers in my hand and my reading glasses perched on the end of my nose.

"Here, let me do that," he said, advancing into the bathroom.

"No! I've almost got it. Get out of the light."

I couldn't suppress a small yelp of pain as I finally jerked free the sliver of glass from the bottom of my foot. I winced again when I swung myself over to the bathtub and cranked up the hot water. I felt

Red kneel beside me, a washcloth in his hand. I let him soap the cut and rinse it, then dry my foot on a fluffy towel. The bleeding had nearly stopped by the time I swabbed it with disinfectant and allowed Red to apply two Band-Aids.

He would have carried me back to bed if I'd let him.

Instead he followed as I limped into the bedroom and retrieved a pair of flip-flops from the closet.

"What are you doing?"

"Cleaning up the mess," I said, edging around him.

"Already done. I swept the glass and screwed a piece of plywood from the garage over the hole in the door. It'll do until we can get the glass company in here."

I stopped and stared out toward the deck. "Thanks. How about the blood on the steps?"

"Sorry, I don't do floors," he said, and I knew he was trying to get some reaction out of me.

"You go back to bed. I'll take care of it."

"Bay." The warm laughter had left his voice.

I two-footed the steps and opened the doors under the sink where Dolores kept the day-to-day cleaning supplies. His hand on my shoulder fell just short of gentle.

"Bay, damn it! Turn around and look at me."

"What? If I don't get the blood out, it'll stain—"

"Forget about the goddamned floor! I think you're in shock or something. You need to get some rest, get off that foot. Now quit screwing around and let me take you back to bed."

"Back off, Red." I tried to force a smile, but my face just wouldn't cooperate. He opened his mouth, but I cut him off. "I mean it. *You* go back to bed and just leave me the hell alone!"

The last came out more strident than I'd intended, but it did the trick. Red stomped down the steps, muttering to himself. I caught the words *stubborn* and what might have been *pain in the ass* before he disappeared into the bedroom.

I carried the wood floor cleaner and a rag and settled onto the top step. Absently, I worked at the darkened streaks of blood that had pooled in the grooves while I fought the urge to pound my fists or fling dishes against the wall. The anger surged through me in waves, bouncing around in my chest until I felt as if it would explode.

I was angry at whoever the scumbag was who was getting his jollies by terrorizing me in the middle of the night. But I was more angry at *me,* for allowing myself to be intimidated, quivering in fear, waiting for Red or one of the sheriff's deputies to rescue me. For the past few years—ever since Rob's murder, really—I'd worked at becoming self-sufficient, relying on nothing and no one to keep me safe and happy. And here I was sliding into the role of a helpless, feeble woman counting on her man to scare the bogeyman back into the closet.

"No more," I said into the predawn stillness of the house. *I would find out who was trying to frighten me and why. And put a stop to it. Me.*

I took a last swipe at the floor, threw the rag in the trash, and limped down into the great room. On the sofa, I pulled the afghan around me, leaving free the hand firmly gripping the Seecamp. I watched the sun slip up over the horizon, its streaks of orange and gold glistening across the top of the ocean before I finally pushed myself up and dragged my throbbing foot behind me into the bathroom.

Time to get dressed for church.

CHAPTER
TWENTY-NINE

IT WAS LARGER THAN I'D EXPECTED BASED ON THE limited amount of information I'd found on the Web site, but the parking lot was crowded when I pulled beneath an overhanging branch of an arching live oak a little before ten. The sky to the west was darkening, another line of rain showers, I thought. A sudden breeze rippled through the drooping leaves of the venerable old tree.

Judging by the vehicles arrayed in neat rows on the rough gravel, it was a congregation of modest means. Lots of pickup trucks and Chevrolet and Ford sedans. Only a couple of older SUVs. The Jaguar looked decidedly out of place. On impulse, I backed around and tucked it between some sort of outbuilding and the side of the church.

I slid out of the car and kicked off my flip-flop, forcing my swollen right foot into the navy pump. It hurt like hell, but I didn't want to call attention to myself any more than I had to. I reached behind me and slid out Romey Gadsden's walking stick. That and the limp—along with my unfamiliar face—would certainly make me stand out, but it couldn't be helped. Navigating in high heels with only one working foot wasn't possible without something to lean on. I hoped Mr. Rom would understand.

It was slow going over the gravel. A young couple with an adorable black-haired little girl smiled shyly as we approached the short flight of steps at almost the same moment. The woman swung the child up onto her shoulder while her husband paused to offer me his arm.

"*Señora? Permítame?*"

"Thank you." I hobbled up the steps with his hand firmly under my elbow.

"*De nada,*" he said, moving off to rejoin his family.

I slipped into the last pew, empty except for an old woman at the far end, head bowed, gnarled fingers working her rosary beads. I slid my shoe off and propped my foot on the kneeler in front of me.

The sanctuary filled rapidly, a low murmur of conversation spreading out as friends and families greeted each other. Most of the faces were Latino, and I could pick out only a little of the Spanish that rippled around me. There were a few other Anglos scattered throughout the modest space, but we were definitely in the minority.

At precisely ten o'clock, the priest made his entrance, and the service began. Outside, the light faded as the storm edged closer. Organ music filled the room, and I did my best to follow the unfamiliar ritual, rising and sitting with everyone else, just as I had done earlier at Theresa Montalvo's memorial service on Hilton Head. I understood very little of the Mass itself, but the warmth and obvious faith of the people around me gradually calmed my fears of making a mistake, and I found myself wishing I could follow the actual words. In almost no time, it seemed, I was rising with my fellow congregants to receive the priest's final blessing.

While people moved out into the center aisle, I sat down, forced my bandaged foot back into my shoe, and turned to gather up my things. As I glanced up, my eye lighted on a familiar face, a white one, talking animatedly to a swarthy man in a shiny gray suit. I ducked my head, fumbled a tissue out of my purse, and held it against my face. I counted slowly to fifty before risking another glance, but the pair had already moved past. I rose and pushed myself into the stream of stragglers, nodding and smiling at the soft greetings of strangers, and leaned on Romey's walking stick as I inched my way toward the door.

I kept my quarry in sight as the pair stopped to exchange a few words with the priest before moving down the steps. I edged out of line and bypassed Father Cordero, nodding in his direction and ignoring his obvious interest in the newcomer limping out of his church. Wind whipped my hair, and thunder rumbled overhead. The two men paused a moment before shaking hands and turning in opposite directions. For the second time in less than a week, I saw the boy's hand slide smoothly into his pocket.

I didn't have to think about which one to follow.

Keeping myself behind the knots of worshippers chatting on the narrow walkway in front of the church, I crept cautiously after Jason Early.

He drove the same white Dodge Neon he'd used to whisk Serena Montalvo away from her sister's memorial service. I stumbled to the Jaguar and pulled out of the parking lot, allowing a couple of pickups to get between us. The recession away from the church rolled sedately down the narrow two-lane blacktop, most of the vehicles peeling off as we neared the interstate.

I followed Jason up onto I-95 North, my mind whirling with unanswerable questions about what the hell he was doing in a Hispanic church in Savannah. But I'd last seen him with Bobby Santiago's girlfriend. And where Bobby was, I would likely find Dolores. I hunkered down for the chase, a little concerned that my gas gauge hovered at under half a tank.

As we rolled into South Carolina, the storm hit, pelting the windshield with raindrops the size of quarters before settling into a steady downpour. I edged up a little closer to the Neon, worried I might lose him in the gloom, although there wasn't any place for him to go except at the exits. Eight miles later, he surprised me by cutting off the freeway at the Hilton Head sign. I stayed back as he brought the Neon to a stop at the head of the ramp and banged my hand on the steering wheel when he turned left.

He was on his way home.

I hesitated, then whipped the Jag across the lanes, the tires taking a moment to bite on the slick roadway. At the dead end, we went right, toward Ridgeland. With the sparse traffic on 17, I had to keep well back, but I thought I knew his destination, and a few miles later he proved me right. The little car bounced over the ruts, past the abandoned gas station. The headlamps skittered across the old plywood covering the windows, making it appear, for just a moment, as if someone had switched on a light inside. Then the car disappeared around the corner.

I pulled off onto the gravel apron in front of a boiled peanut stand, its weathered boards swaying a little in the wind. *Now what?* I asked myself and felt the disappointment sitting like a hard lump in the pit of my stomach. I was damn sure Jason's bizarre mother wasn't harboring three "spic" refugees in her front parlor. So where were they? Dolores had her own rental car, but it only made sense to me that they would all be together.

Unless Jason had only come home for a little while, maybe to change clothes. I stared across the road toward the dilapidated house.

Who was the man Jason had been talking to in front of the church? Maybe I'd made the wrong decision to follow Early. Maybe I should have stuck with his friend.

The windows fogged up as I sat brooding in the rain, and I flipped on the defroster. The haze began to clear just as an old truck suddenly lurched from behind the derelict gas station and pulled out onto the empty road. It looked as if someone had taken a baseball bat to the entire expanse of faded green metal. I couldn't really see the driver, but there seemed to be at least two people in the cab.

I counted to ten, jerked the car into gear, and spun gravel as I set out in pursuit.

*   *   *

"Where the hell are you?" Red's voice barked at me from the cell phone.

"We're just coming into Hardeeville on 17."

"Do you even know who it is you're tailing?"

I took a long calming breath. "It's someone from Jason Early's house, maybe him, maybe not. But these people are connected to Dolores and Bobby."

"You don't know that. What if it was just some guy sleeping off a drunk behind that old gas station? What if he spots you and gets pissed off?"

"Are you coming or not?" I'd called Red for backup, expecting him to share my hunch that the battered old truck might lead me to my missing housekeeper. Apparently I'd overestimated my powers of persuasion.

"I can't drop everything and run just because you've got some screwball idea stuck in your head. I told you we were working on it. Back off and let us do our job."

Yeah, right, I thought. What I said was, "Look. Even if it turns out to be a wild goose chase, at least I'm doing something."

I hadn't meant it as a criticism, but Red took it that way. "You call running off half-cocked 'doing something'? Use your head, Bay." I could almost see him scowling. "Don't do anything stupid."

"Thanks for your help." I stabbed the Off button with my thumb and tossed the cell onto the seat beside me. "And the hell with you," I said aloud to the empty car.

Up ahead, the traffic signal turned green, and the truck took a right. I followed sedately, bumping across a set of railroad tracks so uneven the Jag rocked from side to side. The rain had let up a little, and a few pieces of blue sky peeked out from time to time. The truck kept to the speed limit down a road I'd never been on before. Through the slower beat of the wipers, I could definitely see two heads through the hazy back window of the truck.

At another T-intersection, I watched them go right, and I thought we must be close to the Savannah River. On the left, large houses sat well back from the road behind rolling lawns. Trying to hang back and still keep my quarry in sight, I caught a glimpse of a historical marker, but the mist from the river obscured most of it. Something about Huguenots, I thought. Maybe some of my ancestors.

I jerked myself back to the realization that the truck ahead of me had disappeared at almost the same moment the rain stopped. I gunned the engine and nearly missed the overgrown entrance to a defunct housing development, its faded sign announcing expansive homes on large lots, many directly on the river, at affordable prices. Apparently someone hadn't agreed with the developer's assessment. I slowed and turned into the weed-choked drive. On the right, two houses, almost completed, stood forlornly amid rain-soaked vegetation that seemed to be reclaiming the land.

No sign of the truck, but I followed the cracked roadway at a crawl. Even with the windows closed, I could hear the swift rush of the river ahead. Above me, the sun popped out, glinting off the pools of standing water. I rounded a bend, overhung with willow branches, and slammed on the brakes.

The truck had been pulled sideways across the narrow road, blocking my path. The driver's door opened, and a swarthy man with wide shoulders slid to the ground and faced me. Dressed in a sweat-shirt, jeans, and jacket, he stood over six feet tall, his black hair slicked straight back off a striking face. He flicked a cigarette butt into the weeds and stared at me, his gaze more perplexed than angry.

I slid my bag onto my lap and wrapped my fingers around the pistol.

With a slow, steady gait, he approached the Jaguar. I pushed the gearshift into reverse, left the motor running, and slid the window down a couple of inches. I rested the gun on my thigh, where he could see it. I was armed, inside a locked car, with a clear avenue of escape behind me. I lifted my chin, ready to demand some answers, when movement from the truck caught my eye.

I realized I had misjudged his passenger when a huge dog jumped down onto the roadway and bounded toward me.

CHAPTER
THIRTY

¡SIÉNTATE!"
 I heard the sharp words through the crack in the window and watched the dog drop immediately onto its back haunches. The man spoke more softly, and I missed the next instruction, but the animal's ears pricked to attention.

Now that I could see it up close, the dog looked to be a combination of mostly German shepherd and some other breed that gave added depth to its chest and shoulders. Its coat, too, had more black in it than a purebred shepherd's, glistening with raindrops dripping from the overhanging branches of the trees that lined the narrow roadway.

Over the sound of the river, I could hear the deep, rolling vibrations in its throat, somehow more menacing than any outright bark or growl.

Waving a pointed finger at the dog, the man turned his attention back to me. I wiped sweat from my right hand on the skirt of my suit and regripped the pistol. I sat up straighter as he approached the car.

"Buenos días, Señora. May I help you?"

His smile seemed sincere, the puzzled lift of his brows genuine when his attention fastened on the gun in my lap. Something about the eyes, though, even before he'd spotted the pistol. Wary. Alert.

Certainly not a match for the unconcern in his voice and the slouch of his powerful shoulders.

I nudged the window down another inch, and he had to lean over to speak through the opening. It put him at a disadvantage. After admonishing the dog, he'd shoved both hands in the pockets of his Windbreaker. Nothing telltale bulged, but I kept my gaze on his right arm.

"Maybe," I said in answer to his question, pitching my voice toward the crack of the open window. "I'm looking for some friends of mine. I thought you might be able to give me some information."

"What friends are these, *Señora*? I am new to America. I know only my cousin and his family. And my coworkers, of course."

The accent was almost right, but the syntax rang false, especially for someone who claimed to have been in the country only a short time. Dolores had lived here for years, and she still sometimes sounded as if she'd just encountered English, was still translating from Spanish in her head before she spoke. And *coworkers*. That wasn't a word you learned right off the bat.

"Your English is very good," I said with a smile. "You must be an accomplished linguist."

He scrunched up his face, shaking his head as if in confusion, but again the eyes gave him away. He had understood me perfectly.

"Why you follow me, eh?" The amiable grin wobbled a little. As if in answer to the change in his tone of voice, the dog growled low in his throat.

"*Azúcar! Silencio!*"

At his words, the dog dropped to the ground, its ears now flattened against its massive head.

I tightened my fingers around the gun. I loved animals, but I'd shoot this one in a heartbeat if he made a move toward the car.

"*Señora?*"

"I saw you pull out from the Earlys' driveway. I'm certain Jason knows where my friends are, but his mother won't let him talk to me." I didn't have to feign the concern that wrinkled my forehead. "I'm worried about them."

"I do not know this Jason." His face closed into a scowl. "And why does a rich Anglo lady care about Chicanos?"

"Who said they were Mexicans?"

Our eyes met through the narrow crack of the window, and I watched the mistake register on his rugged face. In a second, he'd regained control.

"I know only my cousin. I no can help. You go away now, *Señora*."

His nearly black eyes held mine. It might have been wishful thinking that I saw a flicker of something like regret behind his intimidating gaze. And something almost familiar.

His next words dispelled any idea I had that this man might be reasoned with. "Better for you. Better for *everyone. Comprende? Márchese!*"

"Wait!" My fingers twitched on the pistol, but he seemed to sense I wasn't prepared to shoot him in order to win his cooperation. "I don't mean anyone any harm. Dolores Santiago. She's my friend. And her son, Roberto. They may be in trouble. Please. I just want to find them. Help them, if I can."

I could tell I was wasting my breath, even before he said again, in English this time, "Go away, *Señora*." The man turned his back on me. He snapped his fingers, and the huge dog leaped to its feet. He patted the damp head, and I was surprised to see the long tail twitch as if in pleasure. Man and dog climbed back into the truck, and a moment later I saw the backup lights flash on.

I debated refusing to move, wondering if he'd come back and talk some more, but my gut told me it would be futile. So would tailing him, now that I'd bungled it so badly. I smacked the palm of my left hand on the steering wheel, slid the gun over onto the passenger seat, and began backing away. But not before I'd memorized the license plate number on the truck and stored away the dark, brooding face for future reference.

*   *   *

I didn't recognize the vehicle pulled up in front of Presqu'isle. The bright red sports car looked like some kind of overgrown insect squatting in the gravel of the semicircular drive. I studied its markings as I moved toward the stairs. A Porsche. Virginia plates. It looked vintage, but its finish gleamed in the waning sunlight.

The front steps were still damp from the earlier rain, and I moved cautiously as I climbed up to the verandah. I pushed open the front door to the sound of laughter and the rattle of crystal coming from the front parlor. I slipped off my shoes and limped down the hall, Romey Gadsden's walking stick making a sharp tapping on the heart pine floor.

Lavinia stuck her head around the doorway. "Bay! What a nice surprise. Come in. We have company."

The scowl on her face didn't match the cheerful words. Neither she nor the Judge encouraged visitors, especially not the kind that called for drinks in the formal receiving room my mother had used only on the most august of occasions. I stepped forward, and her puckered frown deepened.

"What's happened to your leg, child? You're limping. And where are your shoes?"

I waved away her concern. "It's no big deal. I stepped on a piece of glass and cut my foot. It's a little swollen." I saw her gaze drop to the carved stick. "I . . . I'm returning it. To Mr. Gadsden."

I watched the question form on her lips, and my mind raced to come up with a plausible reason for me to have the cane in my possession. But I was saved by my father's booming voice.

"Bay, is that you? Get in here, daughter. Come see who just got washed up by the storm."

With a speculative look that spoke far more than words, Lavinia turned and disappeared into the parlor. I hobbled along behind her, cursing myself for being stupid enough to drag the stick along with me. Truth to tell, it had become natural, almost an extension of my arm. I'd be sad to give it up.

A fire burned in the Italian marble fireplace, and Lavinia had obviously finished her holiday decorating. I had an intense flash of déjà vu when I stepped into the room. The aroma of fresh pine lay heavily on the air, and gilded ornaments glittered from almost every surface, including the eight-foot tree towering in the far corner. It looked exactly as it had every Christmas week of my childhood—elegant, exquisite, and untouchable.

The woman who rose from the brocaded wing chair nearly matched me in height. Her gray-blond hair had been piled in a deceptively casual knot on the top of her head. The suit looked expensive and fit her as if it had been hand-tailored, and probably not in America. She forced a smile, glancing sideways at my father before she set her wineglass on the marble-topped table and rose.

"Bay, darlin'," the Judge boomed, "get on in here and give your Aunt Loretta a hug!"

Lavinia brought a low stool with a needlepoint cover worked by some long-dead plantation mistress, and I propped my throbbing foot up onto it, mumbling an explanation about stepping on a broken glass. The Judge seemed unconcerned about my injury, beaming from across the room, his wheelchair tucked next to the fireplace.

"What do you think about that, eh, daughter?" I hadn't seen him grin that much since the Republicans took back the governor's mansion in Columbia.

"Now, Tally, let her be." The woman resumed her seat and crossed her slender legs at the ankles. "There's no reason Bay should remember me. It's been . . . what? Twenty-five years or more? Emmy was still alive, so it has to be at least that, wouldn't you say?"

Emmy? Surely she couldn't be talking about my mother. Emmaline

Baynard Simpson had never been called *Emmy*. Never! At least not in my lifetime.

"I was just about to make tea." Lavinia's eyes darted repeatedly to where I'd propped Mr. Gadsden's walking stick against the love seat.

"That would be nice, thanks." I didn't bother to offer my help, and a moment later Lavinia scurried from the room.

"I thought my mother was an only child," I said. I tried for lightness, but I heard the statement come out sounding like an accusation.

"Of course she was. Her poor mother nearly died giving birth to her, or so the story goes." She raised a perfectly arched eyebrow. "I heard your grandmother sent poor James off to his own bedroom after that. Not that the old scalawag didn't find his comforts elsewhere, eh, Tally? Baynard men weren't known for their celibacy."

She tilted her head at my father, her slow smile and husky voice dripping with innuendo.

"So is *aunt* just an honorary title then?"

The Judge shot me an admonitory lift of one of his shaggy brows.

"Of course. Actually, we'd be more like cousins. Your mother and mine were at Braxton. The two of us spent quite a lot of time together when you were just a toddler. I used to look after you while they planned their galas and teas." She cocked her head toward the dining room. "I can still see them in their pastel dresses, huddled together around that massive old table." She sighed, and a look of genuine regret flickered in her eyes. "Then they had some sort of falling out. If either one of them was still alive, they'd probably have a hard time remembering what it was all about. It's a shame. They might have been a comfort to each other in their last years."

I waited, but she seemed to have run down. Then, suddenly, that arch smile was back on her face.

"Water over the dam. You look wonderful, Bay. The years have treated you well."

She raised her glass in my direction and drained it. The Judge toggled his wheelchair controls and lifted the bottle of deep red wine from the side table. He filled the delicate crystal and poured more for himself. Lavinia stepped into the room and set the silver tea service on the low table in front of me. I glanced up, but she'd already turned away.

"I have some scones ready to come out of the oven. Bay, will you pour?" she tossed over her shoulder on her way out the door.

"Let me," Loretta said. "You just sit there and rest that leg of yours."

Apparently the training our mothers had received at the exclusive finishing school outside Charleston had been drummed into her as well. She poured and served flawlessly.

I accepted the steaming cup, part of the Meissen service, I thought, and nodded my thanks.

"How quaint that Mrs. Smalls still keeps to all the old ways." Her gaze swept the perfectly decorated room. "I thought I'd drown in Southern tradition before I made my escape to college. Polishing silver and dusting baseboards, making calls and writing thank-you notes. I couldn't wait to get out of the nineteenth century. I can guarantee you I didn't need to know how to arrange roses or put up scuppernong jam at Harvard, although some of it did come in handy during my career."

I sipped the tea and tried to decide how old Loretta must be. My mother had chosen to skip the reproductive thing until menopause threw her off, and I popped up unexpectedly. Loretta's mother probably started at a reasonable age, so she could be anywhere from late forties to near sixty. Whatever her age, she'd had some work done, at least a lift here or there. There wasn't a line or wrinkle marring her perfectly made-up face.

"And what career was that?" I asked, more from politeness than from any real interest.

The Judge seemed to be hanging on her every word, but I found her presence intrusive. I'd planned to spend what was left of

Sunday afternoon laying out everything about Dolores's disappearance in front of my father, hoping that, between the two of us, we'd come up with some sort of scheme to find her. I was wondering if we'd be forced to invite Loretta to dinner when her answer snapped my head up.

"I'm an immigration attorney. Or at least, I was. I spent a lot of time with the old INS. My husband was a diplomat. We didn't have children, so I traveled the world with him. There was always a place for me at whatever embassy he got assigned to. It was a wonderful life." Real pain sliced through her next words, but she avoided my eyes. "I lost him about a year ago. Cancer. It got ugly toward the end, so it was a blessing when he went."

"I'm sorry," I said.

She seemed to shake herself then and mustered a smile. "Tally tells me you're a private investigator. How deliciously wicked! Your mother would have been appalled! Doesn't leave you much time for the garden club and the historical society, I'll bet." Her laugh held just a trace of bitterness. "Emmy must be spinning."

At that moment, a scowling Lavinia carried in a silver tray heaped with steaming scones. I could tell she'd overheard that last remark of Loretta's by the thin line of her compressed lips. Despite my mother's autocratic treatment, Lavinia was always the first to rush to her defense.

"How lovely, Mrs. Smalls," Loretta said, accepting a linen napkin and one of the gold-rimmed dessert plates. "And how kind of you to remember that cranberry was always my favorite."

Lavinia ignored her, served my father, and flounced out without a word.

"I think I've given offense," our visitor said with a gleam in her eye. "Remind me to apologize before I leave."

"Nothing to be sorry for," my father said. "It's just that Vinnie's a mite protective of Emmaline, even after all these years."

"It's charming," Loretta said before setting her untouched plate on the side table. "Loyalty from servants is so rare these days."

I bristled, but Loretta didn't give me an opportunity to come to Lavinia's defense.

"Why don't we go out on the back verandah, Bay? I've missed the spectacular Lowcountry sunsets."

Without waiting for a reply, she swept out into the foyer. I hauled myself to my feet, glancing back at my father's puzzled face. I reached for Mr. Gadsden's walking stick and hobbled out after her. I followed the sharp tap of her heels around to the wide back porch with its magnificent view of St. Helena Sound and the tiny islands that dotted its expanse. I dropped into one of the plantation rockers and watched my "aunt" flick a gold lighter and touch it to a stubby unfiltered cigarette. The heavy tobacco smell brought me up short. *Gauloises,* I thought, and a brief pain stabbed my chest at the memory of Alain Darnay, my onetime lover. Somehow I'd always associate the aroma of the strong French cigarettes with his unforgivable treachery.

"So what did you want to talk to me about?" I asked.

Loretta stood at the rail, gazing out across the water, smoke curling around her slender frame.

When she didn't respond, I lifted my leg onto a low stool. "Come on. I haven't fallen off the back of a turnip truck in decades."

Loretta glanced at me over the elegant shoulder of her jacket. "Neither have I. I heard you were sharp. I told them you probably wouldn't buy that I just dropped in here after twenty-five years to renew old acquaintance."

"Almost," I said. "But that last crack about my mother was a little over the top."

She turned and faced me. "Sorry. God, I hate this place! As I said, I couldn't wait to get out. I always felt as if it would smother me one day." She drew again on the cigarette. "Word is you generally stop in at Presqu'isle on Sundays." She shrugged. "So I took a chance. Besides, I haven't seen Tally in way too long." She blew smoke out into the gathering twilight. "I have to say you've got yourself mixed up in a real doozy this time, Bay. Harry Reynolds tells me you probably aren't going to get scared off by any official request, either."

"Are you talking about the FBI guy? The one who interviewed me about the bank robbery?"

"The same. Poor Harry. You put quite a dent in his ego." Her laugh came out like a sharp bark. "He just can't believe the old Reynolds charm didn't even ruffle your feathers." Again she exhaled smoke toward the water. "Implied threats didn't seem to work, either."

I thought back to my conversation with Harry Reynolds in the elegant front parlor. "He seemed to know a lot about me. And my friends." I waited, but she didn't react. "And he's right. I'm not easily intimidated."

"Look, Bay, you're screwing with a very important operation. Just as we're about to get a handle on what's been going down in this stuffy little backwater, you suddenly pop into the picture." She shrugged. "Once I saw your name on Harry's interview report, I volunteered to slide in here and see exactly what you're up to."

"Who's 'we'? Who exactly do you work for?"

The long fingers of her right hand slid into the pocket of the slim jacket and extracted a card. She flipped it into my lap.

Stunned, I read the words aloud. "Loretta Healey, Special Consultant to the President of the United States on Immigration and Homeland Security."

CHAPTER THIRTY-ONE

*D*ON'T BE TOO IMPRESSED." LORETTA HEALEY DUNKED the stub of her French cigarette in the rainwater collected in a plant saucer and straightened. "Big title, not much authority. Luckily, I don't need to do it for the money. Contrary to popular belief, the government can be downright stingy when it serves their purposes."

I stared at her, this elegant woman who had the ear of the president. "What the hell's going on? Why would Homeland Security be interested in me?"

She flicked imaginary dirt from the seat of the rocker next to mine and lowered herself into it. "They're not. Not directly." She fiddled with the gold lighter, flicking it on and off. "Look, I really don't want to get into it now. Unless you want Tally involved?"

I shook my head. "When can we meet? Can you come to Hilton Head? I have an office—"

"I know. That sounds good. Tomorrow, then, say ten o'clock?"

She tucked the lighter back in her pocket and stood in one fluid motion. The look she gave me was both amused and speculative, as if I were some naughty child who just might have the potential to cause real trouble.

I rose with her. "I don't much like games," I said. "I hope you'll be prepared to explain yourself tomorrow."

Loretta patted my arm, the patronizing gesture raising my hackles. "Take it easy, Bay. We're on the same team."

"We'll see," I mumbled and followed her back inside.

Lavinia looked up guiltily from the chair next to the Judge's and jumped to her feet. Her words carried not a hint of her usual warmth. "We take our dinner at noontime, so we generally have a light supper on Sunday evenings. You're welcome to stay, Mrs. Healey."

"Aunt" Loretta scooped up a chic black bag from the wing chair. "Thank you so much, Mrs. Smalls, but I really must be going."

"Nonsense!" the Judge boomed. "Where are you rushing off to? You can't just drop in for an hour after all these years and then dash off again."

I saw Lavinia tense, and her hands were clutched together so tightly I could see the veins standing out. "I'm sure Mrs. Healey has other friends to visit," she said. Only someone who knew her as well as I did could detect the real anger beneath the feigned politeness.

"I'll drop by again before I head back to Washington." Loretta's eyes flicked to Lavinia. "If that's all right."

You would have needed a microscope to detect Lavinia's chin barely dip.

"Of course. Come to dinner. Vinnie'll whip up something special." My father seemed completely oblivious to the undercurrents of hostility bouncing around the room.

"We'll see." Loretta leaned down to plant a lingering kiss on the Judge's cheek. "I'll call." She whirled in my direction. "Bay, lovely to see you again. Thank you so much for your hospitality, Mrs. Smalls," she added, wisely making no attempt to offer her hand to Lavinia.

"I'll see you out." I followed her down the hallway, where she paused at the front door.

"Take care of yourself," Loretta said loudly, for the benefit of those still left in the parlor. More softly, she said, "Tomorrow at ten. Try to stay out of trouble until then."

In a swirl of exotic French perfume, she was gone.

I limped back into the parlor to find the Judge pouring the last of the wine into his glass. From the kitchen, I heard the exaggerated banging of pans and slamming of cupboard doors.

"How about that?" my father said when I sank onto the love seat and swung my legs up onto the brocade cushions. "I don't think I've even thought of Loretta or her mother for twenty years."

"What's she doing here, did she say?" I wondered what kind of tale she'd spun to cover her sudden appearance. I still found it difficult to believe she'd come all this way just to make me feel like a meddling child. I'd need some time alone to sort through all the conflicting ideas banging around in my head.

"Just passing through, thought she'd look up some old friends. She was overseas when your mother passed away, but I remember she sent a nice note and some truly spectacular orchids."

"Mother hated orchids." I wanted no part of my father's fond remembrances. "Lavinia's seriously ticked off," I added.

"Nonsense. What would she be upset about?"

I laughed. "For someone who prides himself on being able to read people, you sure can be obtuse when it comes to Lavinia. You were flirting, Your Honor, and so was Loretta. Don't try to deny it."

He attempted to conceal the little gleam in his eye, but I knew him too well. "Young enough to be my daughter," he mumbled.

"Bullshit. When has that ever stopped a man?"

"No denying she's a fine-lookin' woman," he said, and I could tell he was baiting me.

"You may find this amusing, but I can guarantee you Lavinia doesn't. Get yourself out there and make amends."

"Tempest in a teapot," he muttered, but he set the wineglass on the table and maneuvered his chair out into the hallway.

I followed him and retrieved my bag from the console table. I carried it back into the parlor, propped up my aching foot, and punched Red's number into my cell.

"Where the hell have you been?" he asked without preamble. "I've been calling you for two hours."

"I turned off the phone. You really pissed me off."

"Yeah, I noticed. I'm sorry for that, but I meant what I said. I'm just glad you're okay. What happened with the tail?"

"It's a long story. Look, I just ran into an old friend of the family, an immigration attorney who consults to Homeland Security." I gave him a quick rundown on Loretta Healey and her real reason for showing up unannounced at Presqu'isle. "You have any idea what's going on?"

"Not a clue. Something about it doesn't smell right, though. Are you staying with the Judge tonight?"

"No. I'm going to grab a bite to eat and head on home."

"Then I'll see you there. Probably shortly after eight. In the meantime, I'll do a little nosing around here, see if I can pick up anything about this Healey woman."

Having Red on board quieted a lot of the flutterings in my chest. "Okay. I'll make sure I'm back by then."

"Be careful," he said, and the usual bantering tone was gone from his voice.

I made a conscious decision to leave my father out of the loop. I sidestepped his questions over the almost silent meal around the old oak table in the kitchen. By the time I could reasonably make my escape, the temperature between Lavinia and the Judge had thawed to the point where she had half-grudgingly agreed to whip him up a batch of his favorite peach cobbler for dessert.

The winter sky sparkled with stars as I sped across the Broad River bridge. Lights from the inhabited islands glowed softly in the distance, and I encountered little traffic on the chilly December night. Which was probably why I spotted the tail.

I might not have pegged him if he hadn't hung back when I stopped for the light at the road out to Callawassie. As I accelerated through the intersection, the lights resumed their steady glimmer in my rearview mirror. They rode high, an SUV or maybe a pickup. I shivered, wondering if the man I'd trailed from the Early house on Sunday had decided to return the favor.

I slid my pistol out of my bag and set it on the passenger seat within easy reach.

As a test, I sped up to seventy, fifteen miles an hour over the posted limit. He stuck with me. I wouldn't have minded at all if a sheriff's deputy had appeared, lights flashing, to pull us over. I desperately wanted to know who had me in his sights.

Our little caravan took the ramp toward Hilton Head, and traffic thickened as we neared the island. With Christmas less than a week away, the outlet malls and other stores were still open, even on Sunday night. Without using my turn signal, I whipped into the McDonald's next to Hilton Head National Golf Club and executed a sharp U-turn to face back the way I'd come.

No one followed.

I waited ten minutes before moving out into the flow again, and this time I couldn't pick up any indication of my pursuer. Either he was completely inept, or I was becoming totally paranoid. I wasn't thrilled with either option.

I eased the Jaguar into the garage a little after eight o'clock and shut off the engine. I waited until the door had closed behind me before sliding out of the seat. I held the Seecamp loosely in my right hand as I made my way up the steps and into the house.

I punched in my security code and immediately reset the alarm. In the kitchen, I pulled out the remains of the Frogmore stew and set the pan on the burner. I sat at the kitchen table until I saw the lights of Red's Bronco swing into the driveway. He frowned at the closed garage door, then looked up to see me motioning him around to the front. Again, I disengaged the alarm and threw open the door.

"What's the matter?" he asked, sidling by me. "How come you're all buttoned up in here?" His voice took on a worried edge. "Did something happen?"

I climbed the steps into the kitchen. Despite the abuse I'd been giving it, my foot felt almost back to normal. "I think I was followed from Beaufort, at least part of the way."

He made me sit down and give him every detail. When I'd finished, he leaned back in the chair. "Maybe you're just a little spooked by that Healey woman," he said, his shoulders relaxing. "Lots of people travel from Beaufort to Hilton Head. It's probably just coincidence."

I didn't argue, but it didn't explain the car's hanging back at the light to keep from pulling up directly behind me. I shrugged. Nothing to do about it now, and I liked Red's version of events a lot better than mine.

"You could be right." I rose to stir the pot on the stove. "You find out anything about Healey?"

Red made a ceremony of unstrapping his gun belt and laying it across the built-in desk. "Yes and no."

"That's helpful."

"Give me a second, okay? I checked the visitor logs to see if she'd been at the office, but I came up empty. Of course, if she's official, she might not have signed in. That Reynolds guy from the FBI has been in a couple of times that I know of, and I didn't see his name on the log, either."

"That's it?"

Red crossed to the refrigerator and pulled out a beer. "I talked a little to Lisa, tried to feel her out about any bigwigs from Washington trying to horn in on our case. She claimed she hadn't heard even a whisper."

"Claimed?"

He twisted the cap off the bottle and took a swig. "I have to say she's making me a little nervous lately."

"Nervous how?"

I took a bowl from the cupboard and ladled in the steaming stew. I set Red's leftover dinner on the place mat and handed him a fork. "Thanks. I'm starving." He blew across a hunk of sausage. "I can't exactly say. There's something secretive about her. That's the best I can put it into words. I always have the feeling that she's not being completely forthcoming with me. Like she's holding something back."

I sat down across from him. "Maybe you're a little paranoid, too."

He ate in silence for a few minutes. I stared out into the blackness through the bay window, my mind trying to sort out all the disparate threads of the convoluted puzzle.

"Do you think it could have been Reynolds who took Mr. Gadsden away?"

Red spluttered and swallowed. "The FBI? Why would they do that?"

I shook my head. "I don't know. I've just been trying to figure out why someone would spirit him away from home, obviously take excellent care of him, and then return him unharmed. If it was the robbers—this kid he thought he recognized—why wouldn't they . . ." I stuttered to a halt.

"Kill him?"

"Yes. I mean, what would be the point otherwise?"

"What would be the point of the FBI taking him? If they wanted an interview, all they had to do was knock on the door. He's a witness in a federal crime. They'd have every right to question him. Why would they resort to something so cloak-and-dagger?"

I carried his empty bowl to the sink. "Because they can?"

"Come on, Bay. I know it's fashionable to bash the feds, but they're law enforcement officers. They don't kidnap citizens to interrogate them."

"How about Homeland Security?" I asked, the image of my

"aunt" in her expensively tailored suit rising up in my mind's eye. "You can't say they haven't overstepped a few bounds since 9/11."

"How do the politicians put it? Mistakes have been made, there's no denying it. But shanghaiing an eighty-year-old black man is over the top, even for them."

"Then give me another scenario that makes sense."

I threw out the dregs in the bottom of the stew pot and set it in the sink to soak. Red downed the last of his beer while I waited for a reply that didn't come. I glanced around to see him slumped in the chair, his lips moving slightly as if he carried on some interior dialogue. I left him to it and crossed the great room to the French doors. Outside, the night sky stretched away to meet the ocean, the glimmering stars the only delineation between the two.

I felt as if someone had set me adrift on that endless expanse of water, and the board Red had hastily thrown up to cover the broken panes of glass only reinforced my sense of helplessness. My inability to piece together the events of the past week in any meaningful way had my stomach churning. It was like the first time I'd been introduced to geometry in high school. I'd always been good at math, but I had found myself panicking as I read the first chapters over and over, the concepts failing to take even the slightest root in my brain.

You'll never get this, I remember telling myself, *not if you study for the rest of your life.*

That was how this trouble surrounding Dolores, Bobby, Serena, and Jason Early had been making me feel. And what about Mr. Gadsden? How did he fit into the picture? Or did he? Were these two entirely separate things, the robberies and the death of Theresa Montalvo? Was it my own desire for symmetry, that perfectly balanced set of books, that made me want—no, *need*—to tie it all up in one tidy package?

I sighed and rested my head against the cool glass of one of the unbroken panes. Something wasn't right. Somewhere I'd made an assumption that was skewing my thinking. I felt it niggling at the back of my mind, and I knew picking at it would only drive it deeper. I closed my eyes and let my breathing slow. Behind me I barely heard Red push his chair back from the table.

"Bay—," he began, but I held up my hand to cut him off.

Images flashed through my head like an out-of-control kaleidoscope: Bobby, Serena, Loretta Healey, Harry Reynolds. Jason Early grinning on TV, tucking something into his pocket in the middle of the mall. And in front of the church. His mother, that strange look on her face as she clutched the chain of the lunging—

"The dog!" I said out loud, and part of the pattern clicked into place.

CHAPTER
THIRTY-TWO

ERIK FOUND ME THE NEXT MORNING, JUST BEFORE nine, scurrying around the office, setting the stage.

"What's up?" he asked, sliding his laptop onto the reception desk. "Do we have a client?"

"Not exactly. Can you rig something up so you can hear what's going on in my office?"

"Why?"

"Can you do it? Even if you have to leave, can you make it so you can hear from, say, your car?"

"You're not making sense, Bay. Why would you want to eavesdrop on yourself?"

I drew in deep breath and willed myself to a calm I didn't feel. "I tried to call you last night. Didn't you get my messages?"

His face flushed. "I . . . I turned off the cell. And I . . . wasn't home last night."

I looked up into his eyes flickering away from my gaze, guilt like a flashing neon sign on his face.

"I don't care where you slept, Erik. Or with whom. We've got less than an hour to set this up. I'm being *interviewed* by someone from Homeland Security. I'm betting they won't let you sit in, but I want a witness. And a recording, if possible."

"Homeland Security? Jesus, Bay, what's going on?"

"I think this whole mess with Dolores and Bobby is about to get simpler, but I don't trust this woman, even if she is an old friend of the family. I promise I'll explain everything later, but right now I need to make sure she doesn't try to screw me over. Can you rig something up?"

"Sure. Fire up your computer." He turned back to the desk and whipped open his laptop. "Wait!" he called as I turned for my office. "I have a better idea."

He pulled his BlackBerry from his pocket and began punching buttons. "This will work. Give me a few minutes. I have to reprogram a couple of things."

"Hurry. I have something else I need you to do before she gets here."

I watched him drop into his chair, his thumbs flying over the tiny keys. In my office, I checked the mini-fridge for supplies, laid out a fresh legal pad, and pulled my notes from my bag. I ran through them again. There were still huge gaps in my theory, but I hoped my conversation with Loretta Healey would fill in some of them. Not intentionally, of course, but that's where Erik came in.

"How are you coming?" I called just as he stepped into the doorway.

"Just leave this on your desk," he said and handed me the PDA.

"Can I put it in the drawer?"

"Better if it's out in the open. It won't be beeping or flashing lights or anything like that. It's a perfectly legitimate piece of equipment. No reason anyone should even give it a second look."

"How does it work?"

Erik stared at me for a moment. "You really want me to get into packets and Bluetooth and all that? Trust me, you'll have a recording. And if I get tossed out, I've fixed it so I can use my cell to listen in." His frown deepened. "What do you think's going to happen? I mean should I be prepared to charge in here and kick some federal government butt?"

I smiled, which had been his goal. "No, I don't think it'll come to that. I'm probably being paranoid, but . . ."

"Understood. What else do you have for me?"

I handed him a slip of paper. "Red ran a license plate for me last night. See what you can find out about this guy."

"Jesse Cardenas," Erik read aloud, then looked up. "What's our interest?"

"He's mixed up with Jason Early and his crazy mother, which means he has some connection to Dolores and Bobby. At least that's my working premise at the moment."

I remembered the dog the strange woman had barely restrained the first day I'd called on her, looking for Jason. The same animal that had leaped from the seat of the pickup truck I'd tailed through the rain on Sunday. Although I'd seen it the first time for only a few seconds—and from a distance—I was convinced now it was the same dog, riding around with a man whose heritage was definitely not Anglo. Which meant Jason's mother wasn't quite the bigot she'd made herself out to be. So why the games?

"What kind of information am I looking for?" Erik asked.

"Anything you can find. Use the sites we set up for running the background checks for the recreation board. I'm betting this guy has no history, at least none that can be verified."

"Illegal?"

"Maybe. Or maybe just a false identity. If so, we need to find a way to crack it."

When Erik didn't respond, I looked up to find him staring at the floor. He looked as if he'd rather be somewhere—anywhere—else.

"What's the matter?"

I had to strain to hear his answer.

"I wanted to tell you . . . I mean, face-to-face, not over the phone, but maybe this isn't a good time."

"Tell me what?" My stomach lurched.

He straightened and looked me in the eye. "It's about Dolores.

Well, not her exactly, but . . . you know, the family. You asked me to check them out, remember?"

I nodded. "Their immigration status." I'd wondered why it was taking Erik so long to gather the information, but another part of me hadn't been prepared to hear bad news, so I hadn't pushed. "What did you find?"

"You really want to get into this now? I mean, with everything else—"

I fought to keep the fear out of my voice. "You brought it up. Just tell me."

"Okay." He paused and squared his shoulders. "I think Hector is using someone else's identity and has been for years."

Loretta Healey breezed in at exactly ten o'clock. She'd traded in her beautifully tailored suit for slacks, sweater, and a wool blazer, but the calfskin briefcase swinging from her hand told me she still meant business.

I introduced her to Erik, who rose to follow us into my office, when Loretta proved the accuracy of my initial prediction.

"We need to speak alone," she said crisply and turned her smile on Erik. "No offense, Mr. Whiteside."

Erik nodded. I glanced over my shoulder as I ushered the woman into my office and got a discreet thumbs-up sign from my partner.

I purposely avoided allowing my eyes to linger on the Black-Berry tossed carelessly atop a pile of papers on the corner of my desk. I closed the door behind us and slid into my chair.

"I have appointments this morning, Loretta. Can we keep this brief?" Seizing control of the situation right up front was a lesson I'd learned from the back of the courtroom, watching the Judge in action.

She set her briefcase beside her chair but made no move to open it. "It was great to see your father again yesterday," she said, her smile seeming genuine. "I'd heard about his strokes, of course. I was pleased to find him looking so well."

"Lavinia takes excellent care of him," I said. "If it wasn't for her, he'd probably be in some sort of care facility. She's very protective."

That brought a ladylike laugh. "So I noticed. And she has an excellent memory. She certainly remembered how much I hate cranberries."

Serves you right, I thought. Out loud I said, "Did you flirt with him in front of my mother, too?"

The smile slipped a little, but she held on to it and shrugged. "I always had something of a crush on Tally. Schoolgirl sort of thing. I'm sorry if you and your . . . Mrs. Smalls were offended. Just a harmless little game."

Harmless? I thought. Depended on your point of view. I made a show of studying my watch. I expected Loretta to reach for her briefcase at that point, but again she surprised me.

"You need to back off this investigation of yours into the death of the Montalvo girl."

Even though I'd been expecting something along those lines, her stark command startled me. "What do you know about it?" I asked and was pleased when I managed to keep my voice level.

Loretta leaned back in the client chair. "I know your housekeeper's son is romantically involved with the victim's sister. I know they've gone to ground, along with Mrs. Santiago. I know you've already figured out that the wrong girl got killed. If you're half as smart as I remember, you know Serena Montalvo is still a target. What you don't seem to have grasped is that sticking your nose in is putting them at greater risk."

Her words sounded familiar. Who had said almost the exact same thing? We stared at each other while I replayed recent conversations in my head. *Angie!* Delivering a message from her father. My stomach lurched.

"You know where they are? Do you have them stashed? Are they under arrest?"

She raised a hand. "None of that needs to concern you."

"Don't give me that crap! These are my friends. Where the hell is Dolores?"

Loretta glanced toward the door. In a moment she had jumped from her chair and jerked it open. Through the gap I could see Erik bent over his computer, his face betraying nothing, although I could bet he'd heard my last shouted question.

"Mr. Whiteside," she said, all smiles and good cheer, "I wonder if I might ask you a favor."

Erik clicked on his own personal charm, and I watched Loretta's bunched shoulders relax a bit. "Anything I can do, ma'am," he said.

"I got a late start this morning, had to race off without my coffee. I see you don't have a machine here, and I was wondering if you'd mind making a Starbucks run."

Her face lit with the same seductive smile she'd used on my father. I trusted Erik was made of sterner stuff.

"Certainly." He rose and slipped his jacket from the back of his chair. "What's your pleasure?"

She grinned. "Just a straight latte. None of that foam and cinnamon stuff." She pulled a twenty from the pocket of her blazer, almost as if she'd been prepared to get Erik out of the office on this pretext.

"I'll bring you a chai, Bay, all right?"

"That'd be great." I held his eyes for just a moment when he slipped his cell phone into his pocket.

He nodded. "Back in a few minutes."

"Thanks so much, Erik," Loretta said and waited until he'd closed the door behind him before turning back to me.

I'd taken that brief lapse in her attention to ease open the drawer where I'd put the Seecamp during my earlier preparations. The sight of it calmed me.

"Charming young man," Loretta said, resuming her seat. "You're a lucky woman, Bay. Now, where were we?"

"I believe you were about to tell me where you're holding my housekeeper and her son."

She laughed. "*I'm* not holding anyone. I'm just a consultant to Homeland Security. An insignificant cog in the wheel of keeping this country safe."

"Oh, I'm sure you're being too modest. You seem to know a lot about this poor teenager's death, her sister, and my friends. I'm wondering why."

The amiable smile faded from Loretta Healey's face. "Wonder all you want. Here's the bottom line: Stay out of it. You're floundering around in a federal investigation. This isn't a request, Bay. Do I make myself clear? Your curiosity has the potential to jeopardize an important operation that may be vital to our national security."

"Ah, yes. National security. The Holy Grail. A lot has been done in its name over the last few years. It seems to me, though, that the Constitution's still in operation. Or did I miss something?"

I had nothing but respect for the job being done to protect us after 9/11, even though there had been regrettable excesses. But I wanted to wipe that smug, superior smile off my "aunt's" face, rattle her if I could. At this point, I didn't give a damn about anything but making certain Dolores and Bobby were all right. I'd deal with the fallout later.

"We aren't discussing ordinary thugs and robbers here," she said. I could tell by her tone that my words had stung. "Immigration isn't just about some itinerant farm workers sneaking across the border. Not anymore. The stakes have been raised since the towers went down. It's become organized and well-financed." She paused for a breath and lowered her voice. "Look, Bay. You've got a nice little business going here. Concentrate on finding errant husbands and doing background checks. Leave this kind of stuff to the people trained to handle it."

"Like you?" I didn't even try to hide my contempt. "Are you telling me you're some sort of undercover agent?"

That made her laugh. "I'm not anything but an old immigration lawyer who's learned a few things along the way that the government thinks they can make use of. I'm not into danger, Bay. I'll leave that to you." She sobered. "What I am today is a messenger, one they thought you just might listen to. Harry Reynolds handled things badly, I know. I'm the second team." She paused again. "You are seriously jeopardizing an ongoing federal investigation," she repeated as if she'd memorized the exact words. "You need to back off. Now."

"Or what?" I asked.

I wasn't sure if the pained expression was genuine or just part of her act. "You've got a good thing going here," she said again. "You need a license, right? From the state?"

I didn't need her to spell it out, but I was damned if I'd let her see it mattered. I shrugged. "I don't have to do this for a living. Matter of fact, I don't have to do anything. But just because there isn't a piece of paper on the wall doesn't mean I'll stop helping people. You can just make it a little more difficult for me, that's all."

Her fist hitting the desk made me jump, and my hand twitched automatically toward the pistol in the drawer. "Damn it, Bay! I'm not the enemy here! As an attorney, I don't like some of this any better than you do. But I'm convinced they're right, at least in this instance. Will you take my word that your housekeeper and her son are safe?"

I watched her weigh whether or not to tell me more. I waited. Silence often worked better than demands.

"Look, there's a lot I can't talk about. A lot I wish I didn't even know. But I can tell you this: We—*they*—have your friends under surveillance. Nothing's going to happen to them. I meant it when I said this may have international implications. You have to leave it alone."

We were still staring at each other when the outer door opened, and Erik sidled in, two large Styrofoam cups balanced against his chest.

"Sorry I took so long," he said. "Lots of other folks with the same idea, I guess."

He handed one of the cups to Loretta. "Plain latte." He dug in his pocket. "And your change. Bay?"

I took the other container. "Thanks."

He slipped off his jacket and draped it back over his chair. "Excuse me, but I have some work to do."

Loretta closed my door and pried the top off her coffee. She inhaled the rising steam and sipped cautiously. The interruption seemed to have broken the atmosphere of confrontation, at least temporarily.

"Nice kid," she said, and I nodded.

"He has a real knack for the work."

An uneasy silence settled over us as we drank. This time, I broke it first. "How can I be sure you're not just telling me what I want to hear? Are you prepared to answer some specific questions?"

"About what?"

"You said we weren't dealing with ordinary thugs and robbers. Does that mean this spate of holdups around the county is linked to Theresa Montalvo's murder?"

"I can't answer that. Mainly because I don't know. I've told you everything I can." She reached down and pulled her briefcase onto her lap. "Except this. These people—my *associates*—aren't fooling around. Take my word for that. They can make your life very difficult if you try to fight them."

"Do you hear yourself?" I slapped my cup down on the desk. "Does this sound like the country we grew up in?"

"Look, Bay, we're not the enemy. But we're talking about our national survival here. Desperate times call for desperate measures. I don't know who said that, but it's certainly apropos these days."

" 'They that can give up essential liberty to obtain a little temporary safety deserve neither liberty nor safety.' Benjamin Franklin," I shot back.

Clutching her coffee, Loretta Healey rose. "You want a quotation? How about 'Death to America!'? Shouted daily in squares in Baghdad and Tehran and a dozen other places by a few million radical Islamists. Surely you're not naïve enough to believe the only people sneaking across our borders are looking for honest work and a better life." Poised with one hand on the door, she expelled a long breath and turned back to study me. "I have a feeling I've just been played, but it was cleverly done. We can debate political philosophy another time, Bay. Just remember what I said. And we can continue this conversation here or somewhere a lot less comfortable."

She stepped into the outer office. "Thanks for the coffee run, Erik. Nice to meet you."

"My pleasure," he said, rising to open the door for her.

A moment later he stood in front of my desk. "Well?" he asked. "You heard?"

"Most of it. What was that Ben Franklin stuff you were spouting?"

"I wanted to see how far she'd go in defense of her position. I don't think she's a true believer, but she certainly has the company line down pat."

"Any other impressions? Does she really know where Dolores and her son are hiding?"

"Maybe not. But she knows people who know." I stared over his shoulder. "I wonder if it would do any good to tail her."

"Doesn't sound like a good idea to me," he said, following my gaze. "She seemed pretty adamant about our staying out of it."

I smiled. "Oh, yeah. If I'm not mistaken, she just threatened to have me thrown in jail."

CHAPTER
THIRTY-THREE

HE SILENCE OF THE EMPTY OFFICE WRAPPED ITSELF around me as I studied the printouts Erik had laid on my desk a few minutes before heading off to scare up some lunch. He'd placed the file on Hector Santiago on top, but—coward that I was—I'd slipped it underneath his research into Jesse Cardenas, the man I'd tailed from Jason's house in Ridgeland.

I chewed on the eraser end of a pencil, wishing for the millionth time since I'd quit that I had a cigarette. Maybe I'd get a pack and keep them in my desk drawer, just for emergencies, I thought. *Yeah, right.* One puff and I'd be hooked again. Nicotine and I could never peacefully coexist.

Erik and I had spent the time after Loretta Healey sailed out of my office discussing the ramifications of her visit. My partner had voted for caution, and I wasn't totally against the idea, but I wasn't backing off my search for Dolores. The woman's words had alarmed me more than soothed me, and I'd said as much to Erik.

"But if the feds have her in their sights, that's a good thing, right?" he'd asked. "I mean, those guys are pretty competent."

"I'd like to think so. But it sounds more to me as if they're using Dolores and Bobby—and particularly Serena—as bait. They're not in protective custody. They're still running around out there somewhere with the bad guys looking for them. There's a chance they could get caught in the crossfire if things go wrong."

Erik grudgingly agreed but still advised taking it slowly. I promised him I wouldn't do anything rash or stupid—at least not without checking with him first. He failed to see the humor. I tried to remember that he'd come close to dying the past summer, quick action by Ben Wyler having saved Erik's life—at a cost no one had ever expected.

I gave him my word I'd be careful.

I forced my attention back to the pages Erik had printed out from his research on Jesse Cardenas. He had a green card, with an address in Chicago, along with a South Carolina driver's license and clear title to the truck I'd tailed. He was employed by a local landscape company on Lady's Island as a laborer and lived outside Yemassee. As Erik noted on the research, it was no longer possible to tell from the first three digits where a Social Security card had been issued unless it had been applied for prior to 1972, so that provided no usable clue.

All his paperwork seemed on the up-and-up. I flipped back to the license info. The picture was grainy, but it looked like the man I'd encountered. Description fit, too. Again, I had that vague feeling that I'd seen him before, but I had no clue where it might have been. The only chink in his armor was the failure to change the address on his green card when he moved from Illinois to South Carolina. Probably punishable by a fine and a hearty slap on the wrist, I thought.

"Damn it!" I tossed the folder back onto my desk.

Had Red been right? Had Cardenas simply been passed out behind the deserted gas station in front of Jason Early's house? Had I read way too much into the proximity and timing? And yet there was the dog. I felt positive it was the same one Jason's mother had barely restrained that day I'd called on her. What I needed was another look. And an excuse to go nosing around.

The phone rang just as Erik walked back in, bringing a breath of warm air and the unmistakable aroma of a Giuseppi's pizza. "I've got it," he called, but I'd already picked up.

"Simpson and Tanner."

"Bay, it's Lavinia. Do you still want to talk to Romey Gadsden?"

I eyed the walking stick propped in the corner of my office. Although the swelling in my foot had gone down, and the pain had pretty much subsided, I had carried the carved cane to work with me.

"Yes," I said. "Is he coherent?"

"I spoke to Glory earlier, to ask if her father was up for visitors. They didn't keep him in the hospital, but the doctor suggested he take it easy for a couple of days."

"So he's at home?"

"At his daughter's, yes. I volunteered to sit with him while Glory goes in to work for a couple of hours. She can't afford to miss too much time."

"You're there now?"

"I just got here. Romey's asleep, but Glory said it was okay for you to come by while she's gone. If you want to."

I glanced at my watch, then longingly at the slice of pizza Erik was sliding onto a paper plate. "I'll be there in an hour."

"Hurry. I need to get home to your father."

I shoved the pistol and Erik's research files into my briefcase, shrugged into my blazer, and tucked Romey Gadsden's stick under my arm.

"Where are you off to?" Erik asked. "What about lunch?"

"I hope I'm about to get some answers," I said. "And I'll take mine to go."

Of course I ended up with a dribble of tomato sauce on the sleeve of my jacket. I'd wolfed down two slices while negotiating the noonday traffic on Route 278, my mind only half on either task. I kept wondering if Romey would be able to remember where he'd been Friday night. And with whom. I didn't completely understand where his brief disappearance fit into the whole picture, but it seemed important to find out what he knew. And I wondered if anyone from the sheriff's office felt the same, if they'd already pumped the old man. I should have asked Lavinia. Or maybe the FBI had decided to go right to the horse's mouth with their questions about the boy involved in the bank robbery. By the time I pulled into Glory Merrick's driveway, the pizza lay in a hard lump in my stomach.

Jenkins Creek flowed quietly, back within its banks now that the weekend storms had moved out to sea. In the sparkling daylight, the snug cottage reminded me suddenly of Belle Crowder's place outside Sanctuary Hill. I shuddered a little, remembering, as I swung out of the car.

Lavinia stepped out onto the covered porch, and I climbed the steps to meet her.

"He's still asleep. Let's sit out here for a minute."

She hugged the sweater more tightly across her chest and seated herself on one end of an old-fashioned porch swing, hung by chains from the roof. I set my bag on the weathered floorboards and joined her, then passed over Romey's walking stick.

"You never said how you came to have this," Lavinia said, laying the cane across her lap.

I avoided her eyes. "Long story. I'll tell you about it another time."

She sighed and let it go. "He'll be glad to have it back."

"Has he said anything?" I asked. "About what happened to him?"

Lavinia shook her head. "Nothing that makes any sense."

"Then why did you bring me rushing over here?" I tried to keep the annoyance out of my voice. Too many things were breaking at once.

"I wonder how old you'll be when you finally learn some patience," Lavinia snapped back.

I bowed my head. "Sorry. But I'm worried about Dolores and her son." I glanced up, ready to gauge her reaction to my next words. "Loretta Healey came to see me today. At the office."

The scowl didn't disappoint me. "That woman! I never liked her mother, either."

That surprised me. "You remember the mother?"

"She used to be at Presqu'isle all the time when you were just a toddler. Then she and Emmaline had some kind of falling out. Later she came snooping around, saying she wanted to make amends. I didn't trust her. Too sweet and syrupy. Cried at the drop of a hat. And she didn't have any trouble letting your father console her. I was glad when Emmaline sent her packing." She sniffed. "Apple didn't fall too far from the tree, seems to me."

"What did Daddy have to say about her?"

Her face relaxed a little. "He says she's just lonely. He heard she and her late husband had a good marriage, traveled all over the world together. He says she went completely to pieces when he passed away. At least that's what he heard."

I wondered who had been this fountain of knowledge about Loretta Healey and whether this information had been gathered before or after her surprise visit.

"Glory? Where are you, girl?"

The voice, scratchy but firm, drifted out to us on the porch.

"He's awake. Give me a minute." Lavinia stood and carried the stick with her through the door. I could hear her clearly, calling, "I'm right here, Romey. It's me, Lavinia Smalls. I'm comin'.'"

I leaned my head against the hard back of the swing and used my foot to set it into motion. A few birds rustled in the gnarled tree shading the house, and across the creek I watched a red-tailed hawk slowly drifting on the swirling wind currents rising off the Sound. How effortlessly he glided, I thought, and wondered what it would feel like to be cut adrift, floating above everything, no worries other than where my next meal was coming from.

"Bay? Come on in." Lavinia held the door open, and I followed her inside.

The house looked as neat as I remembered it, larger without all the sheriff's deputies filling every room. A small Christmas tree had been added since my hurried visit in the middle of the storm. Lavinia led me to the back where a tiny bedroom had been fashioned from what might once have been a pantry. There was barely room for the single bed, nightstand, and low dresser. None of the furniture matched, all of it old, bits and pieces from other rooms, other times.

Romey Gadsden sat propped up on several pillows, his seamed brown face standing out from the crisp white linens. He wore a long-sleeved flannel pajama top, buttoned up to his chin, and an old tattered shawl draped across his shoulders. His twisted hands lay loosely atop the brightly patterned quilt, but the eyes behind his glasses seemed alert. And curious.

"Well, Lydia! I don't see you for more 'n a dozen years, and here you are twice in one week. It's right nice of you to call, child."

There was no place to sit, other than on the narrow bed, so I set down my bag and knelt on the floor beside him. He raised a trembling hand, and I took it—thin and birdlike—in my own.

"How are you feeling, Mr. Gadsden?"

"Fair, child, just fair. I seem to get so tired lately."

I glanced over my shoulder to where Lavinia stood guard in the doorway.

"We were worried about you," I said, studying his worn face. "Do you remember why?"

"Glory says I got lost t'other night."

"That's right. You had us all pretty scared. I'm so glad you're home safe now." I waited, but he didn't respond, just stared at me with a sad smile. "Don't you remember? Where you went? Or who was with you?"

Behind me, Lavinia cleared her throat. I ignored her.

"It was raining hard," I prodded, "but you didn't get wet. Were you in a car?"

Romey Gadsden's gaze flickered away from me, toward the ceiling, and his voice dropped into a lower register. "My mama saw a man hung on the Mercy Oak. Night riders, it was."

I tried to maneuver myself around to get back into his line of sight. "I know. You told me about that. She turned the men in to the sheriff."

Suddenly, the old eyes blazed. "Didn't do nothin' about it,

though, did he? Said mama was just a child, couldn't arrest nobody on the word of a pickaninny." Again his face changed, the look now sly, secretive. "But her daddy and her uncles knowed what to do. Didn't one of those riders live the year out." He smiled and nodded. "Accidents, they said, but Mama knowed. She tol' me. Accidents." The raspy laugh shook the old man's shoulders.

I turned toward Lavinia, but she simply shrugged. A moment later, Romey's eyes fluttered closed. I waited a few minutes, but his breathing had evened out in sleep. I pushed myself up and tiptoed behind Lavinia back into the living room.

"Sit there," she said, indicating a low sofa with a hand-worked afghan draped across the back. "I was just making tea when you came in. I'll bring it."

I slumped against the spongy cushions, my legs stretched out in front of me, and thought about Romey's story. Twice now he'd made reference to the hanging witnessed by his mother. I did the math in my head. The incident had to have taken place in the early part of the last century, maybe around the time of the First World War. I had no trouble believing the Klan had still been active at that time, although I'd never heard about any particular violence in our little corner of South Carolina. I made a mental note to do some Google searching. Surely the murder would have made the papers, although I might have to make a trip to the library to find any references back that far.

I picked up a loose pillow and tucked it behind my neck. The real issue, though, was why Mr. Gadsden kept coming back to the hanging and the Mercy Oak. The first time, he might just have been making conversation, reminiscing about a significant happening in his family's history. But why bring it up again now? Something must have triggered the memory, something that had happened recently. I looked up when Lavinia carried a tray into the room.

"I know Glory won't mind our making ourselves at home," she said and set the tray on the coffee table. "I brought some banana bread along. There's enough for us to have a slice."

I broke off a moist hunk and accepted the mug she held out to me. "Thanks."

We drank for a while in silence. The sun slipped behind a high cloud, and the room darkened. Neither of us reached to turn on a light.

"Tell me about this Mercy Oak Mr. Gadsden keeps referring to. You said before you weren't familiar with the story about the hanging, but what's so significant about the tree?"

Lavinia leaned back against the plantation rocker she'd settled into, her eyes drifting toward the ceiling. "It's over on Hilton Head, at least the one I've heard tell about, but there are others."

I waited while she gathered her thoughts.

"It used to be against the law for slaves to learn how to read."

I shot her a puzzled look, but her eyes were fastened on some place beyond this quiet room on the edge of the creek. "I know that."

"But the masters wanted their slaves converted to Christianity, even if they couldn't read the Bible. So they'd bring in ministers, oftentimes from up north. A slave could get out of work to attend services, so many of them went without havin' any idea what it was all about. But lots were brought to the Lord, and it was a comfort to them in their . . . situation."

Again I watched her gaze fix on a point over my shoulder. I sipped tea and let her find her own rhythm with the story.

"Some of the plantation owners on Hilton Head got together to build a praise house, a place where the slaves from several plantations could gather and worship." Her sharp laugh held no pleasure. "Guess they figured it would be cheaper that way. Only have to pay one preacher. It was over by Mitchellville. Beach City Road, I think. I believe there's a church there now."

When she didn't continue, I asked, "And the tree is there? Where the old praise house used to be?" Could someone have taken Romey all the way to Hilton Head? But why?

Lavinia nodded. "Over the years, it became a natural meetin' place for the runaways heading out on the Road. That's where it got its name."

It took me a minute. "You mean the Underground Railroad?"

She nodded. "It was the first station hereabouts. If a slave was set on runnin', he could find a few supplies to help get him on his way. Nothing much, maybe a few apples and some cornbread, tied in a bandanna. Enough to get him through a couple of days, across the water and onto the mainland. After that, it was just a matter of prayin' for clear nights so he could follow the drinking gourd."

I'd heard the expression before. And the song. "The Big Dipper," I murmured softly, afraid to interrupt the flow of her story.

"Yes, to find the North Star. Always heading north." She sighed, real pain evident on her wrinkled face. "Some of them made it. Most didn't. Hunger or bad luck or the dogs got them." She shivered. "I hear the dogs were the worst."

My mind flashed to the huge animal, its throat vibrating as it hunkered down in front of my car. I could well believe the dogs were the worst. I glanced over at Lavinia, who had slumped back into the rocker.

"So that's how the Mercy Oak got its name." Another image jumped into my head. The solitary tree I'd noticed on the way to Jason Early's house. "You said there might be others. You mean besides the one on Hilton Head?"

Lavinia nodded. "It was a name given to lots of trees on the Road, especially ones that could be easily spotted, ones that stood apart. An escaping slave would look for them hoping to find more supplies to help him on his journey."

Could that be it? Had Romey Gadsden been taken to the Early house? Had he, too, passed the solitary oak in that barren field almost next door to the ramshackle bungalow? But it had been dark and raining that night. How would he have been able to see it? Or was he already familiar with it from another time? If he'd just confirm . . .

"Glory?" Again the querulous voice drifted in from the makeshift bedroom. "I need to make water."

Lavinia met my blank stare. "He has to use the bathroom," she said and rose briskly from the rocker.

"Ask him where he saw the Mercy Oak," I said, and she stopped to stare into my upturned face. "Please. It's important."

"I'll do what I can," she said and disappeared into the old man's room.

The tea had cooled, and I carried the tray out into the small kitchen where Glory Gadsden Merrick and her family had huddled around the old table just a few nights before, their fear a palpable presence in the cozy room. I rinsed out the cups and set them on the drainboard, then covered the remains of the banana bread with a tea towel. By the time I wandered back into the living room, Lavinia stood in Romey's doorway.

"Ridgeland," she said, "for whatever good it will do you. He means the Mercy Oak in Ridgeland. That's the one where his mama saw the hanging."

"Thank you." I crossed the room and snatched up my bag. "I've got to go."

"But what does it mean?" Lavinia asked, stepping forward, her hands outstretched as if she might try to stop me. "Is Romey in trouble?"

I moved across to grip her fingers in mine. "No. But he might still be in danger. I'm not sure. Can someone—?"

"I'll call some folks." She squared her shoulders, and her chin came up. "We take care of our own. Don't you worry about that."

I nodded. "I'll be in touch. Just make sure Mr. Gadsden isn't left alone. And don't let him tell anyone else about the Mercy Oak."

"Where are you going?" she asked as I turned for the door.

"To get to the bottom of this," I said. "Don't worry."

"Take care, child," I heard her say as I slipped out onto the porch.

Ten minutes later I was speeding across the causeway onto Lady's Island.

And the grille of a black SUV was right on my bumper.

CHAPTER
THIRTY-FOUR

I PULLED OUT THE CELL PHONE AND PUNCHED IN Red's number. He picked up on the second ring.

"Where are you?" I asked before he had even finished saying hello.

"I'm on my way in to the Beaufort office. Why?"

"How long?"

"Until I get there? I don't know, ten minutes maybe? I'm just crossing the Broad River bridge."

"In your cruiser?"

"Yes. What the hell's this all about?" His voice hardened. "Are you in some kind of trouble?"

I glanced into the rearview mirror. Dusk was falling, and I couldn't make out the driver, but I recognized the vehicle. The last time I'd seen it, it had been spraying gravel from the semicircular drive in front of Presqu'isle. Or had it been the one on my tail the night before?

"Bay? You still there?"

"Yes. I'm just through the light on Lady's Island, heading your way. Unless the bridge is open, we should hit the station at about the same time. Wait for me. Don't go in."

"What the hell's going on?"

"I've got a tail, and he's not being the least bit subtle about it. I think he wants me to know he's there."

"Who?"

I checked the mirror again as we crawled forward in the late-day traffic across the swing bridge that could open to allow tall-masted boats to pass up the river.

"I'm pretty sure it's your pal from the FBI. The obnoxious Harry Reynolds."

I turned left onto Bay Street at the foot of the bridge, and the SUV stayed right on me, its high-seated lights filling the interior of the Jaguar. Night had fallen completely by the time I swung onto Ribaut Road and whipped into the justice complex that housed the main office of the sheriff's department. I held my breath. The big Ford slowed, gliding past the entrance, before speeding off with a roar of its huge engine.

I pulled into a restricted parking space and shoved the gearshift into Park. A moment later Red was banging on the window. With a shaking hand, I turned the key off and pushed open the door.

"What the hell was that all about?" Red demanded a moment before he saw my face in the overhead light. In a second, I was in his arms.

"What is it, honey?" His voice had dropped. "You're shivering."

I pushed against his chest until I could look into his face. "Can we talk somewhere?"

"I just need to report in. Come inside for a minute, then we'll go find a quiet place, maybe have some dinner. Okay?"

"Okay."

He gripped my hand, and I let him lead me into the office.

"Be right back. Just sit down."

I dropped into a molded plastic chair set with others along the wall. The dispatcher looked up and smiled, and I forced myself to nod back before she lowered her head to her paperwork. I kept an eye on the door, certain it would fill in a moment with the menacing form of Harry Reynolds.

Don't be ridiculous, I told myself. A few deep breaths later, I felt back in control enough to begin questioning myself. How did I know it had in fact been the same SUV? Black Expeditions were a dime a dozen around the county. Erik drove one. I'd had no clear look at the driver. So why was I so convinced my pursuer had been Reynolds? How would he have known where to find me? Had he been watching the Merrick house for some reason? I suddenly remembered my theory that it had been the FBI who had spirited Romey Gadsden away on Friday night. Had he been the one under surveillance? Had I just been a bonus for Agent Reynolds?

My hand went automatically for the pocket of my blazer where, in the bad old days, I would have kept my cigarettes and lighter. The hunger for a calming hit of nicotine took my breath away. I jumped up, startling the dispatcher, who jerked her head in my direction. I shoved both hands in my empty pockets and studied several notices posted on the bulletin board without really seeing them.

If Romey Gadsden had been taken to Ridgeland, had in fact passed the Mercy Oak near Jason Early's house, then it made no sense for it to have been the FBI who snatched him. What plausible reason could they have had to take him to Ridgeland? My initial guess had been that Harry Reynolds wanted to interrogate him alone, away from the reassurance of familiar surroundings. But Red had been right. They had subpoena power. Romey was a material witness to a bank robbery. They could have had him brought in for questioning with a snap of the fingers.

My eyes wandered the room, finally making contact again with the dispatcher. Her smile had slipped, and I could imagine her wondering about the strange woman prowling the small waiting room. I forced myself to sit.

Mr. Gadsden's revelation provided the link between the robberies and the death of Theresa Montalvo. And that link was the old house behind the gas station. Jason Early's house. Nothing else made sense. Somehow his having recognized one of the robbers had posed enough of a threat that they'd grabbed him from his daughter's house and taken him to Ridgeland. Maybe they wanted to see just how much of a threat he could be to them. If he'd been as muddled as he'd appeared when I'd knelt at his bedside, perhaps that had been enough to convince them. Maybe one of them had a heart after all. They'd decided to let Romey go, certain he posed no real danger. Smart. Another body would only put the local authorities on heightened alert. Better to let the old man babble. Who would believe him? I wondered if Lisa Pedrovsky or Harry Reynolds had made any effort to locate Reynaldo Velez and his mother.

I checked my watch. Red had been gone more than ten minutes. I hoped he wasn't involving the sheriff in my problems, especially not about Agent Reynolds. I should have told him that was just between us. When the inner door clicked open, I felt myself relax, until I saw Detective Lisa Pedrovsky step into the waiting room. She stopped, one hand on the doorjamb.

"Bay! What are you doing here?"

I swallowed the jolt of fear that clutched at my throat, unsure where the reaction had come from. I forced my voice to a calm I didn't feel.

"Waiting for Sergeant Tanner. We have a dinner date."

"How nice." Neither her tone nor her expression matched the innocuous words. Instead of blowing by me, as I'd expected, Pedrovsky crossed the room and dropped into the chair beside me. "How's the investigation going?" she asked.

I stared at her. "What investigation?"

"The missing kids. And your housekeeper. Got any leads?"

Not that I'm sharing with you. The words stopped just short of my lips, but I could see her reading the sentiment on my face.

"We're on the same side here," she said, forcing a smile.

I forced one back at her. "Nothing, I'm afraid. How about you? Any luck on the material witness warrants?"

To my surprise, she leaned back as if settling in for a cozy chat.

"We finished going over the Montalvo girl's car, the one we towed from the airport? Nothing much, except a couple of receipts from fast-food places around the area." She paused and studied my face. "Most of them were for two meals, so we're pretty sure the Santiago kid has been with her right along."

My mind spun in a dozen different directions. "What do you mean right along?"

"There's some damage to the front of the Taurus." She paused, waiting for me to react.

I bit down hard on the inside of my mouth and said nothing.

Pedrovsky studied my face for a long moment. "It's not inconceivable it was involved in the hit-and-run."

The words exploded before I had a chance to think about them. "Are you nuts? You think Serena Montalvo ran over her own sister and left her to die in the middle of the road? Why? What possible motive could she have? And what's your evidence? Did you find any fibers or blood? Did the tires match the skid marks?"

Pedrovsky stared at me, her face impassive under the barrage of questions except for the tiniest lifting of one corner of her mouth.

"Jesus, Detective! You find this amusing? What the hell's the matter with you?"

"I'd watch that mouth if I were you, Mrs. Tanner. This is *my* house you're sitting in right now."

It always amazes me how fast fear can turn to anger. Two sides of the same coin? I clenched my hands in my lap to keep from wrapping them around her pudgy neck. "Don't threaten me, Detective." I glanced toward the dispatcher, who was trying hard to pretend she wasn't straining to catch every word. "Especially in front of a witness."

"You misunderstand me, Bay." Again that smile that never reached her eyes. "I'm just concerned for your safety. You know what they say about playing with fire."

She stood, her compact body tensed as if she, too, held herself sternly in check. I wondered what would happen if the two of us suddenly lost it and began flailing at each other in the middle of the sheriff's office. I was saved from finding out by Red's sudden appearance. He took in the situation and was beside me in an instant.

"Ready?" he said in a calm voice, but I noticed how his eyes stayed fixed on Lisa Pedrovsky.

"More than ready. Have a pleasant evening, Detective."

Red took my hand and led me to the door. I turned as Pedrovsky followed us out.

She waited until the glass panel had swung shut before she spoke. "You're treading on thin ice, Sergeant. You might want to give some thought to where your loyalties lie."

Red turned slowly, my hand still gripped tightly in his. "I'm pretty clear on that, Detective. It's something you should take a look at yourself."

Lisa's face tightened, and involuntarily I took a step back. The finger she jabbed in our direction stopped just short of Red's chest. "You forget yourself, Sergeant Tanner. You're speaking to a superior officer."

"Yes, ma'am," he said, his voice tight with anger. "I know exactly who I'm speaking to."

Pedrovsky's glare swiveled to me. "You may have yourself a tame cop, Bay, but don't think that will protect you. You're in this thing up to your ass, and we know it. Har—" She bit off the name but not quickly enough.

I squeezed Red's hand and stepped back up beside him. "You mean you and your pal, Harry Reynolds? You and the Feeb getting tight, are you, Detective? Pretty strange bedfellows." I could almost feel the waves of anger flowing from her rigid body. "I'd watch my back if I were you. Old Harry doesn't have an ounce of Ben Wyler's integrity. Don't settle for second best."

I honestly think she would have swung on me then if Red hadn't stepped in front of her. "That's a sure road back to writing speeding tickets," he said quietly. "Or back to civilian life. Let's just pretend this conversation never happened. Better for all concerned, don't you think?"

Lisa Pedrovsky drew a shaky breath, and her bunched shoulders relaxed. She nodded once, and her smile made my skin crawl.

"Thin ice, Sergeant," she said softly before spinning on her heel and striding back inside.

We watched the door glide closed behind her.

CHAPTER
THIRTY-FIVE

THE STRANGE ENCOUNTER WITH LISA PEDROVSKY HAD
pretty much blown away my appetite, but Red insisted, so we
settled for a quiet booth in a far corner of the anonymity of Ruby
Tuesday. When the waitress had taken our order, Red slid around
closer and draped an arm across my shoulders.

"Everything okay? You haven't said much."

I studied his face and found his eyes clear and untroubled. "She
could create serious problems for you, Red. She's right about the superior officer thing."

"You underestimate the sheriff. He'd never do anything without
a full investigation, and I've got nothing to hide. Lisa's the one who
should be watching herself. Ever since Ben died, she's been riding
close to the edge. And if they find out she's been cozying up to Agent
Reynolds . . . Well, let's just say—professional courtesy aside—that
won't endear her to the task force or anyone else in the department."

The waitress delivered my tea and Red's coffee and slipped away.

I added sweetener and sipped. "What's her game? Is this really
just a personal vendetta against me, or does she seriously think
Bobby and Serena were involved in Theresa's death?"

He shook his head. "Nothing I've seen so far gives the slightest
hint that those kids are anything but potential victims. I think

you're right about Lisa's motives, but don't let it get to you. Everyone else has their heads screwed on straight."

I watched the Christmas lights strung across the windows twinkle against the night sky and wondered if he spoke for the FBI and Homeland Security as well. Red absently stroked my arm, both of us lost in thought. He was the first to break the silence.

"You said you wanted to talk. Change your mind?"

I sighed and edged a little away from him. My stomach tightened. I'd thought the consummation of our long mating dance would have put to rest any issues I had about trust and sharing. Wasn't that what love was supposed to be about? Giving yourself completely to another person, without reservation or doubt? Then why did I find myself hesitating? Habit? For so long, Red and I had been on opposite sides, the rational cop and the impulsive amateur, both striving for justice, but each needing to go about it in a different way, too often crossing swords—and angry words—in the process.

But we were lovers now, planning a Christmas with his kids, a trial run at being a family. Why was I waffling? If I gave him the connection between the death of Theresa Montalvo and the string of robberies that Romey Gadsden's revelation had cemented in my mind, I could let it go. Red would follow the trail, make the decisions. Use the system to find Dolores and Bobby. I could finish my shopping, decorate the house, try to put myself into the proper frame of mind for the kids. . . . *Stepmother.* I rolled the word around in my head, trying it out. . . .

"Bay? What are you thinking?"

I smiled and chose trust.

"I want to talk to you about the robberies. And the Montalvo girl's death. But you have to promise not to tell me I'm nuts."

"No guarantees," he said with a smile, and I let my head drop briefly against his shoulder.

The warmth and intimacy of the moment didn't last long.

* * *

Less than an hour later, I yanked open the door of the Jaguar and threw my bag into the passenger seat. I jerked as Red's hand clamped around my upper arm.

"Bay! Wait up!"

"Leave it alone, Red."

"Look at me." I struggled against his grip. "I understand what you're saying. I get it, okay? I need time to think." I lowered my voice. "I just want to go home."

He dropped his hand and took a step back. "Alone?"

Weak light from the overhead fixture kept his face in shadow, but I could hear the mixture of pain and anger in his voice.

"Just for tonight." Thank God we'd driven to the restaurant in separate cars, I thought.

"So this is what happens when I don't jump on board with every wacky theory you come up with? I either toe the line, or you kick my ass out?"

I wanted to yell at him to shut up, to stop making things worse. I drew in a long breath of the chill night air. "No. That's not what this is about. I'm not saying you're wrong. But I need to work this out in my own head." I forced a smile. "These are my friends, people I care about. I need to decide what to do."

"I thought I was one of the people you *care* about."

"You are. You're being a jerk about this, Red. One night apart isn't going to change anything. Don't you have things to do? For Christmas and the kids?"

Finally, he moved back, the slump of his shoulders admitting defeat. "Yeah, I got a couple of things to take care of."

"Then go do what you have to do and give me some space to work all this out. What's your schedule like tomorrow?"

"I'm on seven to three, unless another one of those robberies goes down."

"Then we'll hash it all out over dinner."

His hand reached tentatively to cup my cheek. "And we're okay?"

I let my face rest for a moment in the gentle caress of his fingers. "We're fine."

I allowed him to draw me into his arms, his quickened breath ruffling the hair above my ear.

"I won't find all my stuff in a pile in the driveway, will I?"

The laugh welled up and escaped, and I felt most of the tension ease from my shoulders. "Not unless there's more going on you haven't told me about. Like a mad fling with Lisa Pedrovsky or something like that."

"God forbid!" He let me go. "Want me to follow you home? In case your FBI friend decides to tail you again?"

I stiffened a little at the suggestion, but I didn't think he noticed. "I'll be fine. Go buy the kids something outrageously expensive."

I lowered myself into the seat and reached for the open door.

"No kiss?" In the glow of the interior light I could see the little-boy-lost look creep back into his eyes.

I lifted my face, and he kissed me softly. "See you tomorrow," I said firmly and closed the door.

As I pulled out of the parking lot, I glanced in the rearview mirror. Red stood right where I'd left him, staring after the Jag's retreating taillights.

I drove in a fog, although the sky above me blazed with stars. Thoughts whirled and spun in a fuzzy cloud inside my head. Which was why it took me a moment to realize my cell phone was ringing. I had just rolled down off the Lemon Island bridge, and I swung into the deserted parking lot where an old antique store had been torn down to make way for the widening of the road and a boat ramp. I pulled in alongside mounds of dirt piled higher than the roof of the Jag and shoved the gearshift into Park.

"Erik, what's up?"

"Did Angie Santiago reach you?"

My stomach contracted into a knot I'd become all too familiar with lately. "No," I said.

"She called the office a couple of times this afternoon. Have you been home?"

"No," I said again. "I'm just heading that way out of Beaufort."

"I'll bet if you check your machine you'll find she's been trying to reach you there, too."

"What did she say?"

"She said she needs to talk to you right away." One of his famous dramatic pauses, and then he added, "She says they heard from her mother."

Sweat trickled down between my breasts, and I slid the window open. The breeze off the water made me shiver a little.

"Did she leave a number?"

He recited it to me, not the Santiagos' home phone. Her cell maybe? And why hadn't she called me on mine? I was positive she'd reached me at least once on my cell. Or maybe she hadn't. Didn't matter.

"I'll call her right now," I said. A thought struck. "Where are you?"

His hesitation could have given me my answer. "I'm at Steph's place. You know, Ben's old house."

Stephanie Wyler had inherited outright her father's renovated bungalow in Sea Pines. The rest of his estate, which had been surprisingly hefty, she'd shared with her sister.

"Keep your cell on," I said. "We may need to be on the move."

"Why? You think something's going down?"

I wanted to share it all with him, but there wasn't time. "Maybe. Just be ready."

"Call me back," he said. "After you talk to Angie."

"Will do."

"Bay, wait!"

"What?"

"There was another message, too. From Gabby Henson."

I groaned. "I'm sure she called to beat me up again for not get-ting back to her about the hit-and-run. How many expletives did you have to delete?"

His laugh made me feel a lot better. "Two or three. But she said she had some information about what Serena Montalvo was involved in and that you'd want to hear it."

Gabby could be a pain in the butt, but I knew her sources were as good as any reporter's in the area. After our most recent encounter, I had programmed all her numbers into my phone.

"I'll get back to her. Right now I want to see what Angie has to say."

"I'll wait to hear from you," Erik said and hung up.

I clicked off and almost immediately the phone chirped in my hand.

"Angie?"

"Uh, no. Is this Mrs. Santiago?"

The denial was almost out of my mouth when I remembered my earlier deception. A young man's voice, deep Charleston drawl. I swallowed and ordered my heart to slow down. "Is this Mr. Picker-ing?"

"Chad. Yes, ma'am. I'm really sorry it took me so long to get back to you."

I had to search for the reason I'd called the dorm monitor in the first place. And pretended to be Dolores. Ah, of course. James Fen-wick. But using the roommate as a means of tracking Bobby down had become moot a long time ago.

"I appreciate it, but I've found the information I need. Thanks for calling." I knew I was being rude, but I needed to speak to Angie.

"No problem, Mrs. Santiago. You know, Bobby's a real good kid. Tell him I'll see him in January."

Please God, I thought. "Thank you. Merry Christmas."

I hung up before he could reply.

The dampness from the river had begun to settle in a fine mist against my face. I rolled up the window and punched in the number

Erik had given me. On the second ring a breathless voice erupted from the speaker.

"Mrs. Tanner?"

"Yes, Angie, it's me. I just got your message. When did your mother call?"

"Late this afternoon. Around four."

"What did she say? Are they all right?"

I heard the little catch in her voice before she blurted, "I didn't actually talk to her. I . . . I eavesdropped on Papa. He kept saying, *'No tengas miedo.'* "

"What does that mean?"

"Don't be afraid," she said and burst into tears.

CHAPTER
THIRTY-SIX

"DON'T CRY, ANGIE. IT WON'T HELP ANYTHING. TELL me exactly what he said."

I heard Angie suck in a long shuddering breath. For the first time I noticed the background noise—a murmur of voices, muted, punctuated by an occasional loud whirring. *Starbucks.*

"Okay." Her voice had steadied. "Papa came home early. He said there wasn't much work, so he told the crews not to come back until after Christmas." She faltered a little. "He . . . he started drinking. He never does that. I mean, I didn't even know we had any liquor in the house. Mom hates it."

Still feeling chilled, I reached over and flipped on the heater. "So then your mother called."

"Yes. He kept calling her *tesoro*—that means 'sweetheart'—and telling her not to be afraid and that everything would be okay. After he hung up, I asked him if it was Mom on the phone, and he said no, but I knew he was lying. Then he went out back, on the deck, and just kept drinking and staring off toward the marsh." Angelina sniffled. "I waited a while, then I went out to sit with him. I told him I was really worried—scared—about Mom and Bobby, and he . . . he started to cry. I've never seen Papa shed even one tear. Not one."

Her own voice cracked again, and I gave her a moment to get herself under control. Hector in tears? The idea of it made the bottom drop out of my own stomach.

"Did he tell you where she was?"

"No. But after I left him, I went to the phone and checked the display. The number was still on there, so I called."

"Good girl! What happened?"

"Nobody answered. I let it ring a long time."

"Do you still have that number?"

"Yes. I wrote it down."

I retrieved a notepad and pencil from my bag. "Let me have it."

"Papa did tell me one more thing," she said after reciting the ten digits.

"What's that?"

"It didn't make any sense to me, but he said that you have to trust family."

"That's it? Do you have any idea what he meant?"

"No. I thought maybe he was mad at me for eavesdropping, but I really don't think that's it."

"I don't either." I couldn't get a handle on how Hector fit into the picture of his son's disappearance, but I knew in my gut he was more involved than he was telling his daughter. Or me. But that was information Angie didn't need to have. "Okay. I'm going to give the number to Erik, see if he can track it down."

"If you find out where she is, I want to go with you."

"Angie, just sit tight. I promise I'll keep you posted on what we find out."

Her voice tightened. "She's our mother. Alex and me. We have a right."

"I'll get back to you," I said. "Don't do anything stupid."

I punched off the phone and immediately dialed Erik. I gave him the number, and he promised to get on it. He'd have to go home and get his laptop with all the search programs, but he thought he might have something within an hour.

"Are you headed for the island?" he asked, and I could hear him moving outside from Stephanie's house toward his Expedition.

"I'll let you know," I said and hung up. I pulled the car into gear and coasted out onto the deserted highway.

The question gave me pause. After my abortive conversation with Red, my intention had been to scout out the Early house in Ridgeland, see what I could spot. Back at the restaurant, he'd told me the feds had hinted there was some sort of illegal activity around the place, but Harry Reynolds had been tight-lipped about exactly what it was. Apparently the cooperation highway ran in only one direction with those guys. I'd pounced on the information, convinced it corroborated my conviction that the robberies and Theresa Montalvo's death were tied together.

Red had tried nicely to debunk my theory, poking holes in every scenario I proposed. It had taken us almost through dinner before he'd gotten around to outright scoffing. Speeding along into the darkness, I could hear his voice, rational and patronizing, ringing in my head. . . .

"You can't connect the fact that Mr. Gadsden recognized one of the robbers with the hit-and-run." I had opened my mouth, but he'd steamrolled over me. "Do you have any idea how many solitary oaks there are around here? Just because the old man was babbling about this Mercy Oak doesn't mean it's the one by the Early house." Again he'd forestalled my interruption with an upraised hand. "And what if it is the same tree? It's a coincidence, Bay, pure and simple. I'm more interested in who took him away Friday night and why."

"That's what I'm trying to tell you," I'd said, my voice rising in the quiet restaurant. "Romey Gadsden saw one of the robbers, could identify him. They took him away to see if he could do it again, if he was a reliable witness. He's easily muddled, and they decided he wasn't a threat to them, so they brought him home. But it was someone connected to the Early house. That's where Romey saw the tree. And Jason Early is up to his eyeballs in the hit-and-run. He knew the victim, and he's been running all over the damn county with the dead girl's sister and Bobby Santiago."

Red ignored most of what I'd said and fastened on a single point. "You give this bunch too much credit. You honestly believe they just let the old man go? I haven't seen anything yet in all the jobs they've pulled that says they're a kind and compassionate group of criminals."

"Bullshit! You said yourself—or someone did—that they've threatened guns but never produced any. Until the bank, when Romey and Lavinia got hurt. And even then they didn't shoot anybody. They hadn't committed any violence up until then and not since, right? Maybe it's all about the money. Maybe they don't want to hurt anyone."

"Altruistic armed robbers?" The sneer in his voice had sent me right up the wall. "Maybe they're donating what they steal to charity. Maybe it's a combination Santa Claus/Robin Hood scenario, is that what you're suggesting? And even if you're right, that still doesn't connect the robberies to the Montalvo girl's death."

"Think about it, Red." It had taken a huge effort to hold my temper in check. "It's the phone calls, don't you see?"

Sometime in the short drive from Romey Gadsden's house to the sheriff's office—with Harry Reynolds's grille on my bumper—that little flicker of a connection had suddenly burst into flame, and I knew what had been nagging at me since the night of the old man's disappearance.

"There was no way anyone could have known that I had any interest in the robberies last Monday night when I got the first threatening call, right? The only thing I'd done to stir anybody's pot that day was talk to Mrs. Early. And that happened *before* the bank job even took place."

"So? I don't see where you're going with this."

I knew Red wasn't being deliberately obtuse, but I was also certain he'd bought into the official party line and my theories were poking holes in it. It was a knee-jerk reaction. I'd expected better of him.

"It's simple. I'm connected to Theresa Montalvo's death because of Bobby. Romey Gadsden is connected to the robberies." I paused for effect. "But the *same guy* made all the phone calls—the ones to me and the one he left on Glory Merrick's answering machine. I don't believe you can't see that." He opened his mouth, but I beat him to the punch. "And if you say the word *coincidence* one more time, I swear to God I'll throw something at you!"

"You don't know for certain it doesn't all have to do with the robberies. You're making that assumption because it fits your pre-conceived—"

"Fine! Let's just drop it."

I'd shut up then. Clamped my lips together except for when I was shoveling food into my mouth. Red's efforts to revive the conversation had only made things worse. By the time I'd picked up the check, I'd managed to calm down a little, but by then I'd decided I needed a little space. If I was on my own, then I'd handle things the way I saw fit. I sure as hell didn't need anyone's permission. . . .

The phone rang again as I neared the wide sweeping curve that would be the point at which I needed to decide: right toward Ridge-land or left toward home? I slowed and eased onto the paved shoulder of the road, clicked on my flashers, and picked up my cell.

"Jesus, Bay. Tracking you down is worse than running a crooked politician to ground. Do you ever get off your damn phone? Or are you just not taking my calls?"

"Hello, Gabby. Yes, I'm having a lovely evening, thanks. And you?"

"Cut the crap, Tanner. Things are breaking. I'm doing you a favor here, remember?"

The sigh escaped in spite of my best efforts. "What's breaking?"

"You don't pick up your messages, either, I see. The Montalvo thing. I've got a lead even the cops don't have yet." She paused. "I finally got to interview the parents."

I cringed at the thought of the dead girl's family under the staccato barrage of Gabby's questions. "I thought you spoke to them earlier, right after Theresa's death."

"I did, but they weren't talking, not about who might have done it or why. I understand they've even been stonewalling the cops. Playing dumb. But hey, this is why I get the big bucks. I have a Latino friend, does a column for the paper. She knows the Montalvos. We went together so she could translate for me."

"And what did you find out?" I glanced at the dashboard clock. Erik should be home by now. He could have the location of the number Dolores had called from in a matter of minutes. I realized I had the steering wheel locked in a death grip and consciously relaxed my fingers.

"I need something in return."

Although the reporter couldn't see it, I smacked my fist against the wheel. "I'm not playing that game, Gabby. One kid is dead. There are two other innocent teenagers and the woman who saved my life out there somewhere on the run. If you have information that can keep them from getting killed, too, then you damn well better give it to me!"

"Take it easy, Bay. All I want to know is if Red and the sheriff have figured it out. I hear the local FBI office may be involved, too. If they're planning some kind of raid, I want a heads-up. The girl's family doesn't know the exact location, only that Serena had found out about it. I'm just asking for a little lead time, not an exclusive. I've got my photographer standing by. We can be on the road in a matter of minutes."

My head felt as if someone had stuffed it full of cotton. "I have no idea what you're talking about. Back up. What did Serena Montalvo find out about?"

Gabby spoke as if I were a slightly backward child. "The coyotes. Bringing illegal aliens into—"

"I know what coyotes are. You're telling me you have proof they're operating here?"

"Jasper County. Somewhere near Ridgeland. And it's not exactly proof, just what the girl told her mother. This gang also provides forged documents. Apparently the girl got on to it from a kid in her school who was trying to get a counterfeit Social Security card."

Enrique Salazar, the boy who couldn't claim his college scholarship. "So you're saying these coyote guys killed Theresa Montalvo thinking she was Serena? Because she was about to blow their operation?"

"That's the family's take."

"Then why the hell didn't they tell the sheriff or the FBI or someone?"

The brief silence crackled. "They did tell someone. They told me."

"I'm calling Red."

"Hold on! Wait! These people are scared, Bay. They don't know where their other daughter is. They've only heard from her once since the . . . since Theresa's death. Serena's the only thing that's keeping them from packing up and running themselves."

Gabby's words registered, but only on the edge of my consciousness. The ones that kept flashing in my mind like a giant neon sign were *Jasper County*. And *somewhere near Ridgeland*.

"I have to go," I said.

"What about our deal?"

"I'll do what I can, Gabby. That's all I can promise."

"Tell Red to speak directly with the family. They're ready to cooperate now. Elena and I convinced them it was the only way to make sure Serena is safe."

"Good. Have them call the sheriff's office right away. I'll still give Red a heads-up."

"And don't forget I want in on the takedown."

"Thanks, Gabby. This definitely counts as your good deed for the year."

"That's a relief," she answered, her voice again crackling with cynicism. "I was running out of time."

As I flipped the phone closed, headlights approached from behind. I waited until the vehicle had roared by, disengaged the flashers, and pulled back onto the highway. No question now about which way to turn.

* * *

The little gas station at the intersection was closed, so I pulled in on the far side and shut off the lights. I figured fifteen or twenty minutes would put me in the vicinity of the Early house, especially with the lack of traffic on this chilly December Monday.

I knew I needed to talk to Red. The question was what could I say to make him believe me? He'd already demonstrated his total disdain for my theories of a connection between Theresa Montalvo's murder and the robberies, and Gabby hadn't given me much of anything to bolster my argument. Still, there were just too many damn coincidences piling up, most of them swirling around Jason Early and the dump he and his mother called home.

A vision of him on the lawn in front of Our Lady of Guadalupe flashed into my head. Who was the Hispanic man he'd been talking with? It hadn't been Jesse Cardenas, I was certain of that. His bulky frame striding toward me, the growling dog at his heels, replaced the quiet scene at the church. There was someone capable of violence, I thought. The eyes. Somehow familiar and yet menacing. Why did I feel as if I knew him?

I ran my hands over my face, trying to clear my head. Enough speculation. I needed to make a decision. I'd told Gabby I'd report her information to Red, but something held me back. We were beyond the old competition, and I had learned my lesson about rushing headlong into danger—and in a particularly gruesome and heartwrenching way. But I had a gnawing feeling that things were going bad quickly. I wanted to see the killer of Theresa Montalvo brought to justice. I wanted this coyote operation shut down. But most of all, I wanted Dolores and Bobby safe.

I picked up my cell phone.

"I was just about to call you," Erik said. "I got a lock on that number Angie gave you, but it doesn't make any sense."

"Where did she call from?"

"The number doesn't look local. I thought at first it must be a cell, because they sometimes have weird exchanges, you know? But it's a land line."

I swallowed the lump of urgency in my throat. "So where is it?"

"The phone's unlisted, but I worked a little magic. I had to spend some company money again on one of the services we subscribed to for the background checks."

Again? I thought, but let it go. "I don't care about that. Whatever it takes."

"It came back to someone named Temprano. Have you read—?"

"Did you get an address?"

"Just a post office box, but the zip is in Ridgeland. Bay, listen—"

Again I cut him off. "Wait a minute. Dolores called from a phone in Ridgeland? Are you sure?"

"No, I don't know that's where the phone is actually located. I'm just saying the guy that pays the bills has a PO box there."

There was only one place in Ridgeland tied to all this, and I knew exactly where it was.

"Give me the name again." Something about it had stirred a memory.

"That's what I'm trying to tell you. Have you read the file I gave you on Dolores's husband, Hector?"

"No. I have it here, but I was sort of . . . putting it off. You made it sound as if I wasn't going to like the answers."

"You're not. And you're going to like them even less now."

"What does that mean?"

"Get the file."

I opened my mouth to protest, my heart hammering with the need to get to Ridgeland and find Dolores. But I snapped on the interior light, dumped out my briefcase, and extracted the folder.

"Okay. What am I looking for?"

"The basic thing is that he's using a false name, like I told you earlier. I found the real Hector Santiago living in a little village outside Oaxaca."

"What do you mean, the *real* Hector Santiago?"

"Just what I said. It's all in my report. They're about the same age, but this guy is in a wheelchair. Car accident about twenty years ago."

My head felt as if it would explode. In a wheelchair? Then who . . . "How do you know that? I mean, it's not a totally bizarre name. There have to be thousands of Santiagos in Mexico."

"Read the file," Erik said.

"I don't have time to read the damn file! What does this Temprano guy have to do with Hector?"

Erik ignored my tone. "It's Hector's real last name. The guy the phone is registered to is Jesús Temprano. Probably a relative."

Family. You have to trust family, Hector had said. Angie's long-lost *Tío* Jesús. Her father's brother?

And another elusive connection snapped into place. I'd picked up a smattering of the language from Dolores, and one of the words I remembered now was *temprano.*

Spanish for "early."

CHAPTER
THIRTY-SEVEN

I APPROACHED SLOWLY, CUTTING THE HEADLIGHTS AS I passed Mr. Gadsden's Mercy Oak, and slid into the drive of the deserted peanut stand. I let the car coast around behind the sagging structure and roll to a stop with its nose pointed back toward the highway. There were no lights on in the house behind me, and I prayed the owners had gone away for the holidays.

I popped the trunk and left the engine running while I retrieved my survival kit. After the shootout at the Florida marina that had left my partner dead, I'd thought long and hard about what I might have done to prevent things going so badly wrong. I'd even discussed it with Red, who reluctantly offered some advice. I opened the duffel bag and extracted a dark hooded sweatshirt, ditching my coat and pulling the heavy fleece over my head. I stuffed my hair into a navy Braves cap and slipped a small but powerful flashlight into the front pouch pocket of the sweatshirt along with a prepaid cell phone. No one had the number, because the whole idea was that it wouldn't ring or vibrate at some inopportune moment. It was strictly for outgoing calls—of the emergency variety.

I exchanged my loafers for black sneakers and laced them up. Lastly, I took out the twin of my Seecamp pistol and tucked it in next to the phone and flash. My carry gun I already had securely in the pocket of my slacks. If I were patted down, most people, even most cops, would be satisfied once they found the pistol in my sweatshirt. In the best possible scenario, none of these preparations would prove necessary. But if everything suddenly went to hell, at least I'd be ready.

I closed the trunk lid as quietly as possible and slipped back into the warmth of the car. Across the road, the abandoned gas station squatted like a discarded concrete box, effectively blocking my view of the house behind it. There were no streetlamps this far out of town, and I strained to make out any glow of light that might indicate the Earlys were in residence. I slouched down in the seat and settled in to wait.

Red had been adamant that I stay out of it. I'd promised to sit tight across the road to keep an eye on the place while he organized the cavalry. Convincing his superiors that they needed to move on the Early house could take some time. He'd specifically instructed me not to notify Gabby Henson. I hoped she'd be able to get past it when she found out.

What worried me most was the ponderous way in which the official wheels turned. Someone, probably Lisa Pedrovsky, would be dispatched to the Montalvos' to question the parents and verify the information I'd given Red. He'd also told me they'd need to notify the FBI since they might be riding into the middle of one of their operations, as well as coordinate everything with the Jasper County Sheriff's Office, which had jurisdiction. I'd always been a law-abiding citizen—mostly—and thankful for the constitutional guarantees the Judge had hammered into me from childhood, the protections that separated us from so much of the rest of the world. But sometimes things went wrong while all the *i*'s were being dotted and the *t*'s were being crossed, while everyone's rights, including the bad guys', were being carefully guarded.

Sometimes things went very wrong. Sometimes people died.

I squirmed myself into a more comfortable position. I could be sitting a long time. I fastened my eyes on the rutted driveway leading off from the highway and thought about Dolores and Bobby. Hector had told his wife not to be afraid. And he'd talked about family. It seemed obvious he was protecting someone. Jesús Temprano, his brother? It was the logical conclusion, and yet there was so much about the whole situation that didn't make sense to me. Why had Hector taken on the identity of some crippled guy still living in Mexico? Did the man have a green card? Had that been the lure? I knew Hector had to have valid documentation in order to secure a business license from the town of Hilton Head. But he'd been in the country way before all the heightened scrutiny of the past few years. He'd been married to Dolores long enough to have produced college-aged kids. Wouldn't that cement his legal status? Or were all bets off if he was using a false identity?

I dug the flashlight out of my pocket and found the file Erik had prepared among the muddle of papers still strewn across the passenger seat. I opened it onto my lap and wriggled farther down so I could keep the light of the flash below the level of the dashboard.

Hector Santiago—the real one—had been granted a student visa back in the early eighties, had gone through all the proper channels, everything above board. He'd been a smart kid, a math whiz who'd been sponsored for college by a group of Hispanic-Americans looking to help out poor Mexicans with promise. After graduation, he'd taken a job with a high-tech firm near Los Angeles, obtaining a work visa. Erik's information indicated Hector had been on the path to citizenship when he made a visit home to his family's village. On the way, he'd been involved in a horrific traffic accident that had resulted in his being paralyzed from the chest down.

In a wheelchair, Erik had said on the phone. So how had the Hector Santiago who had married Dolores and fathered her three children come to be in possession of the documents? If they'd been stolen, why hadn't the real Hector raised an alarm?

I switched off the flashlight and let my eyes readjust to the darkness. He had to have agreed to the switch. Maybe they were related, the Santiagos and the Tempranos. Cousins? No way could the paralyzed

Hector return to his job and his new life in the States, so why let perfectly good documents go to waste? Of course, the bogus Hector wasn't a math prodigy with an American higher education. He couldn't just waltz over to L.A. and take up where the injured man had left off. He'd need to start over.

A UPS truck, its driver no doubt working some holiday overtime, lumbered by, and I lowered my head until it had passed. Across the road, nothing moved.

The scenario made sense, but it was all built on speculation and guesswork. We might never discover the truth unless Dolores's Hector decided to come clean. I wondered if she knew, this sweet woman with her Catholic strictures about right and wrong, so ingrained that she couldn't bring herself to tell even the smallest fib. Could she have stayed all those years with a man she knew to be living a lie?

Off in the distance, headlamps approached from the direction of Ridgeland. I waited, prepared to duck out of sight, but the vehicle slowed as it passed the field with the sentinel oak, the edge of the lights brushing across the canopy of the ancient tree. I cut the engine. The battered pickup, the same one I'd tailed from this very spot the day before, made the turn. But instead of bumping along the rutted dirt drive, it swung behind the deserted gas station, almost the exact spot from where I'd seen it emerge on Sunday afternoon. A moment later the lights went out.

I strained my eyes but could detect no movement.

Without the warmth of the defroster, the windows began to fog up. I rubbed a clear spot with the sleeve of the sweatshirt, but almost immediately it misted over. I pulled my hand away from the door handle. Lessons had been learned in that small marina just south of Amelia Island where Ben Wyler died.

I pulled the cell phone out of my pocket and called Red.

"Don't move, do you hear me?"

His raised voice bounced off the cloudy windows of the Jaguar.

"I'm surprised they can't hear you in Pittsburgh," I said through clenched teeth. "Are you coming or not?"

"These things take time." Red spoke more softly, but the hard edge in his voice hadn't diminished. "We're waiting for a Jasper County judge to sign warrants."

"What about the FBI? Are they in?"

"Reynolds has been out of touch. Even Lisa can't reach him."

That simple statement said a lot about Pedrovsky's actions over the past week. I wondered if her interest in Reynolds was personal or professional.

"Is that going to hold things up?" I asked.

"No."

I hoped Red knew what he was talking about. Harry Reynolds had mentioned Homeland Security. So had Loretta Healey. If this innocuous house outside of Ridgeland really was the heart of some coyote operation, ICE would be involved as well. I had a hard time believing all these vast federal bureaucracies would be content to let a couple of small local sheriff's departments grab the kind of headlines such a bust would generate.

"It's the same truck I followed yesterday," I said. "I'm sure of it. Probably the Cardenas guy driving. Something could be going down."

"I don't care if the damn place is on fire. You don't move, got it?"

Red's breath seemed to be coming in short bursts. I could clearly hear him puffing.

"Got it. Are you running?"

"We're rolling. Just sit tight. We'll be there in no time."

I heard the phone click off in my ear.

I tucked the cell back in my pocket and cleared another space in the misted windshield. I blinked twice to make certain the fog hadn't deceived me. There was light coming from behind the boarded-up windows of the gas station. Not much, but in the almost complete blackness of the December night, a faint rim escaped around the graffiti-covered plywood.

I could feel my own breath quicken and fumbled for the phone. No answer. Red would have switched off his cell as he and the other deputies raced toward Ridgeland. Protocol. I hesitated, my hand again wandering to the door handle almost of its own volition. Still I wavered, my own sense of self-preservation warring with my need for action. What if Cardenas was getting ready to run? What if everyone was gone by the time Red and his fellow officers arrived?

A quick look. Nothing more. Just to reassure myself. The justifications finally won out, and I slipped quietly from the Jag. In less than a minute I had sprinted across the deserted highway and flattened myself against the rough concrete of the old gas station. I waited a moment to let my breath quiet, then inched around the side of the building, my right hand secure around the handle of the pistol in my sweatshirt.

At the corner, I inhaled and darted a quick look around the edge. The pickup sat next to what was once the overhead door that allowed vehicles to be pulled inside for repair. *Same license plate. Same truck.* And more light, this time from a smaller entry door left partially ajar. Down at the far end of the driveway, I could barely make out the Early house, its windows completely black and empty.

I ducked back. My heart seemed to be pounding in my ears. I began to work my way back toward the highway when muffled voices drifted out from the dilapidated building. I froze.

Two males. Arguing. In Spanish. I strained to hear the words, struggling to find one I might recognize. Nothing. The tension rose along with the voices. *Loco,* I finally heard, said with disdain, followed by another string that was almost unintelligible. I managed to pick out *hermano.* Brother. Then *muerto,* almost shouted. I bit down hard on the inside of my cheek. I knew that one for certain. Dead.

I eased back toward the corner, taking care to keep my sneakers from scuffing the loose gravel scattered haphazardly across the barren ground. The argument raged on, but I couldn't make out anything else. Suddenly, the screech of a barn owl stopped my heart. Into the silence that followed, I heard its strong wings beating against the chill night air as it soared by me into the darkness. And in its wake, a strong female voice rose in indignation. Again, I couldn't understand the words, but I didn't need to.

Dolores!

I whipped out the pistol and took one step toward the open door, when a hand clamped around my mouth, and I felt myself jerked to the ground.

"Knock it off! I can snap your neck in a heartbeat if you don't lie still!"

The words, whispered in my ear, had the desired effect. I stopped struggling, more than relieved to have been spoken to in English without the slightest trace of accent. I felt the gun being wrenched out of my hand.

"We're going to stand up now. Easy." My attacker's warm breath ruffled the hair on the side of my head as we rose awkwardly. "Back up slowly. No noise."

I thought then about making a break for it. If whoever had taken me down didn't want to alert the men inside the building, he certainly wouldn't risk a shot. But did I want to stake my life on it? And Dolores's? I nodded against the hand still covering my mouth and followed him step by step away from the building. I stumbled when we moved off the crumbled concrete apron and onto open ground, my eyes frantically scanning the surrounding darkness for some means of escape. Or hope of rescue. The night lay still and heavy all around us. I was on my own.

I couldn't judge our destination, being pulled along backwards, concentrating on not tripping. I considered just going limp, forcing my captor to carry my weight, but his strong arm around my neck made me too vulnerable. I'd about decided to risk it when he suddenly stopped. Above me I could see the drooping arms of the Mercy Oak, its wide canopy and swaying clumps of Spanish moss effectively obscuring the building we'd just fled.

"I'm going to take my hand away, Mrs. Tanner. Not a peep, or I'll be forced to put you out. Understood?"

Again I nodded. I sucked in air through my mouth and turned slowly.

Harry Reynolds stepped back, the Seecamp almost disappearing in his large palm. "That was a stupid stunt," he said softly. "What the hell do you think you're doing?"

I stilled the trembling in my legs and stood up straighter. "Dolores is in there. My housekeeper. I heard her voice. We have to get her out of there."

"There is no *we*, Mrs. Tanner. This is a federal matter. You're about to screw up a six-month operation. I could have you tossed in jail for obstruction."

"Why don't you go ahead and get the paperwork started on that? In the meantime, give me my gun. I'm going after my friend."

"I'll handcuff you to this tree if I have to," the FBI agent said, his tone so matter-of-fact I had no doubt he was prepared to carry out the threat. "Now sit down here and shut up. I have some calls to make."

He palmed my pistol and extracted his cell phone from a jacket pocket. His eyes never left me as he punched one button and said, "Office." A moment later, he moved slightly away, his head bowed into the phone, but his gaze still locked on me. He spoke softly, but I managed to catch a single word: *compromised*. I wondered if he was aware that Red and half the Beaufort and Jasper County Sheriff's deputies were about to come charging into the middle of his "operation." I let my eyes focus on the road from Ridgeland, straining for the slightest indication of flashing blue lights.

Harry stopped talking, and I looked back. Another button beeped in the chill air, and he said, "Tactical."

I frowned at him. Was there a SWAT unit nearby? Had I really stumbled into the middle of a raid? I shivered and shoved my hands into the pockets of my trousers. I hadn't forgotten about my backup pistol, identical to the one Harry Reynolds still clutched in his hand, and my fingers closed around the grip. It was an unusual weapon, one the Judge had secured for me from Len, his Hilton Head gun dealer. Handmade and almost undetectable because of its small size, it had one major drawback: its limited range. I was almost certain Harry Reynolds wouldn't be familiar with it. A woman's gun. If I made a break for it, put on an initial burst of speed, I'd be out of his sights by the time the FBI agent had time to aim and shoot. Maybe. And always assuming he didn't pull his own weapon, no doubt larger and more powerful.

I watched him talk tensely into the cell phone and weighed my chances. I had to decide soon. "Tactical" sounded like guys in helmets and body armor carrying automatic weapons. Storming the old gas station could certainly resolve the issue, at least for them. It could also get Dolores and Bobby killed. If I could just keep Reynolds from calling in his troops until Red and the other deputies arrived, maybe they could talk some sense into him. They could surround the building, force whoever was inside into giving up.

But what if they decided to hold the Santiagos hostage, tried to negotiate their way out using Dolores and Bobby as shields? Neither scenario guaranteed a good outcome, but I trusted Red more than the FBI.

I rose up onto the balls of my feet and flexed my knees. I took one sliding step to the right, my eyes never leaving Harry Reynolds's dim form at the edge of the canopy. I inhaled quickly several times, loading my lungs with oxygen. The owl screeched again, and Reynolds jerked his head toward the sound.

In a second, I was off, sprinting away in a zigzag pattern toward the old gas station. I snatched the backup gun out of my pocket as I ran and pumped with everything I had, all those hours of jogging on the beach finally put to practical use. I could feel the skin between my shoulder blades quivering in anticipation of a shot that never came. Instead I heard behind me the pounding of footsteps on the hard-packed earth and the agent's labored breathing.

I guessed I was no more than fifty yards from the building when I felt a rush of air off to my right. I had only a moment to recognize the low snarl before the hurtling body knocked me to the ground, and I felt long pointed teeth sink into my thigh.

CHAPTER
THIRTY-EIGHT

I LOST TRACK OF TIME AND PLACE. MY WHOLE WORLD consisted of teeth and nails, digging, ripping. The massive dog's hot breath and warm saliva, the guttural grunts—his and mine—as we rolled, locked together on the hard earth. I kicked, but the soft soles of my sneakers had little effect. I could feel myself flagging, the weight of the animal wearing me down, my own screams gradually reduced to whimpers as I slowly lost the battle.

I don't remember firing the gun. Neither the shot nor the high-pitched yelp really registered, but I suddenly found myself free. I scrambled away, scuttling on all fours as if I, too, were a wounded animal. Over my own raspy breathing, I heard someone calling my name.

"Tanner! Lie still. You just winged him. I can't see where he went."

My mind couldn't seem to fasten on a single coherent thought. Who was yelling at me? I heard sobbing and realized it was my own. Blue flickers of light danced in front of my eyes, and I retched, my stomach heaving, but nothing came. A hand dropped onto my shoulder, and I jerked convulsively. The gun wavered in my fingers, then was suddenly ripped away.

"Stay still. I've got you covered."

I blinked away sweat mingled with blood and finally made out Harry Reynolds squatting beside me, his body imposed between me and the direction from which the dog had attacked. His dull gray handgun swept the area.

"Where the hell did he come from?" he murmured.

"Azúcar," I mumbled.

"What? Just take it easy. I'm calling for reinforcements," he whispered.

"Sugar. *Azúcar.*"

"Be quiet."

Suddenly, lights flared from the gas station. Voices erupted into the night.

I gathered my last ounce of strength and screamed, "Dolores!"

Reynolds was shouting into his phone. "We're blown! Move, move, move!"

I felt his hand then, gentle on my forehead, and this time I didn't flinch.

Without warning, the pain hit, like a thousand needles. I tried to bite back the moans, but at least one of them escaped to mingle with frantic barking. I tensed and tried to fold my body into itself. I could hear Reynolds, still yelling, but I had no idea what he was saying. Gradually, the sounds of car doors slamming and more people shouting penetrated the fear.

"Here we go," Harry Reynolds said. I felt something, probably his coat, being draped over me, and the sudden warmth stilled some of my shaking. "Don't worry. We'll get her out."

I tried to rise, but not a one of my muscles would obey my brain's command. I surrendered into the soft fabric that smelled faintly of some musky cologne while an amplified voice ordered everyone to drop their weapons and come out with their hands in the air. I thought of a whole pack of dogs, hopping about on their hind legs, their front paws waving above their heads, and I laughed.

"Shock," a strange voice said.

"You got her?" That was Harry, I was almost certain.

"Yeah. Go ahead. We'll take good care of her."

The hands were gentle, turning me onto my back, exploring the ripped and shredded skin beneath my ripped and shredded clothes. Then I was being lifted, and I realized I was coming to my senses again. Unfortunately. With the fog clearing from my head, my brain had a chance to make an accurate interpretation of the pain signals being sent from every square inch of skin on my body.

I cried out as the gurney bumped along the uneven ground, the worst of the torment seeming to be concentrated on my right leg. Someone—a paramedic—had cut away my trousers, and the cold night air felt like burning ice on my wounds.

I turned my head as we approached the ambulance with its back doors yawning open. What I had wrongly assumed to be an abandoned gas station was lit up like a tree on Christmas morning, and dozens of uniforms swarmed the area. Several men sat on the ground, their hands and legs shackled while the khaki tide ebbed and flowed around them. I tried to spot Red, but there was too much confusion.

A sharp flash took my sight away for a moment. Then I heard the harsh voice of Gabby Henson.

"Leave her alone, Sandy! Get these guys on the ground. I want full-face close-ups. Some of them are definitely *not* Latino."

My eyes adjusted enough to make out a dim form leaning over me. "You okay, Tanner?"

I tried to speak, but my mouth had gone completely dry. I nodded.

"You didn't call, but I'm gonna let that slide. Looks like you got trouble enough."

"How . . . ?" was all I could croak out.

"Monitoring the scanner. They tried to keep it off the airwaves, but that's never possible when you got this many cops mobilized for something." She paused, and a little of the tough veneer slipped. "Jesus, you really got chewed up. She gonna be okay?"

One of the men getting ready to hoist me on board the ambulance paused to answer. "She'll have more stitches than I want to think about, but yeah, I'd say so."

A horrible image popped into my head, and I reached out in a feeble attempt to snatch at Gabby's wrist. She leaned closer.

"Rabies?" I whispered.

"They got the animal," another of my rescuers said. "Somebody winged him, but he'll survive."

"Don't kill," I managed to squeak out.

Gabby snorted. "She must be delirious. I'd want the son of a bitch's head mounted on my wall."

"We need to move," the paramedic said, and Gabby stepped back.

I closed my eyes, the pain in my leg blotting out everything else in the universe.

Except for the dear familiar voice, bending close to my ear. For a moment I thought Gabby must be right—I was delirious. I forced open my eyes, and the corners of my mouth twitched in the best imitation of a smile I could manage.

"Ah, *mi pobre Señora.*"

"Roberto and Serena?"

"*Sí. Salvados.*"

Safe.

With great effort, I raised my hand and felt Dolores wrap it with her own, her touch at once gentle and strong.

"*Que Dios te bendiga, Señora.* I knew you would come."

I sighed and slid into darkness.

CHAPTER
THIRTY-NINE

*I*F I HAVE TO LISTEN TO ONE MORE ROUND OF THOSE damned canned Christmas songs, I'm going to go stark raving mad!"

Red laughed and ruffled my hair before pulling up one of the straight-backed visitors' chairs.

"I'm serious," I said. "I want out of here."

"The paperwork is under way. I talked to the charge nurse on the way in."

"Nurse Ratched? She was obviously AWOL when they did sensitivity training."

"Quit bitching, sweetheart. You haven't been the easiest patient in the world, either. Relax. It's almost over."

I sighed and shifted my weight in the hospital bed. I had yet to find a comfortable position for my heavily bandaged leg, which had been immobilized for the first couple of days after the attack. The thigh wound had been deep, tearing the muscle, and would be the longest healing. That pain, thanks to some wonderful drugs, had been reduced to a constant throbbing that kept rhythm with my heartbeat. I had a few puncture wounds on my arms, but the most troubling injury was the ring finger of my left hand. In my half-drugged daze, I'd heard the discussion about amputating it at the first knuckle, but the doctor who'd sewn me back together had managed to save it. It now lay wrapped in thick layers of gauze, propped on a pillow, the slightest jarring sending hot jolts of pain up my arm.

Still, I wanted to go home, to suffer in my own bed. I let my hopes blossom when Red walked in carrying my favorite sweats and running shoes, although it would be a long time before I'd be doing any jogging on the beach again.

"What's the latest?" I asked, carefully reaching for the chai latte Red had smuggled in from Starbucks.

Red didn't need to ask what I meant. I'd been out of it for the first two days, barely registering that my father had braved the stares of strangers to have Lavinia settle his wheelchair next to my bed. I understood they'd been there several times, along with Erik and Stephanie Wyler. And Harry Reynolds. I had little recollection of any of it.

I also hadn't been able to read the papers, although Red had saved them for me. The bust in Ridgeland, the takedown of the coyote operation by both local law enforcement and federal agencies, and Gabby Henson's exclusive interview with Serena Montalvo had dominated the local news. I'd devoured every word that Christmas Eve morning, awkwardly turning the pages with my one good hand.

"Come on," I said when he didn't answer. "I'm going to hear it all sooner or later."

"I don't know where to start. They got everyone, at least the big fish."

"Do you think they were ever in real danger? Dolores and Bobby, I mean? Surely Hector's brothers wouldn't have harmed their own family."

Red shrugged. "Somebody killed Theresa Montalvo. There's no getting around that."

"But which one?"

"Nobody's stepped forward to claim responsibility, but my money's on Domingo Temprano, alias Jesse Cardenas. The lab boys from SLED are going over that pickup of his. They found preliminary . . . traces, but it'll be a while before they can verify a match with the girl."

"Hector's older brother." I shivered, remembering the cold, eerily familiar eyes that had stared at me through my car window. And the numerous dents in his old truck. "Poor Dolores," I whispered. "What about the other one? Jesús."

"I don't know. Dolores says he tried to keep them away from Domingo, even gave them money to hide out. I'm sure he knew Serena could still blow the whistle on their operation, but he seemed genuinely concerned about keeping them all safe."

"Then why were Dolores and the kids at the Earlys' place that night?"

"Domingo threatened Jesús's family if he didn't produce them."

"But how did he know his brother had been helping them?" I said, almost to myself. Then, "Jason?"

"That's my theory. The boy may have ratted his stepfather out, not realizing he was putting himself in danger. He appears to have been playing both ends against the middle for a long time."

"And Jesús is Jason's stepfather, only he and his mother used the anglicized version of the name." I scrunched up my eyes and shook my head. Sometimes the painkillers fogged up my brain. "The paper said they were running illegals in, charging outrageous fees, then black-mailing them into committing robberies in order to pay off the debt. They had an entire gang of desperate men knocking off banks and bars. No wonder you could never get an accurate description of them."

"Pretty damn slick operation, you've gotta admit. They manu-factured fake documents inside that old gas station, too, sort of a one-stop shopping setup. That was Jesús's specialty. Domingo liked to use Jason as a delivery boy, would toss him a couple of hundred bucks for his effort. I think the stupid kid got a taste for the money."

I shifted my leg and winced. "You saw how he and his mother lived. You can almost understand that."

Red laughed. "You apparently never got a look inside the house.

Jason had a sixty-inch plasma TV in his bedroom. The whole place could have come straight out of a decorating magazine. They deliberately kept the outside looking like a dump to discourage anyone from nosing around. Jesús may have been squeamish about murder, but he sure wasn't turning down his share of the profits."

"I'll be damned." Mrs. M. Early had been a good little actress in more ways than one. No doubt the racial slurs were part of her role, too. "I wasn't even close to figuring this out, was I?"

Red smiled and patted my hand. "None of us had all the pieces, which makes it damn hard to finish the puzzle. If you and the FBI and Gabby Henson had sat down and compared notes, you would have put it together." He rubbed his hand across his forehead. "You were a lot closer to the truth than I was. It was always about the money."

Except for Serena Montalvo, I thought. Her motives had become clear in her interview with Gabby. Through her involvement with Enrique Salazar, she'd managed to tag along when desperation to save his scholarship drove him to seek out a forged Social Security card. She'd been a good little detective. She'd befriended Jason, who'd been hanging around the gas station when she and Salazar showed up for the buy. Eventually she figured out that the Tempranos were exploiting their own people—*her* people—and she'd been determined to blow their cover. Her biggest mistake was in not realizing that Jason couldn't be trusted.

"Poor Serena," I said aloud. "Trying to do the right thing got her sister killed."

We both turned as my doctor breezed into the room, his glasses perched on the end of his nose, his long fingers flipping pages on a plastic clipboard.

"So, I guess we're ready to go home," he said in that fake-hearty voice they must teach in medical school.

"I don't know about you, but I'm sure as hell ready."

Red squeezed my right hand.

"We'll give you a prescription for painkillers and antibiotics,

and I want to see you back here in three days. Those dressings have
to be changed on a regular basis to prevent infection. Dirty wounds
like animal bites can turn gangrenous if we're not vigilant."

"Fine. Not a problem."

"Good thing the dog was picked up right away. The owners had
records of her shots, and we verified it with the vet." He paused in
his paper-flipping to look at me. "Rabies treatments aren't pleasant."

"So the dog's okay? They're not going to destroy it or anything?"

The doctor shrugged. "Not my call, but I believe she'll be in
quarantine for another week." He cocked a shaggy eyebrow. "I must
say I'm impressed with your concern for the animal that attacked
you."

"It's a dog. She was just protecting her territory. Reynolds and I
were the trespassers."

"Stay off that leg for at least another week. Use a cane or a walker
when you absolutely need to get around, but rest and elevation will
do it the most good. I'll see you next week. Have a Merry Christmas."

"Thank you," I called to his retreating back, "you, too."

"You heard what he said about using a cane." Red tried to look
stern, but something had his eyes sparkling. "I've taken care of that.
Or rather, one of your friends has."

"What are you talking about?"

Red stepped outside the door and returned carrying Romey
Gadsden's walking stick. He laughed at the stunned expression on
my face.

"Glory brought it by Presqu'isle, and Lavinia sent it over. Seems
you've seriously captured Mr. Gadsden's heart. But he was quick to
point out that it's just a loan. Until you're back on your feet."

The treacherous tears, which seemed to fall so easily of late,
pooled in my eyes. I sniffed them back.

"They took him away that night, didn't they? The Tempranos."

"Yes. Domingo was all for killing the old man, according to
Jesús, but they convinced him Mr. Gadsden couldn't do them any

harm. That boy he recognized from the robbery, Reynaldo Velez? He and his mother had already taken off back to Mexico. That's why we never found them."

"And the poor kid was being blackmailed by Domingo Temprano."

Red nodded. "The boy was paying off both his own and his mother's debts."

I closed my eyes, just to rest them for a moment. When I opened them again, the light had changed, softer and grayer where it slanted into the room through the blinds.

"How long have I been asleep?" I asked, and Red jumped in his chair.

"About an hour. They're ready for you to sign out. Can I help you get dressed?"

He wiggled his eyebrows in a parody of lechery, and I laughed.

"Don't make me do that! It hurts."

It took us almost fifteen minutes to maneuver me out of the hideous hospital gown and into my own clothes. I'd worked up a sweat and had to slide back onto the bed for a moment to catch my breath.

"When do I get more drugs?" I asked, the pain in my leg making my voice quiver. I looked up as a nurse's aide pushed a wheelchair into the room.

"By the time we get home, you'll be due." Red helped me into the chair and laid Romey Gadsden's stick across the armrests.

"Keep an eye on me," I told Red as the girl wheeled me out to the elevator. "I have a bad habit of turning things into bad habits."

"Not to worry, sweetheart," Red replied. "I'm not letting you out of my sight. Except to go get the car."

He took the stairs. By the time the aide and I emerged into the dusk, he had the Jaguar idling at the curb. The air smelled sweet, softer than I'd expected, and the breeze felt more like April than December.

I bit down hard on my lip as they helped me into the front seat, which Red had reclined all the way back so that I could lie almost flat. He eased out of the drive, and I closed my eyes.

I clutched Romey Gadsden's walking stick. "Who left this on my porch? Jesús?"

"Jason. He had a bigger hand in all this than his stepfather is willing to admit. He wanted in on his uncle's action. He must have known about the plan to take out Serena. I'm not buying it was a coincidence he was right there to 'discover' the body."

I turned my head to stare at him. "Maybe he was supposed to finger her for the driver and screwed up." I shivered. "They might even have used him to lure her out into the open. But why stick around and get his name on a police report? It led me right to him and the whole operation."

"Young Jason has a flair for the dramatic. Plus he's not the brightest bulb in the chandelier. Reynolds thinks it was another stunt to try to insinuate himself deeper into his uncle's operation, which Jesús and his mother had been trying to keep him out of."

"I missed so much of it. I feel as if I was running about a half step behind the whole time. Maybe if I'd been smarter, I could have prevented—"

"Don't start second-guessing yourself. Like I said, you had it figured out better than the rest of us. You're the only one who zeroed in on the connection between the hit-and-run and the robbery operation. I should have listened to you."

"Let that be a lesson to you, young man," I said with mock solemnity, and he laughed.

"Reynolds is reluctantly giving you credit for forcing them into launching the operation sooner than they wanted to. Once we got inside, we could see Domingo was getting ready to move on somewhere else. He had most of his counterfeiting equipment all packed up and ready to go." Red's hand rested lightly on my uninjured thigh. "If Reynolds hadn't been following you, the feds might have raided an empty building."

"A nasty habit of his, apparently," I murmured. I fought against the warmth of the heater and the humming of the tires. "What about the threatening phone calls?"

"Domingo. Once you showed up on Early's doorstep, they checked you out. You were definitely someone they didn't want sniffing around their operation. They had no way of knowing how much you knew, and even Domingo was smart enough to figure out they couldn't afford another body that might be tied to them. Especially a high-profile one like yours."

I stifled a yawn. "But Jesse—Domingo—has a thick accent. The man on the phone—"

"He can turn it on and off when it suits him. I sat in on a couple of the interrogations. He's been in this country a long time."

Like Dolores. And her husband. "How deeply do you think Hector was involved in this? Did he know what his brothers were doing?"

"No one's fingered him, but I find it hard to believe he was completely in the dark. Especially after what Angie told you about that last phone call. Almost sounds as if Domingo was blackmailing him, too. Hector had a lot to lose if someone ratted him out about the phony papers. As to what happens to him, that's Immigration's call."

"Poor Dolores," I mumbled and let myself drift off.

CHAPTER
FORTY

THE HOUSE BLAZED WITH LIGHT. THE SHARP TURN INTO my driveway had jostled me awake.

"What's going on?" I asked.

Red slid the Jaguar into the open garage and shut off the engine. Before he could speak, the door at the top of the stairs flew open, and Scotty and Elinor scrambled down the steps. Red's children skidded to a halt next to the driver's door, their faces flushed with excitement. I glanced up to see Dolores Santiago, her hands folded demurely in front of her apron, her face beaming.

"What the hell's going on?" I asked again, and Red smiled.

"A little welcome home party." He climbed out and came around to open my door. "You want to give the walking stick a try, or shall I carry you?"

"I'll manage," I said.

The pain took my breath away, but I ground my teeth and hobbled into the house, the kids trailing behind.

The great room had been transformed. All the greenery I'd abandoned in the garage had been spread across the mantel. Christmas decorations that hadn't seen the light of day since Rob died were tastefully arranged on tables and shelves. A towering pine filled the far corner, its branches hung with glittering balls, strings of pop-corn, and colored-paper chains.

"Do you like it, Aunt Bay?" Scotty had grown an inch since I'd last seen him, and for the first time I realized how much he looked like Red.

"We helped," tiny Elinor with her wispy dark blond hair an-nounced. "I did the purple ones."

Red helped me to the sofa. Pillows had been stacked on the cof-fee table, and I used both hands to guide my bandaged leg onto them. Almost immediately, I felt the pain recede.

"It's absolutely the most spectacular Christmas tree I have ever seen," I said, and Elinor giggled, hopping from foot to foot in her ex-citement. "Thank you both so much."

"Be careful, kids. Aunt Bay's still hurting a little. Don't get too close."

"I have the dinner all ready," Dolores said, stepping into my line of sight. "And for tomorrow, the turkey. Señor Red, he know what to do."

I watched her pull off her apron, her face flushed, though whether from her efforts in the kitchen or embarrassment I couldn't tell.

"Come here," I said, holding out my right hand.

"Un momento, Señora." She turned and motioned toward the kitchen.

A few seconds later, Bobby Santiago, hands in pockets and head down, shambled into the great room.

"Bobby! Are you okay?" I asked.

He nodded without meeting my eyes.

"Roberto. You have words to say to the señora."

"Thank you, Mrs. Tanner," the boy mumbled. "I don't know what would have happened if . . . But I shouldn't have got you in-volved in all this. When Enrique Salazar called me that morning and said he heard Serena had been killed, I . . . I just didn't know what else to do. It was stupid. I should have called the sheriff right away and told him everything. I'm sorry that you got hurt. . . ." His eyes darted to Dolores. "And that everything got so messed up."

I patted the empty cushion next to me. "Sit down, Bobby. Let's talk a minute."

Red ushered his kids up into the kitchen, where I could hear the clink of plates being removed from the cupboards. Dolores stood solemnly beside her son, her hands folded in front of her.

"It wasn't your fault," I said when the boy had perched warily on the edge of the sofa. "I know you were only trying to protect your friend. Is Serena doing all right?"

Now that the danger had passed, I knew she had probably been overwhelmed by the guilt of having been the inadvertent cause of her sister's death.

"She wanted to do the right thing, Mrs. Tanner. She never meant for any of this to happen." He bowed his head and spoke softly. "They're going home. To El Salvador. I don't know if she . . . if they'll ever come back."

The sadness in his voice made tears well in my eyes. I wanted to tell him that he'd get over it, that there would be other girls, but I knew he wasn't ready to hear that yet. I could also have told him that the authorities wouldn't be letting them leave the country until Serena had testified against the men responsible for all this misery. Maybe even including Dolores's husband—Bobby's father.

"If there's ever anything we can do . . . I mean, I can do . . . to make up for—"

I hushed him with a hand on the sleeve of his jacket. "Just do well at college. Become the man your mother wants you to be. And be happy. That'll be more than enough."

"Come, Roberto. We must go now." Dolores slipped an arm around the shoulders of her son as he rose to stand beside her.

"Yes, *amiga.* Go home to your family."

She dropped her head. "*Señora,* we cannot say how much—"

"I did nothing, Dolores, except maybe make things worse. I'm sorry. Will you and Hector be okay?"

She didn't answer, but I watched the sadness settle into her eyes a moment before she crossed herself. "*En las manos de Dios,*" she murmured. In God's hands.

I wanted to say so much more, but the kids had already bounced back into the great room and over to the tree. Hopefully, we'd have time, Dolores and I, to sort out everything we'd been through in the past week. I squeezed her fingers, and we smiled, an unspoken understanding seeming to flow between us.

"Feliz Navidad," she whispered and dropped my hand.

"Merry Christmas," I said and watched her steer Bobby toward the foyer.

"Hasta martes," she added over her shoulder, and my heart rose. *Until Tuesday.*

I heard the door close softly behind them.

"Aunt Bay!" I turned my head at Scotty's excited voice. He and Elinor had squatted beside the tree with its brightly wrapped packages stacked underneath. "There's one for you. From Daddy!"

"No presents until tomorrow," Red spoke sternly. "You know the rules."

I studied his face, surprised to find he looked embarrassed.

"Come on, let's get dinner on the table. I'll bet Aunt Bay's hungry."

"Does it rattle?" I asked this impish version of Red, and he grinned.

He held up the small box and shook it. "No, but I think it must be a pretty good present. Daddy said you were going to be—"

"Scott Michael Tanner! In the kitchen! Now!" Red's booming voice startled both his kids, and Scotty dropped the box back onto the pile of gifts as if it were on fire. "Elinor! You, too."

Both children turned to obey, but Scotty took a detour to place his face close to my ear. "It's a secret," he whispered, and his small hand patted my cheek gently. "And Daddy says you won't even have to change—"

"Scotty!"

The boy pulled away and darted for the kitchen.

I fastened my gaze on the small square box atop the mound of gaily wrapped presents and closed my eyes.

I didn't know whether to laugh or cry.

ML $\frac{7}{09}$